DARK
FRONTIER

ALSO BY MATTHEW HARFFY

Bernicia Chronicles
The Serpent Sword
The Cross and the Curse
Blood and Blade
Killer of Kings
Warrior of Woden
Storm of Steel
Fortress of Fury
For Lord and Land
Forest of Foes
Kin of Cain (short story)
Shadows of the Slain

A Time for Swords series
A Time for Swords
A Night of Flames
A Day of Reckoning

Other novels
Wolf of Wessex

DARK FRONTIER

MATTHEW HARFFY

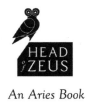

An Aries Book

First published in the UK in 2024 by Head of Zeus,
part of Bloomsbury Publishing Plc

9 7 5 3 1 2 4 6 8

A catalogue record for this book is available from the British Library.

ISBN (HB): 9781804548592
ISBN (E): 9781804548622

Cover design: Jessie Price

Printed and bound in Great Britain by
CPI Group (UK) Ltd, Croydon CRO 4YY

Head of Zeus Ltd
First Floor East
5–8 Hardwick Street
London EC1R 4RG

WWW.HEADOFZEUS.COM

For Ashley and Leanne Dawkins, friends to ride the river with.

Chapter One

Gabriel Stokes looked down at the corpse. The young man's unseeing eyes stared back at him. They seemed to accuse him, Stokes thought, though he'd had nothing to do with the boy's death.

He sighed, sensing the familiar hold of the dead heavy upon him.

Casting his gaze over the dead body, he took in the details as he would with any crime scene. He hadn't been a serving police officer for months, but those habits he had acquired over the last seven years could not be forgotten so quickly. The deceased was scarcely more than a child really. Perhaps eighteen years old. He had the gaunt look of one unaccustomed to regular meals. His sallow cheeks and wispy moustache reminded Stokes of countless such young men who lined the Port of London docks and the airless, smoggy streets of Whitechapel in search of a mark, or a way to make a bob or two. He had seen many such boys in the army too. The lucky ones made something of themselves. Most were not lucky. This stranger's expression was one of surprise, shocked perhaps at his own lack of fortune. His gimlet eyes, gleaming with cunning and bravado in life, now grew rapidly dull in death.

It had been the shouting that caught Stokes' attention. He had been looking down the dusty street, wondering if he had missed John at the station. He'd sent a telegram ahead, as John had requested, but there had been no sign of his friend on the short raised timber platform, nor in the dusty Union Pacific building next to the water tower and windmill.

Taking only his valise and leaving his travel chest at the station baggage room to be collected later, Stokes had headed into the small town. He had just made up his mind that he would look for a hotel and go about finding a coach, or perhaps a horse, that might carry him to Thornford's ranch in the morning, when a barrage of angry insults and jeers had cut through his weariness. There had been an edge of danger in the raised voices, a sharpness that Stokes' years in the army and the Metropolitan Police had taught him not to ignore. His instincts, though dulled by tiredness now, had always served him well. He had dropped his valise on the board sidewalk, leaving his hands free, and watched the young man swagger out of a building that bore the sign CENTRAL HOTEL SALOON AND BILLIARDS. The boy had been cock-sure, voice strident with drink, as he'd stepped through the door in a cloud of cigar and pipe smoke that rolled out of the busy saloon.

Stokes took a long breath. The smell of the smoke was now mixed with the unmistakable tang of black powder from the three shots that had been fired. There were several other scents mixed in. The sooty steam from the train that still hissed and spouted thick clouds of smoke back at the platform where its tender was being refilled. The sour reek of manure from the cattle ready for loading in the lots. The sharp smell of beer and cheap liquor. And the stink of sweat from the unwashed men who had tumbled into the street after the loud-mouthed boy.

If he closed his eyes, he could have been back in London. All Stokes had wanted was some peace; to breathe the air of the wide open spaces he had so long dreamt of. How naive he had been. It was true that the gorges, forests, mountains and endless plains he had seen as the train trundled west had been breathtaking, but he had yet to find in America the unfettered freedom and fresh air he yearned for. He wondered again

2

about his decision to come here. It had taken him weeks to travel this far and little of the journey had been pleasant. At times, looking out over the vastness of the Atlantic from the deck of the RMS *Etruria*, or staring at distant snow-draped peaks in Wyoming and the rolling nothingness of the prairies of Nebraska, he had managed to distract his thoughts from the dark paths down which his mind seemed intent on taking him. But for long stretches of the ocean voyage aboard the cramped steamer, and then the seemingly interminable hours of the rocking train journey, he had found himself alone with his melancholy. All that had changed was the scenery; the despair remained.

Perhaps Harriet had been right. She had said it was madness. But he could not return to London. Not after everything that had happened there, and he could not stay with Harriet and Eliza in Wiltshire any longer. He loved both his sisters dearly, but the sprawling house was too full of memories.

Stokes was being jostled by the crowd around him now and he sensed the danger had not passed. This was no time for reminiscing. Allowing his training and instincts to take over, he cast a last glance down at the boy, to make sure he had missed nothing.

The young man's shirt was threadbare and his trousers patched, but his boots looked expensive, as did the hat lying on the ground where it had fallen beside the corpse. The heels of the boots were adorned with large spurs, such as Stokes had seen worn by some of the riders at Buffalo Bill's Wild West show at Earl's Court. Beside the boy's right hand, in the mud, lay a short-barrelled revolver.

Stokes' ears were ringing. The crack of the pistol shots had all but deafened him. The doomed boy had fired twice, both bullets missing their mark. The third shot had come from the man who had stepped out after him.

He looked old enough to be the father of the youth he had killed. Even his grandfather, Stokes thought. The man's grey hair hung down in unruly greasy waves over his shoulders. His face was weathered and wrinkled, his long moustache white and his cheeks bristled with several days' worth of stubble. His clothes were simple, chosen for comfort rather than fashion. His hat and jacket were dusty; the trousers, tucked into supple riding boots bearing short spurs, showed signs of wear, perhaps from long days in the saddle.

The man might be old, but Stokes had witnessed how deadly he was. As the boy ranted and screamed, the grey-haired man had watched, hand resting lightly on the butt of his holstered pistol. He didn't move and had said nothing for a time until he uttered the few words that had sent the boy into such a blind rage that he had jerked his revolver out of its holster and fired wildly. The old man had not flinched, though there had been less than ten feet separating them. An instant later, his revolver, a gleaming Remington, had appeared to leap into his hand. It had barked once, silencing the boy and his frantic shooting forever.

"You son of a bitch!" shouted a long-faced man with pox scars on his cheeks who had followed the boy out of the billiard hall. "You killed Wyc." His face was growing redder by the second. "You didn't need to kill him." His hand dropped to the dark wooden butt of the revolver he wore in a black leather holster on his right hip.

"Done a lot of things I didn't need to," said the old man who had shot the boy called Wyc. "Killing your friend ain't one of 'em." The barrel of his Remington did not waver as he pulled the hammer back with his thumb. He had fired only one shot, but the bullet had caught Wyc in the chin and exited from the back of his head, leaving a hole the size of a teacup saucer.

Several men had come out of the billiard hall with Wyc, voices raised and joining in his brash insults, but Stokes noticed that none of them had been foolish enough to reach for their own guns. Most had already fled, running off as the shots were fired. The few that remained now edged away from the angry man who vented his ire at the calm, grey-haired shooter.

The pock-cheeked man swallowed, perhaps suddenly aware of his predicament. He was staring into the smoking barrel of a revolver in the sure hands of a proven killer. His fingers trembled above the butt of his handgun.

"Halt," Stokes said, his voice cutting through the hubbub. "Both of you." Everybody turned to look at him. Everybody except the old man with the Remington. His hand did not move and his gun remained trained on the red-faced cowhand. Stokes was used to having his voice listened to, but nobody here seemed inclined to obey him. He took a step closer and snapped his fingers.

"Give me the gun," he said to the old man, using the tone he had employed when ordering men in battle, or in the slums of the East End. "There is no need for any more violence. I am a witness that you did not shoot first. Now, uncock your pistol and hand it over." He held out his hand and was pleased to see it was not shaking.

The old man did not move.

"You ain't from around these parts," he said, without taking his eyes off the pock-faced man.

"No," replied Stokes, pulling himself up to his full height of six feet and two inches. "I am from London. I was in the police force there," he added, thinking the comment might lend weight to his position. He regretted saying it as soon as he uttered the words.

"Well, policeman. You're a long way from home. You can put your hand away. Ain't about to give you my cannon. Don't know how you do things in London, but this is Oregon, and here we keep ahold of our guns while there are snakes around who might need shooting."

"Who are you calling a snake?" spluttered the furious man.

A thin smile played across the old man's face as if he was enjoying himself.

5

"You, Rab Tovey," he said, still smiling. "You and your dickless friends. You're worse than Wyc there. At least he had the sand to draw on me. You're too much of a coward to clear leather. You're all wind." He paused, as if waiting for a response. "Well, if you ain't gonna fight, pick up your dead and get."

Some of the colour drained from Rab Tovey's cheeks.

"Why, you son of a bitch. If you didn't have the drop on me, I'd fight you. But everyone knows you're a killer."

The old man's eyes narrowed and grew cold and hard, all humour gone.

"You say you know I'm a killer, Tovey. And still you've called my good Ma a whore twice. Perhaps you're a brave man after all. I've killed men for less. So tell me, which is it? Brave or stupid?"

The crowd had fallen silent. Tovey chewed his lip, caught in an agony of indecision. Neither man paid any attention to Stokes. The men around Tovey moved further away from him. The air crackled like it did before a thunderstorm. Any second the storm would come and there would be another corpse beside Wyc. Perhaps more than one. And for what? Too much whiskey and some clumsy insults. Stokes contemplated making a grab for the gun in the old man's hand, but immediately dismissed the thought. He had seen the ease with which he had killed, and despite his age he looked strong. Feeling foolish, Stokes lowered his arm. He should not have got involved. This was not his fight.

The locomotive let out an echoing whistle in a great plume of steam, breaking the tense spell that had fallen over the gathered men.

"What's going on here?"

The loud voice came from behind Tovey and a fat man pushed his way through the crowd. He wore no hat and his hair was an unruly mess, as if he had just been woken up. He was in his shirt sleeves, and the shirt was untucked. The long tails of the garment hung halfway down his thighs, reminiscent of a nightgown and further enhancing the impression he had recently been asleep.

The newcomer was bleary-eyed and sweaty, and it would have been easy to disregard him but for the Winchester rifle he held in his hands. He actioned the lever, chambering a cartridge, and levelled the gun to cover both the old man and Tovey. Stokes took a step away from them, lessening the chance of a stray bullet finding him.

"Lower the smoke wagon, White," the newcomer said, quickly assessing the situation. "There'll be no more shooting here unless I'm the one doing it. Now, holster your handgun."

The old man fixed him with his cold eyes for a few seconds, then, without a word, he uncocked his revolver and slipped it into its holster without looking down.

As soon as the gun had been lowered, whatever bravery Tovey possessed returned along with his rage.

"Now see here, Deputy," he said, "that bastard White killed Wycliff Furlong. He wasn't nothing more than a boy."

The fat man stepped close and looked down at the prostrate form of the dead boy.

"He was man enough to have a gun." He bent down and scooped up the revolver from the muddy street. Standing straight again, he rested the stock of the Winchester on his hip and raised the pistol to his nose with his left hand. "Old enough to pull a gun and fire it too, it seems to me. If he was stupid enough to draw on Jedediah White, I'm guessing he got what was coming to him."

"Now listen here, Josh—" Tovey said.

"That's Deputy Briggs to you."

Tovey sputtered, his face flushing once more. The portly deputy stared at him, unblinking.

"Now listen here, Deputy," Tovey said at last, and Briggs nodded. "White here shot Wyc in cold blood."

The deputy held up the pistol he had retrieved from the ground.

"That's not how I see it."

"Well, you wasn't here to see it."

Some of the other men spoke up, lending their voices to the protests against the man they called Jedediah White, emboldened by the fact that the old man's gun was no longer pointing at anyone. Their voices rose in pitch and Deputy Briggs looked about him, his air of control slipping, looking more like a drunk who had just been roused from sleeping off the effects of a long night.

Briggs tried to speak, but nobody was listening. In the distance, the train's whistle sounded again and the locomotive began to move with a squeal of metal on metal and the slow rhythmic thump of the steam engine. The men raised their voices to be heard. Briggs was growing increasingly agitated. Stokes felt sorry for him. He knew all too well what it was to be harangued by a group of angry men all defending their friend. He was contemplating stepping in to help the beleaguered deputy when Briggs lifted his Winchester off his hip one-handed and fired it into the air.

The sharp report of the rifle silenced the crowd.

"I didn't see what happened," Briggs said, now that he had their attention, "but I got eyes, and a man with half a brain can see what went down here. Wyc pulled his sidearm on Jed." He inspected the revolver in his hand quickly. "And Wyc must have been drunk or just a bad shot, 'cause he got off a couple of shots before White plugged him."

"He was provoked!" shouted Tovey.

"I don't care how much provocation there was. If your man shot first, no judge is gonna convict White for defending hisself."

Tovey's face took on a sly look.

"You gonna arrest him then?" he said. "He should answer to a judge for what he done."

"I suppose I should..." Briggs said uncertainly.

"Ain't nobody arresting me today," said White, his tone flat. "You said it. All I did was defend myself."

"And if that's true, you will be free just as soon as you stand before a judge."

"And when would that be?"

Briggs sniffed.

"A few weeks." He shoved Wyc's revolver into his belt. "A month perhaps. Judge Olmsted had an apoplexy couple weeks back, poor man. We're waiting on a new judge."

"I ain't sitting in your jail for a month, Briggs. Got nothing against you, but I doubt you could keep me safe from the likes of Tovey and the rest of the Cabin Creek boys. Likely as not they'd throw me a necktie party before any judge came to town."

The deputy was becoming flustered. He could sense the situation unravelling again. The sounds of the train were fading now as the locomotive picked up speed, pulling its carriages towards the setting sun.

"Now listen here, Jed—"

"No, you listen to me," interrupted White. "I'm needed back at the ranch and I ain't done nothing wrong. Ask this gent." He turned towards Stokes.

"Who cares what this easterner says?" sneered Tovey.

Briggs ignored him.

"Who are you?" he asked.

"My name is Stokes."

"He's a lawman too," interjected White.

Briggs looked Gabriel Stokes up and down, taking in the wrinkled dark suit and narrow-brimmed hat.

"That right?"

"Until this year I served in the Metropolitan Police Force of London."

"London, England?"

Stokes didn't know of any other Londons.

"The same."

Briggs' eyebrows rose. His eyes flicked to the bag Stokes had dropped on the sidewalk.

"Just arrived?"

"On the train from Granger, Wyoming, yes."

Tovey stepped forward, his fists clenched at his sides.

"You're not gonna listen to this damned Englishman, are you, Josh?"

"I've told you already, Tovey. You need to refer to me as Deputy Briggs."

"Well, hell," said Tovey. "You know me. This foreigner just stepped off the train and you're gonna listen to him over me?"

"I'm getting tired of hearing your voice, Tovey. If you don't shut up, you'll be spending the night in the calaboose."

"You'd have to hear me all night then," replied Tovey testily. Briggs glared at him. Tovey stopped talking.

"Did you see what happened here?" the deputy asked Stokes.

"I did," he replied. "You have a keen eye. It was as you described it." Briggs stood a little taller, enjoying the praise from a fellow professional. "They stepped out of the saloon and the deceased was shouting and insulting this gentleman." Stokes indicated White. "Calling him a liar. And other things."

"He ain't no gentleman," said Tovey with a snort.

Briggs and Stokes ignored him.

"Mr White exchanged words with the young man," Stokes said.

"What did he say?" asked Briggs.

Stokes drew in a deep breath. He didn't wish to repeat White's words, but he owed it to the deputy to give him all the facts. He cleared his throat.

"He said that the boy's mother was a..." he hesitated. "That she was a lady of ill repute and..." He faltered again, before rushing on. "That she pleasured Indians."

Someone in the crowd let out a barking laugh.

White spoke up.

"I said his whore of a mother sucked redskins' pizzles for whiskey. That's what I said."

10

"You see?" said Tovey, his face redder than ever. "How's a man to stand for such talk?"

"That's fighting talk all right," said Briggs, shaking his head. "But I've heard worse, and it seems to me that nobody forced Wyc to pull his pistol. Is that so, Mr Stokes?"

"Quite so. The boy unholstered his revolver and fired twice, just as you surmised. Mr White here then drew his own revolver and shot once, killing the boy instantly. You arrived shortly after."

Deputy Briggs said nothing for a time, mulling over what he had heard and weighing up his options. Without warning, he worked the lever on his Winchester, shouldered it quickly and aimed it at White. The grey-haired man's hand dropped to his Remington, but he did not draw it. White was clearly no fool. No matter how fast he might be, he had no hope of beating the deputy.

"Mr Stokes," Briggs said. "Would you be so good as to disarm Mr White?" There was a waver in his voice, but Stokes noted that the man's rifle was steady enough.

Stokes looked about him at the expectant faces of the onlookers. Tovey was grinning in triumph. One of his comrades whooped at the turn of events. Beyond them, on the dusty street a large wagon laden with lumber was being hauled towards them by a team of six mules. The sun was setting, and the sky was afire. The hills in the distance were shadows that promised forests and cool streams. Stokes sighed. He wished he had ignored the fracas outside the saloon. He really had not wanted to get involved, but here he was. He had travelled halfway around the world but was incapable of escaping the violence of men.

"Mr Stokes?" the deputy repeated, the quaver in his voice more evident now.

There was nothing for it. Briggs was in a difficult spot. He could not leave the poor deputy to deal with this alone. With a nod, Stokes moved close to White and pulled the Remington from its holster. The man smelt strongly of whiskey, sweat and horses. He made no attempt to prevent Stokes from removing his gun. Stokes noticed that the man wore a second revolver on his other hip. It had been hidden by his faded black frock coat. Stokes tugged the other pistol from its holster too. It was identical to the first, but with an ivory handle, rather than dark wood.

"Any other weapons?" Stokes asked.

White turned his cold eyes on him for the first time and Stokes understood why Briggs was nervous.

"There's a Derringer in my left boot and a knife on the back of my belt."

"Thank you," Stokes said, taking those weapons too. The Derringer was a tiny pistol that held two shots and would only be effective at very close range. The knife, sheathed in buckskin, was as big as a butcher's cleaver.

Stokes stepped back, holding the weapons awkwardly.

"Next time just get 'em to unbuckle their gun belt," said Briggs.

Stokes felt his face grow hot. He was not accustomed to dealing with such heavily armed suspects.

"I am not planning on disarming any more men," he said. "Would you like me to search him?"

Stokes had learnt the hard way never to trust someone being taken into custody. The long scar along the back of his left hand was a constant reminder. He had been arresting a drunken Turkish sailor. The man had been quiet and obliging and Stokes had relaxed, believing him cowed. The sailor had pulled the razor from his sleeve and it had only been luck and instinct that had prevented Stokes from having his face slashed. Instead the man had cut deeply into his hand. It had bled terribly and even now, nearly seven years later, his grip was not as strong as it had once been.

"I don't think that will be necessary," said Briggs. His confidence was returning now that White was no longer armed. "What do you say, Jed?"

"I ain't carrying no more weapons. If you don't believe me, I could strip right here in the street."

"Keep your clothes on, old man," Briggs said. "Tovey, have one of your boys send for the undertaker. See to your man and then I want you out of town first thing tomorrow."

"But, Josh—" he caught himself. "I mean Deputy Briggs, we only got into town a couple hours ago."

"And you've had more than enough fun. Unless you want to end up in the jail with White, you'll be gone before I come down to the hotel for my morning coffee."

"It ain't right," Tovey grumbled.

"It is what it is, but Marshal Mathey isn't here, so what I say goes, and I say you get out of town, the lot of you. You can come back for the trial. Until then, see to Wyc and get out of Huntington."

The men were not happy, but Briggs ignored them and began leading White in the direction he'd come from. Stokes clumsily picked up his valise, balancing one of the pistols and the huge knife on top of it. He slipped the Derringer into his pocket and, holding the ivory-handled Remington in his left hand, followed Briggs and White.

Chapter Two

The Marshal's office wasn't far. There was nobody else in the building. There were two cells at the rear, with the front being taken up by a desk, a couple of chairs, a pot-bellied stove and two cabinets that Stokes thought equally as likely to hold paperwork as ammunition and guns.

Briggs led White to the cell furthest from the front door. The cell doors were made of stout bars and the rear walls were constructed of brick. White sat down on the narrow bed as Briggs pulled the door shut and locked it with a key he took from the desk drawer. Taking his jacket from the back of the chair, Briggs put it on, then slipped the key into the inside pocket. Stokes noticed that the blankets from the bed in the other cell were crumpled on the floor. Tucking his shirt into his trousers, Briggs produced a bottle of whiskey from one of the cabinets. He poured a large measure into a metal mug on his desk, then went back to the cabinets and dug out a grimy glass, which he half filled.

"Thanks for your help back there," he said, pushing the glass towards Stokes and letting out a long breath. Stokes remained motionless. He didn't want to sit and chat with the man, but neither did he wish to appear rude. He had probably already made enemies of Rab Tovey and the rest of Wyc's friends for speaking up on behalf of White. He had only told the truth, but he was a stranger here and had been in town for less than an hour. Not a great start to his western adventure, though he had to admit the West was living up to its reputation of being wild.

The few people he had talked to on the ship and in New York had spoken of the West as a settled and tamed land, but there seemed little tame about the men of Huntington.

Seeing Stokes had made no move to accept the whiskey, Briggs nudged it closer.

"Have a drink, Mr Stokes. It's the least I can do. I know I need one." He took a long swallow from his cup and replenished it from the bottle. His hand shook and he spilt a splash. The smell of sour sweat and whiskey was strong in the office. Stokes wondered how much and how frequently the man drank.

"No, thank you," he said. "I don't imbibe."

It was the truth, but he looked longingly at the amber liquid. He hadn't touched a drop for nearly a year, but he could not deny that it called to him. He was tired and like Briggs his hands had begun to tremble, as they did after any action.

"Where do you want me to leave Mr White's things?" he asked.

"Put 'em on the desk."

The desk was already crowded with a folded copy of *The Oregonian*, an open journal, pen and ink, a lamp, and the whiskey bottle and glass. Stokes deposited the ivory-handled Remington and the Derringer on the cluttered desktop. Dropping his bag on the floor, he retrieved the other pistol and the knife and laid them on the desk too. Concerned that the glass might be toppled and the liquid it held spilt, Briggs snatched it up.

"You sure you don't want any?" he said, holding the glass up. The golden rays of the setting sun seeped through the small window, making the whiskey glow. Stokes imagined the taste of it; the warming sensation of the liquor trickling down his throat.

"No, thank you," he said, turning away and feeling the sunlight on his face.

Briggs shrugged and drained the glass.

"You have something," Briggs said, gesturing self-consciously at his own face.

Stokes reached up and touched his left cheek.

"Other side," Briggs said.

Stokes moved his hand and felt something sticky. He looked at his fingers. The sun from the window made the blood on them bright. He frowned. He felt no pain and did not recall being struck. For a second he was confused, but then, with a twist of his stomach, he understood. It must be the boy's blood. He had been standing very near when White shot him.

Pulling a handkerchief from his breast pocket, Stokes dabbed at his cheek. The white linen came away smudged with dark red. He immediately regretted using the handkerchief. It had been a gift from Rebecca. He hesitated, then continued to clean his face with it. Perhaps it was fitting that every time he looked at the cloth in the future he should recall such a violent death. Tiredness and sorrow suddenly threatened to engulf him. He felt momentarily woozy and reached out to steady himself on the desk.

"You OK?" asked Briggs, looking anxious.

"I'm fine, thank you." Stokes folded the handkerchief and put it back into his pocket. "Just tired. Can you recommend a hotel in town?"

"The Gate City Hotel is clean enough. It's not far."

"If you could direct me, I'd be much obliged."

"Of course." Briggs rose and walked towards the door to the street.

"How are you planning on getting to the JT Ranch?" called White from the cell at the rear of the building.

Briggs turned towards the prisoner.

"Quieten down now, White," he said. "I'm sorry I had to lock you up, but I'll get you some grub soon. Just let me show this gentleman the way to the hotel first."

White's words had sliced through Gabriel Stokes' weary sadness. He halted and peered through the bars into the

16

shadows. White was still sitting on the bunk. His eyes glimmered in the gloom.

"How did you know I was heading to John Thornford's Ranch?" Stokes said.

"There ain't many Englishmen arrive in Huntington," White said.

"Still, I could be going anywhere. Oregon is a big place."

"That it is, which is why I came to Huntington to meet you from the train. Figured you'd need someone to show you the way to the JT."

"You're Thornford's man then?" That made sense to Stokes. John had always been an excellent judge of character and ability. And whatever else White might be, he was certainly capable. "I had started to wonder if he had received my telegram."

He had not wanted to admit it to himself, as it seemed petty, but he had been hurt not to find his friend waiting for him on the platform at Huntington. They had not seen each other for several years, not since John had left England, and while it might have been churlish of him to expect it, Stokes felt it would have been decent for John to at least have made the trip to the station after the weeks of travel his friend had endured to get there. But of course, he told himself, there were many reasons John Thornford might not have been able to make the trip. It was lambing season after all. With the hundreds of sheep on his ranch, John's hands would be full. There was little time for rest on a thriving farm in spring. Stokes looked forward to helping his friend. Working up a sweat in the fields was just what he needed to take his mind away from London.

From Rebecca.

And Jane Adams...

If he could drive himself to exhaustion, perhaps the nightmares would come less frequently. He pushed away the dark memories that lurked just beneath the surface of his thoughts, ready to rise up and grip him in their terrifying, blood-soaked grasp.

"Too busy to come and meet me in person, I suppose," he said.

"I work for the JT," White said. The old man was looking at him intently and Stokes wondered how much of his thoughts could be seen on his face. "But Thornford ain't too busy to come and meet you," White went on. "Fact is, sure he would have come himself, if he could."

There was something in the man's tone Stokes did not like. He felt a cold finger of dread scratch along his spine.

"Why wasn't he able to?" he asked.

Jed White sucked his teeth.

"John Thornford can't do nothing," he said. "He's dead."

Chapter Three

In the first seconds after White spoke from the shadows of his cell Stokes felt himself standing on the edge of an abyss. Surely he had misheard the old man. John couldn't be dead. Stokes was no stranger to the cruelty of the world, but the unfairness of life still managed to surprise him at times. He tried to ask White questions about his friend's death, but he could not find the words, such was his state of shock.

Briggs was embarrassed, unsure how to react to the Englishman's obvious distress. Again he offered him a drink, but Stokes scarcely heard him.

"What of his wife?" he asked, his voice trembling with emotion. "And the children?"

"They're at the JT," replied White.

"Are they safe?" Stokes asked.

"Safe enough. Reckon."

"What does that mean?"

"Well, figure they're as safe as anyone in this territory."

"That doesn't sound safe to me. I have only been here an hour and already I have seen a man killed and learnt of my friend's death." In an effort to regain his composure, Stokes took a couple of steps away from the desk and approached the iron bars of the cells. "What happened to John?"

"Shot." White's tone was curt.

Stokes grasped the bars for support.

"By whom?"

White rose from the bed. The ropes supporting the thin

mattress creaked. Walking forward, his eyes glimmered, reflecting the window like sparks.

"Grant's men," he said.

"Grant?"

"Tom Grant." White's hard tone showed his feelings towards the man. "Cattleman. Owns the Cabin Creek spread. Been trying to get Thornford to sell up and move on. Things turned ugly these past months. Figure he got tired of asking." He bit his lip and chewed at his whiskers. "It will be hard for Mary Ann to run the ranch without the Captain around."

The thought of the woman alone in this violent land, widowed for a second time, with children to care for and a sheep farm to tend to, all in the face of a hostile neighbour who was apparently capable of murder, kindled a flame within Stokes. This was what he needed to distract from his melancholy, to drive him forward, away from the precipice of despair. He had come halfway around the world to be here, arriving just at this time of tribulation for John Thornford's family. Perhaps it was where he was meant to be.

He could imagine Eliza saying it was God's divine will; that he had been sent here for a reason. Stokes was uncertain how he felt about God. He had seen too much evil and suffering in his thirty-one years to believe in a merciful Lord, but he grasped tightly to the idea that he might be able to make a difference to somebody here in this wild land, so far from all he had known. And that by focusing on helping John's family to deal with their grief, he might be able to stave off his own. Yes, he would head for the Thornford ranch and offer whatever assistance he could.

Decision made, he felt the darkness of his mood recede, pushed aside by the necessity to plan and to act. He turned back to Briggs who was standing uncertainly by his desk, whiskey bottle in hand, poised to pour himself another drink.

"Before you get drunk," said Stokes, employing the hard tone that had made a company of Hussars snap to attention,

"I need you to help me find a means of transport to take me to Griffith."

"Now?" replied the deputy, his voice shaking slightly. He set down the bottle. "It's almost dark. The train ain't running that way since the floods last week. There might be a stage heading towards La Grande, but that won't be till Tuesday, I reckon."

"I'm not waiting for four days. What about a horse."

"Well, there's the livery stable. Hofland might have a mount you could buy. If he doesn't, you'd have to speak to one of the local ranchers, I suppose. There's Pryor, but that's a day's ride to the south. The Circle D is closer, but Reed Doherty's an ornery son of a bitch and I doubt he'd sell you a horse anyway."

"Why wouldn't he sell me a horse?" Stokes asked. "My money is as good as the next man's."

"Doherty is rich enough that he don't need your money, Mr Stokes. I don't think he'd take your specie even if you offered to pay him triple what any horse is worth." Briggs looked uncomfortable. His eyes lingered on the bottle. His hand twitched as if it would reach for the whiskey of its own volition.

"Why?" Stokes snapped, bringing the man's attention back to him.

Briggs shrugged.

"Hates the English," White said from behind the bars. "He came to Oregon twenty years ago from Ireland. Says his family were like slaves there. Lorded over and downtrodden. Now he has one of the biggest ranches north of the Humboldt River, and he lords it over everyone hereabouts."

Stokes thought of the irony there, but he'd had his share of run-ins with Fenians back in London to know there would be no point in trying to buy a horse from a man who might sympathise with their cause.

"That leaves me the livery then," he said.

"Know for a fact," White said, "Hofland has no spare mounts."

"How can you be so sure?"

"Stabled my animals there yesterday and he told me so." White offered him a sly smile. "But you're in luck, Mr Stokes."

"How's that?" Stokes certainly didn't feel lucky.

"Came with a horse and a pack mule for you. If you can get me out of here, you'll have your horse and a guide back to the JT Ranch."

"Now listen here," said Briggs, his voice rising in consternation. "You're staying put until a new judge comes to town."

"That'll be weeks," said White, "and you know I ain't gonna be convicted on any charge. It was self-defence as sure as cow shit stinks. How about you let me out on a bond."

"Well, I don't know about that. You need a hearing for that and Marshal Mathey handles the bonds. There's a lot of paperwork." He rubbed a hand over his stubbled cheeks and his eyes flicked to the bottle again. "Besides, I doubt you have the kind of money needed to be released on recog..." Briggs stumbled over the word. "On recognition," he said at last, looking unconvinced he had got it right.

"Recognisance?" said Stokes.

"That," replied Briggs, nodding.

"Ain't got much cash money," said White. "You ain't wrong there. But Mr Stokes here might be able to help me out. I'm good for it, and you'll get it back when I attend the trial."

Stokes frowned. He couldn't escape the feeling he was being tricked, like a tourist betting on a game of three card monte. But he had made his decision and this would move him towards his goal.

"How much money are we talking about?" he asked.

Briggs licked his lips.

"The last bond we took was for a horse thief and that was for five hundred dollars. I reckon for a killing we'd need at least a thousand."

Stokes shook his head. He could have raised those funds in England, but he had promised to himself that this trip would not eat into his family's wealth. He still had plenty of bills to pay back home.

"I don't have that kind of money," he said.

"Thornford told me you was rich," said White.

"Well," Stokes said, fixing the old man with a firm stare, "I am not."

"How much you got then?" said Briggs, suddenly eager to make a deal. "The lowest I could go is eight hundred."

"Why don't I just leave you here, White?" Stokes said, holding the grey-haired man's gaze. "I could just go to the stables and take the horse you brought for me."

White grinned.

"You won't do that."

"Why not?"

"Because you're a lawman and that would be horse thieving. They hang men for horse thieving in these parts."

Stokes could not face the thought of remaining in the town for days waiting for either the train or a stage coach. White had recognised that and, seeing a way to be free of the jail, he was going to hold on to it. The fact that John Thornford's widow had sent him with the horse specifically for Stokes seemed to make no impact on Jed White.

In the end, after much unseemly haggling that reminded Stokes of dealing with the traders and hawkers of Rawul Pindi, he handed over to Briggs seven hundred dollars. He demanded a receipt, which slowed the whole process down and made Briggs scowl as he scratched out the details of the transaction in a large ledger. Stokes felt a fool for parting with such a large sum, but he was damned if he was going to allow the fat deputy to take a percentage off the top to pay for his drinking habit. White had the look of a scoundrel and Stokes was certain that given a choice the man would not attend the trial. But if White imagined Stokes would allow himself to be made a fool of, the old man had underestimated him. Stokes pushed that thought aside. That was a conflict for another day. Now, they had to leave town. That had been the only other condition Briggs had placed on White's release. He was to vacate the city limits before sunrise.

"If any of those Cabin Creek boys see you, there'll be more gun play," he said.

"And more dead Cabin Creek hands," said White in a gruff whisper.

"That's what I am afraid of," said Briggs. "I've had more than enough killing for my liking. I don't want to see either of you in town again until the day of the trial. Once you get to Griffith you'll be Sheriff Bannon's problem."

Stokes agreed to leave Huntington just as soon as they got their animals and his luggage.

The livery stable was the other side of town from the station, but they saw few people on the street. A couple of Chinamen lounged outside one of the last buildings they passed. They stared at them as they approached. A hooded lamp hung from a hook outside the door, casting a pool of yellow light, but doing little to illuminate the men's faces.

"Whore?" one said, his accent strong. "Opium?"

Through the small, steamed-up windows Stokes glimpsed slumped, reclining figures, wreathed in smoke. His step faltered.

"Not tonight, Johnny boy," said White without hesitation, and walked on.

Stokes hurried after him. White glanced sidelong at him, but said nothing.

Brandon Hofland, the hostler, slept in his stable and did not appear to mind having his evening interrupted. He helped them saddle the two horses and the mule. Before they led the animals into the night, White walked along the stalls, inspecting the other horses stabled there.

"What did you see?" Stokes asked as they rode along the street towards the station.

"Grant's cowpokes' horses."

The station master was less agreeable than Hofland about

being disturbed. He came to his door, holding a lamp that illuminated his scowling features, unruly hair and the nightshirt that hung limply over his slender shoulders. He was barefoot, spindly legs protruding from the nightshirt like twigs. He blinked at the two men standing in the dark street outside his house. His features were sharp and wrinkled. His skin looked as grey as his hair in the darkness.

"What is it?" he asked, his tone breathless. "Has there been an accident?"

"No," White replied. "Nothing like that. We just need you to open the baggage room so that this gentleman can collect his travel chest."

"It is the middle of the night," the skinny man said, frowning. "He can come for his things when I open up in the morning. I will be there by six o'clock. Which won't be long at all. Now, good night to you."

He made to close the door in their faces, but White stepped forward quickly and shoved his booted foot into the opening. Stokes wondered briefly whether he could spare any more of his money to compensate the man for being woken so late, but White's next action quickly removed that idea.

Pulling his ivory-handled Remington, White pushed it into the man's face. Stokes noted that White did not pull back the hammer, but the station master didn't seem to feel any less threatened. He made as if to flee, but White grabbed him by the collar of his nightshirt and dragged him into the street.

"You'll open the office now," White said. "Or I'll go into your house, find the key and open it myself. And if I have to do that, guess that means you wouldn't be much use to me."

Stokes said nothing, but he was questioning his judgement in travelling with this man. John Thornford had been a good judge of character, but in the short time Stokes had known Jed White, the man had done little to engender his trust.

They walked their horses and the pack mule to the station. The station master, with a large overcoat over his nightshirt

25

and boots on his unstockinged feet, led the way. White holstered his gun and made no further threats.

At the station, they took Stokes' clothes from his travel chest and stuffed them into the mule's panniers. Stokes wrapped the slim, brass-edged mahogany case he'd carried from England in one of his shirts and secured it as safely as he could on the back of the mule. The case contained a finely crafted Dollond telescope. It had been a gift for John, who had told him more than once in his letters how he loved to look up at the night sky. It was a fine instrument and Stokes knew John would have appreciated its craftsmanship.

When the station master saw they did not mean to kill him, he started berating them again, his furious voice shrill in the cool darkness.

"Pull me from my bed in the middle of the night, would you?" he cried. "Threaten to shoot me, would you? And me simply doing my duty for the Union Pacific railroad. All I do every day is serve the men and women of Huntington and travellers from all over these United States, and this is how I'm treated. I've a mind to tell Marshal Mathey about this. I've never known such a thing, not in all my long years of service."

The man's tone grated on the nerves, but Stokes had some sympathy for him.

"Please accept my apologies," he said. "As I cannot carry my travel chest with me on horseback, please dispense of it as you see fit. It is of excellent quality. If you should wish to sell it, I am more than happy for you to keep the proceeds."

"I should think so too," spat the station master. "It is only right I should receive some recompense for how roughly I have been treated."

The master continued to gripe and moan as they packed, and Stokes was pleased when White and he finally rode away from the town and into the raw chill of the hills, leaving the grumbling man behind.

Chapter Four

Stokes looked back over his shoulder at the shadows of the buildings in the dark valley. Earlier there had been the raucous sounds of merriment from the tavern known locally as Miller Station. Someone had been playing a piano and several voices had been raised in bawdy songs. It was quiet now, and as he settled into the easy gait of the horse, he questioned the sense of what he had done. It might have been better to have waited until morning. He could have headed north alone in the daylight. But in the Marshal's office his thoughts had swirled confusingly, like a murmuration of starlings, refusing to stop for long enough to allow him to think. At such times, he had learnt it best to make a decision and move forward. As soon as he did that, his mind became calm, allowing him to tackle the problems at hand.

This tactic had served him well in both the army and the police force, and here, in this small town just west of the line between Oregon and the Idaho Territory, it had once more proved efficacious. He had watched his father be smothered by sorrow, the weight of his sadness dragging him into melancholy, habitual drunkenness and ultimately death. Gabriel Stokes would not allow such a thing to happen to him. There was no use in worrying whether his decision had been correct. All he could do was move forward. The past was immutable, however much the mind wished to pick over every minute detail in the hope of understanding what had led to a certain outcome.

It was too dark to check his pocket watch, but he knew it must be close to two o'clock and most of the townsfolk were asleep. The cold light from the moon and stars in the endless sky reflected on the small river they had splashed through shortly after leaving Huntington. The Burnt River, White had called it. Stokes imagined it ran into the broad expanse of the Snake River just east of town. There was a light shining in the window of the station office building and Stokes wondered if the angry station master was still there, complaining at having been woken in the middle of the night.

The bay gelding Stokes rode stumbled in the darkness, missing its footing on the loose rocks of the track they followed. Stokes grabbed the saddle horn with his right hand, holding the reins in his left as he had seen White do. For a second Stokes thought his horse might fall, and he tensed, ready to throw himself from the saddle. The last thing he needed was to be crushed beneath a horse. The gelding, that White had told him was called Banner, was small compared to the Arabians and Walers he was used to riding, but it was certainly heavy enough to snap his bones. He remembered Samuel Bastin, who had been a better horseman than he. That had not stopped a tall black stallion from rolling on Bastin and killing him when the animal had been shot from beneath him in Afghanistan.

However, his concerns were unfounded. The gelding did not fall. When they had collected the animals from the livery stable, White had said Banner was as nimble as a mountain goat and Stokes had to admit he was impressed by the horse, despite its small stature. The saddle, too, had been a surprise to him. It was much heavier and the seat broader than the saddles he was used to. He felt as though it gripped him and held him on the horse's back. With his feet in the deep stirrups, the raised cantle behind and high saddle horn in front, he thought he would only fall if the horse itself fell, or decided to throw him.

Bastin had served with Stokes and Thornford in the Tenth Royal Hussars and the thought of his unfortunate death brought back Jed White's news. Since White had told him of John Thornford's death, Stokes had been too busy to dwell on the tragedy. But now, as he grew accustomed to the rhythm of his mount's movements, watching White's back as he rode into the darkness, leading the pack mule behind him, Stokes found his mind probing this new wound he had suffered, the way a tongue will poke at a sore tooth.

He had travelled all this way to see John only to find he had died less than a week before. No, that wasn't accurate. All men died eventually. That was natural. This was murder. White said John Thornford had been shot down in cold blood. Stokes could scarcely believe it. Thornford had always seemed invincible, even on the battlefield in the face of howling Ghazis, bullets and cannon balls fizzing in the hot, smoke-fogged air. He was a colossus of a man who rode like a centaur and whose booming voice was often tinged with laughter. They had become firm friends while serving together in Afghanistan and Stokes had been looking forward to seeing him again. John had always had a way of lifting his spirits. Stokes had clung to that thought through the interminable days of travel. He had hoped that John might be able to drag him out of the melancholic funk that had consumed him these last months.

Instead, Stokes now rode through the night, his thoughts as dark as the world around him. Perhaps he should have accepted the offer of whiskey from Deputy Briggs. There could be little point in temperance and sobriety now. He shrugged off the thought. He knew from bitter experience that while the drink would dull his pain for a time, the day always came when he would have to face what life had thrown at him, and accept the consequences of his actions. He had seen the disgust on Rebecca's face on the mornings after he had allowed himself to succumb to temptation and it had stabbed him like a knife.

But he could not blame her for despising his weakness. He had felt the same pity and disdain many times when he had found his father, slumped in his favourite armchair, insensate and soiled.

No, whatever mistakes he might make, he had vowed he would make them with a clear head. It had been too late to undo the damage to his marriage, but he refused to allow the drink to define him.

He took in a deep breath of the night air. It was clear, carrying only the scent of the scrubby bushes and trees that dotted the hillside, the soil turned by the horses' hooves. There were none of the smells of the city or civilization. He sighed. He could not deny that it felt good to be in the saddle again, especially after so many days aboard the stuffy, confined *Etruria* and then the rattling, crowded, uncomfortable train from Nebraska. He hated to be cooped up and had yearned to be free to ride in the wide expanses of land he had observed from the train's window.

He wished he'd had more time to prepare though. A raw wind blew down from the hills that rose to the north of the town. The setting sun had been deceptively warm, its golden rays turning the snow that still dusted the peaks the colour of molten iron. There was no warmth in the breeze now and Stokes regretted not buying gloves and a thicker coat for the journey. It felt good to be riding and away from the noise and smells of humanity, but he had not prepared for a long ride. White said it would take three, or maybe four days to cover the distance to Griffith, the nearest town to John Thornton's ranch. The railroad had not yet reached Griffith, and it had been Stokes' intention to take a train on the new branch of the Oregon Railroad and Navigation Company to La Grande, a few hours' ride from the ranch. But spring floods had caused a landslip somewhere between Weatherby and Durkee Station, badly damaging the recently laid track. It would be days, or perhaps weeks, before it was repaired. Stokes had heard about the route closure before leaving Omaha, and had thought he might buy a horse, or take a coach to Griffith, if he could find one. In either case, he had thought he would have time to buy whatever he might need, such as a waterproof slicker, gloves and a winter coat. He had not anticipated having to rush out of Huntington in the dead of night.

Stokes patted the gelding's neck and shook his head. Even if they had not left so hurriedly, he no longer had enough money to equip himself properly. That was another setback he had not anticipated. He had imagined the money he had brought from England would sustain him for months. He had been frugal and careful until this point, taking only a second cabin berth aboard the ship and then a second class ticket on the railroad, enduring the cramped hard seat and the noisome passengers. Now here he was, the night after he had arrived in Oregon with less than a hundred dollars remaining in his wallet.

As they rode into the hills, the wind stinging his face and making him squint, Stokes hoped John's children would like the telescope. He felt a pang of guilt that he had not thought to bring anything for his friend's wife. How foolish he was. He had been so full of the idea of the endless land, the soaring hills, the never-ending sky and, of course, seeing his old friend, he had not considered gifts for John's wife and children. And now he would arrive unwelcome into their grief, empty-handed and unable to even contribute financially, thanks to his rash decision to pay White's bond.

Rebecca had been right. He was selfish and thoughtless. He rode on behind White, berating himself silently, shivering and wishing he had thought to put on a spare shirt over the one he wore.

They rode uphill for another couple of hours and Stokes only realised he had fallen asleep when White touched his knee. He awoke with a start. His heart thumped against his ribs and he peered into the darkness for signs of danger. But the night was silent and the breeze had died down. Stokes saw they were in a kind of cleft in the land. The spray of stars in the velvet sky offered enough light to see that a steep rocky slope protected them on two sides from the wind. White's horse and the mule were hobbled nearby.

"Seems like sitting on a train all day is tiring work," said White.

Embarrassed, Stokes swung down from the saddle. He grimaced. His legs were stiff from the ride and he took a moment to massage some life into them, bending his knees and stretching. The dull pain in his left leg reminded him of the lance that had pierced his thigh at Maiwand. He would have died there if not for John Thornford. Now he would never have the chance of repaying his debt.

He staggered over to the mule and started to strip the supplies and luggage from its back. He was ashamed that he had dozed off. Years ago he had been accustomed to hard riding and night marches. City life had softened him. Not softened, exactly. He was still hard, perhaps sharper and deadlier than he had ever been, but survival in London relied on a different kind of toughness. The muscles required to sit in a saddle for hours were not commonly employed in the daily life of a Detective Inspector.

"As I've had a sleep, perhaps I should take first watch," he said.

"I'll light a fire first."

White crouched in the darkness and a few minutes later, the flare of a match lit his face. He nursed the flames, feeding them twigs and dried grass before he was satisfied the fire would not go out.

Stokes had removed the saddle from the gelding and brushed its back with a handful of long grass. While White tended to the fire, he moved to the older man's horse, a large sorrel mare, and curried her too.

"Thornford said you were a horseman," said White.

"He was a better rider."

"Seen few more natural in a saddle." White glanced up from the flames. "But you'll do."

They sat and warmed themselves by the small fire for a while. Stokes was glad to be out of the wind. The fire's heat reflected from the rocks, the dancing flames casting strange shadows on the men's faces.

"This is a good place for a camp," Stokes said.

White placed a couple of larger branches on the fire.

"Indians used to use it. Say what you like about those heathens, they sure knew the land. A man could hole up here for days even in the winter. There's water nearby and plenty of firewood. Game too, though less now than there was."

They sat in silence for a few minutes. Stokes' head was clear now, free from the indecision of despair and the temptations of civilization. He had long dreamt of being here, in this untamed land. He had not imagined what he would find here, but even in his grief and shock, part of him revelled in the knowledge that he was at last in the far west of the United States of America, a place he had only known through letters, newspaper articles, yellowbacks and the romantic vision of the West painted by Colonel William F. Cody and his troupe of rough riders and shootists.

"You think Grant's men will follow us?" he asked, breaking the hush that had fallen over them.

"Reckon they might. It's no secret where we're headed."

"How is it they came to be in Huntington at the same time as you? It is some way from the Blue Mountains."

"They were trailing a herd down to the railroad. They can never get enough beeves in the east."

Stokes stared into the flickering flames. He picked up a stick from the small pile White had collected and prodded the fire.

"There's one thing I've been wanting to ask you since we left the Marshal's office," he said.

"What's that?"

The end of the stick had started to burn, so he tossed it onto the fire.

"How can you be so sure it was Grant's men who killed Thornford?"

White stared at him through the flames.

"Easy. Was there when it happened, and before he died, John told me hisself who shot him."

Chapter Five

When Stokes awoke, the sky to the east was grey. It was not yet dawn, but it was close. Wisps of smoke rose from the fire, swirling around the protected cleft where they had slept. Jedediah White was kneeling, blowing life into the fire and dropping splinters of wood and slivers of bark onto the glowing embers.

Stokes sat up quickly, barely suppressing a groan at the ache in his back and legs from the few hours of riding the night before. He was sure that after a few days he would regain the strength he'd once had, but for now he was ashamed to appear so weak, especially when his travelling companion was easily twenty years his senior.

Climbing to his feet, Stokes walked away from the camp to relieve himself. He would have to regain his ability to ride long distances if he were to be of any use out here in this vast wilderness. He walked back to camp, the sky already lightening as the sun rose behind the hills. The wind came in gusts, rattling the stand of aspens that grew around their campsite. His thin jacket did little to protect him from the chill and he wrapped his arms around his chest.

Pausing, he breathed deeply of the cool air and turned to survey the land being slowly unveiled by the lifting of the blanket of night. They had camped in one of the few wooded areas. The hills were sparsely forested, with much of them rocky and barren, only slightly softened by the scrubby covering of sagebrush and patchy grasses. The terrain made him think of the harsh Khyber mountains mixed with the Scottish highlands.

Thick clouds had rolled in from the north while he slept. The sky had been clear as they had sat by the fire in the night. Stokes thought of what White had told him about Thornford's murder. They hadn't spoken for long. White had pulled a piece of mutton jerky out of his saddlebag and cut a strip off for Stokes. It was as hard as leather, but he had eaten nothing since the morning before when he had bought a piece of fried turkey from a wizened woman on the platform at Pocatello, Idaho. So he had chewed the jerky until it was soft enough to swallow and chased it down with a swig of water from the canteen White had passed him. Stokes had offered again to take first watch, but White had shaken his head.

"Don't reckon you'd stay awake even if a stampede of buffalo came over the rise," he said.

It was true that Stokes had felt his eyelids drooping.

"Don't let me sleep too long," he'd said, as he stretched out beside the fire, wrapped in the thin blanket from the bed roll that had been tied behind his saddle. The ground was hard and the night was cold. He had thought he would lie awake, perhaps for the rest of the night, turning over in his mind all that he had learnt and imagining what he might face in the coming days. But no sooner had his head touched the saddle he had placed on the ground to serve as a pillow, than his eyes had closed and Stokes had fallen into a deep, dreamless sleep.

When he walked back into camp White was preparing coffee in a blackened pot. He had bought a hunk of bacon from Hofland the hostler, and a couple of slices of the meat were already sizzling in a small skillet. The smells emanating from the fire made Stokes' stomach grumble and he remembered once more how hungry he was.

"I told you to wake me," he said.

White didn't look up from what he was doing. With his big

36

hunting knife, he flipped over the pieces of bacon. They spat and popped in the hot pan.

"Reckon you needed your beauty sleep," he said.

His condescending tone annoyed Stokes. But then, Stokes realised, White had seen little to make him feel respect for the Englishman. All he had to go on were whatever tales Thornford had told him.

"I'll do better tonight," Stokes said.

"We'll have ridden a ways before tonight." White's tone said as eloquently as any words that he thought Stokes' chances of staying awake after a whole day's riding were even slimmer than after just a couple of hours in the saddle. White set aside the pan of bacon on the ground. "There are cups in that saddlebag."

Glad to be of any use, Stokes fished in the bag and found two battered tin cups that he carried back to the fire. White filled them with coffee and nodded at the pan.

"Help yourself."

White skewered one of the slices of bacon with his knife, blew on it a few times, and began to eat. Stokes waited for a minute, hoping it would be long enough for the bacon to have cooled sufficiently. In the end, the smell of it was too much to resist, and he reached for his piece. Having no knife, he picked it up, but quickly dropped it back into the pan, sucking the tips of his fingers.

White scoffed and shook his head. Stokes felt his face grow hot, imagining what he must look like to this grizzled frontiersman. He had ridden through fire, smoke and death, leading men into the jaws of hell in Afghanistan. He had witnessed blood and suffering in the dingy tenements and alleys of the East End. Yet here he was burning his fingers on bacon fresh from the pan like a child.

Stokes picked up the cup of coffee and took a sip, careful not to scald his mouth and add to his embarrassment. The coffee was bitter. He would have preferred it sweetened with sugar, but he said nothing. It was pleasantly hot, and he welcomed its warmth.

"Do you think it will rain?" he asked.

White glanced up at the sky, then stood. Sheathing his knife, he sniffed the air.

"Maybe," he said, after pondering for a time. "But don't think we'll get another gully washer like we had last week."

He took a few gulps of the nearly boiling coffee, then tossed the dregs onto the fire.

"When you're finished with your breakfast, clean up and get packed. We got a lot of riding to do."

White moved to the animals and started saddling the horses. Stokes ate his bacon quickly, then drank the coffee that was just about cool enough to bear. As he carried the pan, pot and cups down to the small creek that gurgled near the camp, he tried to shake his feeling of inadequacy. He might not have known this land, but he was no callow boy. He could handle himself in a scrape and he understood people and what they were capable of. He was no weakling, but he knew he must look it to White, with his lack of resilience after a short ride. In his time with the army he had spent many nights under the stars, but he had seldom needed to fend for himself. As an officer in The Prince of Wales' Own Hussars he'd had a batman who had tended to him. And more recently, though serving in Scotland Yard and being exposed to the worst aspects of humankind, at home Stokes still had servants: a valet to dress him, a butler, a cook, a scullery maid and a housekeeper.

Harriet had called him mad to make this trip. She rarely approved of his decisions, and he had learnt to dismiss his sister's criticism. But in this perhaps she had been right. He did feel a kind of madness simmering just beneath the surface of his thoughts. But he refused to give in to it, and he refused to fail at the simplest of tasks required of him on this journey. He had come all the way from Liverpool with emigrants from all corners of Europe. Stokes had survived – even thrived – aboard the ship, and he had coped well enough up to this point. He was no fool. He would quickly pick up what knowledge was needed. He would listen and observe, two skills Rebecca would accuse him of desperately lacking. Despite Rebecca's valid grievances with regards to his attentiveness where she was concerned, Stokes knew he was more observant than most men, and he often picked up snippets of information from people who would rather have kept their secrets. It was these abilities, coupled with his knack for unravelling mysteries from seemingly disparate threads of evidence that had seen Stokes rise rapidly through the ranks of the Metropolitan Police.

His need to prove himself by starting his police career as a lowly Detective Constable was something Rebecca had never understood. His family name would most certainly have opened doors to more lucrative and less taxing roles. Harriet, ever the pragmatist, had scoffed at his decision to join the Metropolitan Police. Neither she nor his wife could comprehend what drove him to debase himself so, to seek out a position in which he would rub shoulders with ruffians of the worst stamp and confront the most despicable evil on a daily basis.

But Stokes had watched common soldiers in Afghanistan make the ultimate sacrifice, following orders given by men unfit to command, and, once he had made up his mind to enter the police, he had been adamant that he would earn the right to any rank he obtained.

Only Eliza had understood, perhaps better than Stokes himself. There was a searing need within him to challenge himself, to fight against the darkness that had smothered their father; the gloom of spirit that Gabriel feared might also engulf him if he let down his guard. In the smog-wreathed streets of the capital his quick wits, unerring focus and doggedness permitted him to combat the wickedness that threatened the inhabitants of the clogged tenements. The more depravity he witnessed, the more his fervent pursuit of justice consumed him. In the end – perhaps inevitably, Harriet would say – his obsession had destroyed his marriage, led him into disgrace and forced him to turn his back on the life he had created in London.

Stokes scrubbed the pan as best he could with some gravel from the creek bed. The icy water hurt his fingers more than the burning bacon had. The fat in the pan congealed, slimy and white, and he regretted making the attempt to clean it. He scrubbed harder, hoping that with friction the fat would wash away, but it only smeared it around the pan.

Cursing under his breath, he went over what White had told him the night before as they had sat beside the fire gnawing on mutton jerky. White had seemed pleased to be able to speak about the events of the week before, and after Stokes had pressed him for details of Thornford's death, the words tumbled out of the old man.

"We were riding, John and me, along a gorge, on the north side of the JT Ranch. Van Orman had told us he'd seen some ewes up that way. It's been cold and if they lamb up there on their own, they're likely to lose the lamb, and often as not die themselves. We knew it couldn't be many head, we'd brought most of them down from the hills already, but old Bear Hunter is usually right about such things and Thornford did hate to lose any sheep if he could help it. So we rode out to find the strays.

"The ravine is on the border between the JT and the Cabin Creek land and we were wary. Lars said to us before we rode out that it wasn't worth the risk, not with it being so close to Grant's spread and the trouble we'd already had from the Cabin Creek boys."

"What sort of trouble?" Stokes asked.

"The shooting kind," White replied simply. He spat into the fire. "A few months back, the Cabin Creek boys killed one of Thornford's men. A Basque shepherd called Burusco. Nobody saw the killing and nobody would speak out against them, but everyone knew who done it. They found Burusco's body at the bottom of a gulch, with fifty of Thornford's sheep around him.

All shot dead and left to rot. If that wasn't enough evidence, one of their signs was pinned to his shirt."

"Signs?" Stokes said.

"Canvas sheets with red text. They started appearing along the edges of land that Grant and some of the other ranchers said was for cattle only. The 'Blue Mountain Sheep Shooters' they call themselves. The signs warned sheep men not to let their animals graze the cattle land, or they would face the consequences."

"Grievous consequences indeed," Stokes said. It always amazed him what would drive some men to resort to crime. He had seen men stabbed to death over a spilt beer and women beaten and slashed with broken bottles for merely having looked at a man with the wrong expression, or for having looked at the wrong man. There was no doubt men would murder over land and its use. That was what most wars were fought over after all. And yet, he had thought the wars in America were over. The War between the States had finished when he was a boy of six, and the Indian Wars seemed won apart from a few stubborn renegades. Stokes had not expected Oregon to be as safe as the South Downs, but he had never expected to stumble into another kind of war; one fought by ranchers and sheep-herders over livestock and grazing rights.

"You're sure this Grant was behind the signs and the killing of this Basque shepherd, Burusco?" Stokes asked.

"As sure as I am of anything that I ain't seen with my own eyes. Grant is part of the group of cattlemen looking to drive off the sheep from the range. He made it pretty clear he would do what it took to get Thornford to up sticks and move away. Offered to buy him out, but Thornford was having none of that. Called Grant a lying cheat and a back-shooting son of a bitch in front of his men." White chuckled at the memory. "Grant didn't like that, I can tell you."

"I can imagine," replied Stokes. "That does sound like John though."

Stokes recalled a time in a mess tent in Afghanistan where Captain John Thornford had confronted another captain for striking one of the sepoys without cause. Thornford's fury had come in a flash, his booming voice carrying to all the men of the camp as he had bellowed the most obscene insults at the sweaty English officer. Faced with such words, many men would have felt obliged to demand satisfaction, but Thornford was known to be a crack shot with a pistol and an accomplished swordsman, so the captain had demurred and apologised to Thornford and then, red-faced, to the sepoy too. If he had not been cut in two by a cannon ball in the disastrous rout of Maiwand shortly after, Stokes doubted the man would ever have lived down the embarrassment of the incident.

"Grant had started to bring in men to his ranch," White went on. "Men that weren't there to punch cows, if you get my meaning."

"Muscle?"

"Guns," White said. "Men like Joaquin Lopez and Bull Meacher out of Arizona. Cadmar Byrne from Deadwood."

"Killers?"

"Each one has killed more men than they've tipped steers between 'em. Only one reason a man hires gun-sharks like that."

"Didn't Thornford hire any gunsmen?"

"He had me." White didn't elaborate, but having seen him kill a man, Stokes needed no qualification. "And the Captain was plenty tough hisself. You know that."

Stokes sighed.

"Not tough enough, it seems."

White frowned.

"Guess no man is when there's too much lead in the air. Though some have that way about 'em. The Captain was like that. Hard to believe he would die of anything, let alone a single bullet."

"Who shot him? The gunsmen?" Stokes could feel his anger

42

building within him at the thought of his friend being gunned down simply for refusing to give up what was rightfully his.

"They were all there," said White. "And a few of the Cabin Creek cowpokes too."

Something in White's tone brought a thought to Stokes.

"Was Wyc Furlong there?"

Jed White peered at him through the flame-flicker.

"He was there all right."

Stokes thought about what he had witnessed outside the Central Hotel Saloon and Billiards.

"What happened in that ravine, Mr White?" he asked at length.

White cleared his throat and spat into the fire again. He stared into the flames as he spoke, not meeting Stokes' gaze, lost in the memories of that day.

"They started shooting from above. I caught glimpses of their hats and faces, but there was nowhere for us to defend ourselves. Thornford saw it and shouted for us to turn and run. Our horses were fresh and the men in the rocks were not that close, so we turned and spurred off down the gulch." White hesitated. Picking up a small branch, he flung it down onto the fire angrily, sending up a shower of sparks into the cold night. "His horse was right behind me. Didn't see he'd fallen until we'd loped a good way." He sighed. "Turned back and could see them up on the cliff. The Captain was in the dust. He crawled behind a rock, but there was a long open stretch between us. Tried to reach him, but those bastards had us both pinned down pretty good. Thornford had been hit. Bad. Must have known he was dying. The sun was going down and I was hoping to get to him in the dark. Figured I might be able to patch him up enough to get him to Griffith. There's a doctor there."

A hush fell between them. The only sounds were the sigh of the wind in the aspens and the crackle of the fire. Far off to the west, a wolf moaned at the night. The sorrowful sound made the hairs on Stokes' neck rise. It was a cry known to him only from stories and he had not been prepared for the lonely wildness of it. In that instant he fully understood that this land was still far from tamed.

"The sun was going down," White finally said into the flame-licked darkness. "Spent the afternoon taking shots up at the rocks. Don't think I hit any of 'em. My horse had run off with my Winchester, so I only had my Remingtons. Might have plugged one of 'em if I'd had a chance to take aim, but I was behind a boulder and every time I stuck my head above it, one of those sons of bitches shot back. I decided to run to Thornford as soon as it was dark enough, but he must have sensed the end coming."

White's voice caught in his throat and he did not speak for a time. Stokes was anxious to hear the rest of the story, but he was also experienced in interviewing witnesses. Oftentimes it was best not to ask questions and to let them speak at their own pace. And so it proved in the darkness beside their small campfire. Jedediah White wanted to tell the tale as much as Stokes wanted to hear it, and when he had composed himself, he went on.

"The ravine was in shadow when John called out for the last time." White bit his lip and chewed on his whiskers before continuing. "Won't never forget his words." He fell silent again and Stokes waited, feigning patience, for him to tell him his friend's final words.

White cleared his throat.

"'Cadmar Byrne did for me,' he said. 'But I saw Grant up there with him. Lopez and Meacher too. I ain't gonna make it. But you make sure my family is safe and you see that son of a bitch Tom Grant and his pistoleros swing for what they done.' He was quiet after that. I poked my hat up a little later before it was dark and nobody shot. I thought it might be a trap, so I waited some more. When I finally broke cover, Grant and his hands had left. By the time I got to John, he was dead. Drilled

44

through the chest." He pointed to a spot just above his heart. "How he lasted as long as he did, I'll never know."

Stokes had tried to make sense of all he had learnt, his mind whirling, while his body cried out for rest after the night-time ride.

"Have you drowned in that creek?"

White's shout cut through Stokes' reverie and brought him back to the present.

"Almost done," he called out.

Hurriedly, he finished washing up as well as he could. The pan was still greasy, and he rubbed his hands on some scratchy dry grass to rid them of the worst of the bacon fat.

Having learnt his lesson with the pan, he merely swilled fresh water in the cups. He rinsed out the pot too, throwing out the mess of black coffee grounds. He was surprised to see a dirty piece of rag fall out with the grounds and splash into the fast-flowing water of the creek. No wonder it had been unpleasantly bitter. Hawking, Stokes spat to clear his mouth of the memory of the foul-tasting coffee.

He splashed some of the cold stream water on his face, then scooped some of the water into his mouth and spat again. Picking everything up, he trudged back to the cleft in the hillside where they had camped. The sky was noticeably lighter in the east now and he could make out more details of the trees and the ground.

He recalled the pain on White's face as he'd recounted Thornford's murder and how he had been incapable of reaching him before he died.

"Why do you think Grant and his men left before dark?" Stokes had asked.

White shrugged.

"Asked myself the same thing. All I can think is they were worried some of Thornford's men might come looking for us. Easy to bushwhack a couple of men in a ravine, not so easy to survive a gunfight with a bunch of men with some sand. I reckon they had thought to take us both at once and be done with it. They weren't prepared for a long gunfight, especially if reinforcements arrived from the JT."

"What happened when you went to the police?"

"The only law out here are marshals and sheriffs," White said. "I don't trust neither. I knew nothing would come of it. Grant is a wealthy man and most of the people of Griffith make their living from him. Sheriff is no exception. But Mary Ann wanted justice, so the next morning I took Thornford's body into Griffith and headed straight for Sheriff Bannon's. Bannon went through the motions, he rode out with me to the Cabin Creek Ranch and asked a few questions of Grant and his boys, but they all swore blind they had been nowhere near the ravine the day before. With only my word against Tom Grant and all his hands, Bannon said there was nothing he could do."

"Did he ask to see where the murder occurred?"

"He did, but said I couldn't prove it had been Grant's men and with no further evidence or witnesses, that was the end of the matter."

White was standing impatiently beside the horses when Stokes got back to the camp.

"What took you so long?" he asked. "You eat something that didn't agree with you?"

"Nothing like that. I was just trying to clean the pan."

White took the pan and held it up to the grey dawn light.

"Well, I swear," he said with a sneer. "It looks dirtier than when I gave it to you. And you wasted all that good grease." He shook his head, shoving the pan and the cups into a saddlebag. "I don't know. I wait all this time and all you've done is pushed some grease around. And what did you take the coffee pot for? Give it here."

Sheepishly, Stokes handed him the coffee pot, glad he had not done anything more than rinse the sooty metal vessel out in the creek. White shook the pot and weighed it in his hand. With a sigh he removed the lid and peered inside.

"God damn it," he hissed. "Now I'm gonna need to start a whole new brew. What kind of a fool empties out a coffee pot."

"The English kind," said Stokes with a sigh. "Sorry. But it had a rag in it."

"Course it had a rag in. Helps with the flavour." White rammed the pot into one of the mule's panniers, then swung up onto his sorrel mare. "Where is it?"

Stokes was checking his gelding's cinch, but found that White had already saddled the mount.

"I threw it away," he said, putting his left foot into the stirrup and pulling himself onto the horse's back.

"God damn it," White said again. "Threw away a perfectly good coffee cloth. Thank God we ain't travelling far together. Who knows what else you might knock into a cocked hat?"

Without another word, White put his heels to his sorrel's flanks. Leading the mule behind him, he threaded his way through the aspens down to the rough road and turned northward. With a sigh, Stokes nudged the gelding and it trailed after the other two animals.

The sun was up now, fighting to shine through the thick clouds. When he reached the road he looked at the land. From atop the gelding's back on the hillside he could see for miles. The scrubby hills were desolately beautiful beneath the lowering sky. A large bird, an eagle perhaps, flapped out of the trees behind them and soared away over the valley. Stokes thought of the lone wolf's cry in the night. It carried such sadness and yet it was also the sound of freedom. As he kicked the gelding into a trot after White, he realised he felt exactly the same way that wolf had sounded. He had brought much of his sadness with him to America, but a new, unbridled sense of freedom welled up within him with each hoof beat as they rode further into Oregon.

Chapter Six

They kept up a good pace all that day. They spoke little. White was stern-faced and responded to any conversation with a couple of words or a grunt. It was clear he had done all his talking the night before. Questions burnt within Stokes, but he decided to press his companion no further as they travelled northward. There would be plenty of time to talk when they camped. Perhaps White would be more prone to speaking then.

A cold sleet began to spatter on them, the wind blowing the drops into their faces, so Stokes rode hunched over, looking down at his horse's neck. Again he wished he had brought a warmer coat and also longed for a wide-brimmed hat like White's. It gave the old man some protection from the worst of the sleet, but Stokes' narrow-brimmed billycock did nothing to keep the icy rain from stinging his cheeks.

The land around them, starkly beautiful and wild in the sunshine, was now grey and uninviting, and Stokes rode in miserable silence, his legs and back aching from the unaccustomed effort of riding so far.

When they halted for a rest at midday, sheltering beneath a huge maple tree and chewing on some more of the tough jerky, Stokes dismounted and stretched. He was pleased to find that the aching in his muscles was less pronounced than it had been the night before, despite having ridden further.

White produced a bottle of whiskey from his saddlebags and took a swallow. He proffered the bottle to Stokes.

"Want some?" he asked. "Will help you keep warm."

Stokes was shivering. His fingers felt frozen and his light suit coat was drenched. He gazed for a moment at the bottle, then shook his head.

"Suit yourself," said White, taking another mouthful before pushing the bottle back into his bag.

They mounted and carried on. The sleet stopped falling, but the breeze was still cold and Stokes rode on in a misery of trembling. The thought of the spirit in White's saddlebag crowded other considerations from his mind. He imagined the burning warmth of the drink. A few mouthfuls would shave away some of the sharp edges of his grief. But he had vowed not to fall into temptation again, and he did not mean to break his promise. Not this time. He was determined to be as good as his word and he would not permit the insidious demon alcohol back into his life.

After a couple more hours the cloud began to tatter and tear. The sun's rays, when they reached them, were warm and the two riders stopped on a rise, basking in a brief spell of sunshine. In the valley below the shadows of the clouds chased patches of light over the land.

Again, White offered Stokes a pull on his bottle of whiskey. While still tempted, it was easier to decline with the sun warm on his face. Stokes took a swig from the water canteen, then pulled out his pocket watch. He hadn't thought about it since the night before and it would need winding. Flipping it open, he checked the timepiece. The small hand in the seconds dial was still moving. It was just after three o'clock. He wound the watch with the key on its chain and slipped both watch and key back into his pockets.

They had seen no other living soul on the road all day, but now an incongruous sound reached them on the wind.

"Is that singing?" Stokes asked.

"Chinamen," White said, pointing into the valley with his chin as he took another mouthful of whiskey. "They like to sing while they work."

Stokes peered down into the valley. He picked out the line of the railroad tracks. Following the tracks with his eyes along the valley floor, he saw a large group of men, perhaps a hundred, swarming like ants over a stretch of track that had been swept away by a landslide. From this vantage point Stokes could see where part of a steep embankment had broken away and slipped down over the iron tracks.

"There must be hundreds of tons of earth and rock," he said. The sight reminded him of the Royal Engineers when they set about building a bridge, or reinforcing a road for the heavy artillery to be hauled up high into the Khyber Pass. The wind changed direction and the sounds of the men's singing died away.

"They'll have it clear in a day or two," said White. "Whatever you say about those chinks, they're no coffee boilers."

Stokes glanced at White, thinking perhaps the man was making reference to the incident with the coffee pot that morning. But White had already stowed his whiskey bottle and spurred his sorrel down the slope. Stokes took a last look around at the hills and the valley before them. From the direction they had come, a flock of quail rose up into the cloud-scattered sky but there was no other living thing to be seen. Pushing the canteen into his saddlebag, he urged the gelding into a trot and headed after White.

A couple more times, snatches of the railroad workers' singing reached them, but the trail they followed swung away from the path of the train track, and soon the day was quiet once more, the only sounds those made by the riders and their mounts. It didn't rain again, but Stokes' clothes were still damp and he remained cold, so when they saw the timber buildings of a town in the distance, his spirits lifted. He kicked the gelding into a short canter to catch up with White.

"You think I could buy a warmer coat there?" he asked. "Perhaps a new hat and some gloves too?" He was aware he didn't have much money left, and he could perhaps get by without the hat and gloves, but the coat felt like a necessity. The thought of riding three or four more days in the wind and rain filled him with dismay.

"Reckon you could," said White, without slowing his mare. "There's a good general store in Durkee. Fair prices, and good quality stock."

"Good. I will endeavour to purchase a coat at the very least."

"Not tonight you won't."

"You think the store will be closed when we arrive?"

"We ain't gonna arrive."

"What do you mean? It must be less than an hour away."

"We ain't stopping in Durkee."

The man's matter of fact tone infuriated Stokes. Perhaps the frontiersman, used to sleeping rough and hard travel, was comfortable in these conditions. He was not.

"Why not?" he asked in a flat tone, doing his best to hide his frustration. "I'm cold and wet. I need a coat and I have enough for us to sleep in a hotel. Perhaps we could even have a hot bath." The thought of relaxing in a tub of warm water brought back memories of returning to the house in Montagu Square. Oswald, the butler, would heat a bath for him and he would sometimes soak in it for an hour, sipping a brandy and feeling some of the grime and squalor of the day wash away.

"We won't be sleeping in no hotel," said White. "And we won't be having no hot bath. We'll be safer in the hills. We'll steer clear of the towns and press on as fast as we can. Less likely to bump into any more of the Cabin Creek boys that way."

"But I'm cold and wet," repeated Stokes, hating the pleading tone that had crept into his voice.

White sniffed and spat.

"Better than dead," he said, looking up at the shreds of cloud and the red-tinged sky. "It ain't raining now and it ain't what I'd call cold. It'll be a dry night. You'll dry out soon enough and we'll be safer up there." He nodded off towards the hills that loomed in the west.

Without another word, White turned his horse's head towards the sun and rode off at a lope, the mule jostling behind him.

With a sigh and a lingering look at the ordered lines of the buildings of Durkee to the north, Stokes swung the gelding's head to the left and followed White.

Chapter Seven

White led them to a stand of pine trees to the north-west of Durkee. A stream ran down towards the town, and after watering the animals, White hobbled the horses and the mule just beneath the edge of the trees. He unsaddled the sorrel, while Stokes undid the front and flank cinches of his own mount, and tugged off the saddle, dropping it onto the damp earth under the trees. Together, still in sullen silence, they removed the panniers from the mule, then the pack saddle. White began to rub down the animals with handfuls of grass.

"Fetch enough firewood to last the night," he said, without looking at Stokes.

With a sigh, Stokes set about the task, sure that this was one thing he could do without error. There was an abundance of fallen twigs and branches beneath the pines and he had soon collected several armfuls of fuel and dumped the wood in a pile beside the saddles, panniers and saddlebags.

White, who was pulling the coffee pot out of his bag, glanced at the heap of firewood.

"You really are cold, ain't you?" he said with a twisted grin.

Stokes said nothing. The truth was he had warmed up while collecting the wood, but he would not give White the satisfaction of telling him so. Looking up through the branches and needles of the pines, he saw the sky was darkening. Here, in the shelter of the trees, it was already gloomy.

White hunkered down and set about lighting a fire. He was clearly expert at the task and within a few minutes, even with the damp wood, he had a sizeable blaze going. Thick smoke billowed from the flames, curling up and through the canopy of foliage above them. Stokes watched the smoke rise into the branches.

"If we're being followed," he said, "won't the smoke give our position away."

"It's almost dark," said White. "The trees will break up the smoke and give us cover from being seen."

Stokes looked at the clouds of smoke wafting up from the fire. He was not convinced, but said nothing further, not wishing to embarrass himself again.

White soon had coffee boiling. On tasting it, he complained that it was weedy. To Stokes it tasted altogether more pleasant than the thick bitter brew of that morning, but he decided not to comment. He offered to cook some more of the bacon and White handed him the big knife and the slab of meat.

"Don't suppose you can fry bacon wrong," White said. "Just don't burn it."

He sat with his back against a tree trunk and took a sip of whiskey. He watched Stokes slice off four strips of bacon and place them in the pan that he had balanced over the fire on three rocks.

"Wait for the flames to die down," White said. "The bacon will burn like that." He pulled out the makings of a cigarette and rolled one deftly with his left hand. "Smoke?"

Stokes would have preferred a cigar, but he nodded his thanks and accepted the thin cigarette. Taking the pan from the fire, he set it on the ground. Using a twig, he lit the cigarette and breathed in the smoke deeply, enjoying the sensation. He was reminded of the smog of London, but this smoke was fresher, cleaner, and he sat back with a sigh of pleasure. His back ached much less than he had thought it would. He rubbed at his left thigh, but even the old war wound pained him less than it had the night before. He looked up at the dusk sky through the interwoven boughs of the pines.

"The clouds have blown over," he said. "Looks like you were right and it won't rain tonight." He flicked a glance over at White, who was lighting his own smoke with a burning stick. White caught his eye and raised an eyebrow.

"Course I'm right," he said.

Stokes smiled. "It will be cold though."

White prodded at the fire with the stick, then threw it into the flames. "You'll be warm enough, just so long as you don't let the fire go out." He took another gulp of whiskey, but didn't offer the bottle to Stokes.

Stokes took another drag from the cigarette. It burnt down quickly, the tobacco fine and loosely packed. He finished it and tossed the butt into the fire.

"I won't let it go out," he said. He wanted to ask White more questions about Thornford's killing. About Grant and his hired gun-sharks. But before he could speak, White let out a puff of smoke and said, "Now, you gonna cook that bacon, or what?"

While Stokes set about frying the bacon, taking care not to burn it, White heaved himself up and wandered off into the shadow of the trees, presumably to relieve himself. Stokes watched the sizzling bacon by the flickering light of the flames, turning it every now and again with White's big knife. It smelt wonderful. And White had been right again. It was indeed warm here beside the fire in the shelter of the trees.

A few minutes later, White strolled out of the darkness. Stokes had not heard him approach and the old man's sudden appearance startled him. He did his best to disguise his surprise, but evidently White had not missed it.

"You'd better keep your wits about you tonight, Mr Stokes," he said. "I need to get some sleep. That bacon smells cooked to me."

Stokes ignored the rebuke. It was warranted after he had

fallen asleep the night before. In the army a man who fell asleep on guard duty would be flogged. He considered himself lucky to have got away with it with only a few jibes from White and a feeling of shame.

They ate in silence, both hungry after the day's ride. Stokes' stomach still grumbled, and he wondered how long they could survive on jerky and bacon alone. As if White had read his mind, he pushed himself up and said, "Got some beans in my bags. I'll boil us some up tomorrow with a bit of that bacon. If we have time I'll maybe make us some biscuits too."

Stokes wondered how on earth White planned on baking biscuits with no oven, but he decided not to show his ignorance on the matter. He would observe the man and find out soon enough.

It had not been dark for long and White was already shaking out his bedroll beside the fire. Stokes reconciled himself to receiving no answers to his questions. And he could hardly blame the man for being tired. As far as Stokes knew, White had stayed awake the whole of the previous night.

"You take first watch," White said, wrapping a blanket round him and placing his head on his saddle. "And don't fall asleep. I'll forgive you for last night, but this land is still wild. Won't forgive you many mistakes."

Stokes stood, deciding that if he was standing it would be impossible for him to nod off.

"I won't be doing that again," he said.

"Wake me at midnight." With that, White closed his eyes and started to snore.

Chapter Eight

Stokes fought against his tiredness, but it felt as heavy as a buffalo robe wrapped about him. The night closed in as black as ink and whenever he stood still for any length of time, he yawned and his eyelids began to droop.

Leaning against a pine he felt himself beginning to slip. His eyes snapped open. He had fallen asleep standing up and he berated himself silently for his weakness. But when he went back to place a fresh branch on the fire, he looked at his watch by the light of the flames and saw that only minutes had gone by since he had last checked the hour.

The wind whispered through the trees and the longer he spent staring into the darkness, the more his mind began to play tricks on him. He thought he saw shadows moving in the night. He imagined wolves or even bears creeping close to the camp. But if there were any such predators nearby, they did not show themselves.

A few times he heard night creatures shriek in the woods or in the valley below. He did not recognise the bestial calls and he wondered whether they might be made by owls or some other nocturnal hunter.

For the most part, the hours on guard duty were long and monotonous. Stokes longed for sleep and to be free of his dark thoughts, but time seemed to move more slowly than ever, and when he was not seeing imaginary beasts in the gloom, his mind conjured images from his past.

He saw Rebecca, as he had last seen her. Her face beautiful despite the tears that streaked her high-boned cheeks.

Then, unbidden, other faces, pallid and blood-smeared swam before his mind's eye. Annie Chapman. Elizabeth Stride. Mary Jane Kelly, her once pretty face gashed beyond all recognition.

He saw again the tiny shape of Jane Adams. Or what was left of the poor child. Then, finally, the tongue-jutting stricken features of Frederick Cooper as he had answered for his crimes on the gallows of Newgate Prison. Stokes had been glad to watch the man hang, but even death had not seemed enough. Not after what he had done.

In the end, Stokes decided to rouse White at quarter to midnight. He wasn't sure he would be able to keep his eyes open any longer and he didn't want to fall at the last fence.

White came fully awake in an instant. Looking up at the night sky, he nodded, as if he could tell the time from the few stars he could see through the trees. Perhaps he could. Stokes was beyond caring.

"All quiet," he whispered.

He was dimly aware of White rising as he lay down, pulling his blanket around him. He was asleep in seconds, and mercifully, he did not dream.

The crack of a gunshot awoke him. He could not tell how long he had slept, but it felt as though only minutes had passed. It was still dark. His heart hammered as more gunshots rang out. The shooters were in the trees, and the bright flame flashes from their gun muzzles lit their faces for an instant like the flicker of lightning.

"Save your bullets," snarled a voice Stokes did not recognise. "He ain't there."

A couple more shots boomed out from beneath the trees, lighting up the shapes of several men and making the boles of

58

the trees stand out like pillars in a candlelit cathedral. Then the shooters obeyed the voice and stopped firing.

Stokes had not moved. He was breathing heavily, unsure what to do. He was unarmed, and felt dreadfully exposed, lying as he was within the pool of light cast by the fire. His ears were ringing from the shots, and he could hear the pounding rush of his blood. Forcing himself to remain still, he listened for the slightest indication of where their attackers were.

He strained to hear for a minute or more, but after a few seconds of urgent whispering, the words of which he could not make out, all was silent. He had seen at least four gunmen by the muzzle flashes, and they had all been on the north side of the clearing.

Where was White? Had they already shot him? No. If they had, they would have moved into the camp. White must be out there somewhere in the dark, and they knew it. They were wary of him. Perhaps they had not even noticed Stokes lying in his bedroll beside the fire. That would not last. They would see him soon enough and might decide to reduce their enemies' number. He was defenceless there, in the open.

Still there was no sound.

Stokes readied himself, tensing his muscles ready for action. He had made up his mind not to remain lying there, an easy target for the shooters. Without warning, as quickly as he could, he flung off his blanket and ran for the cover of the hobbled mounts.

His left thigh was stiff, but despite his limp, he was fast. He ducked around behind the animals at the same instant that two shots were fired from the trees. The mule let out a shriek and started bucking. Three more shots came in close succession, all from the same location off to the south-west.

A gurgling cry issued from beneath the trees.

"I been hit, Bull! The old son of a bitch got me."

"Shut your mouth, boy," growled the first voice Stokes had heard.

"I'll kill the rest of you too, if you stay there." The gruff voice was White's, and the second he spoke, another two shots whined through the tree trunks and a man squealed as a bullet splintered a tree near him.

"Run away now, boys," shouted White, as the men scattered and fell over each other in an effort to find cover. This time White's voice came from the west. Stokes could not understand how the old man had moved so quickly without making a sound.

A flurry of shots boomed out from the trees. Stokes ducked behind the mule, which had stopped bucking, and now stood trembling. But none of the bullets found him or the animals. Then came the sound of men crashing through the undergrowth. A few minutes later, the thrum of hooves reached Stokes. The men were riding hard.

"I winged one at least," said White, stepping into the firelight from the north. "There's some blood there, but I doubt I got him good enough to kill him." He cocked his head and listened to the galloping horses as they retreated into the dark. "But if they ride that recklessly at night, one of 'em is apt to run off a bluff, or break his horse's leg, and finish the job I started."

As he spoke he pulled shells from his belt and pushed them into his Winchester's loading gate. Moving to the horses, he handed the carbine to Stokes.

Stokes was breathless, as if he had run a long way. He took the gun and watched White. The grey-haired man was calm and unflustered. He checked over the horses quickly, patting them on their necks and whispering quietly. When he reached the mule, it shied away from his touch.

"Easy there," he said in a soothing tone, stroking down the flanks of the animal. White sucked his teeth, then went and scooped up some of the ash from the edge of the fire. Returning to the mule, he packed the ash onto the animal's rump, just behind where the pack saddle sat. Satisfied with his work, he patted the mule. When he held out his hand, Stokes handed the Winchester to him.

"That's one lucky mule," White said, returning to the fire and sitting down. "I guess we're lucky too. If that bullet had been a few inches lower, that animal would be no use to us. As it is, it just took a scratch. I've seen mesquite leave deeper wounds on a mount." He placed the carbine on the ground, pulled out his tobacco pouch and expertly rolled two cigarettes. He handed one to Stokes, who accepted it gladly. His hand trembled slightly, but less than it had with the cold the previous day.

"You think they'll come back?" Stokes asked after he had lit his smoke.

"Not tonight. They might try us again, but I think they'll be scared enough not to make another go at us before we get back to the JT. I must be getting old though."

Stokes thought of the quick shots, and how White had moved so quickly and quietly.

"You heard them coming and stopped them," he said. "I'd call that a job well done."

White spat into the fire.

"Fired a half dozen times and only wounded one of 'em."

"It was dark. They were in the trees and you didn't know they were coming."

White's cigarette glowed as he sucked in smoke.

"Right," he said. He blew out the smoke in a cloud that drifted away on the breeze. There was something in his tone that gave Stokes pause.

"You knew?"

White grunted.

"I may be old, but I ain't blind. I thought they might swing round to the north, and they did. I should have killed a couple of 'em at least. I had the drop on 'em, and I only managed to clip one."

Stokes couldn't believe what he was hearing.

"You lit that fire and you knew they were on our trail?"

White shrugged.

"You were cold."

Stokes thought of the long hours standing in the darkness, staring out at the night and imagining dangers. He had believed it was his mind playing tricks on him.

"Why didn't you tell me?" he asked, his voice rising as his anger grew.

"Figured you needed your sleep."

"God damn it, man," snapped Stokes, his fury bubbling over. "I could have been killed."

"Well, you weren't."

"No thanks to you."

"You're not wrong there," said White. "Should have killed a few of 'em, and I blame myself for not shooting more accurately. But you're fine, so simmer down."

Stokes was about to reply with a furious retort, but White cut him off.

"Here," he said, "I got you something." He pulled a pistol from his waistband and tossed it over the fire. Stokes had his cigarette in his right hand, but caught the gun easily with his left. He had played cricket for the regiment and had always been a good fieldsman.

"Found it where I hit one of those bushwhackers," White said. "Must've dropped it."

Turning the gun over, Stokes examined it, squinting to make out the text etched into the barrel by the dim light of the fire.

"Colt?"

White nodded.

"Model 1877. What folks call a Lightning. Double action. Good enough gun I hear, but I ain't shot one. Too much to break in the mechanism. Last thing you want when the shooting starts is a gun that don't shoot. I'll stick with these." He patted the pair of Remington revolvers he wore. "They ain't never failed me."

Stokes' anger had dissipated somewhat, deflected by his interest in the pistol in his hand. It looked rather like a Webley to him. It had a similarly shaped grip, but a longer barrel than the service revolver he'd carried in London. Flicking open the loading gate, he half-cocked the hammer and used the ejector rod to push the brass cartridge out into his left hand. He repeated the process with the other five chambers. He was left with four spent cases and two unfired bullets in his palm.

"It's a .38," said White. "I only shoot .44-40s. Same for the Remingtons and the Winchester. Less confusing that way. So those two bullets is all you got till we stop at a town. No practice shooting for you."

Stokes closed the gate, leaving the cylinder empty. Holding the pistol at arm's length, he sighted down the barrel and pulled the trigger four times. Quickly. The hammer moved back as the cylinder turned, then fell with a click each time.

Opening the gate again, he reloaded the two cartridges.

When he'd arrived in America, he'd had no intention of carrying a gun. He was done with wars and death. He had come here in search of freedom, friendship and the peace that came from hard work on the land. Instead he had found murder and violence. He weighed the Colt Lightning in his hand. It felt good. The weapon was clean, and seemed well looked after. With a resigned sigh, he pushed the pistol into his jacket pocket.

"I don't need to practise," he said.

Without another word, he pushed himself to his feet, tossed his cigarette into the fire, and stalked off into the darkness.

Chapter Nine

The next three days passed without further incident. The days were long, but their mounts set a pace that ate up the miles and Stokes felt himself growing quickly stronger. They travelled along a broad valley of lush grassland and dotted woods. To the west and east hills rose into mountains.

They saw few travellers, and avoided settlements. They skirted Baker City and camped several miles outside North Powder. The weather grew milder and it didn't rain again. The nights were cold, but White found sheltered spots to camp, where even a small fire was enough to warm them. They kept watch at night, but White was proven correct in his expectation that they would not be attacked again. The two men seldom spoke. Stokes was disgruntled. He had nothing to say to White. The only time he addressed the older man was to ask something about the land they travelled through; the name of a tree, or a bird, or the best tinder to use to start a fire. Whenever he asked a question, White would answer politely enough. He seemed perfectly content not to converse with the Englishman, and for long stretches of each day and for hours at night sitting beside the campfire, they remained in silence.

After dark they smoked. Stokes wrote in his leather-bound notebook, a gift from his sister Eliza, while White whittled sticks with his huge knife and drank whiskey from the bottle. The whiskey ran out the night after the attack and White's mood soured noticeably the following day. He was short-tempered with the horses. And the mule, that seemed none the worse for the scoured welt it had picked up from the bullet, received an angry slap when it stepped on White's foot.

"God damn stupid animal," shouted White, mounting the sorrel and riding off, leaving Stokes to take the mule's lead rope.

The outburst seemed to shame White, and later, when they rested at midday, Stokes was walking back from where he had relieved himself behind a clump of sagebrush when he saw White whispering softly to the mule and stroking its nose.

Later that afternoon they spotted a herd of several hundred cattle, but they were a long way off, and Stokes couldn't see any cowhands with them. Shortly after passing the cows, a lone mule deer buck had walked out of the trees some fifty yards ahead of them. Without hesitation, White pulled his Winchester from its saddle scabbard, actioned its lever, aimed and fired. The whole process had taken little more than a second and Stokes had barely registered the animal when the shot rang out and smoke billowed. Banner tensed, its ears lowering, and Stokes held on tight in case the animal might decide to throw him. White spurred his mare forward and slid from the saddle. Stokes thought the old man must have missed the deer. He had only seen it for an instant before White had fired; after that it had been lost to view behind the cloud of smoke from the carbine. But as Stokes rode closer, he saw that the deer must have been in the action of springing away when White's bullet had hit. The animal was sprawled in the brush beside the path, eyes open and staring, tongue lolling. The bullet had taken it in the heart, killing it before it hit the dirt.

It was a fine shot indeed, and he sensed White's pride in his skill, but Stokes said nothing, not wishing to praise the man who had left him as bait for their ambushers. The large buck had a broad spread of antlers, but White discarded the head, using his massive knife to quarter the animal. He expertly removed the saddles of meat from the back and cut out the tenderloins, securing the meat on the mule and leaving the rest of the carcass beside the track.

That night White called a halt and set up camp earlier than normal. The venison was gamy and rich and was a welcome change from the tough jerky, beans and fatty bacon. The following morning, his spirits visibly lifted by the killing of the deer, White made the biscuits he had promised, but failed to deliver the day before. He rose before dawn and mixed dough from some flour, water, grease, baking powder and salt, all of which he kept stored in a thick iron pot on the mule. He cooked the biscuits in the pot, which he sat in the embers of the fire, and used a plate to shovel some of the coals onto the lid.

"Fresh meat of an evening and biscuits in the morning," White said, when he took them from the pot. He blew on one, then tried it. "They'd be better with milk and butter," he said, "but they'll do."

"In England, we'd call them scones," Stokes said. "Perfect with some cream and jam. But whatever you call them," he added grudgingly, "they taste good."

With thin slices of the venison fried in the skillet, he couldn't think of many better meals he'd had, and he had eaten at Café de la Paix in Paris and Verrey's in London. As he packed the mule in the dewy cool of the morning, Stokes marvelled at the speed with which this new life had become natural to him.

Despite the tension between the two men, they had fallen into a relaxed routine. They rode from just after dawn until midday, when they rested for a spell, watering the animals and eating some of the leftover biscuits, jerky, or venison that White had smoked over the fire. As the sun swung into the west, they rode on until an hour before sunset. Then White would unerringly lead them to a suitable spot, secluded and hidden from the trail by trees or the lay of the land.

White made a fire while Stokes hobbled, stripped and

brushed down the animals, then set about collecting firewood for the night. While White cooked, Stokes would take out his notebook and write down some of his thoughts on the day's journey. He had promised Eliza he would write regularly, but so far he had only managed one letter from New York that he had written aboard the *Etruria,* and another which he had penned on the train and given to the surly station master in Huntington to post on his behalf.

"What you writing there?" White had asked, glancing over at Stokes on the night after the attack.

They had barely spoken all that day and Stokes felt little desire to engage the man in conversation. He looked up from where he was scratching into his notebook with a pencil he had bought in New York.

"I'm keeping notes on all the ways you annoy me."

To his surprise, White had cackled with laughter.

"You're gonna need a bigger book," he said through his guffaws.

Stokes shook his head. The man was annoying, it was true, but he was also able, and cool and deadly in a tight spot. All of these traits Stokes recorded in his notebook. He would post a letter to Eliza and Harriet from La Grande, or perhaps Griffith, but these notes were not for his sisters' eyes. They would be terrified to know of the dangers he had faced. Besides, he would not give Harriet the satisfaction of being able to say she had been right. His eldest sister had told him he would not find peace in America. To discover she had been correct would give her a perverse sense of pleasure, he knew, even if at the same time she would be worried about his safety. No, he would write a letter speaking only of the beautiful vastness of the land and how the sky seemed bigger and higher here than anywhere he had travelled to in his life before. He could picture Eliza sitting by the fire in the drawing room, reading his letters aloud to Harriet. He supposed William would hear of his exploits too. He imagined Eliza's husband catching Harriet's eye and shaking his head. Both of them disapproved of his choices, and he would rather not give them further reasons for their censure. Only Eliza would truly miss him.

On the third day after leaving Huntington the shadows of high peaks rose in the north. Where the sky had been grey, it was now the blue of faded denim and the sun was warm.

As they got closer to La Grande, they saw more people on the road. There were riders and wagons, and they passed a flock of hundreds of sheep being driven by two men and a rangy sheepdog. The shepherds were dirty and gaunt, as if they had slept outside for weeks. Stokes nodded at them as he rode past. They scowled at him.

He smiled to himself. He probably looked just as travel-worn and grimy as the two men. He had ceased thinking about his appearance, or how he smelt, but if White's state could be used as a measure of his own, he must look like a scarecrow come to life.

"Is that La Grande?" he asked, heeling Banner into a trot alongside White's mare.

A sizeable settlement was ahead of them, its wide streets straight and lined with buildings. It was strange to be confronted with civilization out of the wilderness. It was as if a town had grown from the very sod of the valley.

White grunted. He had been even more taciturn than normal since his whiskey bottle had run dry.

"I'd very much like to have a bath before meeting Mrs Thornford," Stokes said. "I could buy some bullets too." He rubbed a hand over his chin. "And perhaps get a shave."

"Mrs Thornford don't care about a few whiskers."

"I care."

White made no complaint this time as they headed for the city. Stokes thought perhaps it was because he believed their enemies were no longer behind them, or that La Grande was large enough to provide some protection and anonymity to the two riders, but he knew it was bound to have more to do with the fact that a township of that size would have establishments that sold whiskey.

They left the horses and mule at a livery stable on the edge of town, then parted ways, each eager to go about their business in the bustling city. Stokes bought himself some boots, a wide-brimmed hat and a woollen coat, and then paid a barber for a shave, a moustache trim and a hot bath. By the time he was finished, it was getting dark. Feeling fresh-faced and clean, Stokes went in search of White. He didn't need to look far. He found him, gambling and already drunk, in the largest saloon on the main street.

Stokes could see White was engrossed in the game and there was nothing to be gained from talking to him. So he walked across the street to the Golden Rule Hotel, which he deemed would be more economical than the gaudy establishment where White was playing poker. He paid for a room and ordered a steak and a cup of coffee in the dining room. The meat was well-cooked, tasty and filling, but the coffee, though hot and wet, was even worse than the stuff made by White in his beaten old pot. Not that Stokes would admit that to him.

When he went up to his room, he counted out what was left of his meagre funds before flopping onto the bed.

It was noisy in the room. Doors slammed and someone shouted downstairs. Across the street came the sounds of laughter and music from the saloon. A stage trundled by, the coachman cracking his whip. A couple of horses cantered along under his window. A man raised his voice in anger. Dogs barked.

After the recent night-hush of the wilderness, Stokes thought he might struggle to sleep with this racket. Perhaps he would go down to the saloon and watch White play poker. He needed to remind the man not to get too drunk anyway, as they should be leaving first thing in the morning. But the mattress was soft beneath him and despite the sounds of the city that filtered through the hotel's windows and thin plank walls, moments later, without even pulling off his new boots, Stokes was asleep.

Chapter Ten

It was mid-afternoon when they reached the JT Ranch. After an hour climbing the forested flank of the mountain, they rode around a bend in the track and saw the solid-looking timber house. It stood in a large clearing, with views down to the valley below. Smoke trickled out of the stone chimney. Also in the clearing was a large barn and a couple of smaller outbuildings. A covered log store stood against one wall of the farmhouse, the chopped timber stacked neatly.

Half a dozen horses stood in a corral. Beyond that, there were fenced off sheep pens, each full of animals. Stokes noticed there were many lambs in one, jumping and gambolling, nudging to suckle from their patient mothers. The lambs' tails wagged like excited puppies'.

To Stokes the place had the air of a well-ordered farm. There was nothing flamboyant about it, and he could well imagine that any money it made had been ploughed straight back into the business to hire hands, and to buy new stock and building materials. It was a distant cry from what John Thornford had grown up with in the Cotswolds, with the gently rolling hills, hedgerows and drystone walls of his family's farm, but this had been Thornford's dream.

Stokes drew in a deep breath of the fresh air. His heart ached. He would never see his friend again, but he was glad to finally lay eyes on what had given Thornford such joy. This was a good place, and he saw how a man could be content to settle here.

"It's something, ain't it?" said White, slowing his mare so that Stokes caught up with him.

Stokes' throat was thick with emotion. It had come upon him quickly and without warning, so he turned away and looked down at the valley through the pines. White must have noticed his discomfort, but he said nothing. Stokes was glad of that. White's behaviour had been civilized and friendly all day, something which surprised Stokes, given the night the old man had had.

When Stokes had awoken just before dawn, he had been furious at himself for sleeping so soundly. He was sure that White would be drunk and no use. Stokes had hurried across the deserted street to the saloon that was still open, fearing they would have to spend another day and night in La Grande, or that he would have to ride on alone, leaving White to sleep it off. As he had feared, White was still sitting at the table with three other men. Stokes' anger had flared and he was about to start into a tirade aimed at White when the old man had pushed himself to his feet.

"Looks like it's time for me to make a move, gentlemen," he said, raking in his winnings, which looked to Stokes' unpractised eye to be substantial. "The pleasure has been all mine."

To Stokes' amazement, White, though he clearly hadn't slept and had been drinking all night while he gambled, seemed to be sober and in high spirits.

White had paid for a breakfast of eggs, steak, bacon and biscuits in the hotel. When the coffee arrived, he had sipped it and scowled. He produced a bottle of whiskey from the saddlebags he carried, poured a generous amount into the coffee cup, and tried it again.

"Better," he'd said.

As they had ridden north-east into the foothills and the forests that led towards the JT Ranch and the township of Griffith beyond, White had frequently pulled the bottle out and taken a swig. Stokes couldn't help but think of what the

72

whiskey would taste like. He could feel his resolve weakening, and was glad that White had stopped offering him a pull on the bottle whenever he took a drink.

"Ma!"

The shout came from a boy of about ten or eleven years of age. He had been behind the barn and now ran to intercept Stokes and White as they rode down towards the ranch buildings.

"Ma!" the boy shouted again. "Jed's back."

The boy was slender, with fair hair, very different from the man who had married his mother. Thornford had been thickset, with luxuriant black hair and a huge moustache. Ahead of the boy ran a scruffy-looking dog. It barked a few times, but quietened down at a word from the boy.

"Well, Al," said White. "Any news?"

The boy's face grew serious and he suddenly appeared at once both younger and more world-weary.

"Some of the sheep got shot up on the high ridge couple days back."

"Anyone come to the house?"

"No, sir. We ain't seen nobody here."

White frowned, but didn't comment further. In the distance, Stokes could see three men coming from the sheep pens, perhaps alerted by the dog's yapping. A woman and a little girl stepped out onto the porch of the house. A second later the girl started running towards the two riders.

"Adelaide Thornford," shouted the woman. "You come back here at once."

The girl ignored her and kept on coming.

"Want to ride with me to the house?" White asked, offering his hand to the boy.

The boy grinned and nodded.

Taking the boy's eager hand, White effortlessly hauled him up and sat him on the saddle behind him. The dog barked again and Banner shied, but the gelding clearly knew the dog, and was not overly startled by its noise. White trotted across the clearing towards the house, leaving Stokes to lead the mule behind his gelding.

When White reached the girl, he leaned down from the saddle and scooped her up and sat her in front of him. She squealed with delight. The dog ran beside White's mare, looking up at the children as if it too expected to be given a ride on the saddle.

By the time Stokes arrived at the house, White was handing the girl to her mother. The woman stepped out from the shade of the porch, the afternoon sun landing warm and bright on her smooth features. She was a handsome woman, perhaps a year or two older than Stokes himself. She wore a plain black dress, partly covered by an apron. Her hair was tied up and away from her face. As she looked up at White and quietly scolded her daughter for her disobedience, something of the angles in her face, the shape of her lips and chin, reminded Stokes of Rebecca. His breath caught, then the moment was lost and he saw that while both women were pretty, with high cheekbones and full lips, there was little else in common between them. Rebecca was younger and had no lines of worry on her face. Mary Ann Thornford's beauty was tempered with loss and hardship. She had lived in this wild frontier, was the mother to two children and had buried two husbands. Those experiences had left their mark, giving her a tougher aspect, a tense wariness to her blue eyes. She turned to look at Stokes as he dismounted and he recognised a deep sorrow in those eyes.

"Lieutenant Stokes, I presume," she said, her voice cultured and mellow.

He handed the reins and the mule's rope to the youngest of the three men who had come from the sheep pens, a gangly boy of perhaps fifteen. Stepping up onto the porch, he said, "How do you do?" He took the lady's hand and brushed her knuckles with his moustache. "It is a pleasure to finally meet you,

Mrs Thornford. I am sorry it is not under happier circumstances. And please, call me Gabriel."

"Once a hussar, always a hussar, I see," she said with a slight smile. "Mary Ann. Please." Her eyes twinkled, despite the sadness that lingered there. "John always said you were a charmer."

Stokes felt his face grow hot.

"I don't know about that," he said. "A lot has happened since I left the regiment." He imagined his old friend describing the man he had known when they had served together. The man he had once been. "I was so sorry to learn of John's death. It is a tragedy."

Mary Ann bit her lip and closed her eyes for a second, before meeting his gaze again.

"More than a tragedy," she said. "A crime. It still does not seem quite real. It came as a great shock." She pulled her daughter close to her and reached out a hand to her son. He took it, somewhat reluctantly. "This is Albert. And this naughty girl who does not obey her mother is Adelaide."

Both children, under his scrutiny, became serious. Adelaide stared up at him, suddenly shy, her eyes brimming.

"How do you do, sir?" said Albert. Adelaide performed a clumsy curtsey.

"How do you do?" replied Stokes. "Perhaps you would show me round the ranch later, Albert."

"Albert would be a good scout around the place," said White, swinging down from his saddle. "He knows every inch of this land. Always off somewhere with Pincher, ain't you?"

The boy blushed at the praise.

"Perhaps you can show Lieutenant Stokes around later," said his mother, "if he would like. But first, let's go inside. You boys must be hungry."

"Yes, ma'am," said White. Stokes noted the warmth in the old man's eyes when he looked at Mary Ann and her children.

"I am pleased to see you found Lieutenant Stokes in

Huntington and got him here in one piece. I had expected you sooner. I was growing worried."

"The railroad track is still closed near Durkee," said White. "And we didn't ride hard. Mr Stokes here needed a few days to get used to the travelling."

"No call to ride in London, I expect," Mary Ann said. "Any trouble?"

White glanced at Stokes.

"Not worth mentioning before we eat," he said.

"Point taken," replied Mary Ann, shaking her head and smiling. "You can tell me about that later. Lenny, would you see to the horses, please?" The youth who had taken Stokes' reins nodded. "Where are my manners?" Mary Ann said, as the boy turned to do as he had been asked. "This is Lenny McCloskey. He's only been with us a year, but he is a great asset to the ranch and is wonderful with the horses." Flushing crimson, the skinny boy lowered his head and led the animals towards the corral. "Come to the house for some food when you're done, Lenny," she called after him.

"And this is Mr Giblin," she went on, indicating the broad-chested man who had arrived with Lenny from the pens.

"Lars," he said, his tone curt. He was a squat, solid man, who looked to be close to forty. His hair was blond and he had a full beard that made Stokes think of Vikings.

"Lastly, but by no means least, is Mr Willard."

The third man of the group was old. As Mary Ann introduced him, he took off his light-coloured, dusty, sweat-stained hat, showing the bald top of his head. His pate was pink, but his face and hands were brown and wrinkled as worn leather. His long white hair hung in straggling tails over his shoulders in the old frontier style.

"I ain't gonna kiss your hand, mister," said the old man with a smirk, "but you can call me Amos."

"Pleased to meet all of you," Stokes said.

There was a pump at the side of the house, and Lars washed

his hands and face in the cold water before following Mary Ann into the house. Stokes followed his lead, enjoying the invigorating sensation of the chill water on his skin.

It was a well-appointed, cosy home, which had clearly benefited from a woman's touch. Against one wall stood a dark wooden dresser upon which rested good china plates, a small silver butter dish and what looked like an inkstand. As Mary Ann went to the stove and busied herself preparing food, Albert and his sister set the table.

"Be careful of your grandmother's china," Mary Ann called from the kitchen. "And today we'll use the Sunday silverware."

Stokes watched as the children went about the task they had been set with sombre earnestness. He thought of his servants in London and Wiltshire and how different his childhood had been from that of Albert and Adelaide.

"Is there anything I can do to help?" he asked.

"That's very kind," replied Mary Ann over her shoulder. "But you are our guest. Just take a seat and we'll soon have some food on the table."

He sat on a high backed chair beside Lars. White and Amos had not come inside, instead remaining on the porch where they now lounged and smoked. Stokes wished he had stayed with them, and thought about going back out onto the porch, but he didn't wish to be rude to his hostess.

Lars seemed to share Stokes' feeling of awkwardness, but after a long silence, he cleared his throat and asked him about his journey. The man's English was good, but his accent reminded Stokes of some of the Norwegian passengers he had travelled with across the Atlantic, reinforcing his thought that the man looked like a Viking. Stokes told Lars about the weather on the trip, where they had ridden, the deer that White had shot, and their night in La Grande. He decided now was not the time to speak of the attack, or what had occurred in Huntington.

Soon the food was ready and Mary Ann called the men

in from outside. She carried through from the kitchen serving dishes covered in roast mutton, potatoes and carrots. The men crowded around the table, eyes wide at the silver cutlery and the blue and white patterned porcelain plates.

"The food smells delicious," Stokes said.

"Well, let's hope it tastes as good as it smells," Mary Ann said, dishing out large helpings for the men and smaller portions for herself and the children.

"Mrs Thornford is a good cook," Lars said.

"It doesn't take much to please hungry men," Mary Ann said.

Lars was right. The food was tasty and with the first mouthful Stokes realised how hungry he had been. He had eaten nothing since breakfast. Evidently he was not the only one and a hush fell over the table as everyone ate.

"I hope you have room for apple pie," said Mary Ann, rising when everyone had finished eating.

"Why, it would be an insult not to partake of your pie," said Amos, with a grin. His teeth were surprisingly white in his dark-tanned face.

Mary Ann served them each a slice of pie. Stokes felt full, but he managed all of his slice, then sat back appreciatively.

"Better than the finest restaurant," he said.

Mary Ann smiled at his flattery.

White stifled a belch.

"Young Al told us there'd been some more trouble up on the high ridge," he said. At his words the mood altered, cooling as if a cloud had drifted across the sun.

Lars scowled.

"Reuban and Tanner have gone out that way to check," he said.

"Check for what?"

Lars scraped up the last of the crumbs from his plate on his fork.

"Sign."

78

"I don't like it," White said. "It's dangerous to head over there. There ain't no point looking for no sign." He shook his head. "We know who's shooting the sheep."

Mary Ann's face was pale in the shadows of the farmhouse, but her eyes flashed with anger.

"If we can prove it," she said, "perhaps we will be able to stop Grant."

White scoffed.

"You won't be able to prove nothing. Only one way that man will pay for his crimes." Reaching down for the saddlebags he had dropped on the floor, White pulled out his half-empty bottle of whiskey and pulled out the cork with his teeth.

"That's enough of that talk, Jedediah White," Mary Ann said, halting him before he could drink from the bottle or pour any of the liquid into a glass. "And if you must drink that rot gut, you can do it outside. I won't have you drunk in front of the children."

"I ain't gonna get drunk," grumbled White, but he pushed himself to his feet and went outside without further complaint.

Mary Ann stood and began to clear away the dishes.

"I reckon the rest of you all have work to do before it gets dark," she said.

Taking the hint, the men thanked her for the food and made their way out into the afternoon sunshine. Albert took the plates into the kitchen and was going to follow the men, when he hesitated in the doorway.

"What is it, Albert?" asked his mother.

"Can I show Mr Stokes around now? You said I could later and now it's later."

"And it will be later tomorrow morning," she replied. "You run along with your sister now, but don't go far. It will be sundown soon."

"Aw, Ma," the boy moaned. "I don't want to take Adie."

"Well, you are her brother and you have to. Do as I say now."

Taking his sister's hand, he yanked her after him and trudged out of the house.

Mary Ann let out a long sigh. She suddenly looked exhausted and drawn. Stokes sprang up and took the last items out of her hands.

"Let me help with that," he said, carrying the empty pie pan and spoons into the kitchen. The kitchen was a mess with the detritus from cooking and the dirty plates and utensils. Having become more acquainted with the work of cleaning after a meal he could well imagine how long it would take to clean up the stacks of dishes and piles of silverware. "Shall we heat some water for these plates? I can clean them."

"Nonsense," she said, "go back and sit down. I'll leave those plates for later. For now, I would like to hear all about your journey from England. And about whatever it was happened to you and Jed on the way from Huntington. And I am sure you have questions for me too. Would you like a cup of tea, Lieutenant Stokes?"

Stokes decided not to ask her again to call him by his Christian name. Perhaps she had seen it as forward of him.

"I would love some tea," he said. "I had begun to think that all there was to drink in Oregon was whiskey and coffee."

Mary Ann smiled from the kitchen where she was placing a kettle on the stove.

"The cowboys like their coffee as dark as the night and as thick as molasses. But John never got a taste for it. He had his tea shipped in especially." She held up the tin of Brooke Bond tea to show him.

"Perfect," Stokes said. "I can think of few things I would rather have right now than a nice cup of tea."

A shadow passed across her features and he cursed his clumsiness. Of course there were more important things than tea.

"Good," she said, her smile returning quickly, "then I'll make us a pot of tea and you can tell me everything that has befallen you since you left Liverpool."

Chapter Eleven

When the tea was made, Mary Ann carried the pot, along with a small jug of milk and a bowl of sugar, in on a tray and placed it on the table. She had already brought out two cups and saucers from the dresser while the water was boiling.

"Do you take sugar?" she asked.

"No, thank you."

She smiled, but it was not directed at Stokes. She was reminiscing.

"John had such a sweet tooth," she said, her tone wistful. "He would take two or even three spoonfuls of sugar in his tea."

Using a delicate strainer, she poured the tea. The trickle of the liquid reminded Stokes of pouring absinthe over a lump of sugar on a perforated spoon. Mary Ann lifted the jug.

"It is ewe's milk, I'm afraid," she said, waiting for his response.

He raised an eyebrow. Smiling, he held out his cup.

"I am not one to turn down a new flavour," he said, holding out his cup and pushing away the memories of raucous, debauched nights dancing with the Green Fairy.

She splashed in some milk, then served herself. Stokes sipped the tea and nodded appreciatively.

"You get used to it in time," she said, an apology in her voice.

"It tastes fine. Certainly a lot better than Jed's coffee. That stuff is like tar." He chuckled. "He didn't like it when I cleaned out his pot, I can tell you."

She shook her head in disbelief and smiled. This time she was looking at him and he felt the smile's glow.

"I can imagine," she said. "Jed puts great store by that old pot. Says the old grounds give it a better, richer flavour."

Stokes whistled quietly.

"That is one way of describing it. You know I found an old wash cloth in it?"

"Oh my!" She laughed for a few seconds, her grief dispelled briefly.

Stokes studied her over his cup. She was a beauty indeed. And again he saw in her features similarities to Rebecca. Mary Ann might be harder, more worn and weary by experience, but he could see exactly what had attracted Thornford to her. There was a vivacious, unsuppressable energy barely contained beneath the surface. Life had done its best to dull her charms, but it had failed. If anything, the lines around her eyes and the hard set of her jaw only highlighted her natural allure. Noticing how he was looking at her, Mary Ann's smile faded quickly. She took a sip of tea.

Concerned that he might have embarrassed her with his staring, Stokes focused on his tea cup. The sheep's milk gave it a slightly sour flavour, but it was not unpleasant.

From outside came the sound of the dog barking and the children shouting. Mary Ann tilted her head, perhaps listening for signs of danger. They heard White's voice as he called something to the children, then Albert and Adelaide laughed. Mary Ann relaxed.

"When you first saw me on the porch," she said, breaking the silence that had settled between them, "you looked as though you'd seen a ghost."

"Not a ghost," he said, surprised by her observation, "but you do remind me of someone."

"Yes? Who?"

He took in a deep breath. He considered side stepping the question. He really didn't want to talk about himself. But Mary Ann was staring at him, her pretty eyes clear and open, so he told her the truth.

"My wife," he said.

It was Mary Ann's turn to look uncomfortable.

"I'm sorry. John told me of your…" She searched for a polite term. "Your troubles."

Stokes recalled the long days in the East End, surrounded by depravity, blood and death. The late nights, drinking until he could barely see. The sweet smell of the opium as he lay dazed on soft pillows, lost to the world, safe from his nightmares. Rebecca had been supportive at first, solicitous and sad for him, but her compassion had soured, turning into tears and recriminations, then furious shouting and broken ornaments as tempers flared. And finally, and the hardest to bear, resignation and indifference. The surrender of a love spurned and lost.

He remembered his encounter with the reporter, Fred Bullen; the explosion of rage that led to the tense, uncomfortable meeting with James Monro, Commissioner of Police of the Metropolis, in which words such as 'disrepute' and 'disgrace' were bandied about. Stokes had been so full of sorrow and whisky, so horrified by what had befallen Jane Adams, that he could barely recall the incident. He could not deny what he had done. His knuckles were bruised and scabbed and there were several witnesses. And yet, even though his actions had cost him dearly, he felt no remorse at beating Bullen senseless. By Stokes' reckoning, the newspaperman had deserved every savage punch.

"I didn't tell John everything," Stokes said. "It was too much for letters. Besides, it was not my place to burden him with my worries."

"John was your friend. He would never have considered you a burden."

Stokes smiled bitterly. He had few friends, perhaps none as steadfast as John Thornford.

"John was a good man," he said.

"He was." She sighed. Her eyes filled with tears, but she blinked them away. "He spoke highly of you too, Gabriel. He couldn't believe it when he heard what had happened with your wife. He said he had never known a truer man than you. I remember those words clearly. He admired you, and thought it unjust that you should be so ill-used."

Stokes drained the tea from his cup. His throat was thick with emotion.

"There is little to admire about me, I'm afraid," he said, when he was sure his voice would not betray him. "And I cannot blame Rebecca for leaving me. I was no longer the man she married. I did not give her the life she expected; the life she deserved."

Rebecca had not really left him, but that was something he would not recount. He thought of the night he had come home to find her with the young man. Rebecca had sent the servants away and the man had been buttoning his shirt when Stokes had arrived. Even then he had failed her. Rebecca had flushed at his appearance, expecting that he might fly into a frenzy; fight her lover; defend his honour. Instead, he had said nothing. Snatching up a bottle of Buchanan's, he had turned and walked back out into the early morning drizzle that slicked the streets and reflected the light from the gas lamps.

It had been a few hours later when he had run into Bullen gloating to a couple of reporters from *The Star* about how he had fabricated the letters received by *The Illustrated London News*. The messages had supposedly been from Jane Adams' murderer and had included dreadful, lurid descriptions of the girl's last moments. The writer of the letters implied the girl had enjoyed his advances before he had given in to his lustful appetites and butchered her. Publication of the salacious letters had nearly doubled the readership of *The Illustrated*

London News overnight. The letters had been a huge distraction, making the Metropolitan Police's task of finding the killer much more difficult and, worst of all, they had caused the poor girl's parents untold suffering heaped on their already boundless grief.

When Stokes had stumbled upon Bullen outside the gin shop, he had already known it was too late for his marriage. Rebecca had given him enough chances to amend his ways, to come home at a reasonable hour, to remain sober, to take her to restaurants, the theatre, the opera. There had been rumours about her behaviour for months, but he had disregarded them.

Dejected and drunk as he had been, Stokes had made no attempt to hold back his anger at the sneering reporter. Bullen hadn't stood a chance. Stokes' resentment at his own weakness lent a viciousness to each blow. He cursed Bullen's callous cruelty as he slammed his fists into the reporter's pudgy face, and he damned himself for allowing the evil of the city to best him; to steal what happiness he had possessed.

"All I gave Rebecca was misery," he said with a sigh. "When she left, I realised she was right. Being surrounded by crime everyday had taken its toll, not just on our marriage, but on me." He rubbed a hand over his face, smoothing down his moustache. "No, I can't blame her for what she did."

"You are stronger than I. I know it is wrong of me," Mary Ann said, her expression glum, "but I blame John for dying."

Her words shocked Stokes.

"He could hardly help getting shot, Mary Ann." He barely knew this woman, but their shared grief made him feel close to her. He wanted to reach for her hand, but he kept his hands on the table.

"Still, I blame him," she said. "He insisted on coming here. I followed him like a good wife, but if he had not been so stubborn, he might yet live. It's not right to have to bury two husbands." Her voice cracked and she stopped talking.

"If John hadn't been stubborn," said Stokes, again

considering reaching for her hand and once more discarding the idea, "he wouldn't have been the man I knew, or the man you married."

She smiled at that. Taking out a small handkerchief, she dabbed at her eyes.

"I know that, but I am so angry at him for leaving us alone here."

"You're not alone," Stokes said, then hearing how that sounded, he went on quickly. "You have Jed and Lars, and the other hands. And Albert and Adelaide too."

"And now you are here too," she said, looking at him unblinking. "How long will you stay?"

He looked down at his cup and saw it was empty. He swallowed against the dryness in his mouth.

"As long as I am welcome."

The sounds of the sheep bleating in the pens drifted to them. Stokes turned and looked out the window. The sun was low in the sky and being on the eastern side of the mountain, the farm was already in shadow. The interior of the house was gloomy. Soon they would need to light the lamps.

"You know," Mary Ann said, "when John heard you had left London, he said to me you were a man who needed a purpose. That's why he invited you here. He said you would drive yourself and your sisters mad with nothing to occupy your mind."

"He knew me better than I gave him credit for," Stokes said. It was true that he lived in constant fear that he might one day succumb to the same melancholy that had driven his father to his own destruction. He had never voiced his fears to Thornford, but his old friend had always been a good judge of character.

Mary Ann's expression was solemn.

"Perhaps you can find a new purpose here."

He shrugged.

"Maybe. America is the land of opportunity, is it not?"

"So they say."

"I have not been here long, but I haven't seen many opportunities. It seems hard enough just to stay alive."

Mary Ann bit her lip, her grief returning to her face in an instant. To cover her emotions she poured more tea.

"I am sorry," he said. "My words are clumsy. I've spent too long with Jed."

"What exactly happened on the trail?"

"It started memorably. Minutes after stepping from the train in Huntington, I saw Jed White shoot a man."

Mary Ann went pallid at the news.

"Oh, dear Lord," she said. "Who?"

"One of Grant's boys. Wyc Furlong."

"Did he kill him?"

"A bullet to the head will usually kill a man." He told her of White's arrest and how he had paid the bond for his release.

"I am mortified," she said. "The man has been loyal to us, but we'd heard stories about his past. It is said he was a killer down on the frontier with Mexico, but I had never truly believed it. He's been nothing but kind to the children. John was pleased with Jed's reputation, and hoped it would keep Grant away." She smiled without humour. "That clearly didn't work. I will see you get your money, Gabriel."

"The money is unimportant. All that matters is that you and the children are safe."

"Well, I am glad you managed to get Jed out of jail and get here without any more trouble." His face must have given him away, for she hesitated, peering at him in the gathering gloom. "Something else happened?" she asked.

Stokes told her of the attack near Durkee. Mary Ann was clearly shaken.

"You're sure it was Grant's men?"

"White was certain of it. I couldn't say for sure, but I think he was right. He injured one of them," he added, as if that might improve the news. "We saw blood beneath the trees where they attacked from." Seeing the worry in her face, he went on quickly. "We didn't have any more trouble after that. We slept in the wilderness until we reached La Grande, and we didn't see any of Grant's men there."

Mary Ann sighed. In the gloaming she looked drawn; older than her years.

"John wanted to avoid a war with Grant," she said. "But I don't see a way now. The only thing I want is to be left in peace to raise my children and the sheep. Is that so much to ask?"

Stokes didn't know what to say, so kept quiet. He caught himself thinking of White's whiskey bottle and how a few mouthfuls would take the sharp edges from this awkward, painful conversation. He cast about the room for something to distract from such thoughts.

Spying a lamp on the mantelpiece, he stood and moved to it. His legs had stiffened up while he had sat and his lower back ached dully. His limp was pronounced as he shuffled over to the fireplace.

"Matches?" he said, not seeing any to hand.

"In that tin, beside the fire."

He pulled out a match and struck it against the side of the tin. The wick caught and he lowered the glass chimney. The room was bathed in the lamp's warm glow. Mary Ann was watching him closely. In the golden light, she was even more radiant, her features softened by the shadows.

Stokes stretched, grunting as his back popped. Hobbling back to the table, he set the lamp down between them. He sat and absently rubbed at his left thigh.

Mary Ann watched him for a few seconds, then stood abruptly. He made to stand too, but she waved her hand.

"No," she said. "No need. Wait there."

She disappeared into the back of the house, where he heard her rummaging in a drawer or perhaps a chest. Outside, he could still hear the sheep. Every now and again the dog barked, and the children laughed. For a time he had heard White and old Amos Willard talking quietly on the porch, but they had fallen silent some time ago. He wondered if they were still there, smoking and drinking in silence, or if perhaps they had wandered away, or even dozed off. Before he could go and have a look out the front door, Mary Ann returned. Her hands were full. Quickly, but carefully, he put the pot, jugs and cups onto the tray and slid it to one side.

Gently, Mary Ann laid a dark jacket onto the white table-cloth. It was dark blue, with gold brocade and buttons. Stokes recognised it at once as Thornford's dress uniform jacket. Atop the jacket, Mary Ann placed a sabre in a polished metal scabbard. Stokes recognised that too. Lastly, she put a small wooden box on the table and opened it, revealing several medals. The first were campaign medals, some of which Stokes also possessed. He ignored those and lifted the last one from the velvet-lined box.

Lifting it up, he examined it in the lamplight. Suspended from a wine-red ribbon, the bronze cross was decorated with a crown surmounted by a lion, and the inscription 'FOR VALOUR'.

"The Victoria Cross was the only medal John cared for," Mary Ann said.

Stokes closed his eyes and for the briefest of moments he thought he could hear the wails of dying men, the screams of eviscerated horses, the thunder of the cannons and the fizzing spit of musket balls as they burnt through the clouded air. His hand again fell to his thigh and he recalled the searing pain of the lance.

"He certainly deserved this," Stokes said, placing the medal back in the box. "He saved my life that day."

"I'm glad he did."

Stokes said nothing. Instead, he reached for the sabre. His father had commissioned it from Thurkle of Soho as a gift to John after he saved Gabriel's life at Maiwand. The date of the engagement was engraved on the scabbard, along with Captain

Thornford's name above a Crown over the Prince of Wales' feathers, a U-shaped scroll with 'Prince of Wales' Own' on the left side and '10th Royal Hussars' on the right. The hilt was ornate, with delicate etching on the pommel and guard. Drawing the blade free of the scabbard, Stokes held it at arm's length, tilting it left and right, feeling the weight and balance of it in his hand. Despite the finery and decoration, it was a fighter's weapon, light and strong, made of the finest steel. It had been years since he had last used a blade such as this, either on the parade ground or in combat. To hold such a weapon brought flooding back the sensation of galloping alongside his comrades, sabres lowered, feet pushing himself up in his stirrups, leaning over the horse's neck, ready to plunge the sword into whichever enemies of the Queen were foolish enough to oppose the might of the great British Empire.

"I never had a blade as fine as this," he said, sliding the sabre back into the scabbard.

"John never spoke much about that time, but when he did, he talked of you. He said you were a better swordsman than he."

Stokes let out a bark of laughter.

"Then he lied. He was one of the best swordsmen in the regiment, if not the whole army in Afghanistan."

She placed a delicate hand on the jacket, touching gently the gleaming brocade.

"He was so looking forward to seeing you, Gabriel," she said.

"And I him. Of the few friends I have, John knew me the best."

"Well, you had shared much together."

"Yes," Stokes said simply. There was nothing else to say. It was true, there was a bond with fellow soldiers that could never be broken, and it could never truly be understood by others; not parents or siblings, and certainly not wives.

"John wasn't surprised when you became a lawman."

"That's funny," said Stokes. "I was quite surprised myself. My family were merely disappointed."

"He said you always had a burning need to seek justice."

Stokes stared into the lamp's flame, thinking of the past.

"I think he was right." That need had cost him Rebecca. "But I have resigned from the Metropolitan Police Force."

"There is still much injustice in this world."

"Too much for me to put right," Stokes said, smiling grimly.

She was staring at him. Her fingers lightly touched the medals in the open box.

"John needs justice," she said, her voice timid, barely more than a whisper. "I need justice."

Stokes pushed himself to his feet and walked to the window. Outside it was still surprisingly bright. From the encroaching darkness in the house, he had thought it must already be dusk. The sun was behind the mountain, but there was an hour of daylight in the sky yet.

Albert and Adelaide were throwing a stick for the dog. The animal scampered back to them, dropping the stick at their feet, wagging its tail furiously. Beyond the children, the men were working with the sheep in the pens, checking their feet and separating those animals with signs of damage or toes that needed trimming. White was watching them, leaning on the fence, cigarette in one hand, the half-empty bottle of whiskey in the other.

Beyond the land that Thornford had cleared, the pines and firs grew thick and tall. The setting sun still reached the tops of the highest trees, and glimmered on water far off down in the valley. The sky in the east was a clear azure, devoid of clouds.

This was a fine land. John Thornford had worked this part of it, making it his own. A place where he could bring up his family and live out the rest of his days, far from the world of warfare and killing he had known for two decades. He had been older than Stokes by some fifteen years, but he was a good man and had found himself a good woman. He had deserved to live for many years yet.

"I came here not just to see John," he said, without turning away from the window. "When he wrote to me, he spoke of the wide open land. He said I would love it here, and I can see he was right. It is stunning. Like nothing I've ever seen before." He drew in a long breath. "I was lost in London. I had seen too many things. I couldn't rest or sleep. I lost my wife because of it. And my position in the police. I thought that here I might find some peace."

"I'm not asking you to fight, Gabriel," Mary Ann said. "All I want is justice."

Stokes let out a long breath. He had known when he heard of John's murder that he would help his friend's widow. He was never going to refuse her request.

"It may well be that one might not come without the other," he said, turning back to her. "I can't promise you the outcome, but you have my word, Mary Ann." He felt there was an inevitability in his words, as if fate had brought him to this place in just this moment of time. He spoke the next words with the cold finality of death. "I will do my best to bring to justice the men responsible for John's murder."

Chapter Twelve

Stokes spent the night in the bunkhouse with the rest of the men. Albert asked Mary Ann if he could sleep with the ranch hands too, but she shook her head.

"I need you to be the man about the house," she said. "You can't leave Adie and me all on our own."

The boy looked dejected, but he nodded seriously and did not complain.

The men smoked, drank whiskey and played cards by the light of a hurricane lamp. Stokes joined in the cards and conversation for a while, but it wasn't long before his head was nodding. It had been a long day, so he pushed himself up and laid down on an unoccupied bunk.

He listened to the relaxed chatter as he lay there in the shadows. There was a familiar camaraderie that reminded him of the army. Lars was quiet, but was clearly respected by the others, even by Jed White, who seemed to respect very few people. Amos was the grizzled, experienced hand who appeared to know the most things ranching and to have an opinion on everything else. They made fun of Lenny, the youngest member of the outfit, but it was light-hearted and Stokes could hear the affection in the older men's voices. The boy seemed to hear it too and he took their jibes in a good-natured fashion.

After agreeing to look into Thornford's murder, Stokes had at first been filled with a sense of dread. He knew so little of this land and its ways. What use would he be? But after a short while, that feeling of anxiety dissipated and for the first time in months, perhaps years, he felt himself relaxing, as if a spring that had been coiled too tightly was unwinding within him. Perhaps Thornford had been right and what he needed was a purpose. Whatever the truth of the matter, he fell asleep feeling more at ease than he could remember, the sounds of the men washing over him.

He awoke in darkness. He could see nothing, but heard whispers.

"What's the matter?" Stokes hissed.

"A couple of the ewes are not waiting till morning," came the reply. He recognised the raspy voice of old Amos. "Go back to sleep, English. Me and Lenny will take care of it."

The door creaked open, revealing the purple night as the two men slipped outside. Stokes lay on the thin, lumpy mattress and listened as Lenny and Amos trudged away, their murmured voices soft and soothing. In seconds, he was asleep again.

When next he woke, it was morning. Lars was stepping through the door, pulling his braces over his shoulders. The only other person that remained in the bunkhouse was White. The old man broke wind loudly, then sat up, scratching behind his ear.

"I feel as if a horse kicked me in the head," he said, groaning.

"Nobody forced you to drink that much whiskey," Stokes replied, feeling righteous that he was now abstemious and at the same time feeling envious of White's indulgences.

"If I couldn't drink," said White, rubbing the sleep from his eyes, "there would be little enough to make life worth living. I discovered long ago that being drunk makes most adversities seem more bearable."

Stokes could not argue with that. He sat and put on the boots he had bought in La Grande. They pinched his toes a bit, but White had told him they'd stretch in time. Standing, he massaged his thigh.

White was already on his feet. He took a big swallow of whiskey straight from the nearly empty bottle beside his bed.

"I'm running low again," he said, shaking his head. "I swear that old bastard, Amos, has been drinking my whiskey while I slept."

"I don't think you need much help," Stokes said.

White shook the bottle, then lifting it to his lips, he drained it empty with a couple of gulping swallows.

"I think you might be right, Mr Stokes," he said, ramming the cork back with the heel of his hand. "But the problem of my missing whiskey can wait till after breakfast. If I'm not mistaken I can smell biscuits, and Mrs Thornford's are even better than mine, which is saying something."

Stokes couldn't smell anything beyond the stale, sweaty air of the bunkhouse, but he followed White out into the fresh morning. Low cloud had covered the sky overnight, making the ranch and surrounding land seem more sombre and less welcoming. Taking a deep breath, Stokes found White's sense of smell must be more acute than his, for on the clear breeze wafted the scent of baking.

Mary Ann welcomed them back into her house, where the table was set simply with enamelled plates and tin cups.

"Good morning," she said brightly as Stokes and White entered. She bustled in the kitchen. "There is coffee in the pot," she called out. "And I can make tea if you would prefer."

"Coffee will be fine," replied Stokes, not wanting her to go to any unnecessary effort.

She carried through a plate laden with biscuits and another piled high with thick slices of bacon.

"Albert," she said, "go and tell the men that breakfast is ready."

Without a word, the boy scurried out of the house, followed by his younger sister.

"We don't have a ranch cook here," Mary Ann said, bringing in a third serving plate, this one covered in scrambled eggs, "but I like to make sure the boys don't work on empty stomachs. Please, help yourselves. Don't wait for everyone. We don't stand on ceremony here."

White didn't need to be asked twice. He took three biscuits, several rashers of bacon and began to shovel eggs onto his plate.

"Now, Jed," Mary Ann said, her tone reproving. "Leave enough for everyone."

Abashed, he pushed some of the eggs back onto the dish, then returned one of the biscuits.

Stokes was serving himself some eggs when the door opened.

"Look who's here, Ma," said Albert, his young voice high with excitement. The boy and his sister came into the house followed by two men Stokes had not seen before. The first was tall and slim and looked to be in his mid-twenties. His arms and legs were long, and he moved with a graceful alacrity that made Stokes think he must be a capable man in a pinch. The man removed his hat and slapped the dust off.

"Tanner," said Mary Ann, "don't do that in here." She stood up and shooed him out of the door.

"Sorry, ma'am," he muttered as he left.

The second man was considerably older than Tanner, but Stokes could not be sure of his age. It could be anywhere between forty and sixty. The man wore no hat, and his hair was long, even longer than Amos' and White's frontier style. It was plaited in two braids that hung down over his shoulders. His face was broad and flat, weathered from a life outdoors. There was something about the man's demeanour, the cool way he surveyed the room and its inhabitants, that marked him out from the other men. His attire set him apart too. He did not wear the plain work clothes of the other hands. His clothes were made from soft, tan buckskin, and on his feet were moccasins, in place of the sturdy boots favoured by the rest of the men. Stokes could not hide his curiosity at the man's apparel.

At first he thought he must be an Indian, but he dismissed that idea immediately. He had seen the noble Sioux warriors in Colonel Cody's Wild West show, and had seen many photographs of America's brave savages. This man had blond hair, darkened with dirt and grease, but it was fair nonetheless. And his eyes were a piercing, icy blue, incongruous and bright in the reddened, tanned face.

"This is Mr Van Orman," said Mary Ann, indicating the older of the two newcomers, "and this is Tanner."

"Strickland," said the tall man, holding out his hand to Stokes. He had left his hat outside and his face was flushed.

Stokes shook the young man's hand, rising to his feet as the men entered, followed by the other hands who had been in the sheep pens.

"How do you do?" he said. He gave a nod. "Strickland. Van Orman."

He offered his hand to the strange old man. After a brief hesitation, he clasped it briefly. His handshake was firm, his skin callused and cool.

"Reuban," he said, before sitting at the far side of the table.

"Or you can call him 'Bear Hunter'," said old Amos, pulling up a chair.

"No," said Van Orman, fixing Willard with a stern glare. "Just Reuban."

"Come on now," said Mary Ann, ushering the men to the table. "The food is getting cold. You can tell us what you found on the ridge once you have eaten."

While the men were being introduced to Stokes, sitting themselves down and serving food onto their plates, White had not lifted his attention from his plate. He had wolfed down his food, and now, as the men fell quiet to eat, he pushed himself away from the table.

"Don't you want to hear what old Bear Hunter found?" asked Willard.

"I'll hear soon enough."

Pouring some more coffee into his cup, White took it with him and walked out onto the porch.

The men ate in silence for a time. The food was good and White had been right, Mary Ann's biscuits were better than his. Stokes had concluded that nobody was going to mention White's rudeness, when Amos spoke up.

"Jed don't like no redskins, on account of his family got themselves scalped by Comanches."

Stokes glanced over at Reuban. It was true he was dressed like a savage, but there could be no doubt he was a white man.

"Van Orman doesn't sound like a Comanche name to me," Stokes said.

Amos laughed at that. Reuban looked up and met Stokes' gaze. His eyes were hard, like stones.

"My parents were white," he said. "They came from Wisconsin and settled in Oregon back in 1860. I was ten when they died. After that, I lived with the Shoshone."

"I am sorry to hear that."

"Why?" asked Van Orman, looking genuinely puzzled. "People die. And the Shoshone were good to me."

"Jed can't forgive Reuban for living with the red boys," said Amos. "Thinks he's some kind of traitor."

"But he was only a boy," Stokes said.

"I ain't a boy no more," said Reuban, chewing on a piece of bacon rind. "But it ain't Jed's fault. A man can't choose how he feels, especially when it comes to the death of his family. The Comanche made war on his kin. He cannot forget that. I understand him. I ain't forgiven those who make war on mine."

Another awkward silence fell over them. Stokes did not want to rake over the coals of any old fires, so instead, he finished the food on his plate.

"Well, what did you boys find up on the ridge?" asked Amos as the men finished eating and pushed their plates away.

"It is bad," said Reuban. "They shot a dozen sheep. Left them to rot."

"Someone needs to plug those sons of bitches!" said Tanner Strickland.

"Tanner!" exclaimed Mary Ann.

"Sorry, ma'am," Tanner said, glancing at the children. "But it sticks in my craw that Grant can get away with this."

Stokes thought of the wolves he had heard at night on the trail.

"Is there any chance the sheep were killed by an animal?"

"Animals don't shoot guns," said Reuban.

"Is there a way to prove that it was Grant's men though?"

"I seen the tracks," Reuban replied. "They were Grant's men all right. Jackson Pailing, Hunter Randle, Keith Sheldrick, Cullen Towns. They were all there. They shot the sheep from horseback. Using their Winchesters."

"How can you be so sure of all this?"

"The shooting is easy enough. They didn't pick up their brass." Reuban fished in a bead-covered tasselled pouch he wore on his belt and pulled out a handful of spent cartridge cases. He dropped them on the table.

"And what about the identity of the men? You said they were mounted, so I presume you could count the number of horses," Stokes was almost talking to himself, trying to imagine the scene and understand what had taken place. "But how do you know who rode them unless..." He paused, thinking about some of the cases he had worked. He recalled one particularly brutal murder, where a jealous docker had stabbed his pregnant wife. They had secured a conviction because of a footprint left in the poor woman's blood. The husband's right boot had a distinctively-shaped gouge in the sole and this detail saw him swing. "Unless," he went on, "they dismounted and you recognised their shoes perhaps."

"No, they stayed in their saddles," said Reuban. "They did not dismount. Not on the ridge anyway. But it was the men I said."

"How can you be so sure?"

Amos reached for the last biscuit.

"Bear Hunter don't need to see a man's boot print," he said, "to know who was on a horse. The man tracks better than most Indians. They say he could follow the sign of an eagle on the wing."

"Anyone who says that is foolish," replied Reuban, "but I know these horses and the men who rode them. They all work for the Cabin Creek Ranch."

"I doubt that would stand up as evidence in a court of law," said Stokes.

Lars had been silent throughout breakfast, but now he slapped his hand hard on the table.

"What more can we do?" he said, his voice raw with anger. "Grant has more men than us. He kills our animals. Has murdered the Captain. The sheriff answers to him. Judge Selby was best man at his wedding. Nobody will stand up to him. Even with evidence, what could we do?"

"I refuse to believe a man can act with impunity," Stokes said. "If we can find enough evidence that points to Grant, someone will pay attention." He finished his coffee. "I will make them listen."

A hard edge had entered his voice and he saw that the men were looking at him differently. Lars shook his head, but Tanner, Lenny and even old Amos looked as though they might actually believe he could do it. Mary Ann's eyes glimmered.

"Reuban," Stokes said, "will you take me to the place where Captain Thornford was killed?"

The weather-beaten man met Stokes' gaze and held it for several seconds.

Lars was still shaking his head, as if bemused.

"Why do you want to see where the Captain was shot?" he asked.

"The scene of the crime is always a good place to start."

Reuban was still staring at him, unblinking, as if weighing

up Stokes' worth against some unknown measure. At last, he gave a curt nod.

"I'll take you," he said. "But first I need to rest. I have not slept in two days and the place is not close."

Chapter Thirteen

After breakfast Stokes decided to make good on his promise to young Albert. The boy had stood by the door awkwardly while the men had left to go about their duties. It was clear he wanted to speak, but had become shy.

"Are you ready to show me the ranch now?" Stokes asked once he had helped carry the dirty dishes through to the kitchen. Mary Ann gave him a small smile of thanks.

"Yes, sir," Albert said, his expression serious.

Adelaide jumped down from her chair and looked ready to follow her brother. Anger flashed across Albert's features.

"Adie," Mary Ann said, "you stay here with me." Adelaide pouted, but her mother went on without pause. "As soon as these plates are clean, I'll need someone to help me make ginger snaps." At the promise of baking sweets, Adelaide lost interest in her brother and the Englishman.

"Then it is agreed," said Stokes, retrieving his hat from the back of a chair. "Lead on, Albert, and I will follow."

He smiled at Mary Ann and stepped out onto the porch behind the boy.

The day was already brightening, the sun doing its best to shine through the grey. There were a few patches of blue where the freshening wind tore at the clouds.

Albert pointed down to where Amos, Lars and the others were busy with the sheep.

"You've seen the sheep pens," Albert said. "So I'll show you the barn."

Stokes followed the boy over to the largest of the buildings. It was constructed from solid timber planking and its high roof was steeply angled. Albert heaved on one of the huge doors. They were perhaps nine feet high and heavy. The boy grunted and pulled, using all his strength until the door swung open.

Inside it was still and quiet, noticeably warmer than the cool air out in the breeze of the morning. Light pierced the gloom through gaps between some of the planks. Motes of dust drifted in the shafts of light.

"We put the horses in here when it's really cold," said Albert. "Lambs too. I like it in here. I like it best down by the creek, but when it's raining or too cold, I come in here where it's quiet."

Stokes looked around the barn. There were bales of hay in one corner. Bridles and saddles in the other, near some barrels and sacks.

"Looks like a good place to be alone," he said.

"Yeah," replied Albert, kicking at some of the straw. "Adie always tries to follow me, but sometimes I don't want to speak to anyone. All the talking gets too loud."

"I know how you feel, but all of Oregon seems quiet to me," Stokes said. "The biggest town I've seen is La Grande and even that was tiny when compared to the likes of New York or London."

"How many people live in London?" Albert asked.

"You know, I am not sure, but I read somewhere over four million live in the city."

Albert whistled.

"I can't imagine that many people all in one place. It must never be quiet there."

"It is the largest city in the world. And you're right, it is seldom quiet. At night it gets better, in terms of noise. But then it is dangerous to be out and about."

Albert moved to where the barrels were stacked and climbed up to sit on one.

"You were a lawman in London, right?"

"A Detective Inspector, yes."

"Ma says you investigated murders."

"I did, amongst other crimes."

"Like Sherlock Holmes?"

Stokes stiffened. He hated being compared with the fictional consultant detective. He had met Arthur Conan Doyle a few years earlier when the writer was researching his first Sherlock Holmes novel. The Scotsman had been pleasant enough, but when Stokes had read *A Study in Scarlet* he had been disgusted. Doyle portrayed the policemen of Scotland Yard as buffoons and Stokes could not shake the feeling that Dr Watson was loosely based on him. Like Stokes, Watson had suffered an injury to his leg at the battle of Maiwand. Then there was the matter of Holmes' drug taking. Stokes had spent several days and evenings with Mr Doyle and was concerned that he had divulged more about his vices than was prudent. If he had learnt anything from the experience it was never to trust a writer.

"No," Stokes said, "Doyle made Holmes up. I dealt with real crimes. Real criminals. And let me tell you, I never solved a crime using the methods Holmes employs in Doyle's stories."

Albert looked crestfallen for a second, but quickly recovered.

"You think you'll be able to prove who killed the Captain?"

"I don't know," Stokes said. "I hope so. I do have one thing in common with Holmes."

"What's that?" Albert sounded excited at the prospect.

"I hate the thought of killers walking free."

"Me too." Albert fell silent and his brow furrowed. Stokes stood quietly, content to leave the boy to his thoughts. "With so many people in London," Albert said at last, "there must have been a passel of shootings."

"Less than you'd think, actually. There aren't as many guns as here."

"So how do people defend themselves?"

"The English haven't needed to defend themselves like that for a long time. At least, not in England. We don't have Indians, wolves or bears. Nothing like that."

"But there are bad men." It was not a question.

Stokes sighed. The inevitability in the boy's statement saddened him.

"Yes," he said, "there are bad men."

"And the lawmen protect the good people from them."

Stokes wished it were that simple. He thought fleetingly of all the corpses he had seen in the last seven years. All the good people he had failed to protect.

"That's right," he said.

Albert had picked up a few strands of straw and was absently plaiting them together as they talked, his fingers quick and nimble.

"Did you carry a gun as a lawman?" he asked.

"Sometimes."

"Did you ever shoot anyone?"

The boy's questions were incessant. Stokes found it amusing that Albert had said he sometimes found talking intrusive and wanted to be alone and in peace. He himself felt he was being interrogated, but he also wanted to learn as much as possible. Besides, he liked the serious-eyed boy. He could close down this line of questioning, but he chose not to. He pondered his reply.

"Not as a policeman," he said, sure that the boy was clever enough to hear the unspoken meaning in his words.

"But you have killed people?"

Stokes was uncomfortable, but he would not shirk from the truth.

"Yes," he said. "In battle. Fighting for my Queen and country."

"In Afghanistan?"

"Yes, where I met your father. Where he won many of his medals."

"He wasn't my father," Albert said, his tone bitter.

"No," said Stokes. "I'm sorry." He didn't know what else he could say.

Albert's eyes glimmered with unshed tears and Stokes wondered if he was thinking of his real father. The boy had surely been too young when the man died to remember much about him.

Albert cuffed at his eyes.

"Captain Thornford was a good man," he said. "I didn't mean anything by what I said."

"You only spoke the truth," said Stokes. "I lost my father too. I know how it feels."

Albert concentrated on the plait of straw for a minute.

"I've been thinking about my father a lot since..." His voice trailed off. He sniffed, keeping his eyes fixed on his hands and the woven straw.

"Losing one's father is a terrible thing, but to find another one, a decent man, and then to lose him must be intolerable." Albert glanced at him. A tear welled up and dropped down his cheek and he brusquely swiped it away on his sleeve. "I know John wasn't your father," Stokes said, "but you can mourn him as if he were. To do so won't lessen the memory of your father and certainly doesn't reflect badly on you. It takes a strong man to allow himself to grieve."

Albert did not look up for a long time. Stokes wanted to give the boy space, so walked over to the saddles and tack, inspecting the harness and listening to the sounds of the farm filtering through the gaps in the barn's planking. When he heard Albert jump down from the barrel, he turned back to face him.

Albert's face was stern. He was not weeping, but the mood between them had grown sombre.

"You know," Stokes said, "John said something to me once that I never forgot."

"What was it?"

Stokes smiled, remembering Thornford's loud, cheerful voice.

"He said that life is too short to waste any of it being miserable." Stokes thought of all the long days he had wasted wallowing in self-pity, his mind confused by opium and absinthe. He chuckled without humour. "It is a worthy thought," he said, "but at times it's not easy to live by such words. But how about we try, at least for this morning?"

"Try what?" asked Albert, his young face pale in the shadows of the barn.

"Not to be miserable," said Stokes. "The sun is trying to come out and we have the whole ranch to explore."

"OK, then," said Albert, forcing a smile.

Despite the sadness lurking within him, heavy as a stone, Stokes grinned in return.

"Good," he said. "Didn't you mention a creek?"

Albert led him to the north of the ranch buildings, leaving behind the noise of the bleating sheep and the men calling out to each other and every now and then whistling at the dog. They were soon in the shade of the pines. The only sounds here were the whispers of the wind through the branches and the chatter of birdsong.

They reached the creek soon after. It ran through a deep cleft in the ground, the walls overgrown in places with grease-wood and sedge. Albert showed him a steep path down into the ravine. It had not been a long walk from the farmhouse, but as they descended down to the creek bed where a stream of water flowed, Stokes felt they could have been hundreds of miles from the nearest human being. Little wind reached them. Only moments before, the morning sunshine had felt warm on their faces, but here it was chill, in deep shade, and their breath billowed about them. Stokes' new boots rubbed painfully, but he was glad Albert had told him to wear his coat.

The foot of the ravine was wider than Stokes had imagined

and there were many areas of flat stone at the edges of the water. Weeds and mud were caught in the branches of some of the overhanging trees. Some way further downstream a tree had toppled down to lie wedged across the canyon. Great clumps of flotsam and jetsam clung to the snapped and rotting boughs.

"I can see why you like this place," Stokes said.

"It's better in the summer," Albert said. "Unless it rains. Sometimes, even when it's sunny here, it's raining up in the mountains. It's too dangerous to be here then."

Stokes glanced up at the shredded clouds. It felt to him like there might well be rain somewhere nearby.

"Shouldn't we get out of here?" he asked. "It could be raining upstream."

Albert shook his head.

"We'll be fine. Reuban taught me how to tell when it's raining up in the hills."

"And Reuban's never wrong?"

"Not with things like that. He can track, hunt and read the land as well as any Indian."

Stokes thought of the buckskin-garbed, fair-haired, blue-eyed man.

"I've never met anyone like him before," he said. "Does he have any family?"

"The Shoshone killed his parents. His brothers and sisters too, I think." Albert picked up a stone and tossed it into the stream. "Amos told me that Reuban's uncle spent years looking for him after the Indians took him. He even got the army to help. They travelled all over Idaho, Washington and Oregon. They eventually cornered Bear Hunter in Utah."

"So Bear Hunter is Reuban's Indian name?"

Albert shook his head. Scooping up another stone, he skipped it on the water so that it bounced up and landed with a clatter on the far bank.

"No, sir," he said. "It was the name of the Shoshone chief.

In the end, Bear Hunter had to give Reuban up to his uncle and the army. Amos says that Reuban was painted like a savage when they found him." Albert touched his cheeks, perhaps imagining having paint daubed there. "He was about the same age I am now. He fought and scratched and didn't want to be rescued."

"They say blood is everything," said Stokes, "but I'm not so sure. Family is important, but who is to say we can't choose ours?"

Albert threw another stone.

"I guess," he said after a while. "I suppose Reuban felt he'd found another father, only to be taken away from him."

Stokes picked up a stone and weighed it in his hand. It was cold and damp, smooth but encrusted with wet sand. He brushed off the dirt.

"How long did he stay with the uncle?"

Albert shrugged.

"Not long. His uncle sent him back to Wisconsin for a while, but when the uncle died, Reuban ran away and headed back west. He lived with the Shoshone for years. But Bear Hunter and his family died of small pox. Lots of the tribe did. The ones who lived blamed Reuban and threw him out."

Stokes sighed.

"I thought we'd agreed we weren't going to be miserable."

"I know," said Albert, with an apologetic shrug, "but so much of life is just plain sad."

"I can't argue with that," Stokes said, trying to shake the sorrowful mood that threatened to envelop them. "How did Reuban end up working on the JT Ranch?"

"The Captain gave him a job. None of the other outfits would have him. Men don't like Reuban much. I guess they remember the olden days and the Indian Wars."

Stokes smiled at that. The last of the tribes had not yet been subdued. There were still renegades who resisted the American government, as they were driven onto reservations. Custer and his men had been slaughtered at Little Bighorn by Sioux, Cheyenne and Arapaho not fifteen years before, but of course, that was ancient history to Albert. He had not even been born then.

"I suppose they do," he said. "Reuban said so himself. It's not easy to forget such things."

"I know it. But I wish Jed would not be so rude to him. It makes me feel bad. Reuban's always been good to me, and I like him. But I like Jed... Mr White too."

As far as Stokes had seen, there was little about Jedediah White to be liked. But Stokes had seen how the old frontiersman behaved with Mary Ann and her children and he could not deny the man had a softer side. No doubt life's hardships had buried deep whatever softness there was in White.

"Did I hear my name?"

The voice startled Stokes and he turned quickly, his heart thumping. White was picking his way down the path they had followed. The top was dense with undergrowth, but Stokes had not heard a sound as White approached.

"It is best not to eavesdrop on conversations, Mr White," Stokes said, somewhat pompously. White's sudden appearance had unnerved him, reminding him he had lived in the largest city on earth for years and had become accustomed to its thrum. He was not attuned to the sounds and rhythms of the land.

"I ain't to blame. You boys speak loud enough to be heard in San Francisco," White replied, with a crooked grin. He swept his gaze over the two of them. "Good to see you getting acquainted. Here, I brung you a present."

He handed Stokes a belt coiled around a holstered pistol. Stokes recognised the gun as the Colt Lightning.

"Took the liberty of cleaning it," said White. "You don't want to be shooting a firearm without checking it first. The belt was Captain Thornford's," he added. "Mary Ann is happy for you to have it, seeing as you were his friend."

Stokes saw a pained expression flicker across Albert's face.

"Albert should have it," Stokes said. "I have no need of a gun belt."

"Young Al ain't gonna be carrying a shooting iron for a few years yet. If you're looking into Thornford's shooting, you don't want to go unheeled."

Stokes glanced at the boy. Albert nodded.

"Put it on, Mr Stokes," he said. "Jed's right. No use in having a gun if you don't carry it."

Reluctantly, Stokes buckled the belt around his waist. The weight of the revolver felt strange against his hip.

"Very well," he said, "but the belt is yours when I leave."

At the mention of leaving, Albert's face crumpled and Stokes thought the boy might cry. Stokes cursed himself for a fool.

If White had noticed the boy's distress he said nothing. He held out the box of pistol shells Stokes had bought in La Grande.

"Thought you should get in some practice," he said. "In case you need to use this smoke wagon."

"I don't think that will be necessary," Stokes said stiffly. "I know one end of a pistol from the other."

"No doubt, soldier," said White, "but it ain't never hurt no one to practise. And don't be telling me stories of your soldiering days. I know you and the Captain did your share of fighting, but an unused knife gets rusty. And don't you go worrying about the noise. I already told Mary Ann and the boys we'd be doing some target practice down here, so they won't come a running."

"Can I shoot too?" asked Albert.

Stokes had been prepared to reject altogether the idea of shooting, but seeing how the boy's face lit up, his resolve weakened. Still, he wasn't sure what to say, not knowing what the boy's mother's thoughts might be on the matter. Before he could broach the subject, White clapped Albert on the shoulder.

"Sure you can, Al," he said. "Ain't never too soon for a man to learn to shoot."

Albert beamed. He looked the happiest Stokes had seen him.

"Wait a moment," Stokes said. "Have you asked Mrs Thornford if it would be all right for the boy to shoot?"

"Have you shot before, young Al?" White asked.

"I done a bit before," Albert replied.

"See?" White said to Stokes. "It's fine."

Albert looked from one man to the other, then, unable to keep quiet, he blurted out, "Ma don't like me shooting. She shouted at Pa when he showed me how to shoot a rifle last summer."

Stokes shrugged at White, as if he had won. Albert's use of the term "Pa" made him raise an eyebrow, but he did not mention the change in the boy's term for John.

"Well, you know what?" said White.

"What?" Stokes replied, expecting from the man's tone he was not going to like what White had to say.

"There comes a time in every boy's life when he has to do what he believes to be right, not what his Ma tells him."

"Now see here—"

White cut Stokes off.

"It seems to me there can be no more pressing time for a boy to learn how to defend hisself from bad hombres than when his pa has been shot by a murderous son of a bitch."

"There is no need for such language, White," snapped Stokes. His voice had taken on the tone of command and even the slovenly old man stood straighter, as if he remembered a time when an officer's presence meant standing to attention and saluting. "However, you make a compelling point."

"I often do," said White, chortling to himself. "I often do. Besides, what Mary Ann don't know can't hurt her, can it, boys?"

Chapter Fourteen

White took a piece of driftwood from the rocks, where it had been deposited by a past flood, and propped it up some fifteen yards away.

"That's not very far," Stokes observed.

"Far enough," White said. "Anything further than that and you want to be shooting a rifle. That Lightning is only good for up close and personal altercations."

Stokes drew the Colt from the leather holster. Checking the cylinder, he saw that one chamber was empty.

"Don't trust no revolver," White said, by way of explanation. "Seen a gun discharge by mistake more than once. One time saw a Texas Ranger fall off his horse and shoot his darn foot almost clean off, all without pulling his pistol. Always leave the chamber under the hammer empty after that. Besides, if you need more than five bullets, you probably lost that fight."

Stokes pointed at White's gun belt where his two large Remingtons were holstered.

"Why do you need two pistols then? That gives you ten shots."

"When you've angered as many men as me, you might need ten bullets to be safe. Now I will say you can be a testy son of a gun, but I still doubt you have as many enemies as me."

Stokes thought of all the men he had put behind bars and sent to the gallows. All of them had families and friends.

"You might be surprised," he said. "You haven't known me long."

"True. Perhaps you'll prove me wrong. Stranger things have happened. Now, you ready to shoot, or are we gonna flap our gums all day?"

Stokes closed the loading gate and held up the revolver.

"I'm ready," he said.

"Show me what you got."

Stokes sighted down the Colt Lightning's five and a half inch barrel. It was longer than his service revolver, but the grip, so like the Webley he had been issued in London, felt familiar and comfortable in his hand. With his thumb he cocked the hammer, let out a breath, and pulled the trigger.

The pistol bucked in his hand. The report was loud in the creek canyon, the sound rolling away, then echoing back to them. The smoke from the shot clouded the cold air, hanging around them like mist with no breeze to blow it away in the sheltered creek bed.

The shot had kicked up pebbles and dust about a foot to the left of the target log.

"In the general vicinity," said White, "but never a bad idea to practise, eh? If that had been a Comanche, he'd be scalping you now."

"Luckily for me," said Stokes, "there aren't any Comanches around."

He rolled his head, loosening his neck muscles, and raised the gun again. Cocking the hammer, he aimed for a second and squeezed off another shot. He was ready for the pistol's recoil this time and the bullet splintered the top left edge of the log.

"Not bad," White said. "Remember, that there is the gunsmith's favourite. One of those new double-action revolvers. You don't need to cock it with your thumb."

Stokes took a deep breath. The smell of the black powder brought a flood of memories, both pleasant and less so. The shooting competitions at Wimbledon Common and the games of cricket in the summer sun on the green afterwards. The crash of cannons and the booming thunder of hundreds of guns fired

114

in volleys at the Afghans who came on relentlessly through the fog. The screams of men and animals. He had not wanted to shoot, but he could not deny that the revolver felt good in his hand, and with each shot it felt as though a tiny fragment of his pent-up grief and sorrow was also being fired away from him.

"Do you think I can hit it with the next three shots?" he asked Albert.

The boy's eyes were wide and he held his hands over his ears against the roar of the pistol, but he nodded, smiling broadly.

"I reckon you can, Mr Stokes," he said, his voice high with excitement.

"Let's see, shall we?"

Without warning, he lifted up the gun, aimed and pulled the trigger three times without pausing. The three reports blended together and met the sound of the echoes rolling back along the ravine. Stokes' ears rang, but he could not keep the smile from his own face. The cloud of gun smoke had almost obscured the log, but he saw that the first two shots had hit the target, toppling it over in a cloud of splinters and dust. The third bullet had missed, hitting the rocks a couple of feet behind the fallen log.

"You might not get scalped after all," said White, with a twisted smile. "Now, how about you give young Al a chance to show us both how it's done."

Stokes ejected the spent brass and showed Albert how to load the chambers.

"Go ahead. You can load all six," he said. "We're going to be emptying the cylinder in a couple of minutes."

When the gun was loaded, Stokes and White stood behind the boy and offered him advice.

"Hold it in both hands," Stokes said. "Like this. It doesn't have much of a kick, but it will take you by surprise, so hold it tight. I don't want to have to explain to your mother how you got a black eye."

Albert held the gun at arm's length. His face was a mask of concentration as he looked down the barrel.

"You just need to make the sight at the end of the barrel line up with the groove near the hammer. Place that on what you want to hit and pull the trigger."

Albert grunted with the effort and the gun shook in his hands as he put pressure on the trigger. The hammer moved back slowly.

"Careful now," whispered Stokes. "Take a breath."

The hammer fell and the gun fired with a boom and a billow of smoke. The water of the stream splashed where the bullet hit.

"Damn it," Albert hissed.

"Remember, I missed my first shot too," said Stokes. "And I've shot many times before. Take a deep breath and let it out slowly."

The second shot was closer, but still wide of the target.

"Just aim like you're pointing your finger," White said.

A third shot rang out and the driftwood splintered.

Albert let out a squeal and jumped up and down, waving the pistol in the air.

"I got it!"

White lashed out a big hand and caught the boy's wrist. His face was stern, his voice hard.

"When you got a gun in your hand, it's for shooting, not for shaking about. Don't point a gun at nobody or nothing you don't want to kill, and don't be flailing about like a mad man with a loaded pistol in your hand."

"Sorry," Albert said, downcast at the rebuke.

"It's no matter, Al," White said with a smile. "Everybody has to learn. The only fool is the one who don't listen. Just remember what I told you. Now, you still got three shots left. Let's see if you got your eye in."

Albert concentrated and aimed, hitting once more and narrowly missing with the last two shots.

"We'll make a shootist of you yet," said White, taking the revolver from the boy and handing it back to Stokes.

Stokes had just opened the loading gate and begun ejecting the brass when White yelled.

"Cover your ears, boys. My big gals are not as quiet as that Lightning."

Without waiting for their reaction, he pulled his two Remingtons, somehow cocking them both and firing in the same instant. The log shattered and jumped. He had drawn the pistols and fired more quickly than Stokes would have believed possible if he had not witnessed the feat with his own eyes. And White did not stop firing. In no more than two or three seconds he had fired all ten of the bullets in his guns and slid the smoking revolvers back into their holsters without looking away from the target. The reports from the larger calibre revolvers were deafening. Thick smoke clogged the creek bed, briefly obscuring the driftwood log. When the smoke dissipated somewhat, Stokes saw the wood had been obliterated. All ten .44 calibre bullets must have hit home.

"By gum," said Albert, giggling at the shock of the sound and quantity of smoke. His hands had remained clamped tightly over his ears, but now he dropped them to his sides and hurried forward, making the smoke whirl about him. "You done destroyed that log," he said with a whistle.

"I may be getting old," White said, "but I ain't blind yet. That ain't much more than a dozen paces away."

"That was quite something," Stokes commented. "I saw some good shooters in Colonel Cody's show but I always wondered how much of that was trickery. I won't deny it's impressive to see such accuracy coupled with speed."

"I ain't fast," White said, shaking his head. He pulled the ivory-handled revolver from its holster and reloaded it quickly with bullets from his gun belt. "If you want to see a real shootist, you should see John Wesley Hardin. I seen him once in El Paso. He shot all six bullets from a pistol into a playing card in less time than it would take me to draw and fire once."

"Some men are just naturally gifted, I suppose," said Stokes, reloading his revolver from the box of .38 cartridges.

"Hardin's gifted at killing, that's for sure." White holstered the now loaded Remington and proceeded to reload the other one. "I ain't never met a meaner snake than John Hardin, and I've run with some rough crowds. He might well be gifted at shooting too, but you know why he's the best I ever saw?"

"Why?" asked Albert, his eyes wide.

"Because he practises every day and twice on Sundays." He ruffled the boy's hair and Albert laughed. It was good to see him happy and Stokes was pleased he had not fought White on the decision to let the boy shoot.

"Well," he said, "you heard the man. No time like the present. Let's get in some more practice while we can."

They shot several more rounds with the Colt, using stones and logs as targets. Stokes took turns shooting with Albert. The boy got better quickly and was soon hitting four out of five times. Stokes liked the weight and aim of the pistol and was content with his own accuracy. He could not imagine ever being able to draw and shoot as quickly as White, but he was reassured he would be able to hit a man if he was called upon to defend himself or others.

Stokes looked at his watch. It was nearly midday. He would call a halt soon. He already felt comfortable with the revolver, and Albert was getting tired, his shooting less consistent. White hadn't fired again since his impressive display with the two Remingtons. His ten rapid shots appeared to have satisfied any need he felt to practise, and he was seemingly content to have shown the Englishman and the boy his superior skill with firearms.

"One more turn," Stokes said, handing Albert the pistol.

"Oh, do we have to stop already?" Albert's tone had taken on a whiny edge, another sign he was getting tired, Stokes thought.

"Yes, I only bought a hundred rounds. At this rate I won't

have any bullets left if I need to use the gun against anything other than trees and stones."

To his credit, Albert did not complain further. He took the pistol and held it in his two hands as he had been shown.

"I'm going to try for that rock a ways up there. The light one sticking out of the bushes."

Stokes followed his gaze to where a rock, paler than the others, jutted from the ravine wall. It was surrounded by greasewood bushes, giving it the appearance of a small stone island rising from a sea of green.

"That's thirty yards if it's an inch," White said. "Think you can hit it?"

"Yes, sir."

Stokes wasn't so sure. Albert's concentration had been wavering, and even at the shorter distance he was now missing around half of the shots he took. He said nothing though as the boy took aim and fired.

The bullet shook the bushes, but did not hit the rock.

"You were just a little low there, young Al," White said. "You almost got it."

Frowning with concentration, Albert aimed again and fired. This time a large chip of stone flew off the rock.

"Told you I could hit it," crowed the boy, justifiably pleased with himself.

"That's some good shooting."

The low, almost whispered voice came from behind them. Stokes cursed at having been surprised again. But White, as fast as a cat, had pulled his ivory grip revolver and spun around, gun cocked and trained on the newcomer.

It was Reuban Van Orman. He stood very still. The only difference to his appearance at breakfast was that he now carried an old Winchester rifle.

"Jed, it's just Reuban," Stokes said, keeping his voice calm. It was the same voice he employed when talking to violent drunks, which he supposed was apt. "There's no need for your gun."

For a few seconds he thought the old man might shoot, but then, slowly, White lowered his pistol, easing down the hammer gently. He adjusted the cylinder to leave an empty chamber beneath the hammer and slid the weapon back into its holster.

"I could have shot you," he said, sounding as if he regretted missing the opportunity.

"You could have shot me many times before today, Jedediah," Reuban replied, meeting White's angry glower with his own unblinking calm stare.

"What do you want?" asked White, his expression sour.

"What I wanted was to rest," replied Reuban with a thin smile, "but with you shooting like it is the Fourth of July, I decided that was a waste of my time. I have come for Mr Stokes."

"What do you want with him?"

Stokes bristled at being talked about as if he wasn't present.

"Reuban has kindly agreed to show me..." Stokes hesitated, flashing a glance at Albert. He didn't wish to remind the boy of his grief, but could see no alternative. "To show me where Thornford met his end."

The elation Albert had felt moments earlier leached from his face. Stokes squeezed his shoulder and held out his hand for the pistol. Albert begrudgingly gave it up without a word.

"Why d'you want to go all the way up there?" asked White. He was suddenly surly. It had been hours since he had emptied the dregs of his whiskey bottle and Stokes wondered how long the man could go without another drink. "I told you what happened."

"You did," Stokes said, nodding. "But I prefer to see things with my own eyes when I can."

White scoffed and spat into the stream.

"It's dangerous," he said, pulling his tobacco and papers from his pouch, and rolling a cigarette.

"I'll be careful."

And with that Stokes pointed the pistol at the pale rock and fired off two quick shots. They both hit their mark. "But you can come along and protect us if you want."

White struck a match on his fingernail and lit his cigarette. He took a long drag, then blew out a plume of smoke.

"I ain't going nowhere with him," he said, tossing the match into the stream.

Turning on his heel, he stalked away without another word. Stokes watched him climb out of the ravine. He was soon lost to view in the woods.

"Well, Reuban," he said, "it looks as though we'll have to make do without the pleasure of Mr White's company."

Chapter Fifteen

Stokes watched Reuban Van Orman with a mixture of awe and incredulity. They had been travelling for over three hours, most of that uphill. Stokes rode Banner. The gelding was strong and sure-footed on the shingle of the slopes, and the muddy dappled shade of the woods they passed through. Even so, the animal was blowing from the exertion of the climb.

Reuban appeared unaffected, and he was on foot. A huge, cream-coloured shaggy dog trotted through the trees nearby.

To Stokes' surprise, Van Orman had refused a mount, saying he preferred to be close to the ground. He then issued a piercing whistle and the big dog had lumbered out of the shade of the trees, tongue flopping and looking for all the world as if it was grinning. Van Orman called the animal Tooyakeh and said it kept coyotes and even wolves away from the sheep. The dog looked soft to Stokes, but it was certainly large enough to put off predators.

Stokes thought the small man would struggle to keep up, but in actuality he was leading the mounted Englishman along tracks and trails at a speed Banner could only just maintain. Every now and then, Reuban would pause and examine something, an impression in the earth, a scratch on a rock, or a scuffed strip of bark on a red cedar, before continuing.

Stokes noticed none of the signs that seemed so clear to the older man, and he wondered what else he was missing about the land they travelled through. But both Banner and he were glad of the short rests, while Reuban scanned the earth. Tooyakeh flopped to the ground, but kept his head up, scanning the forest all about them, ears twitching at every sound.

"What do you see?" Stokes asked the first time they halted.

"Sign," Reuban replied, offering no more detail.

The second time Reuban stopped they were on the edge of a wooded bluff. The ground fell away to the valley below. The sun and wind had scattered the clouds of the early morning and the afternoon sky was a brilliant blue. Far out over the valley, a couple of large birds drifted, gliding on huge wings. Beneath them, a smudge of smoke coloured the sky. Closer to where the two men were on the bluff, Stokes could make out the roofs of the JT Ranch buildings and the thronged sheep in the pens, but they were much too far away for any sound from the ranch to reach them.

"See anything?" Stokes asked, glancing at where Reuban was peering closely at a twig.

"Sign," Reuban said again. Stokes wondered if the older man was making fun of him.

"Is that Griffith down there?"

Reuban didn't look up, but nodded.

"What birds are those?"

Reuban stood and followed the progress of the pair of birds for a few seconds.

"Buzzards," he said.

"And where is the Cabin Creek Ranch?"

Reuban pointed along the valley.

"North of the JT a ways. A couple hours' ride, twice that from Griffith."

Reuban was clearly a man of few words. He pressed on, and Stokes followed, pleased to be riding. He would never have been able to keep up the pace on foot. It was warm in the sunshine, but cool when they passed through the shadows of trees and rocky outcrops. Stokes was glad he had brought his coat. It would be dark soon and the night would be cold. Reuban had also told him to bring his bedroll. The small man had his own blanket rolled and tied to his back, though Stokes wondered if Van Orman would even feel the cold. He seemed as at home in the wild as Tooyakeh.

Stokes was sure it would be cold in the night, but at least they would eat well. When Mary Ann had heard they were heading into the hills, she had given Stokes ample food for the two of them. Reuban had looked amused at the amount of provisions she gave them when they would only be out for one night. As Stokes was shoving the pemmican, bacon, mutton and hardtack into Banner's saddlebags, Mary Ann had gone back into the house, returning with a rifle in a saddle scabbard, along with a bullet belt.

"This was John's," she said. "Take it."

Stokes already wore the Colt on his hip and didn't feel the need to carry another weapon, but the look in her eyes made him reconsider. Stokes had seen enough violence since arriving in Oregon to know that his feeling of safety was at best wishful thinking.

He pulled the rifle from the leather scabbard. It was a Winchester '73. A fine weapon and it looked clean and well maintained, just as he would have expected of a firearm owned by Thornford.

"Thank you," he said. "Hopefully Reuban can keep us out of trouble." He smiled at Mary Ann, but she merely looked worried.

He slung the bullet belt over his shoulder and attached the scabbard to the saddle.

Reuban had not smiled either.

"I don't look for trouble," he said. "But often it finds me anyway. Some things a man can't hide from."

Without another word, Reuban had started to walk towards the woods, Tooyakeh loping beside him, leaving Stokes to finish his preparations and follow behind.

Now man and dog were jogging along a relatively flat stretch of trail, a ridge that ran roughly north to south. On the north side Stokes caught glimpses through the trees of a secluded valley. It was already in shadow down there, but he could see that it was lush with grass and shrubs. The westering sun flashed through the firs and pines as he rode. Ahead, above the trees he saw several large birds. The sunlight caught on something in the trees off to the left. It was bright, red and white; out of place in the shadowed woodland ridge of muted greens and browns.

Riding closer, Stokes saw what it was. It was just as White had described it to him. A cloth sign nailed to the bole of a tree about six feet off the ground where it could not be missed.

The red ink had smudged slightly in the rain, but it was still clearly legible.

It read:

Warning to Sheep Men – You are hereby ordered to keep your sheep on the south side of the plainly marked line or you will suffer the consequences.

Signed
Blue Mountain Sheep Shooters

Now that he had seen the sign, Stokes could make out many more, at regular intervals along the timbered ridgeline. Reuban was waiting for him patiently. Tooyakeh had not lain down as he usually did when they halted, but stood, nose twitching and body stiff. As Stokes rode up, Reuban pointed, but said nothing.

It was then that Stokes noticed the smell. It was a scent he recognised all too well, and his stomach churned. It was the stench of death. The stink of bloated, rotting flesh.

On the north side of the ridge, scattered between the trees, lay the carcasses of several sheep. Black crows and large, red-faced, dark-winged vultures hopped on the corpses, pecking and tearing at the flesh. Reuban clapped his hands together and some of the birds flapped up into the air, slow and heavy with gorged meat. Tooyakeh took a few steps towards the sheep carcasses and the birds, but stopped at a harsh word from Van Orman.

"Is that Cabin Creek land?" Stokes asked, pointing down into the northern valley.

Reuban shook his head.

"Open range," he said. "But the cattlemen say the sheep eat too much grass. Their cows need more space and more grass."

Stokes surveyed the slaughtered animals. Many of the birds, seeing that the men and dog posed them no threat, fluttered back down to resume their feast. He thought of the arrogance that had led to this. The land here looked richly fertile. There must have been enough grass for everyone in this vast wilderness.

The breeze blew the smell of putrefaction into their faces, making Banner snort and stamp. Tooyakeh growled deep in his throat.

"Show me where Captain Thornford was killed," Stokes said, turning Banner's head away from the sheep-strewn slope.

"Not far now," said Reuban, heading northward along the ridge.

As he followed, Stokes looked back over his shoulder. More of the dark birds were returning to the bodies and he wondered how long until the vultures and coyotes would have picked the sheep bones clean. The bones too would eventually be swallowed by the inexorable natural cycles of the wild. In time all evidence of this crime would have vanished. Stokes felt the anger burning deep within him coalesce and harden. He would not allow those responsible for this, or his friend's murder, to go unpunished.

He could not.

If Grant believed he could kill with impunity, Stokes would make him reconsider.

As they rode away, Stokes knew with a sudden certainty that he would not rest until he had brought Grant and his men to justice.

Chapter Sixteen

The sun was low in the sky when they reached their destination. Reuban had led Stokes down the ridge into the shadows of the valley where the lush grass whispered against Banner's legs and almost covered Tooyakeh, then up a slope into more sparsely forested land. The trees thinned out and were replaced by scrubby grass and outcrops of rocks. Here, sedge and pinegrass clung to the thin soil, and nettles and dewberries clogged the rocky crevices.

Reuban made his way unerringly up a rocky incline until the almost imperceptible track he'd been following led into a narrow gorge.

From time to time he had stopped to survey the ground. Once he had told Stokes to be silent and had lain down flat, his ear pressed to the earth. After a minute or more, he had stood, brushing off his buckskins and sniffing the air in a way that reminded Stokes of Tooyakeh.

"I don't think anyone is near," Reuban had said. "But ride with care."

Stokes had loaded the Winchester and the Colt before they'd left, and he checked both guns now, suddenly glad he had brought them. The sight of the dead sheep had unnerved him more than he would have expected. This land was far from tamed and he was dealing with men capable of indiscriminate killing of beast and man.

"Follow me," Reuban said, waiting for Stokes at the entrance to the defile. "I will show you where Thornford died."

The cleft in the mountains was wide enough to ride through, and Stokes knew from what White had told him that he and Thornford had been riding along the trail at the foot of the gorge. But looking into the shadowed pass, he felt uneasy, mounted as he was, so swung down from the saddle, securing Banner's reins around a large boulder. Reuban told Tooyakeh to stay by the horse. The massive dog dropped to the ground, propping its head on its forepaws.

"Is this where White waited?" Stokes asked.

"Waited?"

"Jed told me he had to hunker down behind some rocks and wait out the men who had shot Thornford."

Reuban shrugged, his face devoid of expression.

"I don't know," he said. "But I know where Thornford fell."

Stokes started to follow, then hurried back to tug the Winchester from its scabbard. He thought Reuban's answer strange.

"Can't you read the sign to see where White was?"

Reuban continued walking at his brisk pace and replied without looking back. Sounds echoed between the encroaching walls of the ravine and Reuban spoke softly, as if worried he might be overheard. Stokes imagined the booming echo of gunfire in the narrow space.

"This was all trampled by Sheriff Bannon and his deputies. The sign is not clear."

"But you know where Thornford was shot?"

"Yes, I came here before the sheriff," said Reuban. "I saw the tracks of Jed's horse and the Captain's. I followed the sign to where he was shot. And then I climbed up there to see where the killer had shot from."

He pointed up a steep escarpment to a pile of boulders that would provide perfect cover for an ambush. It was just as White had described it.

"But you did not see where Jed waited after he ran away from the shooting?"

129

Reuban shook his head.

"I was not looking for it," he said, matter of factly. "The Captain fell here." He halted at a place where the floor of the ravine widened.

Stokes scanned the skyline. Anyone hidden in those boulders would have had a perfect view of travellers below. He crouched down and looked at the ground, but he could discern nothing in the dust and pebbles to mark this place over any others.

"You're sure he died here?"

Reuban crouched beside him.

"Yes," he said, passing his hand over the ground as he spoke. "The sign was clear. There was blood here in the sand," he circled his hand over a nondescript patch of earth, "before the rains washed it away."

Stokes tried to picture the scene in his mind's eye. His friend lying in pain and fear. The puffs of smoke from the gunfire on the ridge above. The booming crash of the shots. White's returning fire from further back towards the entrance.

"White told me John had found cover behind a rock. Could he have meant that one there?" He pointed to an outcrop a few paces away. It was covered in lichen.

Reuban moved to the rock and examined it and the ground around it for some time.

"Perhaps this is the rock White was talking about," he said.

"So Thornford died there?"

"No, the Captain died here, where I told you. The sign was clear. Even a child would have been able to read its story."

Stokes very much doubted that any child would possess such skill, but then he thought about what he had heard of Van Orman's childhood and said nothing. Looking up at the rocks again, then along the narrow ravine between the two steep slopes, Stokes frowned. The ravine was in dark shade, but the sky behind the hills was still a bright and vivid cloudless blue.

"Why did Thornford and White ride this way?" he asked. "Is this a common route to travel?"

"It is the fastest way to get to Mr Rice's spread. Especially if they had ridden to check on the sheep on the high ridge first."

"Is this Rice one of the Blue Mountain Sheep Shooters?"

"I don't rightly know," said Reuban. "I doubt it."

"Why? Is he not a cattleman?"

"He is, but he is friendly with the Thornfords. He rides over with his wife and daughters some Sundays."

"So he wouldn't help Grant?"

"I don't reckon so," Reuban said. "But I ain't him. I am a good tracker, but I can't read the sign of a man's thoughts. There's no telling what a man might do until he's done it."

Stokes walked back and forth, thinking. He lowered himself onto his haunches behind the low rock and peered up at where Reuban had said Thornford's shooter had been positioned. Then he walked back to where Banner was tethered, judging the distance and the time it would take to turn a horse and gallop back from the attack. He looked at the ground for prints or anything that might help him see better what had happened here. All he saw were the hoof prints of a shoed horse. Banner's, he concluded.

He trudged back to where Reuban waited patiently.

"Why did the men wait here," Stokes asked, "unless they knew Thornford and White would be travelling this way?"

"Man," said Reuban.

"What?"

"Man," Reuban repeated. "Not men."

"What are you talking about?"

"There was only one man up in those rocks."

"What? White said there were several men. He named some of them."

Reuban's expression was flat.

"I know what Jed said," he replied, his voice low.

"Are you saying he lied?"

131

"I ain't saying nothing," Reuban said, meeting Stokes gaze with his cool blue eyes. "But there was only one man up in those rocks. And the shot that killed the Captain came from up there."

Stokes rubbed a hand over his face. None of this made sense. He could feel the beginnings of a headache, the sort that would linger for hours or even days. He was filled with a powerful longing to find a bottle and drown his grief and confusion under a cascade of whiskey. It was a good thing they were far from a saloon. He closed his eyes, turning over everything White had told him.

"You are certain the shot came from up there?" he asked, removing his hat and rubbing his temples.

"Yes."

"And there was only one shooter?"

"Yes."

Stokes shook his head in an effort to clear it, then replaced his hat.

"Show me," he said.

Without a word, Reuban set off up the steep incline. Even as quick and nimble as he was, he needed to grip rocks and wheatgrass to pull himself up.

Stokes followed more slowly. It was not a treacherous climb, but it was steep and required focus. He struggled a couple of times due to the Winchester in his hand, once dropping the rifle with a clatter and almost losing it. He had thought about leaving it at the bottom, but rejected the idea immediately.

By the time he reached the patch of earth behind the boulders where Thornford's murderer had hidden, the Englishman was drenched in sweat. He wished he had removed his coat before scaling the escarpment. Once he was on relatively flat ground and able to stand safely without fear of slipping, he shook off the woollen garment. He immediately regretted the decision. The freshening breeze gusted up here, high above the sheltered ravine. His shirt was plastered to his chest and he shivered as the wind quickly cooled him. He pulled his coat back on, then inspected the rifle. It was badly scratched from the fall, but seemed to have suffered no other ill effects.

Reuban waited for him in silence, seemingly oblivious of the chilling effects of the wind, despite not wearing anything thicker than a buckskin shirt.

Stokes squinted down into the shadowed ravine, sighting down the Winchester's barrel. It would have been an easy shot.

"How can you be so sure there was only one man up here?" he asked.

"Ain't much room," Reuban said. "To get a shot into the ravine, you need to step on the piece of earth you're on right now."

It was true, there weren't many places where you could get a clear view of the trail below, and to reach them all, you would need to pass over the small patch of earth.

"It had been raining the day before Thornford was shot," Reuban said. "I came up here the day after and there was only one set of tracks up. One man. The heel of his left boot was cracked."

Something in the dirt and grass that sprouted around the largest boulder caught Stokes' attention. He bent and picked it up.

"That's where the man leaned to aim," Reuban said, pointing at the big rock. "Had a smoke while he waited, I guess."

Stokes looked at the small object in his hand. The tattered old butt of a cigarette. He rubbed it between his thumb and forefinger. A few flakes of tobacco crumbled as the paper, weakened by exposure to rain and sun, shredded apart.

As far as he knew, Reuban didn't smoke. Stokes wished he had bought tobacco and papers in La Grande. He could use a cigarette now and had been relying on White's supply ever since Huntington.

"Jed doesn't seem to like you much," he said, thinking about the old man's reaction to Van Orman.

Reuban shrugged.

"Jedediah don't like nobody," he said. "'cept perhaps Mrs Thornford and the young 'uns."

Stokes glanced at Reuban in surprise.

"I don't think he's sweet on her or nothing," Van Orman said, holding up a callused hand. "Truth is, I think she reminds him of his ma."

"Mrs Thornford is a good woman," Stokes said.

Reuban nodded.

"And the Captain was a good man. Only man in these parts would give me work."

"What will you do now?" Stokes asked.

"I was hired to work the ranch," Reuban said. "Figure I'll stay on until Mrs Thornford says she don't want me around." He watched the flight of a bird far away above the valley. "Or until she moves away."

"Do you think she will?"

Reuban was silent for a time. He stared off into the distance, at the forested slopes of the mountain to the south and the hazed peaks further to the east. They were purple in the distance.

"She is a strong woman," he said at last. "But if Grant has his way, she'll have to move. He won't make it easy for her to stay."

"If I can prove what he did here, he won't be in any position to force her to leave."

Reuban looked at Stokes, his blue eyes narrowed.

"It will be difficult," he said. "Most of the ranchers owe him, and he owns half the town."

"Well," said Stokes, turning to make his way down to the floor of the ravine where Banner and Tooyakeh waited, "he doesn't own me."

Chapter Seventeen

That night they made camp in the valley. Reuban found a dip in the ground, surrounded by red cedars on three sides. He lit a fire using only friction. Taking a stick, he rubbed it in a groove that he cut in a larger split log. After a minute or two, tendrils of smoke drifted up from a tiny ember. To this he carefully added some dry fungus that he took from a small pouch hanging around his neck. Then, he gently deposited the smoking tinder into a ball of bark and twigs and blew softly on it until it first billowed smoke, then burst into flame. He placed the ball on the ground and began to feed the flames with twigs. The whole process didn't take much longer than it had taken White to start a fire using a match.

Darkness fell quickly beneath the trees in the valley, but the site Van Orman had chosen was warm. Banner was hobbled nearby and Stokes could hear the gelding cropping at the grass and scrub. Tooyakeh wandered out into the night and Stokes wondered where he had gone, but Van Orman seemed not to notice or care.

The two men spoke little, but they ate well, making a stew of some of the pemmican and mutton Mary Ann had given them. The hardtack was too hard to eat as it was, so they crumbled it into the slumgullion. The smell of cooking brought Tooyakeh back into the camp and Reuban let him lick the remnants of the thin stew from the pot.

Mary Ann had given them coffee too, which seemed to please Reuban more than anything.

"I need me a pack mule," he said, "so I can carry coffee and a pot." He sipped the hot drink in the darkness. The red light from the flames gave his face a ruddy complexion and Stokes thought that with his long plaited hair and stern expression he looked more like an Indian than ever.

When they had finished eating, Reuban rose and moved away from the fire. Stokes thought he could just discern a pale smudge that might have been Tooyakeh out there in the dark.

"I'll keep watch," Van Orman said from the darkness. "And Tooyakeh will warn us if any critters come near."

"Wake me when it is my turn," Stokes said, shaking out his bedroll beside the fire. He lay the Winchester beside him, and the holstered revolver beneath the saddle upon which he rested his head.

He listened to the night for a time, remembering to wind up his pocket watch before sleep claimed him. He could just make out the time by the firelight. It was only just after eight o'clock, but he fell asleep in minutes.

Stokes awoke in the darkest part of the night. The fire had died down to dim embers. He thought about blowing life into it and adding some more wood, but he was warm beneath the blanket. Only his nose was cold in the night chill. He listened for what had woken him, wondering if it had been Reuban, for surely it must be his turn on watch. He pulled out his pocket watch, but couldn't make out the hands in the gloom. A soft breeze rustled the tops of the red cedar trees. There was a sound, thin and distant. He strained to hear more clearly. He thought it might be the lowing of cattle.

"Reuban," he whispered, not wishing to call out and shatter the still of the night.

No answer.

"Van Orman," he tried again, but still there was no reply.

He lay there listening to the soft sounds of the darkness for what seemed a long time, but in reality it was only a few minutes before he once more fell fast asleep and did not awaken again until dawn paled the sky above the mountains to the east.

When he woke, Reuban was preparing coffee and frying bacon. Tooyakeh was sitting hopefully nearby, tongue hanging from drooling lips, eyes unmoving as he stared at the cooking bacon.

Stokes sat up and rubbed the sleep from his eyes.

"I must apologise," he said, embarrassed. "It would appear that the Oregon air has much the same effect upon me as the waters of Lethe."

Reuban glanced up from the fire.

"Lethe?"

"A mythical river. Drinking from its waters would make one forget the past. Whenever I sleep here, I seem to forget to rouse myself when it is my turn to stand guard." Stokes stood and stretched. His leg pained him and his shoulder muscles felt tight.

"Never heard of the Lethe," said Reuban. "Is it in England?"

"No. The underworld." He sniffed. "Though perhaps there is little difference."

"I never heard of no river that makes you sleep," said Reuban, handing him a cup of coffee. "You didn't wake 'cause I didn't wake you. Figured you needed the sleep."

Reuban's words stung, reminding him of what White had said to him.

"Next time, wake me up," he said. "I can do my share. Did I hear cows in the night?"

"A sizeable herd is being pushed along the valley. I went and had a look a while back."

"Grant's men?"

"Reckon so," said Reuban, removing the bacon from the fire and placing the skillet on the ground between them. "Better eat up. They're still a ways off, but we should head east through the trees. Don't think we should want to meet them."

Stokes bridled at the thought of retreating from Grant's cowhands. Then he recalled the quick savagery he had witnessed in Huntington, and the attack in the trees near Durkee.

"How many are there?"

"Can't tell for sure, but a few hundred head of cattle. Reckon seven or eight cowpunchers. Maybe more." Reuban used his knife to cut a piece of bacon, then, as if he could hear Stokes' thoughts, he added, "Enough to make us disappear."

They struck camp, putting out the fire and covering it with earth. Reuban trotted off into the forest, Tooyakeh close behind, with Stokes following them on Banner. They soon came to a stream. They filled their canteens, then let the gelding drink. Tooyakeh drank long and noisily beside the horse.

"This is the stream that runs close to the JT," Reuban said. "You'll have to dismount soon. The stream is easy to follow, but travelling on horseback will be difficult."

Van Orman was right. As they moved further down the mountainside, the trees grew more closely together and the forest floor became tangled with ferns and blackberry brambles.

Stokes led Banner, while Reuban picked out a path.

"Don't touch that plant," he said at one point, indicating a stunted bush with white flowers that were just budding. "Poison oak. Make you itch so much you'd wish you didn't have skin."

Despite the jumbled roots and plants in their path and the low branches that kept Stokes out of the saddle for most of the journey, it was downhill all the way and they made good time. They were back at the ranch before midday.

Albert saw them first and ran out to meet them with Pincher. The smaller dog sped up to Tooyakeh, who did his best to appear disinterested, though Stokes noticed his long tail wagged slowly. Banner nickered a greeting.

"Did you find anything?" Albert asked, breathless from his run out to the approaching men.

"Easy there, Albert," Stokes said. "I don't want to tell you now just to have to repeat everything for your mother."

When they reached the house, Mary Ann was standing on the veranda with Adelaide.

"You boys must be hungry," she said with a strained smile. Her eyes looked bruised and tired, and Stokes wondered how much sleep she'd had since her husband's murder.

"I can't speak for Reuban," Stokes said, "but I for one am still quite replete from breakfast."

"We ate like chiefs," said Reuban, grinning. "We had so much food."

"Tea then?" Mary Ann said. "Coffee?"

"Are there biscuits?" Reuban asked.

"I thought you were full," she said.

He grinned, his teeth white and strong in his weather-beaten face.

"There's always room for a biscuit."

She smiled.

"Come inside then and tell us what you learnt."

Chapter Eighteen

It was mid-afternoon when Stokes rode down the main street of Griffith. On the outskirts of town he passed three sawmills, steam engines cranking and the buzz of their whip saws humming like angry wasps. Huge piles of planking were stacked ready to be carried away and the warm spring air was redolent of wood sap, sawdust and smoke.

Several hundred yards from the first town building, Stokes saw a large contingent of Chinese men working on the railroad. Dozens of them were labouring in silence, the only sounds the clang of their long hammers as they struck the spikes into the sleepers to secure the tracks. None of them looked up at Stokes as he passed on the bay gelding, but the greasy-faced man who sat in a folding chair to supervise the workers followed him with his gaze. The man's eyes were deep set and small, like a pig's.

John had written to Stokes of the excitement in the town at the arrival of the Oregon Railroad and Navigation Company. It looked to Stokes as though trains would be in Griffith very soon. The station building was almost complete, with men climbing on the roof and driving nails into wooden shingles.

After the noise and industry on the edge of town, Griffith was a rather small affair. A scattering of timber buildings centred on a straight street. The town planners clearly had grand ideas for the township, as there was a grid of streets and avenues laid out that went all the way down to the Grande Ronde River that ran more or less north to south through the green valley.

Stokes looked about him warily. He was acutely aware that he was alone. Mary Ann had offered to send Lars Giblin with him, but Stokes had declined. He thought it best that he have a look about the place without the presence of hands from the JT Ranch colouring people's view of him.

He had first considered heading into Griffith with Jed White, but on enquiring after him, Amos had told him that he'd ridden into town early that morning.

"He needs to buy supplies, if you catch my meaning," he said, with a crooked smirk.

Stokes knew exactly what the old man meant. White was clearly a capable man, but the claws of vice were sunk into him so deeply he could scarcely function without a drink to steady his hand and settle his mood.

Stokes had contented himself with a cup of tea and a biscuit. While he ate and drank, Mary Ann had asked what he had discovered up in the hills.

"I'm not sure yet," he'd answered. "But it was good to see the place. And Reuban was a great help." He had seen the disappointment in her face, Albert's too. "I need to understand things better. Investigations like this take time. But I give you my word. I'll do everything in my power to make the men responsible for John's death pay."

A buggy pulled by a chestnut pony passed him on the street. It was driven by a handsome woman with a younger woman sitting beside her.

"Good afternoon, ladies," Stokes said automatically, doffing his hat.

The younger of the women blushed and giggled. The older woman's lips pressed tightly together and she cracked the whip over the pony. The buggy sprang forward and when Stokes looked back over his shoulder, he saw the girl had craned her neck to get a better look at him. He offered her his best smile.

He had seen the ladies come out of a shop on the left of the street and on a whim he trotted Banner over there.

141

Dismounting, he tied the horse's reins around the hitching rail and stepped up onto the wooden sidewalk. He stretched and rubbed his leg. His thigh had pained him since the climb the previous afternoon, followed by the walk down through the forest that morning. It was stiff now, and he massaged it as he looked up and down the street. Removing the rifle scabbard from his saddle, he stepped up to the store front that the ladies had recently exited.

The sign was clean and looked freshly painted. It read: McCall's General Store. Groceries. Dry Goods. Hardware.

He had been thinking about starting with the sheriff, but if Bannon was truly in Grant's employ it might be best to speak to him later. This store was as good a place as any to begin to get a feel for the town and what the people thought of the recent goings on between the sheep farmers and the cattlemen.

He looked briefly through the window, then pushed open the thin timber door. A bell on the door frame tinkled. The shop was well stocked, shelves piled high with all manner of goods. The air was heady with a melange of aromas. Leather polish, camphor, kerosene, coffee and molasses vied for supremacy over myriad other scents, from textiles, tools, foodstuffs and medicinal remedies.

A middle-aged man, wearing a clean brown apron, stepped out from a back room. He was balding and short, his eyes inquisitive behind small round spectacles that were perched on a bulbous, red-veined nose.

"Good afternoon, sir," he said, his tone avuncular and welcoming. "What can I do for you today?"

"Good afternoon," Stokes replied, removing his hat. "I find myself without tobacco."

"Then you are in luck, sir." The man began to pull items from wooden drawers and place them on the counter. "I have some fine cigars and cigarillos. All the way from Havana." He lowered his voice and leant forward, a twinkle in his eye.

"They say they are rolled on the thighs of virgins." He winked. "Or are you perhaps looking for pipe tobacco?" He produced a tin, placing it beside the boxes of cigars. "Do you have a pipe?" He turned and opened a cabinet with several pipes on display.

"I had been thinking about buying tobacco and papers—"

Before he could say more, the small man closed the pipe cabinet and pulled open another drawer.

"Why, of course," he said. "I stock the best rice papers and fine American shag tobacco."

Stokes didn't much like being interrupted, but the man's bustling energy amused him.

"I *had* been thinking of papers and tobacco," he said, "but your tale of the virgins has given me an appetite for those cigarillos."

"Why, of course," said the man with a conspiratorial smile. "What red-blooded man could resist? I smoke them myself on occasion, though I haven't told Mrs McCall about the young ladies in the warm climes of the Caribee." He winked again. "They really are a fine smoke too. Especially with a good brandy." He moved quickly along the counter and pulled a bottle from a low shelf. "Could I tempt you? You sound like a man of fine taste, if I may say so. From the east, no? Boston, perhaps?"

"A bit further east than that," replied Stokes. "No brandy, thank you. But I'll take twenty of the cigarillos and half a dozen of those cigars."

"Why, of course, sir." The shopkeeper began putting away the other items on the counter. "Would there be anything else? Cartridges perhaps?"

"Actually, yes. I'll have a box of .38 Long Colts for this revolver." He pulled the Lightning from the holster and placed it on the counter.

The shopkeeper stiffened and drew in a breath, as if he expected Stokes to shoot him there and then. Or, thought Stokes, as if he had recognised the weapon. McCall regained his composure quickly, and pulled a small box from beneath the counter.

"They come in boxes of fifty. How many would you like?"

"Two boxes should suffice," Stokes said.

"Planning on some target practice?" McCall said with an ingratiating grin.

"I suppose that depends on what targets present themselves."

"Why, of course," McCall replied. His tone was pinched, his movements nervous as he added the two boxes of shells to Stokes' goods.

"Anything else?"

"A box of lucifers, please."

"Why, of course."

McCall fished out a small box of matches, placed it on top of the other items and proceeded to wrap them all expertly in brown paper. He did not look up but tensed noticeably when Stokes retrieved the pistol, slipping it back into the holster.

"You are from England, then?" McCall asked, pulling a length of twine from a large roll.

"Yes." Stokes looked out the window. Three men were riding past, the one in front vaguely familiar.

"And what brings you all the way to Oregon?"

"I wanted to see the land."

"It is beautiful," said McCall. He finished tying the string around the parcel he had made, then used a small, sharp knife to cut the cord. "For the next few months you'll have clement weather, if you are staying. But I would leave before winter though, unless you like the cold. It gets bitter up here. I keep thinking about moving to California, but Mrs McCall won't hear of it."

"What won't I hear of?"

On hearing the voice, McCall jumped. Such was his shock he dropped the parcel he had been holding out. Stokes caught it one handed.

"Well?" said the woman who stood in the rear doorway.

She was considerably taller than her husband, with a long chin and high forehead that was wrinkled from frowning. She was scowling now. "You haven't been telling him your ridiculous tale about the Havana cigars and the native girls, have you?"

McCall flushed crimson. Stokes felt sorry for the man. He gave a slight bow.

"This must be your daughter, Mr McCall," he said. In his experience women responded well to such flattery. Mrs McCall's expression only hardened.

"I am his wife," she snapped. "And who might you be?"

"Forgive my rudeness," he said. "My name is Stokes. How do you do?"

"Judging from your accent," she said, looking him up and down, "I'd say you are a friend of Captain Thornford's."

"I was," Stokes said.

"Terrible what happened to him," she said.

"What did you hear?" Stokes asked. "I've only recently arrived and all I know is that he was killed."

"Shot," Mr McCall said, happy that the subject was moving away from the rolling of Cuban cigars. "Killed up in the hills. Tragic."

"You know who shot him?" Stokes asked.

"Nobody knows that," McCall replied.

"The man who pulled the trigger knows," Stokes said, his tone growing hard.

"Why, of course, but with no witness I don't suppose we'll ever know."

Stokes glanced out the window again.

"The hands up at the JT Ranch believe Tom Grant was behind the killing," he said. "Some sort of dispute over grazing rights."

"We know nothing about that," said Mrs McCall. "But I can assure you, Mr Stokes, it could not have been Mr Grant or any of the Cabin Creek crew."

He swung back to face her.

"You seem very sure of that."

"And I am, sir. Thomas Grant is my brother-in-law. He is a good man and an upstanding citizen of this county. Anybody who says otherwise is merely envious of his success. That is ever the way with those less fortunate. They cannot bear to believe that someone has made something for themselves by dint of hard work and nothing more. They must always seek to besmirch a wealthy man's character. It would do them better to simply work hard themselves."

Stokes cursed inwardly. He had thought to get a feeling for the mood of the townspeople and the first ones he spoke to were family of the very man trying to force the Thornfords from their land.

"Well," Stokes said, keeping the tension from his voice, "I am sure Captain Thornford worked as hard as any other man. All he wanted was to make his ranch a success, and to provide for his family."

"Of course," she replied, her tone softening somewhat. "I did not mean to imply otherwise. But there are always elements who seek to stain the reputation of good men like Mr Grant. It is sad and it is infuriating."

"I have found that a good man's reputation is difficult to tarnish. I am sure your brother-in-law's actions can speak for themselves."

He met her gaze unblinking until she looked away.

"If that is everything," said Mr McCall into the awkward silence.

Thinking of Thornford and his family had reminded Stokes that he had bought nothing for the children. The telescope was still in its polished wooden case with the rest of his belongings in the bunkhouse. He would give it to the children, when he found the right moment, but he didn't want to return to the ranch empty-handed from his visit into Griffith. Not after Mary Ann had shown him such hospitality. He'd seen some books on a shelf on the far wall of the store. He went over and flicked through them. Selecting two, he returned to the counter. The McCalls watched him in silence.

"I'll take these, too, and a quarter pound of those lemon drops."

"Why, of course," said McCall as he pulled down the jar of sweets, weighed them out, then slid them into a paper bag.

"If you would be so kind as to wrap the books," Stokes said.

McCall promptly did so, tying the parcel with string and handing the package and the bag of sweets to Stokes. All the while Mrs McCall stood behind the counter, her lips pursed and her brow furrowed as she glowered at the Englishman.

Stokes paid for his purchases, frowning at the thinness of his wallet.

"Mrs McCall." He bowed, before putting his hat back on. "Mr McCall."

"Thank you for your custom," McCall said automatically as Stokes opened the door with a jangle of the bell. "Have a nice day."

Stokes nodded to the shopkeeper standing beside his tall, stern wife. Again he felt sorry for the man. Pulling the door closed behind him, he stepped back out onto the wooden sidewalk.

Chapter Nineteen

Outside the general store, Stokes looked both ways along the street. There were a few people going about their business, but it was not busy. He could see the sign of the Lady Elgin saloon further down on the far side of the wide, rutted mud road. He shoved the items he had bought into his saddlebags, and hung his rifle scabbard from the pommel, all the time feeling that he was being watched.

Untying the reins, he stepped into the stirrup and swung up onto the saddle. He glanced at the store. The McCalls were both peering at him through the window. Mr McCall looked embarrassed to have been caught staring at the Englishman, but Mrs McCall met his gaze defiantly. Tugging the brim of his hat politely, Stokes reined Banner around. He had passed a livery stable on the edge of town near the station building. It was a warm afternoon and he'd noticed a water trough outside. The gelding would welcome a drink and a town hostler would be as likely as anyone to have dealings with all the ranch hands and cowpokes in the area. Perhaps he would be able to help Stokes get a feel for the mood in town.

Touching his heels to Banner's flanks, he set off at an easy trot. Turning in the saddle, he was not surprised to see Mrs McCall come out of the store and hurry down the wooden sidewalk. News of his arrival would not take long to spread. He was contemplating following her, to see who she would relay her news to first, when the boom of a gunshot rolled down the street like a clap of thunder.

The shot came from the edge of town and the report was followed by coarse laughter and the sounds of horses stamping. Harsh voices shouted, but Stokes could not make out the words. Ignoring Mrs McCall, he spurred Banner into a lope.

There was a large house at the end of the street. A small brass sign gleamed on the dark, painted door, but Stokes was riding too fast to make out the words engraved on it. Passing the building, he saw the source of the commotion. Tugging on Banner's reins, he slowed the mount as he took in the scene.

The three mounted men he had seen from the store were circling their horses around a prostrate figure. From the man's clothes and the straw conical hat that had been knocked from his head, Stokes could see he was Chinese. He was pleading in heavily accented English, begging the men to let him go. He tried to get to his feet, but one of the riders jerked his horse to the right and the man stumbled and fell, sprawling in the muck. Stokes saw then that the cowhand had roped the poor man, and the rawhide lariat was secured around his saddle pommel, as if he were tying a steer for branding.

The other two riders laughed, their voices jagged and grating against the man's pitiful wails for mercy. One of the men had a pistol in his hand. Stokes had thought there was something familiar about the mounted men and now he saw why. As one of the horses wheeled about, the sun shone on the rider's pocked cheeks. Stokes recognised the man immediately. Rab Tovey.

As he watched, one of the riders, a burly man with a broad, vicious-looking face beneath a round-crowned bowler hat, kicked out from his saddle, catching the defenceless Chinese man in the face as he was attempting to climb to his feet. Seeing the three armed and mounted men tormenting a single unarmed opponent filled Stokes with a sudden searing rage.

Gone were his plans to investigate the mood of the towns-folk before proceeding with his inquiries. The same anger that had seen him beat Fred Bullen now burnt away all rational thought in a blazing rush. Without hesitation, Stokes kicked Banner's flanks and the gelding responded instantly, bunching the huge muscles of its rear legs and leaping forward into a gallop.

The three horsemen were engrossed in their sport. They had not noticed Stokes coming round the corner and now he rode at a run out of the shadow of the large house and straight towards them without warning.

Stokes bared his teeth as he rode, tugging the Colt Lightning from its holster. Banner responded like a steed bred for battle. They were only fifty or sixty yards distant, and the gelding had not reached his top speed, but he did not shy away. At the last instant, Tovey must have seen or heard Stokes' approach, for he tried to swerve his horse away. He was too late. Banner hit Tovey's chestnut mare, the glancing blow making the horse rear and buck.

Stokes hung on to the saddle horn and gripped Banner tightly with his legs. He was close to Rab Tovey and swung his revolver hard, catching the man across the forehead. Tovey's eyes glazed and he lolled in the saddle, his revolver toppling from his hand as he stared about him in a reeling daze, blinking and trying to focus.

The big man with the bowler hat was quick. His hand dropped to the pistol he wore at an angle on the left side of his belt. He was already sliding the gun free of the leather, but stopped when Stokes aimed the Lightning straight at his chest. They were no more than ten feet apart and the Englishman couldn't miss.

Stokes did not look away from the wide-faced man, whose hand rested on his pistol grip. The man's eyes were small, hard as flint and as cold as a winter's night. The eyes of a killer.

The third rider was skinny, as if he had never eaten a square meal. His bony, raw, angular face was partially hidden beneath a dusty, wide-brimmed brown hat and a shaggy mop of dark hair. But Stokes had seen enough of the man's features to see his right cheek was scabbed with a series of incisions and deep scratches. Stokes thought he'd recognised him, and the man confirmed it as soon as he opened his mouth.

"That's the son of a bitch who stopped us finishing Jed White in Huntington," the man said.

Banner was blowing and shaking with nervous energy. The gelding had a warrior's heart and wanted to prance and turn. It was all Stokes could do to keep the beast still enough for him to remain facing his foe. Stokes was certain that to turn his back on him would be a fatal mistake.

"That's my gun," said the scrawny-looking man.

"Is that so?" replied Stokes, not taking his gaze from the man with the bowler hat and killer's eyes. "I took this pistol from a coward who tried to shoot me in cold blood."

"Who you calling a coward?" said the man, his nasal voice rising to a shout.

"Shut your mouth, Hunter," said the broad-faced man.

"But, Bull," the thin man called Hunter whined. "That gun—"

"I said shut up." The man Hunter had referred to as Bull cut him off, his voice as hard and cold as his eyes.

For a couple of seconds it seemed that the thin man would protest further, but in the end he merely nodded.

"Must be another gun like mine," he muttered.

"I'm sure there are many guns like this one," said Stokes, his aim not moving from Bull. "But if you had one like it, you'll know it is an accurate firearm. Now," he nodded to the man on the ground, "let him go. If there is one thing I can't abide, it is bullies and cowards."

None of them moved except for the Chinese man, who pushed himself up with a groan. He looked about him, eyes wide with fear.

"Go," said Stokes, without looking down. "You're free."

After the briefest of hesitations, the man slipped the rope from his torso. There was blood trickling from his nose and split lip, but other than that he seemed unharmed. He bowed to Stokes, then scurried off.

Bull narrowed his eyes. His fingers twitched on his pistol's grip. He did not blink as he stared at Stokes.

"I could take you," he said, tapping gently the butt of his gun.

Stokes felt as though he were staring into the eyes of an animal. He dared not look away. To show fear now would prove disastrous. Nudging Banner forward, he crowded the man. He raised the Lightning's muzzle and pointed it directly into Bull's face.

"You might be fast," he said. "But are you fast enough to draw before I put a bullet in your skull?"

"You can't shoot all three of us."

"Perhaps not," said Stokes, "but that would be no concern of yours." He cocked the hammer with his thumb. The gun's barrel barely wavered. It was scarcely a yard from Bull's face. "Have you seen what a bullet does to a head at close range? Even a small bullet like a .38. It is not a pretty sight. Now, call your men off and be on your way."

For several seconds none of them spoke. Banner snorted and stamped, but he held himself still, as if he understood his rider's need.

Then, slowly, an ugly smile formed on Bull's face.

"Drop your gun," came a new voice from behind Stokes. To give the order weight, Stokes heard the click of a gun's hammer. "Now."

Chapter Twenty

Stokes tensed. He had been so focused on the three men before him he had not heard a fourth approaching from behind. His mind raced, but he could see no way out of this. He had been a fool to think he could ride up to these men, outnumbered and out-gunned as he was, and win. At least the poor Chinese man had got away. It had not been completely futile. But Stokes cursed himself. He had lost sight of what was important. If he had any hope of bringing Thornford's murderers to justice, he would need to be clever and more careful. Now he would be lucky to escape with his life.

He was about to lower his gun, resigned to failure, when a new, familiar voice called out.

"No, Cadmar," said the voice, "drop yours."

Stokes risked a glance over his shoulder. Some ten yards behind him was a young man astride a black horse. He had a pencil-thin moustache and eyes of the palest blue glared from beneath his black hat. In his right hand he held a polished revolver that glinted in the afternoon sunshine. It was pointed directly at Stokes' head. The shells he could see in the cylinder looked huge, as did the dark, yawning muzzle.

The street was otherwise empty apart from a single figure who stood in the shade of the large house with the brass plaque on the door. It was Jed White. His Winchester carbine was shouldered and aimed unerringly at the back of the mounted man who threatened Stokes.

"I can drop you now," White said in a friendly tone, his voice slurred slightly by drink, "or you and your boys can put away your lead-chuckers and let me shoot you another day when I ain't so drunk."

Stokes looked back at Bull. He had not drawn his pistol, but his hand had grasped the grip, his muscles taut, ready for action. Stokes shook his head slowly and, as their eyes met again, he saw the reality of the situation dawn on Bull.

"You'll get what's coming to you," Bull whispered, then to the man behind Stokes he said, "Let's ride, Cadmar. Now's not the time. Not here. Not like this."

Stokes heard the man's horse approaching from behind, but he did not turn again.

"Hunter," Bull said, "pick up Rab's piece and see he doesn't fall."

The thin fellow jumped down and retrieved the gun that Rab Tovey had dropped.

"I'll be seeing you again," he said to Stokes, spitting into the mud as he jumped up into the saddle.

"I'm counting on it," Stokes said.

Hunter pushed Tovey's reins into his hands, but rode close to him in case he should fall. The man's forehead was split. Blood trickled down his nose, and his eyes were still glazed.

The man on the black horse rode very close to Stokes.

"Next time, Englishman," he said, "you won't be so lucky."

Stokes said nothing. He didn't lower his gun until the four riders were a hundred yards distant and still riding. It took him a couple of tries to holster the pistol, his hands were shaking so.

When he had got the gun back in the leather sheath, he looked back at the large house. White had vanished. Stokes sighed, angry at himself for the recklessness of his actions. He would look for White in a while. He owed the man his thanks at least.

He patted Banner's quivering neck.

"I'll get you that drink now," he said, and the gelding's ears twitched.

Then, remembering the parcels in his saddlebags, Stokes smiled.

"And I could certainly use a smoke."

A grey-whiskered man stepped out to meet Stokes as he rode up to the livery stable. He took hold of Banner's bridle as Stokes dismounted, then led the gelding to the water trough.

"The water's free," said the man. "A brush and a feed will be two bits."

The man had a kindly face and an easy manner.

"Thank you," Stokes said.

Pulling the coins he had been given as change by McCall out of his pocket, he held them in the palm of his hand.

"Two bits," he said, sorting through the coins. "How much is that?"

The man flicked through the coins in Stokes' hand until he found what he was looking for. His fingers were callused, the nails dirt-darkened. Stokes noticed the skin of the two fingers closest to his thumb were a sickly yellow hue.

"Same as a quarter," the man said, taking a single coin. "Twenty-five cents. For that I'll give this fine-looking boy a good currying. Some corn too. And all the water he cares to drink. Name's Hampton."

Stokes shook the man's hand.

"Stokes," he said.

As Banner drank, quietly dipping his mouth into the trough, Stokes rummaged in his saddlebags. Opening one of the packages, he removed the matches and cigarillos.

"Would you care for a smoke?" he asked, offering one of the small cigars to the hostler. The man grinned and licked his lips.

"Mighty generous of you."

He took one and Stokes handed him the box of lucifers, not wishing him to see how much his hands still shook.

Hampton snapped a match out of the box and scratched it to flaring life. Cupping the small flame in his hand, he puffed on the cigarillo, then offered the match to Stokes.

"I seen these in McCall's," Hampton said, blowing out a thick cloud of smoke, "but I ain't never had enough ballast to buy none." He savoured the smoke for a few seconds. "That's good. Thank you."

"You're very welcome." Stokes drew some of the smoke into his lungs, before blowing it out into the bright afternoon air. Hampton was right. It was good. Strong and pungent, and a lot better than White's rolled shag cigarettes.

For a couple of minutes, the two men stood in silence, smoking. Banner finished drinking from the trough and shook his great head. Stokes looked down the street and saw that people were once more moving along the sidewalks. A laden wagon pulled by four oxen trundled slowly towards them. Stokes walked to the corner of the stable and peered north-ward, in the direction the three Cabin Creek men had ridden. There was no sign of them. The sounds of distant hammering from the station and the far-off railroad reached him on the still air.

"Will you be wanting to stable him for the night?" Hampton asked when he returned.

"No, thank you. I won't be staying."

Hampton took a puff of his cigarillo, nodding in appreciation.

"Probably for the best. You won't be wanting to cool your heels here."

Stokes looked at him sidelong.

"Oh? And why is that?" The cigarillo had calmed his nerves, and he smiled at the hostler's obvious discomfort at the question.

"I mean nothing by it," Hampton said. "It's just those

Cabin Creek boys won't take kindly to being humiliated. The stocky fellow is Beauregard Meacher. They say he's killed more than ten men."

"The one they called Bull?"

"Yes, sir. He's a mean one. The ugly rascal you clattered is Rab Tovey. He's a skunk, but I doubt he'd fight if facing a man with sand."

"And the other two?" Stokes asked.

"The scrawny lad with the scratched up face is Hunter Randle. I heard he's wanted in Missouri. He's been swearing blind these last few days that when he finds the man who shot up his face and took his gun, he's gonna kill him."

Hampton's gaze dropped to the pistol on Stokes' hip.

"I didn't do anything to the boy's face," Stokes said. "Someone shot a tree near him and he caught the splinters. Lucky not to lose an eye, I reckon."

Stokes remembered the attack in the darkness and how White had shot into the gloom, the flame-flashes flickering like lightning in the smoke.

"If this is Randle's gun," he said, "the man's a coward who tried to murder me and Jed White in the dark."

"Well, he's a bad egg. Now he's seen you, I'd say he'll likely try again. I'd watch your back, if I were you."

"What about the man on the black horse?"

Hampton sucked his teeth then took a quick drag of his cigarillo.

"That's Cadmar Byrne," he said. "Might not look like much, but he's the worst of the bunch. Killed more men than cholera, or so they say. Knows his horseflesh though, I'll say that for him. He only rides the best mounts. Served in the cavalry for a time, so I heard."

Stokes patted Banner's neck. The horse snorted and rubbed his nose against him, almost knocking his hat off.

"Can I leave him here for an hour or two?" Stokes asked.

Hampton blew out a stream of smoke.

"Sure," he said. "But I'd ride on if I were you."

"Thank you for the advice. But I'll be staying around."

Hampton found something in his teeth and worked at it with a dirty nail for a time. He spat.

"I wouldn't want to see you end up like that friend of yours," he said. At Stokes' sharp look, Hampton pointed to Banner's rump. "Couldn't help but notice the JT brand. You don't exactly sound like you're from these parts either."

"What do you know of Thornford's shooting?" Stokes said, his tone sombre.

The old hostler shrugged.

"Nothing really," he said, stubbing what was left of the cigarillo on the sole of his boot and pocketing the butt. "But Grant and the other cattlemen have this whole valley eating out of their palm. Thornford never stood a chance. It weren't a fair fight from the start."

"You think Grant killed him?"

Hampton held up a hand as he led Banner into the stable.

"I wouldn't go that far." He tied the gelding, then walked back to the wide open doors of the timber building. "I got to be careful," he said, lowering his voice as if fearful of being overheard despite the nearest person being the wagon driver who was well over a hundred yards away. "This stable's all I got." Hampton bit his lip. "Grant and the other ranchers use my services more than your friend Thornford ever did. I can't afford to cross 'em." He stared at the wagon and the four oxen heaving it along the rutted street. "But that don't mean I got to like 'em. Or how they conduct business. You saw Cadmar, Meacher and the others," he hissed, his voice barely above a whisper. "Grant's got more of that kind riding for his brand. They don't look like no cowpunchers to me."

His eyes focused on something in the distance. Stokes followed his gaze. Two men were striding towards them along the street. The taller of the two wore a black, broadcloth suit. The shorter man was dressed in nondescript brown trousers and a plaid shirt. As they walked past the slow wagon, the sun gleamed on the silver badges both men wore pinned to their breasts.

"Sheriff Bannon and Deputy Stockman," whispered Hampton. "Careful. Whatever you say will make its way back to Grant within a day or two."

He turned and walked into the stable, leaving Stokes standing alone in the afternoon sunshine.

Chapter Twenty-One

"What's the meaning of this?" Sheriff Bannon said as he reached Stokes. "Who are you?"

Stokes had taken the measure of the two men as they approached. The black-suited sheriff was tall and broad-shouldered. He was probably in his mid-forties, his bushy moustache peppered with grey and his stomach bulging slightly over his belt. A large revolver was holstered on his hip. He walked with a comfortable, self-assured purpose and would have seemed in complete control of his surroundings if not for the fact he was accompanied by the shorter, younger man. The deputy looked less like a county sheriff and more like a ranch hand in his worn and patched brown trousers, faded plaid shirt and scuffed, heeled boots. He walked off to one side and a couple of paces behind the sheriff, his eyes nervously flicking to left and right in search of threats. He carried a double-barrelled shotgun.

Stokes held out his hand.

"My name is Stokes."

Bannon looked at his hand as if he'd been offered a rotten fish. He did not shake it.

"Well, Stokes, I'm Bannon and I'm the sheriff here. And I don't take kindly to guns being fired on my streets."

Stokes looked at the other man, expecting an introduction, but Bannon seemed oblivious and made no mention of the man carrying the shotgun.

"I can understand that, Sheriff," replied Stokes, keeping

his tone mild. "It does not do to have men disturbing the peace."

"That's right," said Bannon, a bit nonplussed that this stranger was agreeing with him. "There is a city ordinance forbidding the shooting of firearms within Griffith city limits except on the Fourth of July and New Year's Day. I'm afraid there's a fine of ten dollars for breaching said ordinance."

Bannon's officious nature oozed from him like a bad smell. Stokes had seen countless such men in the army and the police. Self-important men who enjoyed the sound of their own voice and loved nothing better than to order others around. Stokes' hands were steady now and he decided he would have some fun with this pompous prig. He took a last drag on his cigarillo, dropped it and ground it under the toe of his boot.

"Well then, Sheriff," he said, "I have some bad news and some good news for you." Stokes smiled. "Which would you rather have first?"

"I fear the bad news is all for you, sir," Bannon replied. "You will be ten dollars poorer or, if you cannot pay the fine, you will have to spend a couple of nights in our new jail."

"That leads me to the bad news I have for you," said Stokes.

"What is it, man?"

"The gentleman who discharged his firearm in *your* street is no longer in town."

The Sheriff bridled at Stokes' tone.

"I have it on good authority that it was you who fired your pistol," Bannon said, his face reddening. "You were seen in an altercation with some buckaroos."

"Well, I can assure you whoever gave you that information is mistaken. All I did was disarm the man who was shooting and prevented him and his friends from further abusing a poor Chinese labourer. If I had known there was a sheriff in town, I suppose I might have sent for you, but there really was no time for that. I used to be a public servant myself, so I understand how difficult it can be to keep the peace."

"Public servant, you say."

"Yes. A policeman. Though on *my* streets guns were never as common as they are here."

Bannon opened his mouth, then closed it. He seemed caught between wishing to continue with his plan to condemn Stokes and his genuine interest to learn more of the Englishman's past.

"Where did you serve?" he asked at last, his curiosity clearly having won.

"It was nothing like here," Stokes said with a thin smile. "I worked the East End of London."

"You were a lawman?" asked Bannon, sounding incredulous. "In London?"

"Yes," replied Stokes. "Detective Inspector at Scotland Yard."

Bannon's face had grown increasingly red. Stokes could not tell if Bannon thought he was lying to him, or if he was embarrassed.

"It is thanks to our shared profession," Stokes continued, "and the skills I learnt on the job that I am able to bring you the good news."

"And what is that?" Bannon said, uncertainty in his voice.

"I know the identities of the men who were brawling and disturbing the peace. So it should be an easy enough thing for you to ride out and arrest them."

"I won't be riding out anywhere," spluttered Bannon.

"Don't you want to even hear who it was?" Stokes asked, sounding shocked.

It was clear Bannon knew full well who Stokes had confronted, but he swallowed his anger down and glared at the Englishman.

"OK, tell me."

"Beauregard Meacher, Hunter Randle and Rab Tovey. Tovey did the shooting."

Bannon stared at him for a long time.

"You'd better watch yourself, Stokes," he said. "People

round these parts don't take kindly to wiseacres from England. You wouldn't want to end up like your pal, Thornford."

Stokes' smile vanished.

"What do you know of Thornford's murder?"

"Nothing," Bannon said, looking uncomfortable. "Who knows who shot him?" He looked as if he regretted bringing the subject up, but he couldn't close the door he had opened, so he squared his shoulders and spoke with loud conviction. "Thornford was a troublemaker. He got what was coming to him."

Stokes clenched his fists. He wanted to leap forward and punch the smug lawman in the face.

As if he sensed Stokes' thoughts, the silent deputy raised the shotgun and pulled back the hammers. Stokes took a steadying breath and held himself still with difficulty.

"Are you a troublemaker, Stokes?" asked Bannon. When Stokes did not reply, the sheriff sneered. "I think you are. Well don't be getting any ideas. This is not England. Your name and your past don't mean nothing here. Don't cross me. I'm warning you. If you do, you'll regret it."

"I'm not here to start any trouble," Stokes said, keeping his voice flat and not much louder than a whisper. Despite the anger that threatened to engulf him, he forced himself to lower his gaze. Now was not the time for open conflict with the sheriff.

"Good," Bannon said. "If you behave yourself we can all get along."

Spinning on his heel, he walked away without looking back. The deputy carefully lowered the hammers on the shotgun, then, without a word, he followed behind Bannon.

Stokes watched the sheriff and deputy walk away. No, he thought, he wasn't there to start trouble. But by God, he planned to finish it.

Chapter Twenty-Two

"Why, if it ain't Lieutenant Stokes! Welcome, Gabe!" Jedediah White's voice was brash and loud in the hush of the Lady Elgin. Being late afternoon, the place was quiet. A balding man in shirt sleeves and an apron was cleaning a table near the front window.

The saloon was clean and appeared to be well maintained. A large mirror was mounted behind the bar. In front of that were stacked scores of glasses, small, large, and stemmed. Dozens of bottles of differing size and shape were on display in a glass-fronted cabinet. The bar top appeared to be marble and it gleamed, reflecting the light from the window. The floor was smooth varnished planking. At the rear of the space there was a large iron stove, its metal chimney disappearing into the ceiling. The ceiling itself featured elegant plaster designs and elaborate covings and cornices. The whole affair had an opulence that was out of keeping in this Oregon backwater. Stokes wondered how such a place could hope to recoup the investment of its proprietor. Perhaps whoever owned the establishment was pinning their hopes to the railroad bringing an influx of visitors to the town; it would certainly need more than its current clientele to turn a profit.

But Stokes had to admit the decor was inviting. As were the smells he would always associate with such places. The sour scent of spilt beer, that could not be removed, no matter how often a bar was cleaned. The sweet smells of the different spirits and mixers. The tang of skin and sweat, and damp cloth, and, hanging over everything, the acrid bite of smoke.

Stokes' mouth watered and he swallowed. He had not been prepared for the effect the saloon would have on him. He halted in the doorway.

The only patrons were White and three other men sitting around a table at the rear. On the table were cards, ivory chips, coins, dollar bills, glasses and a half-empty bottle of whiskey. Jed and two of the other men held cigarettes. The fourth man, a portly fellow with a thick, black bird's nest of a beard had a clay pipe jutting from his mouth. The air above the men was fogged with smoke.

Stokes had come down the street to thank White for his help with the Cabin Creek men. He was already regretting his decision. In fact, apart from the items he had bought in McCall's, he wasn't sure coming into town had been a good idea. All he had achieved was to show his hand. If Grant hadn't known who he was, he would hear all about him soon enough from his hired guns and Sheriff Bannon.

"Say hello to the Lieutenant, boys," White crowed. "He's a great man. Friend to the redskin and saviour of the Chinaman!"

White laughed loudly. He drained his glass and slammed it down on the table. A stack of ivory chips toppled over and several of them clattered to the wooden floor. A slight man with sallow, stubbled cheeks and black greased-back hair swore and stooped to retrieve them.

"Watch it, Jed!" he said, his tone sharp.

"Why?" slurred White. "What's *it* gonna do?"

He cackled at his own joke and slapped the table again, sending more money onto the floor.

"God damn it," snarled the man closest to White, catching the whiskey bottle before it too fell. He wore a dark suit and shiny black shoes. His face was soft and pasty. He looked like a banker, or a grocer; out of place gambling and drinking in a saloon with the other rough types at the table. But Stokes knew all too well that appearances could be deceiving. Anyone could be caught in the jaws of vice.

"If you're offering," White said, holding out his glass to the man.

The soft-faced man hesitated, then, with a shake of his head, he poured a drink for White and refilled his own glass. Stokes watched the amber liquid sloshing as the man raised the glass to his lips and took a deep swallow.

"Don't just stand there looking stupid, Lieutenant," said White. "Buy us another bottle of whiskey."

A few seconds earlier Stokes had been ready to thank White for intervening in what looked set to become a very sticky situation. He held one of the Cuban cigars in his hand and would have happily bought White a drink as a show of his gratitude. But in an instant, all feeling of goodwill that he'd felt towards the man had evaporated.

"You, sir, are drunk," he said, his words clipped.

"That I am, Gabriel, my boy," said White, chuckling. "That I am." He took a slow sip of his whiskey and then placed the glass carefully back on the table. He moved as though the table were rocking back and forth like a ship in high seas and he was scared the glass might slide off, or that he might miss the table altogether. "I play my best poker drunk."

"I'm heading back to the ranch," Stokes said. "Can you ride?"

"Of course I can fucking ride!" bellowed White. "I ain't dead. I been riding since before your daddy rode your ma!" Turning to the man who had been cleaning tables and who had now returned to the bar, he called out, "Another bottle for the table. My English pal here is paying."

The barman looked over at Stokes, who still stood in the doorway. Stokes licked his lips. The whiskey had called to him. He could almost taste the burning heat of it in his mouth and throat. Again, he thought, he owed White his thanks. Not just for coming to his aid against Meacher and the others, but for reminding him so persuasively what a fool a man becomes when he succumbs to the temptation of the demon drink.

"Are you sure you will not come with me, Mr White?" he asked.

"I ain't leaving here until I cleared out all these boys," he said. "You go and fraternise with that savage Van Orman. Or maybe you can find a chink in town to starch your shirt collar."

Stokes sighed. He put the Cuban cigar in his jacket pocket and looked questioningly at the barman.

"Bottle's a dollar," the man said.

Stokes nodded. Walking to the bar, he placed a dollar in change on the shiny counter. The barman swept the coins into his apron pocket, then, uncorking the bottle, he set it down on the lustrous marble.

Stokes turned to leave.

"Hey," called White from the back of the room, "ain't you bringing the bottle over?"

Ignoring White's shouts, Stokes walked back out into the golden light of the afternoon.

Chapter Twenty-Three

It was dark when he arrived back at the JT Ranch. Despite the warmth of the afternoon, after the sun had set the air grew cool and by the time Banner carried him along the track and into the open area between the ranch buildings, both Stokes' and the gelding's breath was steaming in the air.

On the ride, Stokes had had plenty of time to think over what he'd learnt. At first he had thought perhaps the Cabin Creek men he had confronted might waylay him on the road. He'd kept his eyes open, scanning the trees that lined the trail, but after a while he decided it was unlikely. They didn't know he was planning on leaving town so soon, so they would be just as apt to have ridden back to the Grant spread than to lie in ambush for him.

And he had learnt little new about Grant. He had already known the man was rich and influential, and White had told him that Sheriff Bannon was in Grant's employ. He'd found out that Grant's sister-in-law ran the General Store with her husband and that she was loyal to her brother-in-law, which seemed unremarkable. He'd also discovered that the owner of the livery stable wasn't keen on the cattlemen, but was not willing to stand up against them. His livelihood depended on the ranches. The same was no doubt true for most of the townsfolk.

Stokes sighed, pulling his coat about his neck against the night chill. All he had succeeded in doing was tipping off Bannon that he had the skills to investigate his friend's murder and, as if that were not bad enough, he had made enemies of some of Grant's hired guns. Still, perhaps there could be some good to come of that. If it came to a fight, an angry man might make a mistake where a calm one would not. It was a slim sliver of light in what had been a dark and fruitless day.

He saw a light shining beneath the door of the ranch house and wondered if Mary Ann was awake. He contemplated riding over there, but immediately dismissed the idea. It was late and it would not be seemly for him to visit John's widow at such an hour. There would be time to speak to her in the morning.

He pulled Banner's head towards the barn, his mind turning back to the thoughts that assailed him. He needed to unearth the truth of what had happened. For that, more than opinion and speculation was necessary. If he was to bring Thornford's killer to justice, he required hard evidence. Proof that would be irrefutable and would stand up in a court of law.

The other horses in the corral nickered in welcome and Banner whinnied in response.

"Yes," Stokes said, absently patting the gelding's neck, "you're home, boy."

Then there was what Van Orman had shown him up in the mountains. He couldn't decide how what he had discovered in the ravine fit in with everything else. Stokes' mind was tugging at threads of ideas, hoping to unravel answers that so far eluded him, but no matter how hard he concentrated, the truth did not reveal itself.

His thoughts were interrupted by Pincher's barking from the darkness. A moment later, light spilled out from the house as the door was flung open. Stokes blinked against the sudden glare. Mary Ann stood there, her slender figure silhouetted against the lamp light.

"If you've come looking for trouble," she said, her voice trembling with emotion, "you've come to the wrong place."

Stokes saw then that she had in her hands a double-barrelled fowling piece. It looked large enough that if she fired the thing, the recoil would knock her from her feet.

"I come in peace," Stokes said. "It's me, Mary Ann. Sorry if I startled you."

Stokes sat quietly while Mary Ann moved about the kitchen. The clink of cups, the rasping of a knife sawing into a loaf of bread, the pouring of water and Mary Ann's shuffling movements around the space were comforting to him in a way he could not easily define.

He was not used to such a homely setting and was unaccustomed to hearing the sounds of food and drink being prepared for him. And yet he could not deny he enjoyed being looked after in this way.

He touched the parcel that lay on the table. He had taken it from the saddlebags when Lenny had offered to unsaddle Banner. The boy had come out of the barn when he had heard their voices. Stokes had thanked him and then made his way over to the house. He'd decided he could give Mary Ann the books he had bought. It would not be wrong to converse with her briefly on the veranda. This was not Mayfair, and there were no nosey neighbours to gossip about the widow and her late-night gentlemen callers.

But Mary Ann was either oblivious or uncaring of the impression she might give and she had ushered him inside.

"You must be cold and hungry," she said. "I'll make tea."

"I really shouldn't," Stokes said, but she was having none of it.

"Nonsense. Come inside out of the chill. Lenny will take care of Banner."

"Is he sleeping in the barn?"

"Yes," she replied, leaving him to sit himself at the table while she went into the kitchen. "One of the mares is in foal and having a hard time of it. Lenny has a way with the horses.

It's not the first time he's done this. He'll stay with the mare until the foal comes. The horses like his company and respond better when he is with them. He has a gift."

Stokes thought of the boy and how Banner had reacted to seeing him, nuzzling into Lenny's neck as if greeting another horse. It was a gift indeed. Lenny would never struggle to find a job if he could handle horses well. If he left the JT, perhaps Hampton could use another pair of hands. Stokes was staring into the lamp, its light blinding him as he thought of the future.

And the past.

Pulling his gaze away, he looked into the shadows, blinking at the afterglow images of the lamp. Lenny shouldn't have to look for new employment. He had a job here and seemed content enough. But Stokes could not devise a clear path that would see Thornton's widow able to stay. If he could not prove Grant was guilty of murder, or otherwise dissuade him from his bully tactics, it might be best for her to leave with her family and start a fresh life somewhere else.

Mary Ann came in from the kitchen carrying a tray. She placed it on the table, glancing at the parcel.

"I bought you something in town," Stokes said.

"Oh, you really didn't need to do that," Mary Ann replied. They both spoke quietly, conscious that the children slept in the next room. She took a plate with a thick ham sandwich on and placed it before him. Then she poured the tea.

"I'm sorry to have disturbed you so late," Stokes said. He'd glanced at his watch while he waited. It was after eleven.

"I don't mind." She set the pot down and passed him his cup. "I can't sleep anyway. I try, but ever since... I just lie there with my eyes open and my head full of dark thoughts."

"I know what that's like," he said. The smell of the sandwich and the steam wafting up from the teacup made him realise how hungry he was.

"That might help you pass the time when you can't sleep, at least," he said, handing her the parcel.

"Really, you shouldn't have." She looked down at the brown paper tied with twine. Her eyes glimmered in the lamp light. She was very pretty.

"It's the least I could do," he said, turning his attention to the sandwich. "Open it while I eat this. I'm famished."

She untied the cord and Stokes made a start on the sandwich, savouring the soft bread and the salty ham. There was creamy butter too and he was surprised by a sudden biting piquancy.

Mary Ann looked up from where she was unwrapping the books.

"I hope you like the mustard. I didn't think to ask, but John loved it so on ham."

"It is delicious," he said, and meant it. He coughed and took a sip of tea. "It did come as a bit of a surprise though. Have you read that?" He nodded at the topmost book, a novel call *Ardath*. "The other one is for Albert really, though Adelaide might well like to listen and look at the pictures."

Mary Ann offered him a smile that lit up her face. The weariness and pain fell away and she looked like a girl.

"I loved *A Romance of Two Worlds* and *Thelma*. I didn't know Marie Corelli had written another novel. Thank you, Gabriel. It really is most kind of you." She looked at the other book, *Winning His Spurs* by G. A. Henty, flicking through the pages and seeing the illustrations of knights and castles. "And Albert will adore this. I'm sure you are right and Adelaide will like hearing the stories too. Perhaps there are princesses in distress. What girl doesn't like to imagine herself as a princess being rescued by a dashing knight on a white charger?"

"Oh, I almost forgot," he said, pulling a paper bag from his jacket pocket. "These are for Adelaide. But I hope she'll share with her brother."

Mary Ann looked inside the bag, then, with the same girlish, mischievous smile, she took one of the sweets and popped it into her mouth.

172

"She will share with her mother too," she said.

"Even if she is not aware," he said, returning her smile.

Finishing the sandwich, he pushed the empty plate away.

"Thank you," he said. "I should turn in."

"Tell me what you found in town first." Her expression was sombre. "I was worried when you weren't back by nightfall. When I heard just the one horse I wasn't sure who it might be. Didn't you find Jed?"

"I found him." Stokes refilled both their cups from the teapot. "But he was less than amenable to returning with me."

"Drunk?" she whispered, as if speaking the word any louder would make it worse.

Stokes nodded.

"Does he do that often?"

"When he does, it's in town. John made it very clear he would not abide drunkenness on the ranch. I do worry about him though. He has such a temper when he drinks."

Stokes peered at her in the golden lamp light.

"Has he ever raised a hand to the children? Or to you?"

"No, no," she said, sounding half horrified and half amused at the idea. "Nothing like that. But I know how he is. It's as if he is looking for a fight sometimes."

"He's not the only one." He told her about his run in with Meacher, Byrne and the others. She listened, shaking her head. Whatever joy she had found in the books and the sweets was gone now and she scowled as he recounted how Bannon had confronted him.

"I'm not proud to say the man rubbed me up the wrong way," Stokes said. "I've seen his kind all my life and I struggle to keep my mouth shut when faced with their petty vindictiveness."

"You're as bad as Jed," she said, offering him a thin smile that took some of the sting from her words.

"You don't know how right you are," he replied seriously. "We all have our demons."

She stared at him for a time.

"Drink?"

Stokes' face grew hot from embarrassment. He had never spoken of his vices with anybody before. Not even with John Thornford. He had alluded to some of his problems in letters, but Thornford had never asked for details, perhaps thinking Stokes would speak to him more openly when he was ready. Stokes was ashamed at how he had allowed himself to become controlled by such base desires and addictions.

"Amongst other things," he said, his voice a hoarse whisper.

"But you have beaten your demons."

He let out a long breath.

"I'm not sure that any man who falls foul of the demon alcohol can ever say he is free of its power. Not completely." Seeing the concern in her face, he offered a smile. "Don't worry. I am not drinking. And I have no plans to. But it is not such an easy thing as saying I have overcome it."

She sipped at her tea.

"John would wake up screaming sometimes," she said, her voice distant with memory. "He would never speak of those nightmares, but I know they were about Afghanistan. It cannot be an easy thing to leave war behind."

"We saw terrible things there," Stokes said. "Great things too. Acts of incredible bravery. Selflessness. On both sides. And then, such..." He searched for the word. "Such savagery. I thought never to witness the like again."

"And yet when you sold your commission you became a police officer in London, investigating some of the worst crimes imaginable."

"In hindsight, perhaps a poor choice."

"I'm not so sure. I don't know you well enough yet, but John said you would be the perfect man for the job. He said you would never rest until a crime was solved and the guilty put behind bars or swinging from a rope."

"Well, he was right about never resting." His tone was bitter.

"You suffer with nightmares too?"

"It's a rare thing for me to have an untroubled night," he admitted.

"I can only imagine the things you saw in Afghanistan."

He recalled a flashing image of a screaming Ghazi, bloodied tulwar in hand. The stink of gunpowder smoke. Hot blood on his thigh. Searing pain.

"The dreams were of the war at first," he said. He drank some tea and was pleased to see his hand was not trembling. "After a time they were replaced by worse things. More recent memories."

"The Ripper murders?"

In an instant his memories were awash with the blood of the poor wretched women. The horror of those autumn nights of 1888 still hung on him like the stink of dried sweat. With each of that butcher's victims he had thought things could get no worse. That was before Jane Adams. He stared into the lamp's flame, willing it to burn away any images from the Adams case that threatened to swim up to the surface of his thoughts. He shuddered.

"I'd rather not talk about it," he said. "Especially at night."

"I'm sorry," Mary Ann said.

"The evil that men do is no fault of yours."

"But you came here in search of peace, and all you have found is more misery and death."

"Oregon has certainly not been what I expected," he said. "But I am already sleeping more soundly than I have in years. The land and the air itself is a balm on my soul."

"I am glad," she said. "But it is a hard land. Unforgiving."

"It is no paradise on earth, that's for sure. It would be better without the likes of Grant and his hired killers preying on innocent folk."

"What do you plan on doing next?" she asked, setting down her teacup in the saucer with a clink.

"Well, Grant knows I'm here now, or he will soon enough, so as I see it, there is only one place I can go next."

"And where is that?"

"I will ride out to the Cabin Creek Ranch and speak to Tom Grant himself."

"The man is a brute," she said, aghast. "It will be no use. He will never admit any involvement in John's murder." She fixed her gaze on Stokes. Her eyes were large. Dark and fathomless in the gloomy room. "It will be dangerous."

"It might be," he admitted. "But if they kill me, you'll have more evidence against Grant."

"Don't say that," she said, her voice sharp with anger.

"Sorry," Stokes said. "I spoke rashly. But don't worry. I can take care of myself."

"So could John." Mary Ann's words were acerbic.

"I know he could," he said, ashamed of how his words had come out. "What I meant to say is that I aim to speak to Grant openly. I'll take Jed and maybe some of the other hands with me. Make it clear that we won't go quietly. From what I hear of this Grant he's a bully, but he's no fool. He won't risk an open fight with Jed and me. Being a rich man is of no use in a graveyard."

"But why take the chance?" she asked, struggling to keep the anger from her tone. "It is foolish to confront him."

"Let's call it a calculated risk. I want to meet the man and hear what he has to say."

"But to what end? Grant's a liar."

"I don't doubt that, Mary Ann," Stokes said, pushing himself up from the table. "But there is a lot you can tell about a man by looking him in the eye, even if he is lying as you do it."

Chapter Twenty-Four

"You really plan on doing this?" Old Amos Willard was leaning against the barn watching Stokes as he readied Banner for riding.

"I do." Stokes tightened the cinch then stroked his hand along the bay gelding's flank. Banner snorted and stamped, one iron-shod hoof sending up a puff of dust. Lenny had done a good job with the horse; his coat gleamed. He looked rested and raring to be on the move once more. He was nothing like the tall Arabians Stokes had ridden when he served in the Tenth, but this little horse had heart and he was quickly becoming in Stokes' eyes the best horse he had ever ridden. Banner was eager to please, clever, sure-footed, brave and seemingly able to travel all day without tiring. Add to that a smooth gait and it was a real pleasure to ride the gelding. Despite knowing he was heading towards danger, Stokes had risen from his bunk keen to be in the saddle.

In spite of the conversation the night before, and the memories that had been stirred within him like old embers being turned over and coaxed back into life, he had slept soundly, unmolested by the nightmares that so frequently plagued his nights. He wondered at the ease with which he found sleep here. He had said the land was like a balm on his soul and he could think of no better way to describe it. He grieved for his friend and burnt with the desire to see Thornford's killer brought to justice, and the need to see Mary Ann and her children safe from harm, and yet, despite the bleak situation – or perhaps because of it, he mused – he woke each day more rested than he had been for months.

"I wouldn't ride in there alone," Amos said. "Those sons of bitches will as soon shoot you as talk to you."

Stokes picked up Thornford's Winchester and slid it into the saddle scabbard.

"You might well be right, Amos," he said. "But I don't plan to go alone."

"Taking Jed with you?"

"I think it for the best."

"Well, I can't disagree with that," said the old man, spitting a squirt of tobacco juice into the weeds that grew against the barn wall. "He's a good man at your side in a tight spot. If he can see straight."

Stokes had been thinking about that. He had hoped White might have returned during the night, but there was no sign of him. He had briefly considered asking some of the other men, Lars or Tanner, to go with him, but had quickly disregarded the idea. They were strong men, and no doubt game enough, but they were not killers, and he did not wish to put them in undue danger. His life was his own to risk and he cared little if it should be lost in the endeavour. And he doubted White felt much more strongly about preserving his own skin. If the bullets began to fly, he could think of no man better to have with him. The two of them would not be killed easily and would give pause to their enemies.

A nagging voice whispered that Thornford had been a more than capable man and he had been killed easily enough. What if Grant's men lay an ambush for him too?

Lenny stepped out of the barn and grinned at the two men.

"Foal come at last?" Amos asked.

"Yes, sir," Lenny said with a broad smile. "A stallion. Black with white socks. Mother and child are both well and on their feet." The young man's eyes were red and there were dark smudges beneath them. He had barely slept, tending to the mare all night, but as he turned to the east, allowing the morning sun to bathe his face, no amount of weariness could dampen his joy.

"That's welcome news," Stokes said. "Thank you for caring so well for Banner too, even when you were already so occupied. I appreciate it."

Lenny beamed.

"I didn't mind. Banner's a good boy, ain't you?" He rubbed at the horse's forelock and Banner tilted his head, as if listening to the boy.

"That he is." Stokes stepped up into the saddle. "Now, I'd better be going. No way of knowing what state Jed will be in when I find him."

"Nothing a strong cup of coffee can't fix," said Amos, with a crooked smile. "Or perhaps two, if he's really been paintin' his tonsils."

Stokes raised an eyebrow. He wasn't sure Amos was right about that, but then again, he had seen White drink upwards of a bottle of the stuff that passed for whiskey here and still be able to ride and shoot straight. And the more he thought about it, Mary Ann and Amos were right. It would be foolhardy to ride to the Cabin Creek Ranch alone.

"I should be home before nightfall," he said, spurring Banner into a quick trot. He smiled as he rode. He had only been at the JT a few days and already he referred to it as home. Well, for the time being it was, he supposed.

He looked about him at the forested slopes of the Blue Mountains. The day was already bright and once the morning cool was dispelled by the rising sun, it would be warm. Over the valley a couple of buzzards flew, soaring slowly as if suspended from the dome of the sky. Yes, there were worse places to call home. If things went well, he would write to Eliza in the evening and tell her about Griffith, the ranch, Mary Ann and the children. She would be anxious for news about how he did.

Swinging round a bend in the trail, the sun momentarily

blinded him as it flashed between the trees. He blinked and saw movement downhill on the trail about a quarter of a mile distant. Dust hazed in the morning sunlight, kicked up into the air by the hooves of several horses.

Reining in, Stokes raised his hand to shield his eyes from the glare. There were half a dozen riders and they were coming at a lope. He scanned them, looking from horses to men in an effort to identify them. At first there was nothing to distinguish them. They could be any horsemen, but their speed spoke of urgency and Stokes was suddenly certain they were not friendly. They were closer now, the shade of some tall fir trees dappling them as they came up the slope.

Banner shifted nervously beneath Stokes. The gelding's ears dropped flat and his nostrils flared.

"Easy, boy," Stokes said, patting his neck as he peered at the approaching riders. Then, with a jerk of the reins that made the horse snort, he tugged Banner's head around, back towards the JT Ranch. He kicked in his heels and Banner leapt forward. Stokes let the horse have his head and he galloped over the ground they had so recently passed.

It was Meacher's broad face that Stokes had recognised. He had not bothered trying to pick out any of the other faces. There could be no doubt where the men came from. These were not friends and there was not much time to prepare for their arrival.

Chapter Twenty-Five

Stokes galloped into the ranch, a great cloud of dust following in his wake. Wheeling Banner around in a circle, he surveyed the buildings, the animal pens and the nearby fields. The only person he saw was Amos, who was leaning on the corral fence, chewing tobacco.

Pulling the Colt Lightning, Stokes held it above his head and fired off three quick shots. Without waiting to see the reaction the shots provoked, he rode Banner over to the barn, leaping off at a run before the horse had stopped.

Lenny was there, bleary-eyed, but alert enough to catch the reins from Stokes.

"Get Banner inside and grab your rifle. Keep a watch on the ground out front from the barn window."

"Wha—?" Lenny blinked.

"Grant and his men are coming."

That seemed to sharpen Lenny's senses.

"My rifle is in the bunkhouse," he said.

"The Captain's Winchester is in the saddle scabbard. It's loaded. Take that."

The boy blinked and rubbed at his eyes. He looked very young.

"I ain't never shot nobody," he said.

Pulling .38 calibre shells from his saddlebags, Stokes stuffed a handful into his jacket pocket and reloaded the three empty chambers.

"Pray you don't need to now," he said, without looking up. "But if the time comes, I need to know you will do what needs to be done." He grasped the young man's shoulder and stared into his eyes. "Can you do that?"

"Yes, sir," Lenny said. His voice trembled, but he stood upright.

"Good man," Stokes said. "Now, quick about it. There is no time to waste."

Trusting that Lenny would follow his orders, Stokes hurried towards the house. Mary Ann was on the porch, shotgun in her hands, her eyes wide and frightened.

"It's Grant," Stokes snapped. "He'll be here with his men in a couple of minutes."

Glancing back, Stokes saw that Amos was hobbling as fast as his old legs would carry him towards the bunkhouse.

"I'll get my old Henry and cover you from there," Amos called out. Stokes nodded his approval.

"What is it, Ma?" Adelaide poked her head out from behind her mother's skirts.

"Go inside, Adie," Mary Ann said, keeping her tone calm with evident effort. "Albert!" she called. When no reply came instantly, she shouted again, her voice cracking. "Albert!"

"I'm right here, Ma," Albert said. He was standing in the shadows of the open door, just behind his mother.

"Take your sister in the house and hide where your father told you."

Indecision flashed over the boy's face. His eyes flicked towards the trail. The dust from Stokes' galloping arrival still lingered in the air like the ghost of a memory. The distant thunder of hooves reached them.

"Go on, Al," Stokes said. "Do what your mother says. There's no time to argue."

"Come on, Adie," Albert said without hesitation. Grabbing his sister's hand roughly, he dragged her into the house. She protested, but he ignored her, pulling her after him.

"Where are they going to hide?" Stokes asked.

Mary Ann looked as if she didn't understand him. Panic was rising up within her, but as he watched, she took a hold of herself, setting her jaw and squaring her shoulders.

"The far corner of the house," she said, her voice surprisingly steady. "It's rock there on two walls and it's behind the stove and chimney. John said it would be safe there."

"That sounds right. Good." Stokes' mind was racing.

"Shall I keep hold of this," Mary Ann asked, raising the shotgun.

Stokes paused in his assessment of the situation for a second. "Is it loaded?"

"Of course."

"Good. If things go bad, fire off both barrels and get inside the house. Have you got more shells in there?"

"Beside the door. In a box."

"If there's fighting, reload and take what shells you can and hide with the children. If anyone comes through the door, you let them have it."

Mary Ann nodded grimly. Her face was very pale.

"You think it will come to that?"

"I don't know," he replied, his tone curt. "But we should prepare for the worst. Lenny is in the barn and Amos is in the bunkhouse. Who else is around?"

As if in answer, he spotted Lars sprinting up from one of the fields. The blond man was red in the face and panting.

"Just you?" Stokes shouted, pleased to see the man had a Winchester in his hands and a revolver on his hip.

"Tanner and Reuban left early for the high ridge." Lars was breathless from the run, but even winded and sweating, there was a solidity about the man that Stokes liked.

He wished the extra men were at the ranch, but they would have to make do with what they had.

"Hunker down behind the kitchen wall," he said to Lars. "Don't show yourself. If shooting starts, you come out and pick off as many as you can. Lenny and Amos will be shooting from the barn and the bunkhouse."

"Shouldn't I wait and speak to them?" Lars said. "It don't feel right to run and hide."

"This is not about what feels right," snapped Stokes. "This is about winning or losing. Life and death. The children are in the house. Get out of sight. Now."

The thrum of hooves on the trail was loud. A light breeze shivered the tops of the pines and for an instant it appeared as though the horses passing beneath were making the boughs shake.

"Now, Lars. Quickly."

Without another word, Lars ran around the side of the house and was lost from view.

"Mary Ann," Stokes said, taking another quick look around the yard at the buildings and the crossfire he had created. "Go back up onto the porch. Open the door and stand with your back to it. Anything happens, don't worry about me. Remember what I said. You fire both barrels at the men and move into the house. Take the shells, reload and protect your children."

"What are you going to do?"

"I'm going to meet them."

And with that he walked out to where all of the shooters in the buildings would be able to see him. He touched the Colt's smooth grip, checking it was still there, even though he had only just reloaded it. He was aware of his limp and his left leg ached as he walked. He stopped moving as the six horses came galloping into sight. They did not slow as they pelted across the dusty earth towards him.

Stokes stood his ground, hands on his hips.

Chapter Twenty-Six

As the six riders galloped towards him, Stokes was able to take in details. Along with Bull Meacher in his dome-crowned billycock, he saw the raw-boned features of Hunter Randle beneath his dirty, broad-brimmed hat.

Beside Randle rode a man with an even larger hat. It was so wide it might have seemed humorous if it had been worn by a different man. But the face under the sombrero was hard with dark gimlet eyes. The man's skin was tanned and his long moustache black. Silver glinted from his horse's tack and saddle and the sun flashed from the oversized rawls of his spurs as he hauled his mount to a halt.

Off to Stokes' right, placing him nearer to the bunkhouse and the barn was another rider he didn't recall having seen before. He was a broad-shouldered black man who rode with such languid ease he seemed to be lounging in the saddle. His close-cropped beard was dusted with grey, and he gave off an aura of self-assurance as his gaze roved over the buildings.

At the front of the group came Cadmar Byrne, riding the same black horse as the day before. The young gunman seemed amused to see Stokes standing alone before them. Offering him a smile, Byrne tipped his hat as he slowed his mount.

The leader of the band was a barrel-chested man in a dark suit. He had a full beard of black hair streaked with white, like veins of silver in basalt. His horse was a fine beast, tall and long-legged, its coat white and sleek. If it seemed out of place amongst the other horses who were more like ponies, so did its rider amongst the rough men. It was not just that his attire was more expensive, though this was true for all of them apart from perhaps Cadmar Byrne, who seemed to have a similar taste for the sartorial in his black suit and polished boots. That was where the similarities ended. The man who rode at the head of the group seemed to dwarf the men around him. At first Stokes had believed the man to actually be much taller than the others, but as he grew nearer, he realised that was an illusion, partly caused by the stature of the man's horse, but there was more than that. He had an air about him of someone who expects to be obeyed. A powerful persona. He reminded Stokes in that regard of Captain John Thornford.

All the men were armed. Stokes kept his hands at his sides and made an effort not to flinch when the dust cloud rolled over him as the horses clattered to a standstill.

Before anyone could speak, a sudden raucous barking came from behind the house. The men turned to look as one. Their horses jostled nervously.

Streaking towards them, all flashing teeth and hackles raised, came Pincher. He did not know these riders and he clearly meant to make his displeasure at their arrival known.

Where Banner and the other JT Ranch horses all seemed content to ignore the dog, perhaps even enjoying his yapping welcomes, the Cabin Creek horses were not accustomed to Pincher's antics. Some of them shied away. Men cursed, wrestling to keep their mounts under control. The tall Arabian stallion the leader rode was more skittish than the rest. At the dog's approach, it sidestepped, kicking out and almost unseating its rider.

Cadmar Byrne nudged his horse closer to his employer. He reached for the stallion's bridle, but it shook its head, spun about and kicked at the dog again, narrowly missing the animal.

For a time it seemed that the big bearded man on the stallion would be thrown, but then there was a deafening crash

186

and a cloud of smoke. He had pulled a revolver from a saddle holster and shot at the dog. For the briefest of moments there was a shocked silence, as if the horses, men and dog all held their breath, then Pincher recommenced barking.

The man had missed.

The rider's gun barked again, much louder than the dog. This time his aim was good and he hit the poor animal. Pincher yelped. Blood splattered the dust. The dog's left hind leg had been shattered by the bullet and now hung by a sliver of fur and skin. Letting out the most pitiful howl, Pincher struggled up and ran away as fast as its three good legs were able to bear it. The ruined limb dragged behind it, leaving a trail of blood on the dusty earth.

The rider was red-faced. Sawing the bit into his horse's mouth, he got the animal under control and swung it around to face Stokes.

"That's what it gets for barking at me," the man sneered. Meacher and Randle laughed. "You want to bark at me some, Englishman?" The man's beard jutted defiantly and he grinned, happy to have sent the dog away and pleased with the sound of his own voice.

Beyond the house, they could still hear the dog's whimpering moans. Stokes supposed it would be dead soon.

His hand twitched. It was all he could do not to pull the Colt Lighting and begin firing. The large man still held the revolver across his saddle. It was a big gun, a Colt Dragoon, and with it in his hand, he might well shoot Stokes before he would be able to clear the holster. If the cattleman did not shoot him, no doubt Byrne or one of the others would kill him soon enough. But perhaps his death was a price worth paying, Stokes thought. If he could kill the leader, the others might be able to take down the remaining Cabin Creek riders from their hidden positions.

But it would be risky. A few seconds would pass before they would commence firing, and when the lead began to fly, Mary Ann might be hit by a stray bullet. And the odds were not great, even with the hidden riflemen. Lenny was an uncertain quantity. Stokes had no doubt that Lars and Amos would acquit themselves well, but the boy might lose his nerve or prove a terrible shot. And even though Mary Ann had a weapon, from the doorway she was too far away to kill a man with the shotgun.

No, there were too many imponderables. If it became necessary to fight, the men hiding with rifles would give the JT Ranch a chance at victory, but it was only a slim chance and not one they should gamble on, especially with Mary Ann and the children in the house.

Struggling to control his mounting anger, Stokes clenched his fist and moved it slowly away from the pistol's grip.

"Mr Grant, I presume," he said.

"One and the same," replied the bearded man. "And you must be the Captain's old army buddy."

"My name is Stokes. Captain Thornford was my friend."

"Well, I am sorry for your loss then. Losing a friend is never easy." Grant frowned and sounded sincere, then spoilt the effect with a lopsided smirk. "They say back east that the West has been tamed. No doubt the Captain would have disagreed with that assessment."

Stokes clenched his fists more tightly. He would not be goaded into action.

"What is your business here?" he said.

"My business is my concern," Grant said, his tone suddenly glacial. "And unless you own this land, I suggest you shut your mouth and let me do the talking. I have a proposition for Mrs Thornford there." He looked at Mary Ann standing on the veranda with her back to the doorway.

He kicked his horse forward but Stokes stepped in close and grabbed the animal's bridle with his left hand. The men behind Grant tensed. The one with the black moustache and huge hat suddenly had a revolver in his hand. Stokes had not seen the man move, but there was the pistol pointed directly at his face. He wondered if he had misjudged the situation, but it was too late to worry about that now.

"If you have something to say, Grant," he hissed, "you can say it from here. You seem to like the sound of your own voice. I'm sure you can speak loud enough for Mrs Thornford to hear you."

"Easy there, Lopez," Grant said, waving a hand. The man with the drawn gun uncocked it, but did not slide it back into his holster. "Mr Stokes here don't mean me no harm, do you now?" Grant was staring down at Stokes. The broad smile on his face didn't reach his eyes. They were cold and hard, like shards of slate.

"I'm not so sure about that, Grant," Stokes said in a quiet voice. "I think it would be normal for me to wish harm on the man who killed my friend."

Grant's smile disappeared.

"I didn't kill him," he said. "I told Mrs Thornford that already. How many times must I say it?"

"I suppose until people believe you," replied Stokes. He studied Grant's features. "I'm not sure I do."

"God damn it, man," Grant said. "Was I sorry to see him gone? Not at all. The man was as troublesome as a mesquite thorn in my foot, something his friends seem to share with him, if you are anything to go by. But I didn't kill the man."

"Perhaps you didn't pull the trigger." Stokes scanned the hard-bitten faces of the mounted men behind Grant. "Which one of your killers did it?"

"I didn't shoot the man and neither did any of my men. Captain Thornford had a passel of enemies. Any one of them might have plugged him. Or it could have been someone riding through." He sneered as he looked Stokes up and down. "We get all sorts of scum drifting through these parts. No telling who Thornford might have upset. Now, I'm tired of these baseless accusations. Especially when I come with a neighbourly offer for the Captain's widow. I just hope for her sake she isn't as stubborn as her late husband. Or you, for that matter."

Stokes moved closer, gripping the horse's bridle tightly.

"Don't you dare threaten her," he said.

"I have no reason to threaten anyone. I've come with an offer that I would strongly advise her to take."

"My husband already rejected your offer," Mary Ann called from the porch. "If you thought by killing him I would accept it, you have a lot to learn about women."

Grant let out a loud sigh.

"I did not kill your husband, ma'am," he said, speaking slowly, as if to a simpleton. "But I am not insensitive of the predicament you find yourself in. The life of a sheep farmer is hard. My boys tell me they've seen quite a few dead animals up in the hills already."

"Because they shot them!" Mary Ann's voice cracked with emotion.

"Well, we don't want to see harm come to any more animals, do we?" Grant said, baring his teeth in a wolfish smile. "Or to anyone. This land is no place for a woman on her own. I'm willing to up my previous offer by ten percent. I suggest you take it. There is no telling what might happen to a woman on her own out here far from town."

The sound of a rifle lever being actioned was loud in the still air. They all turned towards the bunkhouse. Amos stood there, part-hidden in the doorway, Henry rifle aimed at Grant. Even if the old man was only a mediocre shot, he could scarcely miss at such a range.

"If you threaten Mrs Thornford again," Amos said, "I will drop you from that saddle like the varmint you are."

"I can take him, boss," whispered the black man, barely moving his lips.

Stokes seized the opportunity of Amos' distraction to draw the Colt Lightning and press it into Grant's side. "If anyone shoots," he hissed, "you'll be hit first."

Grant's face flushed with fury. All his men had their hands on their guns. A couple of them had their revolvers in their hands. They looked as taut as piano wire, thrumming and eager to snap into action.

Lars chose that instant to show himself. He stepped partway around the stone wall of the farmhouse, his rifle aimed and ready.

"I've got Byrne," he said.

The riders' eyes flicked in his direction. Cadmar Byrne twitched and his horse shook its head.

"And I got Meacher," said a young voice from the barn, snagging everyone's attention.

To Stokes' ears Lenny sounded terrified, but to his credit he held the Winchester steadily aimed down at the cluster of riders from the hay loft window.

Mary Ann, her face pallid, but with colour high on her cheeks, stepped down from the veranda and strode purposely towards the horsemen, raising the shotgun as she came. She didn't stop until she was a yard away from Grant.

"I'm not much of a shooter, Mr Grant," she said, sweeping the muzzle over the men, "but I don't think I can miss at this range. Do you want to take that chance?"

"You're making a big mistake," Grant said, staring at her. There was no sign of a smile now. "I'm offering you a fair price. This'll be the last time I do. Next time I won't be so understanding."

"I thought you said there wouldn't be a next time," Mary Ann said, pulling back both hammers on the fowling piece.

Grant glared at her. His knuckles were white where he gripped the Colt Dragoon on his lap. The man was almost trembling with rage. Stokes thought they might have pushed him too far, that he might throw it all away and start blazing with his huge pistol. To remind him of what the outcome of that would be, he jabbed the barrel of his gun into Grant's side.

"Whatever you're thinking," he said, his voice barely above a whisper. "Don't."

Grant glowered down at him.

"I doubt we'll speak again," he said. Rage burnt in his eyes and his words carried an unspoken threat.

Stokes forced a cool smile.

"Planning on leaving the area, are you?" he replied. "I hear Montana is good for cattle if you are looking to move."

Grant shook his head.

"Just like John Thornford, ain't you? So brave. Well courage can only get you so far."

Stokes met his gaze and did not blink.

"Perhaps far enough," he said.

"I doubt it." Then, in a loud voice, Grant said, "Come on, boys! I've said my piece. Let's get going." He backed his horse and Stokes released the bridle and stepped away. He didn't lower his gun.

"I know you wanted some fun, boys," Grant shouted, as he wheeled his stallion around, "but the lady don't want no part of us today." He winked at Mary Ann. "But they say the best things are worth waiting for. Come on, boys. The Lady Elgin's open for business. Whiskey and a poke on me."

He spurred his big stallion and it sped off at a gallop. The other men got their horses under control, then followed their boss.

Byrne was the last to leave. He tipped his hat to Stokes and Mary Ann.

"See you soon," he said with his twisted smile. He didn't wait for a reply, but touched his spurs to his horse and loped after the others.

A mist of dust hung in the air behind them.

Amos and Lars stepped from their positions, and a few seconds later Lenny came out of the barn. All of them looked pale and shocked that they were still breathing and had not had to kill anybody.

Having met Grant, Stokes wondered how long that would continue.

Nobody said anything as they watched the riders retreat into the trees. Then the silence was splintered as Albert ran out of the house crying.

"Pincher!" he yelled. "Pincher!"

Again and again he screamed the poor animal's name, but Pincher didn't make a sound.

Chapter Twenty-Seven

Stokes reined in and looked along the valley. The sun was already high over the mountains and the day warm. The sky was a vast, deep blue streaked with thin scratches of white. Stokes patted Banner's neck and took out a couple of the cigarillos he'd bought at McCalls. He offered one to Lars, who nudged his piebald mare closer and took the cheroot with a nod of thanks. Of all the men he could have ridden with, Lars was the best. Stokes didn't think the man liked him much, but he had proven himself dependable and he didn't feel the need to speak all the time.

Stokes wanted silence. The ranch was a lot quieter than London. But still, there were constant distractions. Albert would seek him out, chattering all the while about Indians and animals and shooting. Asking questions about what it was like to fight in a war, about Afghanistan, about being a lawman in London. The boy was often accompanied by Adelaide, who was headstrong and seldom quiet. Her questions were not like her brother's, they were not prone to send Stokes' spiralling darkly into his past, nevertheless, she was insistent and her questioning incessant. He liked the children well enough, but when they were around he rarely got a moment to think. And he needed to think. He felt as though his mind were filled to the brim. If he had some time to himself, he hoped he would be able to sort his thoughts.

He wanted to ride out on his own to survey the countryside, but Mary Ann would not allow it. In the end he had to agree with her that the risk of riding unaccompanied was too great, even though he yearned for some time alone with his thoughts.

He struck a match and offered it to Lars, who bent over in the saddle, cupping his hand. There was barely any wind and Stokes managed to light his own cigarillo from the same flame, before shaking the match out and throwing it down onto the rocky ground.

From this bluff on the east of the JT Ranch land, they could look along the trail that led to the Cabin Creek. There was also a clear view into the east and south. Stokes knew Grant could avoid the trail and send his men over the mountains and across the high ridge, but Tanner and Van Orman were up there. They would hopefully act as a deterrent, or at least provide the inhabitants of the JT with early warning of an approach from that direction. Stokes had ridden up there with Lars the day after Grant's visit to tell the two sheepherders what had happened and to warn them to be careful. They hadn't seen anyone, and Van Orman said he was always careful.

Stokes had suggested they bring the sheep down, but Reuban had refused, saying they needed the good pasture. But he did concede he would not take the flock further west or north over the line drawn through the trees by the Blue Mountain Sheep Shooters' signs. Tanner and he would trail them south for a few days, then loop back towards the JT. Stokes couldn't command them to do otherwise. He wasn't happy about it, but that would have to do.

That had been yesterday. Grant's visit had been only the day before that. Since then they had heard nothing more. Stokes wondered how long until the cattleman's next move. When the time came, Stokes thought they would be lucky to get away without shots being fired, or blood being spilt.

Grant didn't seem to be a man who would sneak about in the shadows, though he must have guile to have become so powerful. Like a man with a hand full of aces, he seemed very sure of himself, convinced that he would prevail. Stokes had seen how Grant had ridden his men straight into the JT. This was a man who attacked things head on. Stokes wondered at that, thinking about Thornford's murder and Grant's denial of any involvement. He seemed like a man who would revel in overcoming a rival and might even brag about it. Grant controlled the county Board of Commissioners who paid the sheriffs' wages and, with no witnesses of the murder apart from White, Stokes could easily imagine the man gloating to Thornford's widow and friend. The man had no problem making clear threats. And yet, instead of boasting, he had been resolute in his denial. One thing was certain though: Grant had hated being turned away from the JT. He had been humiliated, and Stokes was sure that would not be the end of the matter.

He puffed at the cigarillo, enjoying the taste of the smoke on his tongue. He watched the stripes of cloud-shadow roll slowly over the land below and down the slopes of the peaks far off to the east. There was no other movement in the wide valley.

"We'd better be getting back," said Lars, stubbing out his cigarillo on the heel of his boot, then tossing it away. "Mrs Thornford will be mighty annoyed if we're late for the picnic."

Stokes smiled and checked his watch. He wound it quickly, then put it back in his pocket. Lars was right. It would be after midday by the time they got back and Mary Ann had been adamant that nothing would stop the planned Sunday luncheon the JT Ranch was due to host. The hands had all been given tasks to make the place look more presentable. Lenny and Amos had given the barn doors and the bunkhouse window frames a fresh coat of paint. Lars had been tasked with cleaning the outhouse and fixing the door on the small building so that it didn't swing open with the slightest wind. Stokes had been given the job of pulling up the weeds that grew alongside the bunkhouse and repairing the corral fence, both of which he had done in the morning before they had ridden out to talk to Van Orman and Tanner. Even Jed White had helped without too much complaint when Mary Ann had asked him to saw planks to the right length to be placed on sawhorses and used as a table.

White had ridden into the ranch late on the Friday afternoon of Grant's visit. He had been sullen and grumpy, complaining that he had been forced to leave the saloon after Grant's crew turned up.

"It was either that," he said, "or start shooting. And I doubt that would have ended well for me."

He was still drunk and staggered when he dismounted, but he had clearly been in control of his faculties well enough to be able to judge the situation in Griffith. No matter how good White might be with his Remingtons, alone against the six men who had ridden to the JT, Stokes didn't rate his chances. Neither did White, it seemed, for he had ridden for home. But not before stocking up on whiskey. He unloaded half a dozen bottles from his saddlebags, carrying them reverently into the bunkhouse and threatening to shoot anyone who touched the liquor without asking first.

"I'm a generous man," he slurred, "but I won't be abiding theft of my gut warmer."

Stokes wondered how long six bottles would last. It seemed White's drinking had become worse since he had returned from collecting Stokes in Huntington, though of course, it could simply be that he now had more access to liquor than he had on the road. Neither Mary Ann nor the ranch hands commented on White's state, and it was true that once he had slept off that drunk he'd acquired in town, he kept his drinking in check enough so as not to appear inebriated.

When White heard about the encounter with Grant, he had been set to ride off and fight the Cabin Creek men right then and there, chances of survival be damned. Stokes had stopped him, and for a time he had thought they might come to blows, such was White's anger. But in the end he had talked him out of acting rashly.

197

"What good would it do Mary Ann if you rode off and got yourself shot?" he said, placing himself squarely between Jed and his horse.

"I could at least plug that rascally son of a bitch," White said, his bloodshot eyes blazing.

"I had my gun on the man," Stokes said, "and believe me, I was tempted."

"Then why didn't you? You could have ended this thing right there."

"But it wouldn't have ended anything. Innocent people might have been killed."

"You're just yellow," White spat.

Stokes' anger had flared then.

"I'm no coward, Jed. And I won't have you call me such." He glared at White, who chewed his moustache, but offered no apology. Stokes chose to let it go. It would do no good for them to be fighting each other. "Who's to say who might have been killed if I'd shot Grant? Mary Ann? Albert? Adelaide? Is that what you want?"

"Course I don't," grumbled White. "But you had the man there. You could have claimed self-defence. It might have been the best chance we'll get."

"A chance at what? Murder? That is not the right way. There are laws."

"Laws? You're a fool." White spat. "There is no right way here. Just who's left standing when the smoke clears. That's the western way. And that's what Grant and his killers have coming to 'em."

"Perhaps," Stokes said with a sigh. "But I want to believe they can be brought to justice for their crimes." He placed his hand on White's shoulder and looked him in the eye. "If it comes to a fight, if there is no other option, I'll be there right beside you. I am not scared of the fight, nor even death. But I cannot turn away from the law so easily. What would separate us then from the men we seek to bring to justice?"

"We'd be alive," snarled White. "They'd be dead."

"But could we live with ourselves?"

"Could kill that bastard Grant and sleep like a babe."

Taking a last drag on his cigarillo, Stokes did as Lars had, leaning down to extinguish it against the hard leather of his right stirrup. He enjoyed riding with the comfortable cowboy saddle and wondered whether he would ever ride again with the smaller and thinner English saddle he had used all his life. Not by choice, he wouldn't, he thought. He checked that the slim cigar butt was truly out before dropping it to the ground.

"Come on then," he said to Lars, "time to head h—" He caught himself before he said *home*, "back to the ranch."

Lars pulled his paint mare's head around. He did not comment, but Stokes saw the small smile on the man's face. He was careful not to refer to the ranch as "home" after that first time. It was a mistake to do so. It was not his home. He had only been there for a few days. But he could not shake the feeling that he belonged here. Still, it was folly to think that way. Even if he somehow managed to resolve the issues with Grant, it might be best for Mary Ann to sell. Kicking Banner into a lope along the wooded ridge, he pushed the thoughts from his head, instead revelling in the power of the gelding and the sensation of wind on his face.

After a while he slowed his pace. They were under the trees now and it would not do to be knocked from the saddle by a low branch. Lars had kept up with him easily. The man did not look like a horseman, sitting his saddle like a sack of potatoes and riding with no grace, but Stokes had soon realised appearances were deceptive. Like many of the men in Oregon, Lars had grown up riding in all terrains and seasons. He was as comfortable on the back of a horse as on his own feet.

As they walked the horses through the woods, listening to the birds in the canopy and the dull thump of hooves in the leaf mould, Stokes thought of everything he had learnt since arriving. There had been scant time to stop and think but he vowed that he would make the time that evening to begin compiling a dossier of all the evidence, both real and circumstantial, relating to Thornford's murder. He would also document Grant's threats and any other behaviour that might prove useful as a testament to the man's character. He would go about it in a business-like fashion, taking precise notes of dates and times. He knew what to do. It had been his job for the best part of the last decade. And if he had any hope of having Grant convicted, there was no other way. He would also have to write to Eliza and Harriet, he thought.

When they rode out from under the shade of the pines, Stokes saw that the guests had arrived. Three horses, one of them as tall as a Clydesdale, were tied in the shade of the barn, and a wagon stood before the house. The team of mules had been unhitched and Lenny was leading the four animals towards the barn. A girl in a bonnet walked beside him. She had been talking, but when she saw Lars and Stokes come riding up, she fell silent and looked at them with soft dark eyes.

Stokes felt his spirits lift. The sunshine, the ride through the trees, the prospect of partaking of the sumptuous food he had smelt wafting from the kitchen for the last two days, and now the pretty girl looking at him from beneath long lashes, all combined to fill him with a joyful energy he barely recognised.

With a grin, he lifted his hat and pulled Banner to a halt. Before the horse had come to a complete stop, he leapt from the saddle. He instantly regretted the move as pain shot through his left thigh. His leg almost gave way and for a terrible moment he thought he might collapse before Lenny and the girl. He stumbled forward, then caught himself at the last second. To dissimulate that this was what he had intended all along, he raised his hat high in the air and bowed low.

"Madam," he said, "Lieutenant Gabriel Stokes at your service."

The girl looked at him with an expression somewhere

between amusement and shock, then she laughed, lifting her hand to her mouth.

"How do you do?" she managed through her giggles.

Lenny looked perplexed, unsure what to do next.

"See to those mules," Lars said, dismounting in a more leisurely manner. He touched the brim of his hat. "Miss Cora."

Still laughing quietly, the young woman turned away and followed Lenny towards the barn.

Shaking his head, Lars led his mare after them.

Stokes stood there feeling foolish. When he was sure the girl, Cora, had her back to him, he rubbed at his aching leg. It had been better these last few days as he became more accustomed to riding. Now it throbbed and the memory of the Afghan lance felt very recent. He silently cursed his own rashness. And all brought on by a pretty face. By God, was he so vain? He concluded he must be and began to limp towards the barn.

Sounds of laughter and conversation came from behind the house. He couldn't take long.

"There you are," said Mary Ann, stepping out from the house, "I thought you would be too late for the pork and quince pie." A few curls of her hair had come unpinned and she blew them away from her face. She wore an apron over her black dress and there was colour in her cheeks. She looked very beautiful, but Stokes did not permit his gaze to linger. "I trust everything is in order?" she asked, perhaps mistaking his sudden serious demeanour.

"We saw nothing of concern," Stokes said, his tone rather formal.

"Good. Hurry up and wash your hands, then help me to carry these plates out to our guests. I see you've met Cora." Her eyes twinkled. Stokes squirmed inwardly at the thought she might have seen his pathetic attempt at charm. "I'll introduce you to everyone else." It was the first time Stokes could recall Mary Ann showing any sign of happiness. It gladdened him.

"I'll be with you presently," he said.

He quickly unsaddled Banner and turned him out in the corral, then made his way to the house. The ache in his leg was more remote now and he was smiling ruefully at his own foolishness as he stepped into the kitchen.

A thumping sound welcomed him and his smile widened as he saw Pincher, tail beating against the stone floor at his excitement to see Stokes.

"He'll be running out barking to greet us when we ride in soon," he said, leaning down to stroke the dog. "He'll do well enough with three legs. Better than I can do with two, that's for sure."

"He might not be much of a sheep dog now," Mary Ann said, taking a cake from the oven and placing it on the table, "but I'm glad I didn't let Amos kill him."

Stokes recalled the heated words in the aftermath of Grant's visit. Albert had found Pincher cowering beneath the porch and had crawled in and pulled the dog out. The animal had been in terrible pain, the leg shattered and almost severed by Grant's bullet. But despite its fear and agony it had been as docile as a lamb as Albert lifted him, tears rolling down his cheeks, and carried him into the house.

"It would be kindest if I sent him on his way quickly, ma'am," Amos said. He made to pick the dog up, but Albert cried out and interposed himself. Adelaide clung to her mother's skirts, her face white and tears streaking her round cheeks.

"No," Mary Ann said, her voice firm and final. "We have suffered enough death in this house. If God chooses to take poor Pincher, then so be it, but I will not see him killed while there is a chance he might live."

When Amos saw there was no arguing with the woman, he heated his knife blade in the stove fire, then asked Albert and Stokes to hold the dog still. The animal had whined and whimpered, but had not even shown its teeth as Amos sawed the ruined remnants of the hind leg off. Luckily, there was little holding the limb in place and the sharp knife cut through the furry skin and sinews with little resistance. Amos bandaged the leg with white cotton that Mary Ann had cut from a clean petticoat.

"The hound has heart," he said when he'd finished. "Reckon he might pull through yet. Though his running days are probably over. It's in the Lord's hands now."

Mary Ann touched his arm.

"Then we will pray that He spares him," she said. "Thank you, Amos."

Stokes stroked Pincher's head and scratched his ears, marvelling at the speed of the animal's recovery. The dog lay near the stove, on a bed Albert and Adelaide had made for him out of old saddle blankets.

Mary Ann looked down at Pincher, her features softening.

"He has been in my way all the time while I've been cooking," she said. "I've almost stepped on him more than once, but I couldn't bring myself to move him out of the kitchen." She paused, cut off a thin slice of loaf cake and dropped it on the floor, near the dog's head. Pincher sniffed it, then gobbled it up in an instant. "Truth be told, he's been good company. It's been a joy to see him eating and getting stronger. Bit by bit."

"He's a tough one," Stokes said, standing straight and rubbing absently at his thigh. "I think that toughness runs in this family."

Mary Ann met his gaze for a second. There were tears in her eyes and she cuffed them away quickly as she turned to pick up a plate covered in biscuits.

"Carry these outside," she said, her tone brusque and business-like, "and I'll introduce you to everyone."

Chapter Twenty-Eight

Stokes leaned back and placed his hands on his stomach, stifling a belch. The sun was bright and warm. He could feel sweat soaking into his hat band. White and Lars had fashioned an awning out of some timber poles, rawhide ropes and a sheet of canvas that was normally used to cover wagons. It offered shade to part of the group around the table, and they had seated the children and the womenfolk so they might benefit from the protection from the sun's glare. The men sat in the sunshine.

"I say, Mary Ann," Stokes said, "if you keep feeding me like that there won't be a horse on the ranch that will be able to carry me."

"Papa's horse, Goliath, could manage, I'm sure," Cora said with a mischievous smile. "Perhaps you could use him."

The children and some of the men laughed. Stokes was careful not to join in. He had only met Cora's father half an hour before and he did not wish to insult him. It was true that Thomas Rice was a large man, portly even, and his mount was more akin to a dray than a riding horse or one of the quarter horses the ranch hands favoured. But Stokes was not sure that the neighbouring rancher would take kindly to a stranger laughing at his expense.

Mr Rice frowned and wagged his finger at Cora. He looked ready to leap up and beat the girl and Stokes was pleased with his instinctive decision not to belittle the man.

"You're not so grown I can't give you a good hiding," Rice

said, then, unable to maintain his stern expression any longer, he burst out laughing. "I wonder if Goliath would manage my bulk if I had another slice of that magnificent pie." He looked expectantly at the last piece of pork and quince pie on the long table. Mary Ann quickly scooped it up and placed it on his plate.

"One more slice can't hurt," she said with a smile.

"Tell that to Goliath," said Elsa, the second oldest of the Rices' three daughters.

"Cora," admonished Mrs Rice, "now you've got your sister copying your insolence. You should know better."

"They're only joshing," said Rice, placing a calming hand over his wife's. "I'm big enough to take it." He winked at Cora.

"You are big enough for most things, Pa," she replied. Her face was devoid of expression, but her eyes were laughing.

Stokes allowed himself to smile now. Rice appeared to be a decent, friendly man and the atmosphere around the long, cloth-draped table was convivial.

There had been little in the way of conversation since Stokes had first come from the kitchen carrying the biscuits. Mary Ann had introduced them all to him and quickly they had set to the food, of which there were copious quantities. As well as the biscuits and pie, there were sandwiches of boiled ham and cheese, and buttermilk to drink. Mrs Rice had brought something she had called bear head cheese. It seemed to be a kind of brawn and Stokes had commented on the unusual name, enquiring what the gelatinous concoction was made of.

Mrs Rice had looked at him as if he was simple.

"Why, bear head, of course," she said. "Mr Rice shot a big grizzly down by the creek not last week."

Everyone laughed at the shocked expression on Stokes' face and then again when he smiled after tasting it. It was salty and flavoursome, as good as the finest terrine. Mr Rice had also produced from his wagon a dozen bottles of Eagle Brewery beer that he'd had cooling in a stream until he'd packed them in a straw-lined crate that morning.

Stokes had declined the offer of a bottle, though he could think of little better on this warm afternoon. Despite his self-enforced abstinence, he enjoyed the meal and the cool buttermilk was pleasant enough.

The food was delicious and there had been only small snatches of conversation until everyone started to feel full and push themselves back from the table. The only ones now reaching for seconds, or perhaps even thirds, were Thomas Rice and Lenny, who, despite being skinny as a rake, appeared to be able to eat his own bodyweight and still not be replete.

Stokes looked about him, taking in the scene. Lars, Amos and White sat at the far end of the table, with the sun on their backs. They each had a bottle of beer in their hands and empty plates before them. As he watched, White began dexterously rolling a cigarette with his left hand.

Lenny had managed to seat himself next to Cora and it was obvious that the two of them had been looking forward to this lunch. They glanced at each other with secret smiles and from time to time they would both reach for food at the same time, which allowed them to touch hands, seemingly by accident. Stokes didn't think they fooled anyone and he caught Mrs Rice looking at the two youngsters with a deep furrow between her eyes. Slender and willowy where her husband was stout, Mrs Rice had the look of a stern woman, who rarely smiled. However, the expression she wore when taking in Lenny and her eldest daughter did not appear to be one of disapproval, more one of concern, or even sadness.

Despite Mrs Rice's sombre demeanour, the atmosphere at the table was light and jovial enough. Elsa was about Albert's age, and they whispered to one another, giggling and laughing at whatever silliness they talked about. Stokes wondered how long it would be until the two of them would be cooing over each other like Lenny and Cora.

The youngest of the Rice girls, Florence, was perhaps a year older than Adelaide and the two of them were thick as thieves.

As soon as they had finished eating they slipped under the table cloth, and shortly afterwards the two girls scampered off to play a game of their own devising down by the vegetable patch.

"Mind you don't step on my carrots," called Mary Ann to the girls with a roll of her eyes.

The last two guests were ranch hands from Rice's spread. Their foreman, who Rice introduced as Mayfield Redin, was a stocky man of about Stokes' age. He wore a black hat and had a rugged, weathered face that spoke of endless seasons outdoors. The other man's name was Logan Warnock. He was considerably younger, not much older than Lenny, but with none of the softness of youth about him. Warnock was rangy and hatchet-faced. Neither man spoke much, but they had both met Stokes' eyes when introduced and their handshakes spoke of strong, direct men.

It was evident from the relaxed nature of the Rices and the Thornfords, along with the easy banter between the hands from both ranches, that these gatherings were a regular affair. He could understand Mary Ann's insistence that the picnic should go ahead as planned. In a tough life, such warming moments were rare and fleeting, something to be cherished.

"May I be excused?" asked Cora politely.

"Go on then," said her mother. "But don't be going far."

"I'll be serving composition cake soon," Mary Ann said, "and I don't want to have to holler for all you young ones."

Lenny stood up at the same time as Cora.

"I won't be going too far then," he said. "Ain't nothing gonna keep me away from your composition cake, Mrs Thornford."

Warnock muttered something under his breath, but Stokes couldn't make out what he said. Cora must have heard though, for she blushed. Lenny shot the hard-faced hand a dirty look and strode away with the girl.

"Come and see Pincher," Albert said, standing up. "He got shot." Elsa rose and followed him into the house, wide-eyed with excitement.

"I too am looking forward to partaking of your cake, Mary Ann," Mr Rice said, "but I feel a rest is in order first." He patted his ample belly. He glanced down to where White was leaning back and smoking his rolled cigarette. "If the ladies don't object, perhaps a smoke before dessert would help with our digestion."

The ladies did not demur, so the men pulled out their makings. Stokes offered one of his cigarillos to Rice, but he declined.

"Much obliged, Mr Stokes," he said, "but I prefer a pipe myself." He took out a briar pipe and a small tobacco pouch from which he filled the pipe expertly. Soon all the men were smoking.

"That was a wonderful meal, Mary Ann," Rice said, smiling. "And the bear's head cheese was delicious, my dear." He patted his wife's hand. Turning his attention to Stokes, he said, "You were an army man? Is that where you met John?"

"That's right," Stokes said. "We fought together in Afghanistan from '78 to '81."

"Nasty business, from everything I've read about it," Rice said.

Stokes breathed out a stream of smoke.

"I found little to recommend it," he said.

"The war, or Afghanistan?"

"Both," replied Stokes. "The only good thing to come out of either for me was that I made lifelong friends in the regiment."

"John was your commanding officer?"

"For a time, yes."

"You must have been very young," said Mrs Rice.

"Old enough to fight for Queen and country." Even to his own ears, the words sounded pompous. "But yes," he went on, "I joined the regiment young. My father served in the Tenth Hussars, my older brother, too."

"Do they still serve?" Mr Rice asked.

"Sadly, no. Michael was killed before I was born. In '55, at the battle of Eupatoria in the Crimea."

"I am very sorry to hear that. But your family must be proud of the sacrifice he made."

Stokes had a fleeting vision of his father's screaming face during one of his frequent rages, spittle flying from quivering jowls. Eliza weeping. Harriet scowling from the doorway to the drawing room.

"Yes. Of course," he said, stiffly. "Very proud." Then, to head off further questions, he added, "My father died several years ago."

Of course he would not speak of the unutterable sadness that gripped his father from the instant he'd learnt of Michael's death. Of the cold, forbidding, melancholic man who had been a distant, threatening presence in the echoing rooms of their huge house throughout his childhood. He would say nothing about how his father had ultimately ended his suffering by swallowing a bullet from Michael's Adams revolver, leaving behind more sorrow and devastation for his three surviving children to deal with.

"Do you have any other family?" Mrs Rice asked.

"I have two sisters back in England." He did not mention Rebecca. If either of the Rices noticed the wedding band he wore, they did not comment. Stokes wondered if Mary Ann had told them something of his past. Whether she had or not, he was glad not to have to speak about his wife.

"They must also be proud of your achievements."

"I merely did my duty," Stokes said.

He did not enjoy speaking about himself. There was nothing praiseworthy about him or his past. He caught himself looking at the bottles of beer that bobbed in a bucket of cold water drawn from the pump. One beer would not hurt, surely?

"As it should be," Rice said, nodding and puffing on his pipe. "There is no greater calling than to serve one's country. To risk making the ultimate sacrifice."

Mrs Rice looked at her husband sharply.

"It is a risk all soldiers take," Stokes said. "I saw many

209

good men die. I would have perished at Maiwand, if not for John."

"Ah, yes," Rice said, pointing at him with the end of his pipe. "Got a medal for it, didn't he?"

"The Victoria Cross."

"How many of the heathen savages did he have to kill to get that?"

Stokes frowned.

"There was no counting of kills in the Tenth," Stokes said, his voice clipped. Rice looked uncomfortable under his chill gaze. "A soldier obeys his orders and hopes he is fighting for a just cause. The Afghans were defending their homeland. There were many brave men on both sides. As in any conflict."

Rice grew sombre. He puffed out clouds of smoke as he thought about Stokes' words.

"But you had God on your side, surely. Those savages are much better off under the auspices of the British Empire."

"I am not so sure about that," Stokes said. He didn't wish to be drawn on his thoughts about empire and conquest. His opinions had made him few friends in London. But he was not one to shy away from an uncomfortable truth. "Who truly has the right to own any land?" he said. "Why should one nation rule over another? Should it be that the strongest take what they want simply because they can?"

"It has always been that way," said Redin from the other end of the table.

"But should it be?"

"Well how else would things change for the better?" Redin fidgeted in his chair, looking like a man who wished he had not got involved, but didn't feel he could withdraw from the discussion without losing face. He took a swig of beer. "Civilization must progress," he said after gathering his thoughts. "The strong will prevail over the weak."

"Should it be that way?" Stokes said. "I'm not so sure. What number of deaths is acceptable in the name of progress? And how civilized are we really? After the war I became a police-man in London. The biggest city in the world. The heart of civilization." He scoffed. "You cannot imagine the squalor. The stink. The streets littered with drunks and whores. Rapes and murders almost every day."

"Gabriel," Mary Ann hissed, cutting him off. "That's enough."

Stokes looked about him. He could hear the children talking and laughing from inside the house. By the vegetable plot, Florence and Adelaide were chasing after each other in fits of giggles.

"Forgive me..." Stokes stammered. "I... forgot myself. I did not mean to spoil the picnic. Please accept my sincerest apologies."

There was an awkward silence. Stokes was furious with himself. Where were his manners? He rose from the table, ready to excuse himself with another apology, but Mrs Rice broke the silence before he could speak.

"We lost a son, Mr Stokes," she said. Her face was very pale and her eyes glimmered as if she were on the verge of tears. "Our Henry was killed in battle, just like your brother."

"I'm awfully sorry for your loss, ma'am," Stokes said. "And for my crass behaviour. I have no excuse."

"You have nothing to apologise for," she said. "There is nothing civilized about killing. Henry was killed by the Cheyenne in Nebraska. We call them savages." For a time she watched the children playing. "I tried to hate them," she said at last. "Perhaps I did for a time, but the more I thought about them and the more I heard about what had happened at Antelope Creek, the less I could hate. 'Progress', we call it. All they wanted was to live on land that had been theirs for centuries. How many young men will never grow old? All in the name of 'progress'..." She choked on her emotion and her words trailed off.

"Now, now, dear," Thomas Rice said, patting her hand.

"I agree with you, Mrs Rice," Stokes said. "It is shameful that the cost of the decisions made by old men in power is paid for with the blood of the young."

"However much we dislike it," Rice said, draining his bottle of beer and reaching for another, "it has ever been thus. Powerful men dictate all our lives. Whether president or prime minister." He levered off the metal stopper and took a swallow. "Or cattle baron. We are powerless against them." He stared at Mary Ann and some unspoken communication passed between them.

"You have heard from Grant again?" she asked. Stokes noted that she had not mentioned the cattleman's Friday visit.

"We have," said Rice, setting his bottle down. He picked at some crumbs on the tablecloth, shifting awkwardly in his chair. The wood creaked under his weight. The girls playing nearby shrieked. Rice watched them for a time, then, straightening his shoulders, he turned back to Mary Ann. "There's no easy way to say this," he said. "We're leaving."

"Leaving? But Thomas!" Mary Ann looked from Rice to his wife. "Winnie. No!" She was distraught. "We need to stick together."

Mrs Rice would not meet her gaze. Thomas Rice nodded slowly, accepting her words.

"I know that's what we agreed," he said. "But with John gone, things are different. Grant's offered us ten per cent on his first offer."

"Did you accept it?"

"Not yet. But I plan to." Rice sighed. "Winnie and I have discussed it."

"But what Grant is offering is still not what the land is worth," Mary Ann said. "You know it, as well as I do."

"That's as maybe," Rice said, "but what would you have us do?"

"Reject his offer to start with," Mary Ann retorted, her words sharp. "Like I did."

"It's not so simple," Rice said, leaning forward over the

table and lowering his voice so that the children would not overhear. "You know we've lost a lot of stock already. When Grant came to the ranch on Thursday with his new offer, he threatened us."

"You never mentioned that before, Mr Rice," Redin said, sitting up straight. "That ain't right."

"I'm sorry, Mayfield," Rice said. "I didn't say anything because I knew you and the boys would ride on over to the Cabin Creek guns blazing."

"If Grant threatened you or your family, damn right we'd go on over there and straighten him out. With our fists or guns, it's no matter to me."

Stokes noticed that Jed White was nodding his approval of the foreman's words.

"Well it matters to me," Rice said. "Grant has enough hired guns to kill you and Logan a dozen times over. Davie and Berton already up and left, I can't lose you too."

Warnock slammed his fist into the table, rattling the plates and cups.

"Now see here, Mr Rice," he sputtered. "Berton and Davie had no stomach for a fight, but we ain't no soft-horns. We'd give Grant and his muscle a run for their money."

"I don't doubt your sand, Logan," said Rice in a conciliatory tone. "But no matter how hard you and Mayfield are, you are decent men. Not killers. Grant has the likes of Cadmar Byrne, Bull Meacher and Joaquin Lopez riding for his brand. Those men are stone cold killers. Back-shooters who wouldn't think twice about beefing you. You might take one or two of them, but they would surely kill you in the end and where would that leave us? We would be no better off, and I do not want to see you throw your lives away."

"This land isn't worth it," added Winnie Rice. "We love it here, but it just isn't worth dying for."

Mary Ann was nodding sombrely. She had said similar to Stokes.

"I hear you," she said. "I really do. But what if I told you there was a way you could stay?"

"I can't see how," Rice said. "Not while Grant runs the valley."

"There might be a way we can get rid of him. Once and for all."

Rice looked at her unblinking, as if weighing her resolve. Having made up his mind, he said, "If you have a plan, let's hear it."

Chapter Twenty-Nine

Gabriel Stokes and Jed White rode down the hill to Griffith the following day. The sunny weather they had enjoyed at the picnic had been replaced with a dismal grey. Thick clouds had built up over night and to Stokes it looked like rain was on the way. The morning was almost over but despite the gloomy appearance of the sky, it had not rained and the day had grown uncomfortably warm. They had needed to halt on the ride down from the JT so that Stokes could remove his coat. White had looked on in amusement as Stokes had dismounted, taken off the heavy wool jacket, then stowed it behind his saddle before stepping into the stirrups again. The old frontiersman seemed oblivious to the changes in temperature.

They had ridden out after breakfast when their breath still smoked in the chill air. White had worn nothing heavier than his shirt, but had appeared warm enough. Now, even having removed his jacket, Stokes felt clammy and too hot. White rode alongside him, showing no sign of discomfort.

They had ridden in silence for close to an hour, which suited Stokes. He was nervous and exhilarated, but tired too. He had stayed up late sitting close to Mary Ann, both of them hunched over the table in the pool of lamplight. Each of them had been focused on writing, conferring every now and then in whispers so as not to wake the children. Riding down the wooded slope beside the taciturn White gave him plenty of time to think about what they had been committing to paper. He was still unsure any of it would work, but surely it was worth a try.

"I still think we should ride on up to the Cabin Creek and shoot 'em all," White said, when they were still in the woodland and yet some way from town.

Stokes sighed.

"I understand how you feel, but this way, we could be rid of Grant and nobody else needs to die. We owe it to John to try. He would have wanted us to follow the law."

White hawked and spat.

"This won't be the end of it," he said. "If there ain't no more killing in this matter, I'll give you a golden eagle."

"You already owe me hundreds of dollars."

White spat again.

"I ain't forgotten about that," he said. "I'm good for it."

"Just don't miss your court date, once it has been set."

They rode along for a time, lost in their thoughts. The trees were loud with the sound of birdsong, and despite the anxiety that had twisted into a knot in Stokes' stomach, he did enjoy being in the saddle again. He was also looking forward to going into Griffith. He had several errands to run, and one that was of the utmost importance. He thought of the letters in his saddlebags.

The letter to his sisters had not been difficult to write. In it he spoke of the beauty of the land, and of the people he had met on his travels. He had been careful not to speak of the troubles facing the ranch and made no mention of the confrontations with Grant and his hired thugs. But Eliza knew him better than anyone and she was astute and perspicacious. If they had been speaking face-to-face, he knew it would be impossible for him to hide that something was wrong. In writing, it was much easier to omit and obscure things, and yet he would not be surprised if she wrote back asking him for details of what was amiss. Still, by then the matter would be resolved one way or the other. Then perhaps he would write a letter telling her the truth, but not yet.

The other letter in his bag was thicker and much more important.

"You really think this plan can work?" asked White.

"I hope so."

"If hope was gold dust, we'd all be rich."

"It is worth a shot, at least," said Stokes.

White sniffed. He didn't look convinced, but he said no more.

They passed the railroad, where the Chinese work gang toiled in the heat. The tracks had reached the station. The building looked finished, the roof shingled, the sign affixed above the door. Several men were putting the finishing touches to the raised timber platform that would allow passengers to alight. The warm air was thick with the clangour of hammers. Beyond the station building, the tracks were being continued towards a series of stockyards and loading sidings.

White and Stokes headed towards Hampton's livery stable.

"I'll see that the horses are watered," Stokes said, "then I'll go directly to the Post Office."

"Suits me," said White. "When you're done, come and find me at the Lady Elgin."

Stokes frowned.

"Don't drink too much. I don't want to stay in town long."

"Don't worry about me," replied White, swinging down from the saddle and tossing his reins to Hampton, who had stepped out from the shade of the stable building. "Alpheus," White said by way of greeting.

"Jed," responded Hampton with a nod.

White strode away without a backward glance.

"What's that old coot got to be hurrying for?" Hampton said. "Nobody told me they was giving away rotgut in town."

Stokes smiled and dismounted, careful not to jar his leg. It still ached slightly from his antics in front of Miss Cora the day before.

"Even if Jed has to pay for his whiskey," he said, "I doubt there is much that could slow him down when there's a saloon nearby."

Hampton chuckled.

"For a man who hasn't known White long, you have a mighty fine grasp of his character."

"A man of simple, and rather dubious pleasures. Whiskey, cards, and killing might well sum up Mr White, it seems to me."

"Yes, sir. That about says it all," Hampton said. "Not necessarily in that order. And don't forget sporting ladies."

Together they led the horses to the trough.

"I've not seen him with a strumpet," said Stokes.

"Well, like I said, you ain't known the man long, and much of that time you been up at the JT. The man's a brute, but he ain't an animal. Besides," he let out a cackle, "I don't think he could convince any of the painted cats to travel up to a sheep farm when they make a good living in town."

They watched the horses drink for a while. Stokes removed his hat and wiped his sleeve across his brow. The day was as humid as it was warm. He felt sweat trickle down his spine.

"What brings you to town?" Hampton asked.

Reminded of his task, Stokes went to his saddlebags and fished out the packet of letters.

"Post Office," he said, waving the sheaf of papers.

"Any more trouble with the Cabin Creek boys?"

Stokes looked sidelong at the grey-whiskered hostler, trying to judge his motive in asking. Hampton seemed genuine and friendly, but Stokes reminded himself he barely knew the man.

"No," he said, deciding not to mention Friday's encounter. "No more trouble. Are they in town?"

"Nope, not seen any of the Grant crew since Saturday. A few of 'em came in on Friday afternoon and they painted the town red. They were mighty riled up. Meacher and Lopez got into a slugging match with a couple of teamsters. Lucky for them Sheriff Bannon's in Grant's pocket, otherwise they might still be sleeping it off in a cell." The old hostler looked at Stokes slyly. "I wonder what might have got 'em so hot under the collar."

"I wonder," said Stokes. He produced his last two cigarillos and offered one to Hampton.

"Don't mind if I do." He grinned, popped the cigarillo in his mouth and accepted a light from Stokes, who went on to light his own with the same match.

Hampton puffed appreciatively.

"So you wouldn't happen to know anything about a certain visit to the JT that didn't go as Mr Grant would have liked?"

There was clearly no use denying it. If Hampton had an ulterior motive in any of this, Stokes couldn't see what it was.

"Oh yes, of course," Stokes said with a wide smile. "Now that you mention it. It had completely slipped my mind."

Hampton seemed to think that was one of the funniest things he had ever heard. He let out a barking laugh and slapped his thigh to accentuate his mirth. Stokes watched him in silence, smoking impassively.

Wiping tears from his eyes, Hampton said, "Thought you said you'd had no trouble with Grant."

"That was true. The trouble was all Grant's. Not mine. The only member of the JT crew inconvenienced was the sheepdog. Grant shot him."

"I heard Jackson Pailing saying something about that. That don't sit right with me. Only reasons to kill an animal are to eat it, to defend yourself, or to put it out of its misery."

"I wonder if Grant thought he was defending himself. Little men can get frightened by all manner of things. Even a dog like Pincher. But the truth of the matter is the only misery in the affair was Grant's poor aim. He didn't even manage to kill the wretched creature, despite it being right under his nose."

"That's a sad thing. It's never easy killing an animal that has served you well. I'm thinking perhaps that task fell to you, seeing as how you had known the dog for less time than the others."

"Oh no," Stokes said, "Pincher isn't dead. I would have sent him on his way if it had been needed, but Mrs Thornford insisted we give him a chance." He remembered how that morning, as he came to the house for breakfast, Pincher had risen from his bed in the kitchen and greeted him. The dog seemed able to move about well enough on three legs and its tail wagged furiously as the ranch hands had each taken a moment to pat and stroke him.

"Well, I'll be damned," said Hampton, shaking his head. "I work with animals every day and still they never cease to amaze me."

"I feel the same way about humans for the most part," Stokes said. He puffed at his cigarillo, then added, "You know, there is something that's been preying on my mind."

"What's that?"

Stokes examined the old hostler, staring into his eyes for signs of guile or duplicity. He saw none. He needed information and Hampton seemed as good a man as any to start with.

"I've been wondering why it is that Grant needs so much land. He owns huge swathes of the valley, and yet he seems intent on acquiring all the land he can lay his hands on, through fair means or foul."

Hampton stared him in the eye for a long while. It was the Englishman's turn to be appraised. He sensed the old hostler was weighing up Stokes' chances against Grant. If he'd been a betting man, Stokes wouldn't have placed a wager on himself. The odds were stacked against him. But Hampton apparently came to a different conclusion. He nodded, took a deep drag of his cheroot and said, "There is talk that Grant has signed a big beef contract with the government."

"How big?"

"I don't rightly know. Perhaps big enough that the land he has isn't sufficient to supply the number of head he's promised. Sheep damage the grass, cropping it down to the roots. The longer it's grazed by sheep, the worse things will get for Grant and his associates."

"Any idea when he'd need to fulfil such a contract?"

"Well, I don't know anything for sure, but looking at the way he is dealing his hand of late, it wouldn't surprise me to learn it's tied up with the opening of the railroad."

Chapter Thirty

Stokes' boots were loud on the timber sidewalk. He turned over what Hampton had said about the government contract. It made sense, and if Grant was expected to deliver soon after the arrival of trains to Griffith, it would explain his urgency. Stokes wondered how much money would be involved in such a beef contract. America was a huge place. A big contract would be worth a fortune.

Enough to kill for?

Stokes had no doubts on that front. He had arrested men capable of committing murder for the price of a glass of gin. For the sums of money involved in a massive government contract, some men would do almost anything.

As he reached the Post Office, Stokes realised he was crushing the letters in his hand. His tight grip had creased them, and his sweat had smudged the ink on the letter to Eliza. Forcing himself to relax his grip, he straightened out the papers, checking that the addresses on both were legible. If the letter to his sister went astray, all that would happen would be that Eliza might think him a bad brother. She might worry about him, but nothing more. If the letter Mary Ann had penned did not reach its destination, there could be serious ramifications. They were pinning their hopes on the letter. The gravity of it made his heart flutter. It was a gamble. He felt as though they had staked their lives on a single roll of the dice. He remembered having a similar hollow feeling of dread in the pit of his stomach when he had been ordered to advance at Maiwand. Then, as now, he had pushed forward and done his duty. He rubbed his thigh, thinking of the disastrous conclusion of that attack and prayed that this would prove to have a more fortuitous outcome.

Taking a deep breath, he pushed open the door.

Unlike the doomed attack at Maiwand, posting the letters was a painless affair and over in a matter of seconds. Of course, Stokes had not really expected anything else, but the weight of the message he delivered, and the knowledge that Mary Ann's future was tied up with it, had preyed upon him.

The man behind the counter in the Post Office was small, and smartly dressed in a dark suit. He was slim, his cheeks pink from a fresh shave. His moustache was black and severe, drawing attention to a weak mouth and an almost non-existent chin.

He took Stokes' instructions without comment, almost snatching the letters from him. His movements were fast and jerky, reminding Stokes of a thrush, pecking at a snail.

When the clerk saw the address on the letter to Eliza, he raised his eyebrows and looked up at Stokes.

"We don't get many letters to England," he said.

"I trust that won't be a problem," Stokes replied, his voice cool. Something about the man annoyed him. Stokes' nerves jangled with the anticipation of seeing the other letter safely on its way. Turning around suddenly, he checked the window, half-expecting to see Grant and his men there, coming to stop him from posting the letter. But the window was clear. There was nobody directly outside the Post Office. Inside, the only people were Stokes and the clerk.

"No problem at all, sir," the clerk said, his tone affronted. "It was merely an observation. Your letters will be safely sent on their way."

"Good," Stokes replied. He had no time for pleasantries or good manners.

The clerk peered at the address of the thicker letter, a slight frown passing across his features. He glanced up at Stokes, who met his gaze.

"Something amiss?" he asked.

The clerk ignored the question and went about weighing each of the letters.

"That will be nine cents, for the two letters."

Stokes paid him.

"How long will the letter to Salem take to arrive?"

The clerk didn't need time to think of his answer.

"It should be there within two days. A few years ago it would have taken much longer. A week or perhaps more, but now, with the trains, things are much quicker. Of course, if it is truly urgent, you could send a telegram." He picked up a pad and pencil expectantly.

"That won't be necessary."

The clerk looked disappointed. The address on the letter had clearly piqued his interest and he had hoped to learn something of the message's contents. The night before, Stokes had put forward the idea of sending a telegram, but they quickly discarded the notion. The message was urgent, but Mary Ann pointed out that anything sent via telegraph was not a secret. There would be time for the message to reach its destination and they already knew the recipient would be on his way to Griffith soon enough.

Judging from the inquisitive expression on the clerk's soft face, Stokes wondered whether he could be trusted not to open the letter the moment he left. He would have to assume the man would be above such things, or at least fearful of the consequences of breaking federal law and opening post not addressed to him. One thing he could be sure of though was that if the Post Master owed any allegiance to Grant, the cattleman would know soon enough of the letter Stokes had posted and to whom it was addressed, even if he did not learn of the contents.

Stokes stepped out into the warm street, replacing his hat on his head against the milky sunlight's glare. He strode back the way he had come. There was something else he needed to do before going to meet Jed White. Hopefully he wouldn't be long enough for the old man to get into any trouble. He smiled at the thought. The man was to trouble what manure was to flies. Still, the street was quiet and Hampton had said none of Grant's men were in town. His next errand wouldn't take long.

He felt lighter now. He hadn't realised how tense he had been, but when he had handed over the letter that Mary Ann had written, it was as if a weight had been lifted from him. Their plan was in motion, and all they could do now was wait.

Casting another glance both ways along the street for any sign of Cabin Creek men, he saw none. Without thinking, he dropped his right hand to the grip of the gun on his hip. It was reassuring to know it was there.

Pulling the shop door open, he stepped into the shaded interior of McCall's General Store, enjoying the heady mixture of smells as his eyes grew accustomed to the gloom.

"What a pleasure to see you once more," Mr McCall said. He had been dusting boxes of soda crackers that were stacked high to the left of the door, but now he scurried back behind the counter, as if embarrassed to have been caught away from his post, or, thought Stokes, as though he wanted the protection of the stout timber counter between him and the Englishman who had just stepped in out of the warm midday sunshine. "What can I get for you on this fine day?"

Stokes wasted no time on small talk. He sensed Mrs McCall lurking in the back room, no doubt listening to everything he said and ready to hurry off to her sister and her brother-in-law with whatever she gleaned.

He ordered some more cigarillos, another box of .38 Long Colts, and a half pound of hard candy. He smiled at that, knowing Mary Ann would eat more of the sweets than the children. Taking a quick look at the shelf of books, he spied one entitled *The Baltimore Gun Club*, which he had not noticed on his last visit. He saw it was a translation from a French author and was set to return it, but some distant memory prompted him to leaf through the pages. The book was illustrated, the pictures wonderfully detailed. There were drawings of a great gun and a projectile used to fire men to the moon. With a start, Stokes realised he had read the story and seen the pictures before when he was just a boy. He hadn't recognised the name of the author, Jules Verne, but it was most definitely this story he had read spread over months in the *St James Magazine and United Empire Review*. The story had been called *From the Earth to the Moon* then. He placed the book on the counter too. Albert had loved the book he had bought for him, and this would be a perfect accompaniment to the telescope that had been meant for the boy's step-father. He thought Captain Thornford would have approved of Jules Verne's story of the attempt to conquer the moon itself.

Ignoring Mr McCall's clumsy attempts at probing questions, Stokes paid the shopkeeper, picked up his parcel, and left.

Half a dozen men were riding down the street from the north. Stokes squinted against the bright light, trying to make out their faces. They were riding unhurriedly and he recognised none of them. He had no idea of their business in Griffith, but if it took them to the Lady Elgin, the risk of Jed White being involved in some form of confrontation would grow.

He increased his pace and wondered if they had something cold to drink in the saloon. Perhaps he could buy a bottle of something before they left town. The first thought that entered his mind was the beer Rice had brought to the picnic. Stokes licked his lips, recalling the beads of moisture on the glass bottles. Perhaps it was foolish to go into the saloon, with all the temptations he sought to avoid so readily on display. But he had promised Mary Ann he would not allow Jed to stay in town. Besides, he was thirsty, and he was not about to allow his demons to defeat him. He would face them, and vanquish them.

He was pleased to see the riders pass the saloon. One less thing to worry about. He scanned their faces, certain now that he'd never seen any of them before. They wore leather chaps. Their hats were dusty and their spurs jingled and gleamed as they passed. More than one of the horsemen looked longingly at the open doors of the Lady Elgin as they trotted by. Stokes recognised that look, if not their faces. It wouldn't be long till they returned.

Inside the saloon, he spotted White at the same table where he had been sitting last time. Just as on the previous occasion, there were three men with him, two of whom Stokes recognised as White's previous card-playing companions. The last man was younger and wore the shirt, kerchief, trousers and riding boots of a cowpuncher.

"Come to collect me so soon, Stokes?" White called out. "I ain't hardly had time to wash the dust out of my throat."

"I've done all I needed to do," Stokes replied, his tone serious, though he felt surprisingly contented. "Finish off your hand while I get a drink. It's a tad warm out there."

"Much obliged," White said with a grin. "Come on, lads, time's a-wasting."

Stokes flipped open his pocket watch, checking the time and winding it without thinking.

"Ten minutes," he said. "No more. I promised Mary Ann we would head straight back."

"Hell, I might need more than ten minutes to clean these boys out," White shouted, "but I guess I can make a good start."

Stokes walked up to the bar, checked it was dry and clean, then placed his parcel from McCall's on the marble counter.

"What'll it be?" asked the barman, pushing himself up from where he had been sitting reading a crumpled copy of the *East Oregonian*.

"Something cold."

"I got beer. That's cold enough. Keep it in an icebox."

"Do you have anything in the icebox besides beer?"

"I got sarsaparilla for the children."

Stokes had no idea what that was.

"If it's cold, I'll have one of those."

The barkeep made no comment. The look of contempt he gave Stokes said enough. He pulled a bottle from beneath the bar and poured a glass of dark brown liquid. Stokes sipped it and was unable to keep his face from twisting into a grimace.

"I find it best to just drink the whiskey," said a woman's voice. "That stuff will rot your guts quicker than any spirit."

Stokes had seen the woman coming down the stairs at the back of the saloon, but had paid her little notice. There was no doubt as to her profession. He had seen countless such women all over the world, and they all seemed to wear similar uniforms for their trade. This woman was taller than average, with auburn hair piled high on her head. She wore a gaudy dress, the hem too high for a lady, showing off slender, shapely ankles. The bodice of the dress was tight and low-cut, giving prospective clients more than a mere suggestion of what they could expect for their money. Her cheeks were dark with rouge, her eyes and lashes smoky. Her lips were the bright red of freshly spilt blood.

Her accent caught his attention more than her appearance and he turned to study her closely. She met his gaze without flinching. The smile on her lips reached her eyes just enough to soften her expression. He guessed that beneath all the make-up she was quite pretty. And she was a lot younger than he'd initially thought. No older than twenty, perhaps younger.

He lifted the glass and sniffed it. He took another sip and shrugged. The taste wasn't as bad after the initial shock.

"Sadly, I no longer drink whiskey," he said.

"All the more for me," she replied, sliding up close to him at the bar. "Buy a girl a drink? I'm spittin' feathers!"

He glanced over at White and the others playing cards. His mood was still buoyant from having delivered the letters. Besides, this dollymop might know something useful. In his experience, strumpets were often a waste of time when it came to police work. The officers would kid themselves the women would provide them with useful tips, but more often than not, they simply ended up partaking of the prostitutes' wares, as they partook of publicans' cheap beer. Another perk of the job. The women themselves were frequently so drunk they could barely recall anything of their customers anyway, and it was not as though criminals would give up their plans to the girls they were prigging.

But every now and then a dolly would prove useful. This one seemed talkative and he didn't detect any slurring of her speech, though of course, the day was young. And he was intrigued by her accent.

"A whiskey for the lady," he said, turning to the barkeep.

The barman sneered, and muttered under his breath, "I don't see no lady."

Stokes scowled at him.

"I'll have none of that talk."

The barman grew serious but decided against continuing the conversation. Pouring the whiskey, he returned to his paper.

"Allow me to introduce myself," Stokes said, pushing the glass towards the girl. "My name is Gabriel Stokes."

"Bella," she replied, taking a sip of her whiskey. "Sawrey."

He smiled, partly at her and partly at his own shallowness, wondering if he was any different from the mutton shunters he had despised in London. If this girl had not been pretty, he would most likely have turned her away.

He raised his glass.

"Your good health, Miss Sawrey," he said.

She laughed at that. Her mirth seemed genuine.

"Blooming 'eck, you're the poshest gent I ever seen in here."

"I'm not sure how posh I am."

"Posher than the farmers, miners and cowboys who come in here, that's for sure." Bella looked him up and down, taking in his dusty boots, sweat-stained hat and shirt open at the neck. "You sound like you just stepped off the boat from England, but by the looks of you, I'd say you're well on your way to fitting in here."

"I could say the same for you. Your accent would be more at home in Yorkshire than Oregon."

"Lancashire," she replied. "My family came out west from Morecambe in '83."

Both of them took another drink. Her eyes were dark and sad. He wondered if she was thinking about where she had come from.

"You must have been just a girl then," he said.

"Twelve," she said, drinking the last swallow of her whiskey. "Almost a woman." Stokes watched her as she placed the glass on the counter. It had a crimson print of her lips on the rim. For a fleeting moment he imagined the taste of the whiskey in her mouth. She saw how his eyes followed her movements and sighed. "Well, are you taking me upstairs or not, Mr Stokes? Neither of us is getting any younger."

He took a mouthful of his drink. He thought perhaps he could grow to like its sour flavour, but it would never be as good as a cold beer. It had been a long time since he had been with a woman, longer than he had been without a drink. There was something about this girl. He considered allowing her to lead him up to her room, but immediately discarded the idea. He imagined the squalor of the place, the rumpled sheets that would smell of the stale sweat of numerous nameless men who had gone before him.

"Not today," he said, offering her a smile.

A flash of irritation passed over Bella's face.

"My time isn't free, you know."

"If you have other affairs to attend to, Bella," he said with a gallant bow, "please do not let me detain you."

She glared at him, angry that he was making fun of her. After a few seconds a smirk tugged at the corners of her mouth.

"You're a queer one, and no mistake," she said. "I suppose I don't have anything more pressing to do. But all this talk is thirsty work."

"Of course." He signalled to the barman, who was clearly listening to their conversation from behind his newspaper. "Another whiskey for the lady, please."

This time the barman made no comment about Bella's virtue or lack thereof. Once the whiskey had been poured, she sipped it.

Over at the table in the corner, the three men groaned as White won another hand. The old man grinned, his eyes twinkling as he dragged the pot of coins and bills towards him. The bottle on the table was already half empty. It was going to be difficult to get him to leave, Stokes thought.

"I know who you are," Bella said, quietly. She touched his arm, pulling him further down the bar and out of earshot of the barkeep. Stokes raised an eyebrow.

"I did tell you my name," he said.

"I mean you're famous."

"I am?" Stokes was incredulous.

"You're Captain Thornford's war hero friend who stood up to Bull Meacher, Hunter Randle and Cadmar Byrne. The Englishman who stuck a gun in Tom Grant's face and told him to get off the JT Ranch. Everyone's heard of you. It was all anyone was talking about on Friday night when the Cabin Creek boys came in here."

Stokes said nothing. He sipped his sarsaparilla. It was warming up already, its flavours becoming harsher.

"You had better be careful," she continued in a hushed tone. "The likes of Meacher and Byrne aren't used to men standing up to them. And Grant is used to getting his way."

"I know the type."

"No," she said, her tone growing sharper, "you're not

listening to me. Grant *always* gets what he wants. And everyone knows he wants the JT. And everyone knows he'll get it in the end, no matter what it takes." Her voice caught in her throat. Taking a deep breath, she swallowed more of the whiskey.

"What do you know about it?" he asked.

She turned away from him and stared out through the window at the bright sunlit street. The light picked out the soft down of hair on the curve of her neck. For a time he thought she was not going to answer, but he kept silent, giving her time. At last, having made up her mind, she sighed.

"I didn't come to Oregon to be a whore," she said. She spoke the words like a slap. "Father had a dream and it brought us west. He staked a claim and started farming and mining the land. The winters were tougher than anything we'd known before, but we were not soft southerners like you." A ghost of a smile touched her lips. "Us Lancashire folk are tough as they come. We don't give up easy. Me, my brothers and our ma and pa worked hard and we made a go of it. Life was good for a while. That was before..." Her voice trailed off and she looked back to the light-bathed street outside. There was movement out there. The six riders Stokes had seen before were tying their mounts to the hitching rail.

"Before what?" he asked. He could sense her tensing up. When the cowboys entered the saloon, he was sure her mask would return and she would once again be the no-nonsense mawk. She was a Lancashire girl, after all. As tough as they come.

"Before Grant decided he wanted the claim," she said.

"What happened?"

"Grant got what he wanted."

"And your family?"

Bella sighed.

"Pa made the mistake of standing in Grant's way."

"And your mother? Your brothers?"

A tear trickled from her eye.

"God damn it," she said.

He pulled a handkerchief from his pocket and handed it to her. She dabbed at her eyes. The cloth came back stained with lamp-black.

"I ain't got no brothers or parents no more," she said. "I told you," she hissed, "Grant always gets what he wants." She sniffed. "I was only sixteen when I came to work here."

The realisation struck Stokes like a punch. It was obvious, and he couldn't believe he had not thought of it before.

"Grant owns this place?"

"Who else?" she whispered, her words as dry and bitter as salt. "If he can't blackmail you or buy you, he'll just as soon burn you out. He'll kill whoever stands against him. You should tell Mrs Thornford to accept his offer and get out. While she still can."

"Somebody should stop him," Stokes said.

"My pa tried to stop him," she said, picking up the whiskey glass and draining it in one gulp. "So did Captain Thornford. It ain't worth it."

The cowhands outside on the sidewalk were loud, joking and laughing, in high spirits. Whatever business they'd had must have gone well.

"Thanks for the drinks," she said, then, as the six men strode into the saloon, spurs jingling loud enough to be heard over their good-natured chatter and the clump of their boots, she turned to the door, arching her back provocatively.

"Good afternoon, boys," she said, her tone sultry and welcoming. Her eyes narrowed as she surveyed each of them in turn. "Am I right in thinking you just got paid?"

"Why, yes, ma'am," said the oldest of the group, a brawny man with a thick, black beard. "And we've got the afternoon off."

"Have you been working hard?" Bella asked.

"Why, yes," said a willowy thin boy, who looked not much older than Albert, but was probably sixteen or seventeen. "We been driving a herd from Selah. It's been nearly three weeks and we sure could use a drink."

"You must be tired," Bella said.

"Why no, ma'am," said the boy. "We're set to tear it up, even though it's only Monday!"

"What a pity," she said, coquettishly. "I had thought you might feel the need to lie down. I have a very comfortable bed."

The boy's face flushed scarlet. The other cowhands guffawed and slapped him on the back.

"Looks like she's taken a shine to you," one said.

"I can take a shine to each of you," she replied, gently stroking a finger along the man's arm. "Just as long as you've all collected your wages."

The men laughed. Stokes felt his stomach tighten. He had witnessed such scenes before and these men seemed harmless enough, but he was beginning to wish he had not spoken to Bella from Morecambe. He barely knew the girl, but what he had learnt filled him with sorrow. She was a bright and pretty thing, and if not for circumstance, there was no knowing where her life might have taken her. No, it was not circumstance, or fate that had led her here. It was Grant. Grant had killed her family and forced her into selling herself to every dirty cowpoke and miner who rolled into Griffith with money in his pocket.

Stokes turned back to the bar, not wanting to watch any further. He gripped the bar tightly with his left hand and took a long swallow of his drink. It tasted sour on his tongue.

He heard Bella lead the young cowboy up the stairs, while the others positioned themselves along the long bar. They ordered a bottle of whiskey and six glasses.

"You want a drink, mister?" one of them said.

When Stokes didn't respond, the man raised his voice.

"Hey, you there. You thirsty? Want a drink?"

Slowly, Stokes faced the man. It was the wide-shouldered one with the thick beard.

"No, thank you."

"Why, listen to that, boys." The man chuckled. "This here must be the King of England." He peered at the glass on the bar, wrinkling his nose theatrically. "Are you drinking sarsaparilla? Perhaps this ain't the King, boys. Maybe it's the Queen."

Without pausing to think, Stokes found the Colt Lightning in his hand and pointed at the man's face. The colour drained from the cowboy's cheeks.

"Mister," he sputtered, "I was only fooling with you."

"Well," said Stokes, his voice as cold and sour as his drink, "I am no man's fool."

The cowboy's throat bobbed as he swallowed.

"I'm sorry," he said, his voice croaky. "I meant nothing by it. Can I buy you a drink?"

"No, thank you," Stokes repeated.

White came over from the card table and placed his hand on Stokes' shoulder.

"What's the trouble here?" he asked, keeping his voice light. Stokes could smell the whiskey on his breath. It had been a mistake to come in here.

"There's no trouble," he said. "Is there?"

The cowboy shook his head emphatically.

Lowering the revolver, Stokes returned the gun to its holster.

"Good," White said, clapping Stokes on the shoulder. "Then I got time for one more hand."

"No," said Stokes, his tone brooking no argument. "We leave now."

White stared at him for a few seconds, before nodding.

"All right," he said. "I hear you. Time to leave. But I swear, Gabe, you're more ornery than a mule. Next time we go anywhere, don't you dare tell me to be careful. As soon as I turn my back on you, you're in some scrape or another. There was a grizzly in town, I figure you'd poke it just to see what happens."

Chapter Thirty-One

Tanner Strickland let out a whooping cry, as Gabriel Stokes loped into the camp on the high ridge.

"You ride like a regular buckaroo now!"

Stokes grinned, pulling Banner to a halt, then wheeling him around with a touch of the reins and pressure against his flanks. The gelding responded instantly, spinning on the spot as if dancing. Stokes had ridden every day that week and felt more at home in the saddle than ever. The ride up through the pines to the ridge had further lifted his spirits, though he had been in a good mood since the telegram had arrived for Mary Ann the previous afternoon.

A boy from Griffith had ridden out to the ranch with it. Mary Ann had read the short message in silence. Her hands had trembled as she'd handed it to Stokes.

RECEIVED YOUR MESSAGE STOP HAVE GOOD NEWS STOP WILL MEET YOU NOON 30 APRIL AT GRAND HOTEL

It seemed their plan might actually work. Stokes had been sceptical, as had Thomas Rice when Mary Ann had laid it out to him at the picnic. It was simple enough, but relied on good-will from a very influential man, not to mention some luck.

"Sylvester Pennoyer?" Rice had said in a tone of amazement. "You really think the governor will listen to you?"

"I think he will," Mary Ann said. "Mr Pennoyer is a good

man. My father knew him, and John met him a few times when on business in Salem. They were not close, but he liked John. I think he will be sympathetic to what we have to say. I plan to write to him requesting an audience."

"And then?"

"He will be in Griffith for the opening of the station. Mr Stokes and I will present the evidence against Grant then. With the Governor's backing, we can get Grant indicted."

"I'm not so sure," Rice said, frowning. "Perhaps it would be best if I just accepted his offer. John's dead and who knows what else Grant is capable of?"

"At least give us until we can see the Governor," Mary Ann pleaded.

"What if Grant presses me for an answer? He's not a patient man."

"You can tell him you need time to think. Or that you need to discuss the matter with a business associate…"

In the end she had managed to get Rice to agree to that much, but he had not been convinced their plan would bear fruit. The arrival of the telegram had lifted Mary Ann's mood considerably and she was looking forward to telling Rice the good news when they met for their Sunday picnic.

Stokes reined Banner to a halt. There was a pot sitting by a small fire and he could smell the welcoming scent of coffee over the smoke and the earthy aroma of the sheep. It was cool up here on the mountain in the shade of the trees and a cup of coffee would restore him before he headed back down to the JT. Strickland's mare was hobbled nearby beneath the wide canopy of a red cedar. It whinnied a welcome to Banner as Stokes dismounted.

"I thought you were gonna jump right off without stopping," Tanner said, with a wink.

"I only do that for pretty girls," Stokes replied, wondering which of the JT hands had told him about his showy dismount in front of Cora Rice. The truth was he had been tempted to leap from the horse's back while still in motion, such was his ebullient mood, but common sense prevailed. He had been lucky not to injure himself more badly when showing off to the girl, and his leg had recovered well in the week since then. Tanner Strickland and Reuban Van Orman were certainly not worth the risk of further injury.

He led Banner over to the other horse and hobbled him. Some way down the slope the flock of sheep were grazing contentedly. Tooyakeh was lying in the grass close by.

"Well, there ain't no pretty girls here," Tanner said. "If I spend much longer up here, those ewes are gonna start looking mighty attractive."

Stokes pulled a face.

"I have some good news for you then," he said, taking the parcels of bacon and hardtack from his saddlebags and carrying them over to where Van Orman was sitting near the fire. "You're invited to Sunday lunch at the Rices'."

Tanner whooped again, his loud voice startling the horses and making them snort.

"Miss Cora is a darn sight prettier than those ewes, that's for sure," he said.

"That she is," Stokes said, helping himself to coffee. "Though I think your chances there are slim."

"Oh, I know she's sweet on Lenny," Tanner said. "Though God alone knows why when she could have a real man." He straightened his hat, slapped dust from his leather chaps and struck what he imagined to be an elegant pose.

"Perhaps she prefers someone of a softer disposition," said Stokes, sipping his coffee and smiling. "After all, she was not even impressed with a dashing cavalryman like me."

Van Orman looked up from where he was carving a piece of wood.

"Maybe she is looking for a man who does not discuss the merits of bedding ewes."

"Now see here," Tanner said, flushing scarlet. "I was only joshing."

"Many a truth has been stated in jest," said Stokes, with a glance at Van Orman. The older man's eyes twinkled beneath the brim of his hat, but his expression remained impassive.

"Maybe skip the picnic," he said, keeping his eyes on the piece of wood in his hands, "and head to the vaulting house instead. Sounds like you're in need of a girl before you do something you'll regret."

Tanner's face grew dark and Stokes wondered if Van Orman had crossed a line. But then Tanner's expression softened and he looked at both men in turn, shaking his head.

"You know what?" he said. "You're just trying to rile me up, but you're right, you old two-bit-Indian. I've been up here with just your ugly face, your mangy dog and these sheep for company for too long. As soon as I'm done eating Mrs Rice's fine grub, I'm gonna ride into town and rustle up a poke with that girl they got in the Lady Elgin."

"I seen her," Van Orman said, his expression unchanged. "She's a pretty one. Pretty enough perhaps to help you forget all these woolly beauties."

He laughed. Stokes joined in. Strickland shook his head, scowling at first, but unable to keep the smile off his face for long.

"Damn you both," he said, tossing his coffee away, throwing down his tin cup and stalking out of the camp.

Strickland's reaction only made the two older men laugh harder. Stokes chuckled as he drank the last of his coffee.

"Thanks for the coffee," he said. "See you tomorrow."

"Not me," Van Orman said, still whittling at the piece of wood.

"You're not coming?"

"I'll feel better staying up here and watching the sheep with Tooyakeh."

"Lars said he'd be happy to ride up and take a turn."

"Thank him for me, and the Rices too, for the invitation. But tell Lars he can go with everyone else."

"You're sure? You could ride to the Rice ranch and be back here before sundown. It would only be a few hours."

Van Orman looked up at the sky through the pines. He drew in a long breath, as if smelling the air for sign of trouble.

"A lot can happen in a few hours."

There was no answer to that. Stokes' life had been upended too many times for him to contest Van Orman's words.

"Well, if you're sure," he said, moving over to Banner and mounting.

"I'm sure," Van Orman said. "Something is coming. I don't know what, but I can sense it on the wind."

"Sure you don't want Lars to ride up here? Or me? I could stay tonight, if you want."

"No," Van Orman said, his tone severe. "You'd best be getting back to the JT. Lars and you stay close to Mary Ann and the children. There's bad medicine in the breeze."

"I'll ride up with Tanner on Monday. Bring you some of Mrs Rice's food."

Van Orman nodded and went back to his carving. His words had unnerved Stokes. He wasn't sure if it was his imagination, spurred on by Van Orman's prediction of doom, but the air around him felt charged, as if a thunderstorm was brewing.

He rode close to where Strickland was leaning against a tree and looking at the sheep. Leaning down from the saddle, he offered him a cigarillo. Tanner took a cheroot and lit it with a match he produced from a pocket.

"See you tomorrow," he said.

"No hard feelings?"

Strickland laughed.

"I punched cows from Texas to Montana before I ended up watching woollies for Thornford. I can take more than you two can dish out. Believe me."

"Good," Stokes said. "Keep your eyes open."

"I'll set out early and get changed into my Sunday duds at the JT before you all head off to the Rice spread."

"See you then."

Stokes kicked Banner into a trot. Soon they were deep in the shade of the tree canopy, flashes of light filtering through the branches and leaves as they travelled down the side of the mountain. Banner's footing was sure, his gait comfortable and familiar to Stokes after all the hours of riding.

Reaching an outcrop he had discovered on a previous ride, Stokes dismounted and led Banner along the rocky ground. The soil was thin here and the bluff exposed to wind, rain and snow. Several trees had been toppled in a storm the previous winter, leaving a bare escarpment, surrounded by the shattered trunks of fallen trees. From here he could look out at the valley and he took a moment just to stare over the vast expanse of forest and fertile grassland below.

Banner snuffled at his shoulder and Stokes absently patted the gelding's neck. He looked about, piecing together how the trees had come to fall here. Once he spotted the splintered trunk of a huge fir tree, it became clear what had happened. The tree had snapped, perhaps under the weight of heavy snow or strong winds, and then its massive bulk had wrenched several other smaller trees from the ground, shattering some and ripping others out, roots and all. The soil was rocky and thin, only allowing for shallow roots, and the trees had been unable to withstand the force of the larger tree as it had crashed into them. Several root boles were exposed in a jumble of earth and pebbles.

Stokes stared down in the direction of the JT Ranch, but it was obscured from his view by distance and trees. He wondered about what Van Orman had said. Surely it was not possible that the man could sniff out danger on the wind, as he could read tracks on the ground. The air seemed pure enough to Stokes, carrying no scent that he could discern other than the wholesome, loamy smells of the forest.

Still, Van Orman was almost certainly right. Something bad was coming. Even if the meeting with the Governor went well, Grant would not simply roll over. And much of the evidence against the cattleman was circumstantial at best, or merely hearsay. There was no doubt that the man's character was tarnished, but without more concrete proof of crimes being committed by him or on his orders, Stokes was unsure what they would be able to achieve. And everything would be made even more difficult by the fact the Sheriff was in Grant's pocket too.

He hoped Mary Ann's faith in the Governor was not misplaced.

A flock of birds fluttered up from the forest far below and flew away to the east. He tracked their flight, wondering what type of birds they were. Finches or perhaps quails. He imagined looking at them through the lens of the brass telescope he had brought from England. But of course, even if he had the instrument with him, it would have been impossible to follow the flight of the birds. It had proven difficult enough to focus on the cold grey surface of the moon when he had sat with Albert three nights before. It had taken him several minutes to find the moon and then focus the telescope. He had been ready to give up hope, wondering if perhaps the lens or refractor had been damaged in transit, but then the mountains and seas of the rocky satellite had jumped into crystal clear relief and his breath had caught in his throat. It felt as if he could reach out and touch what normally was so small and distant. Albert had loved staring up at the moon and had asked questions incessantly. After a time it became clear that Stokes was unable to answer most of the boy's queries, but Albert was undeterred.

"I'm going to write down everything I can think of," he'd said. "Perhaps Mrs Mullen will know. Or maybe Mr Verne talks about it in his book."

Albert loved the book Stokes had given him and whenever

he had a spare moment, the boy could be found reading studiously.

Stokes smiled to himself, thinking of Albert's irrepressible nature as he watched the flight of the birds until he lost them against the hazy sky. He wondered whether he would ever return the way those birds flew; across the mountains and wide plains of America and then, ever eastward, over the vastness of the Atlantic Ocean. He could not imagine he would ever feel the urge to return to the life he had left behind. If they could be done with Grant he could see himself settling here, perhaps even being happy again. Something he had scarcely thought possible only a month previously.

Staring out into the bright afternoon light he had a brief vision of standing at the door of a timber house, much like the one at the JT Ranch. There were horses in the corral and children playing on the porch. And at his side stood a woman. In the picture conjured by his imagination she looked similar to both Mary Ann and Bella.

He smiled without humour. His mouth was dry and the sudden craving for a drink made his hands tremble.

His shook his head in disbelief at his own foolishness. He had travelled halfway around the world to be rid of his past, but that did not make it simply vanish. He was still married. At the thought of Rebecca, he sighed. He did not wish to picture her. He would rather live out a fantasy in his mind in which he was wed to a forthright Lancashire lass, a strong woman who would bear them sturdy sons and work the land by his side.

Scowling, he yanked Banner's reins, turning the horse back towards the trail. The gelding rolled his eyes at Stokes, unaccustomed at such rough treatment.

"Sorry, boy," he said, stroking the animal's nose, before stepping up into the saddle.

His mood had soured at the thought of Bella. He had laughed with Van Orman and Strickland, but he hated the thought of the girl selling herself. He knew it was foolish. He barely knew the girl, but the thought of her lingered. She had come to this land as a child and the life she now lived was not what she had once hoped for. But she was still young. She could leave that life behind and start anew.

"By God, you really are a fool," he whispered to himself. Banner's ears twitched, listening, but Stokes said nothing further. Touching his heels to the horse's flanks, they set off once more down through the trees towards the JT.

Chapter Thirty-Two

Stokes rode into the ranch just after three in the afternoon. At once he saw a buggy parked in the shade of the barn. The chestnut pony hitched to the vehicle stood three-legged with its head down, dozing in the warm afternoon. There was no sign of anyone else in the yard, the corral or the fields near the house. The door of the building yawned open, showing only darkness within.

A prickle of unease ran down Stokes' spine. Van Orman's words still rang in his mind and he could not shake the idea that something evil might have befallen Mary Ann and the children during his absence. Unbidden, the image of Jane Adams' bloody corpse bobbed up to the surface of his memory. *God, please, not the children.*

Dismounting and hitching Banner to the rail, he stepped warily up onto the porch, his hand resting on the grip of his Colt.

"There you are, Gabriel," Mary Ann called through the open door. "I was beginning to worry."

Relief washed through him like summer rain. All at once he heard Albert and Adelaide playing behind the house. Pincher was barking with them and the sound further brightened his mood. He stepped inside, blinking in the shade of the farmhouse and taking a moment to compose himself.

"Nothing to worry about," he said. "The boys are fine. Tanner will ride down tomorrow."

"Not Reuban?" Mary Ann asked.

"He says he would rather remain with the sheep."

A gruff voice spoke from the back of the room.

"That don't surprise me none," it said.

Stokes peered into the gloom and saw Jed White sitting at the far side of the table.

"Now, now, Jed," Mary Ann admonished. "I'll have no ill word about Reuban spoken in my house."

White grimaced, drained his cup and rose from the table.

"Ladies," he said, moving around the table and pushing past Stokes. He smelt of sweat, old cigarette smoke and sour whiskey.

As Stokes' eyes grew accustomed to the lack of sunlight, he made out the two women sitting at the table across from Mary Ann. He thought of the buggy outside and immediately recalled seeing them when he had ridden past them in Griffith on his first visit to town.

"Gabriel," said Mary Ann, "let me introduce Abigail Mullen and her daughter, Ruby. Ladies, this is Lieutenant Gabriel Stokes."

"At your service," he said, removing his hat and bowing with a flourish. Ruby Mullen smiled openly at him, her eyes shining. Her mother frowned, evidently displeased to see her daughter's reaction to the tall Englishman.

Mary Ann took it all in and smiled at him, raising an eyebrow knowingly as she turned away from the women.

"Would you care for tea?" she asked.

"I can think of nothing better," he lied, thinking how he would much prefer a cool beer.

"Are you working here on the ranch?" Mrs Mullen asked. Her smile was polite, but her tone made it clear to Stokes that she disapproved of his presence. Perhaps she thought it unseemly for him to have arrived so soon after John's death, though that was hardly his fault.

"For the time being," he said. "I do what I can to help."

"And what then?" she asked. "What are your intentions?"

The pitch of the woman's voice needled him.

"My intentions?" he asked.

Mrs Mullen sniffed.

"Your plans, sir," she said, as if he were an imbecile. "For the future."

"Come now, Abigail," said Mary Ann, returning from the kitchen with a fresh kettle of hot water and a cup and saucer for him. "Lieutenant Stokes is welcome to stay here as long as he wishes."

"You come from London?" Ruby said.

Her cheeks were pink, her eyes thoughtful and shining. She must be the same age as Bella, he thought, though there was none of the world-weary strength in this girl's eyes. Her innocence was attractive in its own way, he supposed, and her tone was certainly much more pleasant than her mother's. He smiled at her.

"I lived and worked there for several years, yes."

"Then I cannot imagine you will wish to stay here for long at all, Lieutenant," she said. "It must be so boring for you."

"Actually, I came here hoping for some peace and quiet. So far I've not had much luck on that front. As to how long I'll stay, I can't really say. But I can see why many men come west. It's a beautiful land."

"It's a hard land," said Mrs Mullen.

"Yes, but even the rockiest of terrains produces beautiful flowers. In Afghanistan I saw the most vibrant poppies growing in the mountains. It looked like nothing could ever survive there, and still flowers flourished." He sipped his tea. "Looking around this room, I am reminded of how beauty can be found in the remotest of places."

Mrs Mullen scowled at his obvious flattery. Ruby beamed and looked at him through her lashes. Mary Ann shook her head slightly and drank some tea. He fancied he saw a thin smile playing on her lips.

"Abigail came to ask after Albert and Adelaide," she said.

"She is the school mistress, you see, and Ruby helps her, teaching the youngest ones."

Mrs Mullen was nodding, seemingly pleased that the conversation was moving onto a topic she found more appropriate, and altogether safer.

"Tomorrow," she said, "it will be three weeks since the children's father was killed, God rest Captain Thornford's soul." She paused what she deemed to be a respectful amount of time before continuing. "I think it is high time for the children to return to their classes. It does not do for them to neglect their lessons. Young minds must be constantly moulded. They should not be allowed to dwell on the sorrows of life. It is not healthy." From outside came shrieks of laughter from Adelaide and Albert, followed by Pincher's frantic barking. Mrs Mullen shifted uncomfortably. "I would have spoken to you about this at church," she said with a sniff, "but we have not seen you there of late. I was concerned for you."

Mary Ann ignored the barely veiled jibe. Stokes admired her self-control.

"I'm sure you of all people understand this has been a trying time, Abigail," she said.

Mrs Mullen's lips pressed tightly together.

"Of course, my dear," she said, her tone losing some of its zeal. "You are in mourning. But you should not cut yourself off from the Lord Jesus, and it would do Albert and Adelaide good to return to their routine of school. In a few weeks they will be free to help you around the ranch all summer."

"Thank you for your concern," Mary Ann said stiffly. "I will send them back to school soon enough. When I am ready to do so."

"You know best, I'm sure." Mrs Mullen cocked her head, listening to the hollers and yells of the children frolicking with the dog in the sun. "But it sounds to me as if they are ready for their lessons once more."

Stokes placed his cup and saucer on the table.

"As you say, Mrs Mullen," he said, "the children's mother knows best. There will be plenty of time for schooling. For now, let them enjoy life."

Mrs Mullen looked at him sharply.

"Do you have children, Lieutenant Stokes?"

"I do not."

"Then I would suggest you keep your thoughts to yourself on the subject of how to raise them."

Stokes took a long, calming breath.

"I am sure you are a fine teacher," he said, "and that you wish only the best for the children and Mary Ann, but please do not presume I am not acquainted with grief. I am sure you too have lost loved ones, and we each grieve in our own way. Mary Ann has told you she will send Albert and Adelaide back to school soon. As she is their mother, there should be nothing more to say on the matter."

He met her furious gaze until she looked away. Ruby was grinning, but she forced a neutral expression before her mother could notice. Mary Ann was embarrassed and tried to smooth Mrs Mullen's ruffled feathers. She made small talk for a few minutes, but the mood was cool now and soon the school-mistress stood and thanked her hostess for tea. She nodded at Stokes, who rose and offered her a formal bow.

"A pleasure, I'm sure," Mrs Mullen said.

"The pleasure was all mine," Stokes replied. Ruby's smile grew wider.

"I'll send them to school soon," Mary Ann said, as the Mullens climbed into the buggy.

"Well, I have said my piece, dear," Mrs Mullen replied. "You know what I think is best."

"I do. And thank you again for visiting."

Ruby Mullen waved as the pony pulled the buggy away. Mary Ann waved back.

"And there I was thinking you were a charming English gentleman," she said.

"My charm may have waned somewhat of late, I'm afraid," Stokes said, raising his hand in response to Ruby.

"I'm not so sure," Mary Ann said. "It seems to work on naive girls. Then again, I seem to recall Cora was none too impressed with you."

"But she likes Lenny," he said, with a small smile, "so I think we can discount her sense of taste."

Chapter Thirty-Three

Sunday dawned bright and clear. The sun was still low in the sky when Tanner Strickland rode down from the high ridge and reported that the night had been peaceful and everything was quiet when he'd left Van Orman.

"I thought I heard some shooting just after dawn," he said, "but it was a ways off. Sounded like it came from the south."

Old Amos scratched his scraggly beard.

"Sound has a funny way of bouncing about in the hills. Might've come from anywhere. Someone hunting mule deer or elk maybe?"

Strickland pondered this.

"Maybe," he said. He did not seem convinced. "Too many shots for that though, I reckon. Perhaps some cowboys were letting off steam in town."

"That's a mighty long way for the sound to travel."

They all agreed about that, but none of them was any the wiser about where the shooting might have come from, so they got themselves ready for the picnic, spit-polishing their boots, stropping razors to get an edge, carrying pails of cold water from the pump. The frenzy of activity reminded Stokes of his time in the Hussars when the regiment was called to the parade ground for inspection. Some of the hands of the JT though, like Amos Willard and Jed White, would never have passed muster in a military brigade. Neither man made much of an effort, leaving their whiskers bristling and not bothering to change out of the clothes they'd worn the previous day. At least

251

they had both risen without complaint. They had been up late the night before drinking a good quantity of White's whiskey supply.

Of all the hands, Strickland was the most fastidious about his appearance. He cleaned himself up and changed into his Sunday best, a dark broadcloth suit with a starched shirt, thin tie with tie pin and black, polished boots. The only thing that was out of place was his hat, which was the same brown, dusty thing he wore while tending sheep or punching cows.

"By Josh and by Joan," said Amos on seeing the young man stepping out of the bunk house in his fresh attire, his cheeks freshly shaved and his hair oiled and combed. "You forgot to buy a new hat. What's the matter, wages not enough to cover pomade and a John B.?"

Strickland flushed.

"It takes me a long time to train a hat to my head proper," he said. "I've had this one nigh on three years and I just about got it sitting right. I ain't about to start with a new one now."

The children were in their best clothes too and each wore smart shoes when they came out of the house, followed by Mary Ann. She wore a plain black dress that was buttoned up to the neck. A small bonnet held her hair in place. Despite the sombre nature of her garb, there was no missing the fact that she was a beautiful woman. When she walked down the steps from the porch, the ranch hands, who had been chatting and ribbing each other about their clothes, fell silent.

Stokes was the first to react. He hurried forward and offered his arm.

"Let me escort you to your carriage, ma'am," he said.

"Thank you, kind sir," she replied with a small curtsy, taking his arm.

Adelaide giggled.

"We don't have a carriage," she said. "Only a wagon."

"With you and your mother aboard," Stokes said, "I feel it deserves to be called a carriage. Don't you?"

"Yes," she said, laughing while Albert rolled his eyes. "Can I take your arm too?"

"Of course," he said, "it would be my utmost pleasure."

In this fashion they made their way to the wagon, while the hands mounted up.

"Lars," Mary Ann said, "could you fetch the basket that's on the table, please?"

Without a word, Lars hurried to obey, returning with a large wicker basket covered in a blue and white cloth. He placed it in the wagon beside Mary Ann and the children. Lenny climbed up with them too.

"Thank you, Lars," Mary Ann said, offering the blond man a smile that lit up her face.

Amos rode up front and whistled long and loud.

"All aboard," he called out, making the children giggle. "Next stop, Picnicville."

It was well over an hour's ride to the Rices' and they were in high spirits, looking forward to the socialising and Mrs Rice's famously generous spread. Stokes looked at Strickland and McCloskey. Both were as clean and well turned out as he had ever seen them and he smiled at the power a pretty girl has over men.

The day was warm and close. It was not too bad while they travelled in the shade of the woodland, but when they passed out from beneath the trees and onto the open grassland of the lower hills to the south of the JT, the sun made them sweat and look forward to a cold drink. Clouds had begun to form over the hills and mountains as they often did as the days warmed. The clouds were white and fluffy, with no risk of rain.

Stokes noticed a darker cloud in the south that spoke of a possible downfall. How annoying it would be if the picnic were spoiled by rain. He squinted into the distance. Surely the solitary cloud could not bear rain.

He felt suddenly cold, as if a chill wind had blown down from the mountains despite the warmth of the day. He shuddered in realisation at the same moment that Jed White called out. That was no cloud.

"Smoke," White said.

"I got a bad feeling about this," Lars said.

Stokes had the same feeling, as if a fist was clenching around his heart.

"Let's have a look," he said.

White, Lars and Strickland were already spurring forward. Stokes turned to the wagon.

"If you hear gunshots," he said to Amos, "don't come anywhere near. We'll ride back to you when it's safe."

Amos nodded. His face was pale. He was old enough to have seen several similar columns of smoke in his day. It never boded well.

"What about me?" Lenny asked.

"Stay here. Guard Mary Ann and the children."

"But what about Cora?" His voice cracked. Fear twisted his face. Tears were not far away, such was his anxiety.

"I'll find her," Stokes said. "Stay here and help Amos guard. Have you got a gun?"

McCloskey patted the Colt on his hip and nodded.

"Good. We'll be back soon."

"What do you think it is?" Mary Ann asked.

He hesitated.

"I don't know," he said, though he had a good idea. He could see from her expression she knew well enough what they could expect to find when they rode closer to the smoke coming from the direction of the Rice Ranch.

Chapter Thirty-Four

The ranch buildings were still burning when the men from the JT rode over the rise. The smell of it was strong on the light breeze. The aroma of burnt flesh was heavy in the smoke. It brought back terrible memories of Afghanistan to Stokes. He hoped the smell was from the animals that had been in the barn when it went up. It had collapsed now, flame-licked timbers jutting into the sky.

The main house was a charred ruin. Flames still danced along tumbled beams and one blackened stone wall remained standing, the chimney protruding incongruously from the fire and smoke.

Three horses lay dead in the yard between the smouldering buildings.

A few chickens pecked in a nearby field and a couple of pigs rooted along the mud down by a small stream that ran close to the house. Other than the animals and the wafting smoke there was no sign of movement.

"No way that happened by accident," White said. When nobody answered, he said, "The barn's a good ways from the house. Unlikely the fire crossed from one to the other."

"But not impossible," Stokes said. "Sparks can fly a long way and settle on a roof."

"I guess," White said. "But if that had happened, figure we'd see the Rices and the ranch hands outside with buckets. And those horses look to have been shot."

"You think the Rices are dead?" asked Strickland. There was a tremble in his voice as if he was going to weep. It made him sound like a boy. Stokes could not blame him.

"Don't know," White said. "Only one way to find out."

He nudged his horse forward and, warily, rolling her eyes, his mare carried him down the slope towards what was left of the ranch.

Reluctantly, Stokes touched his heels to Banner's flanks and followed. Pale-faced and grim, Lars Giblin and Tanner Strickland headed down the rise too.

They hadn't gone far when they saw the first body.

"Over there," Lars said, pointing.

Two booted feet were sticking out from behind a water trough.

The smoke was thicker here, drifting across the open ground as the breeze picked up. The horses shook their heads and baulked. The sweet smell of cooking meat clogged the back of Stokes' throat, threatening to make him gag. Strickland's eyes were wide, his face as white as milk.

"We should go on on foot," Stokes said. "The horses are nervous. Tanner, take the mounts out of the smoke and watch them."

Lars and White glanced at Stokes, then at Strickland. Without a word, they dismounted and handed their reins to Tanner.

"Holler if you need me," he said, leading the horses away.

"We will," Stokes said. Then, remembering what he had told Amos, he pulled out his Colt Lightning. "Going to warn them not to come down here. The children shouldn't see this."

He fired three shots into the air. He ejected the three spent shells, letting them fall to the ground. He reloaded with cartridges from his pocket. Some way off, he noticed the gleam of several brass cartridge casings in the dust.

"The shooting Tanner heard?" he asked, nodding at the brass.

"Reckon so," said White, walking slowly towards the trough and the partially concealed body behind it. The wooden trough was riddled with bullet holes and the water had leaked out from the splintered timber, soaking the earth beneath it. It was close to the barn, but the fire had not touched it. The air was hot here though, making it uncomfortable to get close. But they could get near enough to see who the man was. He wore long-sleeved underwear that was dark with blood. Some of his hair had been singed away and half his face had blistered in the heat of the conflagration, but he was easily recognisable as Mayfield Redin, the Rices' foreman.

Lars spat.

"Redin was a good man," he said.

"Least he died with his boots on," White said.

Neither Stokes nor Lars responded to that.

"Don't touch him," Stokes said.

White shrugged. Leaving Redin's corpse where it was, they moved away from the heat of the barn and continued their search of the property.

"Recognise any of those horses?" White asked.

Lars gave them a cursory glance.

"Don't think I ever saw that paint before. That bald-faced bay neither. There's no mistaking that one though. Biggest horse in the whole valley. That's Goliath. Mr Rice's horse."

As they looked, the massive stallion lifted its head from the ground and moaned in pain. Stokes could see at least three bullet wounds in its side. Its chest heaved and shuddered. Its flank was slick with blood.

"Jesus!" Lars said, taking a step back.

It was a wonder the animal yet lived. And it was clear to all of them it would be dead soon. White drew one of his Remingtons and put a bullet in Goliath's head. He did it so quickly that Stokes had no time to look away. The horse tensed for a second, then was still.

Ejecting the cartridge and reloading the chamber without

257

looking at his hands, White moved closer to the two smaller horses. These were both unmoving.

"Shod, but no brands," he said.

They found Warnock's body down by the stream. The pigs were already snuffling around at the blood on the ground.

"Git! Git!" shouted Lars, kicking at the hogs and sending them away from the corpse.

Acid rose in the back of Stokes' throat. If they had arrived an hour later, the pigs would have been well on their way to consuming Warnock. The poor ranch hand had been shot in the forehead. The back of his skull had a saucer-sized hole in it. His hat lay in the dust nearby. It was strangely clean so near the bloody remains of its owner. Apart from his gun belt and his boots, Warnock, like Redin, was only dressed in a faded red flannel union suit undergarment.

Several brass shell casings lay close to Warnock's corpse. Lars poked them with the toe of his boot.

"Looks like he put up a good fight. Hope he got some of the sons of bitches who did this," he said.

"Maybe he did," White said. "Maybe he didn't. Hard to say. I ain't that good at reading sign." If Warnock and Redin had hit any of their attackers, they had been carried away by their accomplices. Apart from the horses, there were no other bodies, at least not out in the open. None of the men mentioned it, but they all knew what the cloying smell in the smoke meant, and what they would find when the fires died down.

Stokes walked away from the shimmering heat of the burning buildings, breathing deeply of the fresh, clean air once he was some distance from the fires. Lars stood as if rooted in the yard. His eyes flicked this way and that, never settling on any one thing for long. White placed a hand on his shoulder and turned him away, leading him with surprising gentleness after Stokes.

"Tanner," Stokes said, "ride back to the wagon and tell them not to come down here." He used the tone of command he had learnt in the Hussars and he was pleased to see Strickland

258

respond to it well. He straightened and his eyes cleared, losing some of the shock. "Have Amos take Mary Ann and the children back to the JT. Tell Lenny to ride up to the high ridge as fast as he can and to take a horse for Reuban too."

"Reuban don't like to ride," Tanner said.

"I don't care what he likes. Tell Lenny to get Reuban and to bring him back as fast as he can. Then you ride for Griffith and fetch Sheriff Bannon."

"What in the Sam Hill do we need Bannon and Van Orman for?" White said.

"We need to do this by the book," Stokes said. "Whatever we think about Bannon, he has to see this. He has to make a report."

White removed his hat and cuffed at the sweat on his brow.

"But there are no witnesses," he said. "Anyone could have done this. That's what he'll say."

"Maybe," Stokes replied. "That's why we need Van Orman. He can read the tracks of the men who did this. With any luck he'll recognise their prints."

"God damn it," said White, rolling a cigarette. "We know who done this."

"We think we know," Stokes said. "And believe me when I say I want to find whoever did this and bring them to justice. But we need proof."

"What more proof do you need than that?" White swept an arm to encompass the burning buildings and the scattered corpses of animals and men. "Grant told Rice to leave a week ago. And now—" His voice broke. He lit his cigarette and took a drag. "Those poor children."

Stokes took the reins from the horses. Strickland hesitated.

"You think Cora..." His voice was small and uncertain.

"Don't think about that now," snapped Stokes. He could not allow panic to set in. "Go on, Tanner," he said. "No time to waste now. Send Lenny for Reuban and then bring the Sheriff here. And don't let Bannon fob you off. Get him here."

Strickland swung up into his saddle. "You can count on me," he said. His horse, agitated by the smoke and smell of blood on the air, whinnied and bucked for a few seconds, but Strickland clung on, turning the mount a couple of times on the spot until he had it fully under control and then, without another word, he touched heels to the horse's sides and sped off up the rise.

"It can't be," Lars said in a strange voice. Something about his tone drew Stokes' attention. "It can't be," Lars said again. "Jesus, Mary and Joseph," he said in a great rush of breath, "can it be?"

Before Stokes understood Lars' meaning, the burly man began to sprint down the slope back towards the smoking remnants of the ranch.

"By God," White said, watching Lars run.

Stokes followed White's gaze and watched where Lars was running. He could scarcely believe what he saw. Stepping out from the smoking remains of the house came the youngest of the Rice girls, Florence.

Her white night dress was bright against the blackened timbers and dark smoke of her home. Even from that distance Stokes could see that the girl's eyes were wide and staring. Lars reached her and scooped her up into his arms.

"Well, I'll be damned," said White. "Looks like we might have a witness after all."

Chapter Thirty-Five

Florence clung to Lars Giblin's neck. When he started walking towards them, she began wailing. He halted, unsure what to do.

"What is it, child?" he asked, his voice soft.

She whimpered. He started to walk back to Stokes and White, but Florence grew more agitated. She did not relinquish her hold on his neck, but she wriggled and squirmed and made a mewling sound.

"Tell me, child," he said. "What is it?"

She had become so distraught when he moved that he stood still and beckoned to the other two men.

"She don't want me to leave," he called.

"She's just a child," grumbled White, "why don't he just bring her up here."

But they could hear the girl's pitiful crying and see that Lars was stuck, held fast by uncertainty and compassion for Florence and her obvious distress. Quickly tying the horses to a red alder tree, they walked down towards Giblin and the girl.

"This ain't no place for the girl," said White when they were close. "Come on. Let me take her."

But when he reached for her she howled and clutched Lars even more tightly.

"Where did she come from?" Stokes asked. Her nightdress was barely smudged with soot and dust and she had seemed to emerge from the burning house itself. There was no way anyone could have survived inside that inferno.

Edging closer, he looked for a sign of where she might have appeared from. All he saw were the cracked and charred remains of timbers and the blackened stonework of the wall and chimney. The roof must have been made of wooden shingles for it had been consumed entirely. The heat from the house was still unbearable and it held him away with an invisible barrier he could not cross. That Florence might have come from there was impossible.

"Did you see where she came from?" he asked.

"Looked like she stepped out of the house," Lars said, "but she couldn't have. Nothing could live in that."

Florence let out a moaning sound. Lars stroked her back to comfort her.

"There, there, child," he cooed in a sing-song voice. "I'm sorry. Let's go away from here."

She shook her head violently and howled like an animal.

"I see where she came from," said White, who had been moving around and looking at the wreckage from different angles.

"You do?"

"Yeah, look." He pointed to a spot close to the house. "The grass on the sod has all burnt off, but, there, you can see the door."

"The root cellar," Lars said.

White nodded. "The root cellar."

Stokes saw now what they were referring to. A door opened into what had at first just appeared to be a mound of earth, partially obscured by the smoke and debris of the house. The door stood ajar. White and Stokes had the same thought at the same time and hurried forward side by side.

"Hello," Stokes called out. "Anyone in there?"

There was no answer. White didn't wait for one anyway,

but Stokes noticed that he pulled one of his pistols out before he stepped into the dark. Drawing his own Colt, Stokes went in behind him.

The interior of the cellar was much cooler than the fire-heated air beside the burning house. Stokes shivered as the sweat on his back chilled suddenly. Blinking against the darkness, he squinted to see into the shadows. The place was redolent of earth and vegetation. Shelves lined the walls of what was essentially a man-made cave, dug into the ground and covered with a thick roof of sod.

A whimper from the gloom drew his gaze. Holstering his gun, White lowered himself down beside a pale shape on the earth floor. White's sharp intake of breath made Stokes wary of what he had found. He moved nearer.

His eyes had grown accustomed to the darkness now, and there was enough light pooling in from the doorway that he could make out the figure that lay huddled between the shelves of potatoes and beets.

"Cora?" Stokes croaked. He could see enough of her slender form and the shape of her face to know this was the eldest Rice girl, but she was no longer the pretty, vivacious young woman of the week before. Her cotton nightdress was blackened and part of it had burnt away completely, exposing legs that were raw and red from the fire. Her feet and calves were so badly burnt they resembled something a butcher would throw to a dog. Her hands were charred too, and when she turned towards the sound of his voice he saw that the left side of her face was dreadfully disfigured. How she had managed to walk to the root cellar, he could not imagine.

"Who did this?" Stokes said. "Who did this, Cora?"

She shook her head, whimpering with the pain that racked her body.

"Florence?" she said, her voice rasping.

"Florence is safe," White said. "You're safe too now."

"Who did this?" Stokes asked again. If they could get a description of the men who had committed this atrocity, they would be able to seal Grant's fate once and for all.

"I... I... I..." she stuttered. She was trembling uncontrollably. "I don't know. Wore masks."

"Masks?" Stokes asked.

"Hoods." A great convulsive sob gripped her. "Where's Elsa? Where is she? Are Ma and Pa..." Her voice trailed off. Stokes and White looked away. Perhaps she could see the answer in their faces, or maybe she already knew what had happened to her family.

"Stokes," White growled. "Enough of your questioning. Now's not the time. This girl needs a doctor, not a detective."

"You're right," Stokes said. "Forgive me. I'll go fetch the wagon. They can't have gone far."

Hurrying back out into the sunlight, the smoke-stink of the fire hit him again like a slap.

"Cora's in there," he said to Lars.

"She all right?" Giblin asked.

"She needs a doctor. I'm going for the wagon so we can get her to town."

He didn't wait for a reply. Sprinting up the slope to where the horses were tethered, he untied Banner, mounted and galloped northward.

As he rode, his mind turned over what he had seen, piecing together what must have occurred at the ranch. He recalled Redin and Warnock and knew their sightless eyes and pallid features would join those of other corpses that plagued his dreams. But worse than the dead men, he knew Cora's scarred face and burnt limbs would take up residence in his nightmares alongside Jane Adams' tiny defiled body.

Banner was fast, and more than happy to run away from the smoke and the smell of death. It was not long before Stokes saw the wagon. He called out as he approached, but Mary Ann and the children had already turned towards him at the sound of Banner's hoof beats.

"We need the wagon after all," he said. "We've found Cora and Florence. They're alive."

"Thank the Lord," said Mary Ann. "How are they?"

"Florence seems to be unhurt," he said. "Cora needs a doctor. You'd best head straight into town once we have got her on the wagon."

"What about Elsa?" Albert said. "You seen her?"

Stokes hesitated.

"I haven't seen her, Albert," he said.

"Maybe they took her," Albert said.

"Maybe. Reuban will be able to tell us when he looks at the sign. Where's Lenny?" He only then realised the young man wasn't on the wagon.

"The poor boy needed to do something," Mary Ann said. "He was mad with worry. Tanner took him on his horse. They're going to ride back to the ranch and change horses there. Then he'll ride up to get Reuban."

Stokes nodded.

"Good. Best Tanner and Lenny aren't here."

"How bad is she?" Mary Ann asked.

Stokes met her gaze, his expression grave.

"Bad enough," he said, pulling Banner's head back towards the smoke on the horizon.

Chapter Thirty-Six

The flames died out in the long afternoon, but smoke still drifted up from the shattered remains of the ranch buildings. After Amos and Mary Ann came back with the wagon and took the girls away, there was little to do. White wanted to ride to the Cabin Creek Ranch immediately, but Stokes had convinced him otherwise.

"We can't be sure this was Grant," he said, "but even if we knew for certain, what would it gain for you to ride into his ranch and get yourself killed?"

"Ain't planning on getting killed," White said.

"I suppose that is what every man who has ever lost a fight has told himself."

"Every man ain't me."

Lars said little, but his face was ashen. When he handed Florence to Mary Ann, the girl howled. The sound seemed to hurt Lars like a blow. They could hear the little girl's crying for a long time after the wagon had crested the rise.

Stokes could not put the sight of Cora out of his mind. She had been nearly mad with pain, shivering and weeping pitiably as they carried her as carefully as they could out of the root cellar and lifted her into the wagon. The memory of it filled Stokes with bitter rage.

"I cannot believe the law means nothing here," Stokes said.

"Look around," replied White. "How much value you reckon the law has out here?"

"Perhaps the time will come when we'll need to take

266

matters into our own hands," Stokes conceded. He could scarcely believe his own words. But such crimes could not be left unpunished. "One way or another, whoever did this is going to pay."

"We agree on something at last," White said.

Lars nodded. The three of them smoked in silence for a time, each lost in his own thoughts.

As the afternoon wore on, White proposed moving Redin's and Warnock's bodies, but Stokes was adamant that they must be left as they were until the Sheriff and Van Orman had a chance to see where they had fallen.

The pigs had made their way back down to the creek and looked eager to start eating Warnock's corpse. White pulled out a pistol and was going to shoot the animals, but Stokes put a hand on his arm.

"Those girls don't own much," he said. "Are you going to kill their pigs when we could just as easily pen them?"

"Just as easily?" White said, shaking his head. "It's clear you ain't never tried catching a hog."

"Gabriel is right," Giblin said. "They ain't ours to kill. All they are doing is being hogs."

There was a small area with a muddy wallow that seemed to be where the pigs had been housed, but part of the fence had been knocked down, perhaps in the fighting that morning. Stokes and Giblin fixed the fence as best they could. White refused to help.

"Said I wouldn't shoot 'em. I ain't building no fence for them shoats."

They proved as difficult to drive up to the pen as White had said. Stokes and Giblin tried in vain to direct them to the fenced area, but the hogs were too clever and evaded them. In the end Lars mounted up and roped each of them in turn, dragging them squealing into the enclosure.

The shadows were long on the ground by then, the sun touching the peaks in the west. The afternoon was warm and both Stokes and Giblin were sweaty and irritable after wrestling with the pigs while White looked on.

Stokes gazed up the slope and saw a group of riders approaching. It was Sheriff Bannon, accompanied by Deputy Stockman and five other men Stokes had not seen before. They were all well mounted, carried Winchesters and wore revolvers on their hips and badges on their chests. One of the men led a pack mule.

"You took your sweet time, Bannon," said White. "Needed to finish your Sunday lunch?"

Sheriff Bannon dismounted. He ignored White, though his cheeks flushed red and his brow wrinkled as if he'd smelt something bad.

"We spoke to Mrs Thornford on the way here," Bannon said. "Hell of a thing." He surveyed the smouldering remains of the ranch. "Hell of a thing," he repeated. "Mrs Thornford said you spoke to the older of the girls. What did she say?"

"You said you spoke to them," White replied insolently. "What did she tell you?"

"She didn't tell me nothing, Jed," Bannon said with a sigh. "The poor girl was feverish and couldn't speak." He stared down at the destruction of Cora's home. "I wouldn't be surprised if she didn't last till tomorrow."

"Don't you say such a thing," Giblin said. Stokes thought Lars might draw his pistol and shoot the Sheriff where he stood, such was the fury on his face.

"I didn't mean nothing by it," Bannon said quickly. "I pray the girl gets better. Of course I do. But we've ridden hard to get here and all I want are straight answers. Not Jed's horse shit."

"Don't mind him," Stokes said. "It's been a long day for us too, Sheriff, as I'm sure you can imagine. A sad, long and hot day. With nothing but water from the creek to drink."

Bannon snorted, perhaps amused to think of White's

discomfort at not being able to drink anything stronger than water. But his demeanour softened somewhat.

"Well," he asked Stokes, "what did the girl say?"

"We didn't get a lot out of her," Stokes said. "Just that the men who did this wore hoods over their faces."

"So she couldn't identify any of them?"

"Perhaps when she feels better she might be able to tell us more. Maybe she'll remember something about their clothes. Their mounts, their saddles and bridles."

"I doubt a judge would hang a man because a girl thinks she saw his saddle. What about those horses?" He gestured towards the dead horses. They were thick with flies now. In the sky high above them circled vultures.

"The big one is Rice's horse," Stokes said. "The other two none of us recognise. They're shod, but unbranded. The men that did this stripped their saddles and carried them away with them, along with any of their own who were wounded or killed. Seems they were not as sure as you about the identifying qualities of horse tack."

"Or they just liked their saddles," said Deputy Stockman. He was chewing a plug of tobacco. Leaning over in the saddle, he spat a stream of brown juice into the dust.

"You think it likely some of 'em were shot?" Bannon asked.

"More likely than not," White said. "Redin and Warnock look to have put up a fight. Both of 'em were men to ride the range with. They had sand. Reckon they might have evened the score some before they cashed in their chips."

Deputy Stockman slid down from the saddle, throwing his reins to one of the other men.

"That them there?" he asked, pointing to the crumpled shape of Redin's body where it still lay behind the shattered water trough.

"That's Redin," White said. "Warnock's down by the stream."

Bannon wheeled on White.

"What in tarnation are they doing there?" he said. "You been messing about with the hogs and you didn't think to see to the dead?"

Bannon was furious, but his anger appeared to amuse White. He had been saying much the same for most of the afternoon, but now he stared Bannon down, waiting until the big man regained his composure.

"We thought it would be a good idea for you law enforcement boys to see how they fell. Easier for you to picture what happened if we left the... What did you call it, Stokes?"

"The scene of the crime."

"Yeah," said White. "If we left the scene of the crime untouched."

Bannon glowered first at White then Stokes. He looked as though he would say more, but after a few seconds he thought better of it.

"Show me what we got then," he said.

"You'll have to wait for a while yet, I'm afraid," Stokes said.

"Wait? What for? You been waiting all day and we been riding all day. It will be dark soon and it's a ways back to town."

"You said yourself that the children's testimony is unlikely to bear fruit. The men who did this wore masks. They rode unbranded horses and even took away their saddles from the animals they lost."

"I know all that," said Bannon. "So why can't we go and look at the bodies?"

"There might yet be a way of identifying the murderers."

Bannon frowned.

"And just how do you propose to do that?"

"I don't," Stokes said. "But Reuban Van Orman might."

"What in tarnation has that half breed got to do with any of this?"

"He can read sign better than anyone, or so I've been told."

Bannon hitched up his belt and grunted.

"I've heard that said too, but he ain't here. Even if he was, who would listen to a damn redskin like him?"

"I'd listen," replied Stokes. "I would hear what Van Orman can read in those tracks. Perhaps he can tell us who the men were who rode in here and killed Mr and Mrs Rice, Redin and Warnock and at least one of their daughters. Unless they took Elsa away with them."

That idea gave Bannon pause.

"You think they might have taken her?" he asked.

"I don't know," Stokes said. "I can't read sign like an Indian. But she's either in there," he pointed to the smoking remnants of the ranch house, "or they took her. Either way I want to hear what Van Orman has to say on the matter, and having us walking all over the tracks isn't going to help him."

Bannon looked at Stockman, who shrugged. The mounted deputies were grim-faced, but none of them offered an opinion.

"God damn it," Bannon said at last. "I ain't waiting for that breed."

Without seeming to move, Jed White's hands were full of Remington revolvers. One was pointed towards Bannon and Stockman, the other was aimed in the direction of the riders. How White had pulled the guns and cocked them so quickly Stokes could not imagine.

"We've waited this long," White said. "Figure it won't hurt to wait a while longer."

"Damn you, Jed," Bannon said. "I'm the sheriff. You ain't gonna shoot me."

"That may be your firm belief, Sheriff," White said. "You ready to test it? You a gambling man, Bannon? Not sure I'd take those odds."

"You can't shoot all of us," Stockman said.

White twitched the muzzle of his left hand revolver to point at Stockman's face.

"Maybe I can," White said, "maybe I can't. But I sure as hell can shoot you, Stockman."

Bannon's face was crimson. Sweat beaded on his forehead and trickled down his nose.

"You would pull a gun on the legally appointed sheriff and his deputies over a fucking redskin-loving son of a whore like Van Orman?"

"Don't like Van Orman any more than you do," White said. "Matter of fact, I despise the son of a bitch."

"Then why do this, Jed? Has a day without whiskey made you mad? You'd be willing to swing over this?"

"Could use a drink," White said, a ghost of a smile on his lips, "that's for sure. But it ain't nothing to do with that."

"Then why?" Bannon shouted. The horses shied and stamped. "Why bring us out here only to pull your shooting irons on us?"

Jedediah White smiled without humour.

"If it was up to me," he said, "you wouldn't be here and those who did this would be dead. But Mr Stokes, tender heart that he is, thought the law should be called, so you're here. And we're gonna wait for Van Orman."

"But you don't even like the man."

"No, I do not. But I can't deny the man can track."

"You'd listen to that breed?"

"I'd listen to the devil himself if he'd tell me who did this."

And so they waited. Half an hour passed and Bannon tried a few more times to convince White to let them down into the ranch, but White just shook his head. The riders dismounted and grumbled quietly to each other, flicking angry furtive glances at Jed White and the Englishman who seemed to be at the centre of all the trouble in and around town of late.

"Was that absolutely necessary?" Stokes whispered to White when the sheriff and his deputies had withdrawn a little distance from them.

White finished rolling a couple of cigarettes. He handed one to Stokes.

"Maybe it was, maybe it wasn't," he said, striking a lucifer and holding the flame out to Stokes. "But once I make a decision, I don't like to back down, especially not to the likes of that fat bastard Bannon." He puffed his own cigarette to life, then shook out the flame and tossed the match away. "You'd better pray that breed arrives before it gets too dark to see."

Van Orman and Lenny McCloskey rode down the slope towards them a short while later. Their mounts were trembling and stumbling, lathered in sweat and blowing hard. Stokes thought there was a good chance the animals might be ruined after that day's long ride.

McCloskey was ashen-faced as he saw the devastation.

"Where's Cora?" he said. His eyes were wild.

"She's in town with the doc," White said.

McCloskey tugged at his horse's head, turning it around, ready to ride straight for Griffith. White stepped in close and caught hold of his bridle.

"You ride that horse any further, it'll collapse under you before you get to town."

"Then someone give me a fresh horse!" McCloskey yelled, his voice cracking.

"Come down off the horse, Lenny," Giblin said. "Cora's in good hands. We'll get you into town just as soon as you've had something to eat."

Reluctantly, the young man slid from the saddle. Van Orman ignored Lenny and slipped a leg over his horse's pommel and dismounted lightly. His moccasined feet made no sound. He glanced up at the sky. It was a dark blue in the east and molten bronze in the west, as if another ranch burnt just behind the hills.

"It will be dark soon," Van Orman said.

"Christ," said Bannon, "that's the wisdom we've been waiting for? We can all see it'll be dark soon, you heathen."

"The sun is low. Good for seeing tracks. But it won't last long." Van Orman turned his back on the sheriff. "You all walked down there?" he asked Stokes.

"When we arrived first thing. The three of us," he indicated White and Giblin. "Tanner too. And we had to fix that fence and rope the pigs. But we've kept everyone else out since then."

"Good," Van Orman said. "Stay behind me."

Without waiting for a reply, he walked down the slope, pausing every now and then to survey the ground.

Darkness was closing around them when Van Orman was satisfied he had seen enough. Bannon, Stockman and the other deputies followed several paces behind him as he moved about the dusty ground. They grumbled at how long he was taking, but they didn't put much effort into their complaining. Now that Van Orman was there, the men from town seemed as keen as Stokes and White to allow the tracker to do his job.

Giblin and McCloskey were still up by the red alder with the horses. Lenny had his head in his hands. Lars sat close beside him.

"Well," said Bannon, when Van Orman had finished, "can you tell us what happened here?"

"I can," Van Orman said. He walked back towards the horses.

"Well, are you gonna?" Bannon hurried after him. Behind them, the deputies were rolling the bodies in canvas paulins they had brought from Griffith for the purpose.

Reaching his horse, Van Orman took a canteen of water from the saddle and drank. Then he began unbuckling the cinch.

"Now see here, you heathen bastard," Bannon said.

Van Orman pulled the saddle off the horse's back, carried it a few paces and dropped it in the dust.

"There were eight men," he said, beginning to rub down the horse with its saddle blanket. "All mounted. Two got shot. One badly. Fell from his horse. Lots of blood."

"And the girl?" White asked. "Did they take her?"

Van Orman did not look up from what he was doing. He shook his head.

"You're sure?"

Van Orman nodded.

"You can tell all that from the sign?" Stockman asked.

"I can tell about the riders. The ground is dusty. Easy to read, even after they walked all over the place."

"What about the girl?" Bannon asked. "Can you see from the tracks they weren't carrying extra weight?"

"Two of the horses were riding double on the way out. Those tracks are deeper. Easy to read. But the girl is light, too light to see in the horse footprints."

"So how do you know they didn't take her?" snarled Stockman.

Van Orman turned and stared at Stockman until the deputy looked away.

"Because she's dead," Van Orman said. "Down by the creek."

Chapter Thirty-Seven

Stokes stared down at Elsa's tiny body. The hogs had been at her. They'd dragged her into the muddy water and chewed at her a while, covering her in slimy muck, which was why they hadn't noticed her before. Taking a deep breath, Stokes dropped down beside the child and rolled her over. She was stiff. He shuddered at the cold, wet touch of her skin. Her nightgown was dark from blood and muck, her eyes staring. He shut his eyes for a couple of seconds, holding back the screams of anguish he could feel building within him.

Opening his eyes again, he checked the girl for signs of injury.

"I can't see what killed her," he said, keeping his tone flat. The men stood around him, casting their shadows into the already gloomy creek bed.

"The poor thing is covered in blood," whispered Bannon. Like all the other men, his face was pale in the dusk.

"Some of that is from after she was killed. The pigs and the vultures."

Van Orman had noticed the birds first. The men had been intent on keeping the carrion birds away from Redin and Warnock. They hadn't noticed them settling further down the stream.

Stokes completed his assessment of the body. The girl's feet were bare. They were scratched and bleeding, but didn't seem to have been touched by the animals.

"Is there another sheet, or a blanket," he said. "I would like to cover her."

One of the deputies, a serious-looking man by the name of Seb Mooney, hurried to fetch a canvas paulin and handed it to Stokes. He draped it gently over Elsa, letting out a shuddering breath when it covered the child's face. He did not wish to look at those accusing eyes any longer, but he knew they would return to him in his sleep.

Stokes stared at the fiery sunlight that still tinged the west. The forested hills and mountains were dark. He sighed. That such horror should be found in such idyllic country saddened him beyond measure.

"Perhaps Cora got her out of the house and she was already injured," he said, forcing himself to focus on what lay immediately before him. "Or maybe she was wounded shortly after leaving the house. Somehow in the confusion she must have run this way instead of following her sisters into the root cellar."

Van Orman nodded.

"She ran and was bleeding," he said. "Nobody followed. She fell up there." He pointed to the top of the stream bank. "Later, hogs pulled her here."

Several gunshots rang out without warning. The men cried out, pulling their pistols and crouching, uncertain what was happening. Perhaps the men who had burnt the steading had returned. It was almost complete night now.

A few seconds later Jed White appeared at the edge of the stream. Stokes hadn't noticed him leaving.

"What's going on?" asked Bannon, his voice tight.

"Trouble?" said Stockman.

"Only for those hogs," White said, thumbing five fresh shells into his gun. "Let the buzzards and coyotes have them. See how they like being chewed up. Ain't nobody gonna eat their bacon after what they done."

Tenderly, Mooney and another of the deputies wrapped Elsa's broken body in the canvas and carried it out of the creek.

Stokes climbed up the muddy slope, taking in a great lungful of air. It was still bitter with smoke and his stomach churned.

"Thomas Rice and his wife must be in there," he said, nodding at the burnt building. There were no flames now, but wisps of smoke still drifted up from the charred beams.

"We'll pull 'em out in the morning," said Bannon. His voice was unsteady and he let out a long breath. "Hell of a thing." He shook his head as if he still couldn't quite believe what had happened. "We'll take 'em all into town for the undertaker."

White pointed over to the east. On a slight rise was a single oak. In the dim light they could just discern the shapes of three wooden crosses that stood beneath the tree's boughs.

"Reckon the Rices would rather be laid to rest with their kin," White said. "Saw a shovel in the root cellar. You boys bring any more?"

"I got a couple of shovels along with the paulins," said one of the deputies.

"Good," White said. "Let's get digging then. We take turns, we can be done by sun up."

Bannon scowled. He seemed about to protest, but the deputy was already heading to the pack mule.

"Well," Bannon said, "looks like we're gonna spend the night here after all." He didn't sound happy about the prospect. "We did a lot of waiting for you to show up," he said, turning to Van Orman, "but I reckon we would have found that girl by ourselves."

"Maybe," Van Orman said, in a tone that made it clear he thought it unlikely. "But I figure you wouldn't know who done this without me."

"You know the men who did this?" Bannon asked.

"Some."

"You sure?"

"I don't recognise none of the horses," Van Orman spoke slowly, seeming to enjoy Bannon's increasing annoyance with him. "But a couple of the men dismounted to help those who fell. I know their boot prints well enough. Seen them all over the range these last months."

"Well, who was it, man?" Bannon said.

"Rab Tovey and Cullen Towns."

Bannon sighed.

"They work for Grant. You absolutely sure of this?"

"They done it all right. No mistaking the sign of those rascals."

"Jesus," Bannon said. "The horses are unbranded. The children didn't see no faces. We ain't got no evidence. I can't confront Grant based on the word of a breed."

"Can't or won't?" Stokes asked.

"Can't. Won't. What's the difference? You don't understand. Mr Grant's a powerful man."

"I understand perfectly well," Stokes said. "You don't wish to bite the hand that feeds you. That makes sense. But do you really want to accept food from a man capable of this?"

Bannon peered about at the shadows of the burnt buildings. Up by the horses, the men were lighting a fire. Under the oak, Seb Mooney and a couple of the other deputies had already started digging the graves.

"We ain't got any evidence," Bannon said, his tone exasperated. "No matter what that breed says."

"Reuban," Stokes said, "you say at least one of the men was shot?"

"Yes. Hit pretty bad. Fell off his horse. Plenty blood. Tovey got him up on his horse with him."

"It appears to me, Bannon," Stokes said, "that you might not have enough evidence to convict Grant, but you have enough to speak to his men."

"I don't know about that," Bannon said.

"God damn it, man," Stokes said, the disgust at what he had witnessed that day colouring his tone, "you are the sheriff. A terrible crime has been committed. You cannot just turn a blind eye to this. This is not a quarrel between two armed men."

He saw that Jed White was up by the graves, too far away to hear what was said. Stokes lowered his voice anyway. "This is not a man shot to death in a ravine where the only witness is a drunk. Five people have been murdered here in cold blood. One of them was a woman, and another a little girl. If it hadn't been for Cora's bravery, two other girls would be dead too." McCloskey was not near, but Stokes hissed the next words. "And Cora all burnt up. You saw her face. She might yet die from her wounds, but even if she lives, what life will she have now? These crimes are too big. You cannot overlook them, no matter how powerful Grant is. If the Cabin Creek hands were involved in this, they must be brought to justice."

For several seconds Bannon did not speak. Stokes had started to lose hope when the sheriff cleared his throat and spat.

"Damn it all to hell," Bannon said, his voice loud in the gloaming.

"What is it, boss?" one of the deputies by the fire called out.

Bannon sighed, then called back.

"Tomorrow we're riding out to the Cabin Creek Ranch."

Chapter Thirty-Eight

"What can I do for you, Bannon?"

Tom Grant stepped out of his fine house and walked down the stone steps towards the waiting men, none of whom had dismounted. Dust clouded the air from where the riders had loped along the track to the ranch house. Some minutes earlier they had passed beneath the timber arch that bore the Cabin Creek name and an image of the ranch's brand. They had not slowed their pace even when three of the Cabin Creek hands had galloped their ponies out to intercept them.

"This is official business of the County Sheriff," Bannon had shouted, ignoring the cowpunchers' calls to slow down.

Stokes had been impressed with Bannon's mettle. The night before he had thought the sheriff might change his mind in the morning, but the sight of the bodies being lowered into the earth seemed to steel his resolve. In the darkness they had each taken their turns at the shovels, even Bannon. Stokes' hands were sore, his back and shoulders stiff from the effort. He wondered if Bannon's own aching muscles served as a painful reminder of the dreadful crimes that had been committed.

It had been an uncomfortable night. Stokes had wrapped himself in Banner's saddle blanket, but even so he had shivered after his stint digging as the sweat dried under his shirt.

They had found Mr and Mrs Rice soon after sunrise. It was hard to distinguish between husband and wife, such was the extent of the burning. Their bodies were stiff and charred, shrunken husks of their living selves. Lenny McCloskey and one of the deputies had staggered away and vomited at the sight. Stokes had felt his own gorge rise, and all the men were pale-faced and silent as they lifted the bodies and placed them as gently as they were able in the ground alongside their daughter, Elsa, and next to the sons who had been so cruelly taken from them.

The men drank coffee and ate the last of the picnic food Mary Ann had made and had left with them. The night before, they had brought out some potatoes from the root cellar and roasted them in the embers of the campfire. The men from town had brought a little jerky and pemmican with them, but they had not expected to be staying out so had not thought to bring more provisions. The flyblown pigs lay where White had shot them. They were large animals and would have fed dozens of men with their meat, but if any of the men thought it a waste, none of them commented. The thought of eating meat from an animal that had gnawed on Elsa and Warnock's corpses turned Stokes' stomach.

It was a clear day and the sun quickly burnt off the dew and early morning mist that coiled along the creek. The men spoke little as they rode hard northward, past the trail that led to the JT Ranch and further along the valley. When they'd stopped briefly to water the horses in a stream, Stokes noticed Bannon and the deputies checking their guns. He checked that his Colt was loaded and wished he had brought Thornford's Winchester. He wondered if Bannon would stand firm if it came to a fight. Stokes wasn't sure what the man would do, but he had begun to hold a grudging respect for the sheriff. If what he had heard from Hampton about the man was true, Grant had helped him obtain his position. It would not be an easy thing to stand up to the cattleman, but now that the decision had been taken, Bannon seemed to have made his peace with it.

"Easy, boys," Bannon said. "Let me do the talking. I don't want nobody getting shot today."

Lenny McCloskey closed the cartridge gate on his revolver and shoved the gun back into its holster.

"The Cabin Creek boys should have thought of that before they done what they done," he said. "They got it coming to 'em, I say."

"If you can't control your boy," Bannon said to White, "he can just as well stay here."

"I ain't no boy," protested McCloskey, sounding more like a child than ever.

"If he don't calm down," White said, "I'll hog-tie him myself and we can pick him up on the way back."

"You ain't tying nobody," Lenny said, his face red.

It had been a mistake to allow Lenny to come with them, thought Stokes. He was liable to pull his gun at the slightest provocation. Seeing so many armed men, and recalling the scene at the JT and the destruction of the Rice ranch, Stokes had a sinking feeling. This could end very badly and he suddenly had an inkling of Bannon's reticence to confront the cattleman, surrounded as he would be by his hired gun hands.

"Think of Cora," Stokes said.

"I am," said McCloskey, his voice rising in pitch. "She's all I think of. I think of her burnt. In pain—" His voice choked off.

"You should have gone to her," Stokes said.

Lenny reacted as if he'd been slapped.

"I know."

"But you're here now," Stokes said, "so don't go getting yourself killed. We want to bring those responsible to justice. It won't do Cora any good to find out that you've been shot too."

"I do the talking," Bannon had repeated loudly to make sure they all listened. "Just like we talked about." He flicked a look at Stokes, who nodded. "And that is all we do. Nobody clears leather unless I say so."

It was well past midday now and the sun was hot in the

pale sky. The twelve riders were spread out before the huge ranch house. It was a splendid building, its stout stone walls topped with split logs on the second storey. Two thick stone chimneys towered above the shingled roof. The front of the house was lined with a raised veranda. There must have been a cellar beneath the building, Stokes thought, for the veranda was reached by several stone steps. It was not as grand as the stately homes of England, or the Georgian town houses of Bath and London. Nor was it even as obviously opulent as the brownstones in Philadelphia or New York. Nevertheless, the Cabin Creek Ranch house had a rustic charm and exuded an earthy authority. Anybody who saw this building, situated within lush pasture land, forested hills and mountains rising in the distance, could not be mistaken as to the wealth and power of the man who owned it.

Tom Grant knew the impression the building had on his guests as he slowly descended the steps from the veranda. He halted halfway down, so that he was still taller than the men astride their horses. Standing alone before a dozen armed riders, most men would have displayed signs of nervousness. Grant showed none. He appeared at ease as he surveyed them, even pausing to tip his hat.

"Lieutenant Stokes," he said, with a smirk.

"Mr Grant," Stokes replied with a nod.

Bannon and his deputies shifted nervously as if they were the ones outnumbered, rather than standing before a single man. The three Cabin Creek hands who had met them near the ranch entrance clattered up behind the riders, adding to their nervous tension. Stokes glanced over at a movement to his right. Several more men were stepping from what must have been the bunk-house. Joaquin Lopez and Jackson Pailing were amongst them. Pailing carried a double-barrelled shotgun that looked as big as a cannon. From the rear of the house came Cadmar Byrne and Bull Meacher, as if they had been waiting for just this moment to step out into the open. Byrne leaned nonchalantly against the stone wall. Meacher moved away from him and into the sun-light, putting some distance between them.

"Well, Bannon," Grant said, "I don't suppose you rode all the way out here with all these men just to pass the time of day. What do you want?"

Bannon opened his mouth then closed it.

"Out with it, *Sheriff*," Grant said, putting a sarcastic slant on the title. "I'm a busy man, as you well know. This valley doesn't run itself."

Bannon looked like he would rather be anywhere else, but after another second or two of hesitation he mustered enough courage to speak.

"We come to question some of your boys," he said.

"Pertaining to what?"

"Murder." Bannon's voice was flat and heavy.

"Murder?" Grant said. "My goodness. These are proving dangerous times indeed. Who's the unlucky victim?"

"Victims," Stokes said, unable to listen to Grant's supercilious tone any longer. Bannon flashed him a look. Stokes thought the sheriff would be annoyed at the interruption, but he seemed more thankful than angry. "Mr and Mrs Rice," Stokes went on, listing the dead slowly, purposefully. "Mayfield Redin and Logan Warnock. And all three of the Rice girls."

He watched Grant's face for any sign he might have heard any news to the contrary. There was none. No tell-tale twitch or momentary change of expression.

"How dreadfully sad," Grant said. "Murder, you say? How did they die?"

"The Rice ranch was burnt to the ground," Stokes replied.

"Could it not have been an accident?"

"Accidents don't shoot people with a .45," White growled.

Grant stared at him.

"All of this is tragic," he said, "but what has it got to do with me or my men?"

"Van Orman read the sign at the Rice place," Bannon said.

His voice was firm now. Grant's dismissive tone was riling him too, it appeared.

"Oh, did he now? And I suppose he says my boys did this terrible deed?"

"All he said is that two of 'em were there for sure."

"That half breed would say anything to cause me and my people trouble. I can assure you none of my men were anywhere near the Rices' yesterday morning."

Stokes looked at the men who had ridden from the Rice ranch. Their faces were pinched and hard. Lenny McCloskey's cheeks were flushed, his eyes bright. He was biting his lip and his hand hovered over the gun at his hip.

"Easy, Lenny," he whispered. McCloskey made no indication he had heard him.

"All the same," Bannon said, "I'd like to speak to Rab Tovey and Cullen Towns. Hear what they have to say about it."

"Well then, I'm afraid that just like the Rices you're fresh out of luck."

"How's that?"

"Tovey and Towns don't work for me no more."

"When did they leave?"

"Yesterday morning. Asked for their wages and rode on out. Isn't that right, Cobb?"

A tall man with a greying moustache had just come round from the rear of the bunkhouse. Stokes noticed smoke rising from behind the building.

"Yes, sir," he said, climbing the steps to stand beside Grant.

"Cobb Smithson," Grant said by way of introduction. "My foreman."

"Kind of sudden like," said Bannon. "Any idea why they decided to leave?"

"Why do men do anything?" Grant said with a shrug and wry smile. "I have long since ceased trying to understand the mind of men, especially simple cowpunchers who drift from spread to spread. What do you think, Cobb?"

"Figured now the weather's better and the spring round ups are coming, they wanted a change of scenery."

"What about the rest of your men?" White asked, making the words sound like an insult. "They all here?"

"Last I looked," Grant said, his tone suddenly frosty, "Mr Bannon was the sheriff."

"Well, then," said Bannon, "are all your men here?"

"A few are out watching the herd," Smithson said.

"Any injuries?" Stokes asked.

Smithson scowled.

"Injuries?"

"Any of the men got holes in 'em they shouldn't have?" White said.

"None of my men have been shot," Grant said.

"You sure?" Stokes asked. "They have a lot of firepower and accidents happen. These are dangerous times after all."

"No, no shootings, accidental or otherwise. I'm very particular about that. If a man has cause to discharge his firearm, he should make sure he kills what he's shooting at."

He stared at Stokes, leaving the threat hanging in the warm afternoon air. Stokes looked over at where Cadmar Byrne lounged against the house. The smartly dressed gun hand smiled at him. A few paces off to the left, Bull Meacher did not.

"Perhaps your hands are better shots than you," Stokes said. "I have to say I'm pleased that you're not that good with a gun yourself."

"What do you mean?" Grant said. "I can shoot the spots off a playing card at twenty paces."

"And what a feat of arms that must be to watch. But luckily for the Thornfords, it seems you cannot shoot the spots off a dog at two paces."

"That dog lived?"

"It did," Stokes said. "Sometimes one bullet is not enough. But you were telling us that your men had been careful. None of them has been shot."

Grant glowered at him for several seconds. Colour had risen in his cheeks and he was clearly furious with Stokes for making a fool of him in front of his employees. But equally clearly, a man did not get to Grant's position by being a fool. Realising that to continue this war of words would only make him look weak, he took a deep breath and forced a smile.

"That is right," he said, "none of my men have been shot."

"Then you have nothing to hide," Stokes said, meeting his gaze without blinking.

"Nothing whatsoever."

"Good," said Stokes. "Then you won't mind us having a look around the bunkhouse."

Grant glanced at his foreman. Smithson gave a small nod.

"The sheriff can look around, if he wants," Grant said. "The rest of you stay here."

Stokes dismounted.

"Bannon," he said, "shall we?"

Without waiting for a reply, he strode towards the bunkhouse. He could sense Grant's furious glare boring into his back. He wondered how far he could push the man before he snapped. Grant was used to being obeyed, but he knew enough about leading men to know that if he got into an argument with Stokes, he might well lose face. Things could get ugly, and with a dozen men on each side, ugly would quickly become deadly.

He heard Bannon climb down from his big grey mare, then the click of his spurs as the sheriff followed him.

"You got a plan, Stokes?" Bannon whispered as he caught up with him.

"My plan hasn't changed. All we need is evidence."

"You're gonna get us all killed."

"I hope not, but time will tell."

Pailing and Lopez blocked the doorway to the bunkhouse. Close up, Pailing's shotgun looked even bigger.

"Eight gauge," Lopez said with a sneer. "That thing will cut a man clean in two."

"Best be careful then," Stokes replied. "We don't want any accidents. Grant, could you tell your thugs to let us past, please?"

Grant thought about it for a second before saying, "Let them through, boys."

The light inside the bunkhouse was dim, the windows small and grimy. There were rows of bunks, a cast iron stove, and little else. It was not much different from the JT bunkhouse, except bigger. Stokes counted twenty-four beds. He made his way quickly along the lower bunks, pulling back the blankets and sheets, then turning over the thin mattresses.

"Hey," called out someone from the doorway, "what the hell are you doing?"

Stokes ignored the man and carried on turning over the beds.

"I'd like to know too," hissed Bannon. "What are you doing? Grant ain't gonna take much more of this. Dang my melt, I should never have listened to you."

"Did you hear what he said about his men?" Stokes said, keeping his voice low as he looked at another bed.

"Grant? He said his men were nowhere near the Rice spread. What did you expect him to say?"

"He said they had been nowhere near the Rice ranch yesterday morning." He pulled back the sheets from another mattress, letting his words sink in.

Bannon sighed.

"God damn it," he said. "We never said when the Rice ranch was burnt."

"Whose bed is this?" Stokes snapped at the men by the door.

"That was Sheldrick's." Cobb Smithson had pushed through the hands and now walked along the bunks to where Bannon and Stokes were looking down at a mattress bearing a dark brown stain.

"That's blood," said Stokes. It wasn't a question. "Quite fresh too. Thought you said there were no injuries."

"Maybe he cut himself shaving," Smithson said.

"Where's Sheldrick now?"

"Left yesterday."

"With Tovey and Towns?"

"Yep."

"Convenient," Bannon said.

Smithson sniffed.

"Not really," he said. "Need all the hands we can get for the round up."

Stokes walked over to one of the windows that looked out over the corrals. A pile of what looked like sheets was burning there, a dark pall of smoke billowing up from the blaze. Pushing past Smithson and the other Cabin Creek hands crowding the doorway, Stokes went outside.

"What you found?" White called out. He was still sitting on his horse along with the other men. White was the only one of them who did not look anxious under the gaze of so many armed men.

Stokes didn't answer. He ran round the bunkhouse, followed by the Cabin Creek hands. The fire was burning hot and fast, great billows of smoke rolling into the sky. A large metal can was beside the bunkhouse. The smell of coal oil was acrid in the air. It was too hot to get close to the bonfire.

A long-handled axe was propped against the woodpile by the house. Hurrying over, Stokes grabbed it and sprinted back to the fire.

"What in the name of the devil are you doing?" asked Grant, who had come down the steps and was now watching Stokes along with the rest of his men.

Ignoring him, Stokes went to the fire. He could feel his eyebrows singeing with the heat, his eyes watered and his face felt as though it would blister, but he did not hesitate. Using the axe head, he snagged some of the burning material and pulled it free of the flames. Then, when he was a safe distance away, he stamped out the fire and lifted the item with the axe. It was a strip of cloth, charred and blackened at the edges.

"There's no crime in burning soiled linen," said Grant.

"No, there is not," Stokes replied. He stuffed the fabric into his jacket pocket and made his way back to the horses.

"Did you find what you were looking for?" asked Grant.

"I'm not sure," replied Stokes, pulling himself up into the saddle. "Time will tell." Seeing McCloskey was shaking, his hand tight around his pistol grip, Stokes nudged Banner close to the boy's horse.

The cattleman's eyes gleamed.

"Ah yes," he said. "Time. The great healer. It is a true pity that time cannot heal all ills. And if only it were possible to travel backwards in time. The Rices could have accepted my offer. They would have been far from here now and still alive. Now, with no living heirs, the estate will go to auction and I will buy it at a fraction of what I was going to pay Thomas Rice. Every cloud and all that." He grinned.

"You low-down son of a bitch," McCloskey said. He began to pull out his Colt, but Stokes, ready for such a move, gripped the boy's wrist firmly. All around them, the Cabin Creek men lifted their rifles and drew their revolvers. The sound of Winchester levers and pistol hammers being cocked was loud in the still afternoon.

"No, Lenny," Stokes said. "Now's not the time."

"You listen to the Englishman," Grant said. "You need to know when you've been dealt a losing hand."

For several seconds nobody spoke. Lenny shook in Stokes' grasp. With a sudden angry motion, Lenny yanked his wrist free. For a terrible moment it looked to Stokes as if he was going to open fire and they would be cut down in a barrage of bullets. But instead, McCloskey backed his horse, then turned it away from the ranch house and kicked it into a gallop.

"The kid's not as stupid as he looks," Grant said. "Perhaps you are though, Theodore."

Bannon blanched.

"Just doing my job," he said, pulling his horse's head around.

Seeing that the danger had passed, the rest of the men followed the sheriff's lead, backing their mounts, then turning them south. They were keen to put as much distance as possible between them and the Cabin Creek Ranch.

"I'll be seeing you, Theo," Grant shouted after them.

When they were out of rifle range, Bannon shouted over the drum of the horses' hooves.

"I can't believe I let you talk me into riding out here."

"It was the right thing to do," Stokes replied.

"Well, I'm mighty glad you think so. Perhaps you'll sleep easy after this, but I'll have to sleep with one eye open. It doesn't pay to make an enemy of the likes of Grant."

"I haven't slept well for years," Stokes said. But Bannon didn't answer. He had pulled away and galloped after his deputies.

White moved alongside Stokes.

"What did you find back there?" he asked.

Pulling the singed cloth from his pocket, Stokes rode close and handed it to White. It might once have been part of a cotton pillowcase, now it was charred and burnt at the edges. As he held it out to White, Stokes pushed his finger through one of the two holes that were clearly cut into the fabric.

Chapter Thirty-Nine

Stokes pulled his coat about his shoulders and stared out at the night. The day had been warm, but as soon as the sun set the air grew cold. Far off in the darkness he heard the yipping cry of a coyote. By his side, Pincher growled deep in his throat. Stokes smiled at the dog's courage. Three legs and still ready to fight to protect the ranch and its livestock. He wondered how Tooyakeh fared, high up the mountain where Van Orman had left him watching over the flock. When he had asked Reuban about the dog's safety, he had shrugged.

"Tooyakeh is brave and strong," he'd said. "He knows what he must do."

Stretching, Stokes rubbed at his leg and peered into the darkness. He was leaning on the fence of the corral. His muscles ached, his body tired from digging the graves and the day's riding, but still he had accepted the first watch. Sleep was a long way off; his mind full of thoughts and images tumbling over themselves.

The new lambs were safe in the barn along with their mothers. But there were worse things out there than coyotes, wolves and mountain lions. Pushing himself away from the fence, Stokes made his way back towards the house. They'd arrived as the sun was setting. Bannon had ridden on to Griffith, promising to check on Mary Ann and the children. McCloskey had gone with them, refusing to head back to the ranch. The boy had been almost mad with worry. They had not tried to stop him.

"Just promise me you'll get some sleep," Stokes said to him. "And send Tanner and Amos back to the JT. The ranch needs to be guarded."

"I'll tell 'em," McCloskey said, "and just as soon as I know Cora is well, I'll get me some shut eye. But I can't rest till then. And I ain't so sure I'll be able to sleep at all knowing that bastard Grant is still breathing."

Stokes knew how he felt. He doubted sleep would come easily to him either. Not after everything he'd seen these last couple of days. The air was cool and fresh, but even the cleanness of the mountains, forests and streams of Oregon could not soothe away the memories of the recent horrors he had witnessed.

On the porch he could just make out the red glow of White's cigarette as the frontiersman took a deep drag. The ruddy glow illuminated his craggy features for a second, his eyes glowing like coals in the gloom.

"We should have gone straight into town," Stokes said, sitting beside the old man and pulling a cigarillo from the box in his pocket.

"Ain't no point fighting this fight without the ranch," White said.

"Is that what we are doing then?" Stokes asked. "Fighting Grant for the ranch?" He struck a match. Its hissing flare was bright in the blackness. He lit his cigarillo and shook the match out. This had started with him trying to find his friend's killer. There was so much more at stake now.

"Grant wants to take it," White said, sipping whiskey from a coffee cup. "You seen what he's capable of. You're a fighter, just like the Captain. Figure it falls to us to fight for what Thornford built."

Stokes smoked in silence for a time, savouring the taste of the tobacco. In the darkness he could see Cora's burnt face, Elsa's twisted, bloody form.

"I don't know where all this will lead," he said. "Are you sure Mary Ann and the children are safe in town?"

Stokes sensed more than saw Jed White shrug.

"Sure as I am of anything," the older man said. "You heard Grant. He figures all the Rice girls died in the fire. As long as he thinks that, they'll be safe. And Bannon said he'd watch them."

"Do you think we can trust him?"

White took another mouthful of whiskey.

"A week ago I'd have said no, but I seen a change in him today."

Stokes nodded in the darkness.

"I think you're right. There is only so much a man can stomach."

"Reckon what he saw at the Rice spread gave him cause to reconsider whatever deal he'd struck with Grant."

"Perhaps he decided whatever he'd been given or promised wasn't enough for him to lose his soul over."

White blew out a plume of smoke.

"Better late than never," he said. "If it will make you feel better, we'll ride into town tomorrow to help watch over Mary Ann and the kids. Besides, I need some more whiskey."

"God, man. Just stay sober for one more day. That's all we need. Keep Elsa and Cora secret till the Governor arrives and Grant's goose will be cooked."

"Don't worry about me," said White. "I ain't about to let a little whiskey stop me from protecting them. But I ain't so sure it will be over by Wednesday. You really think this plan you and Mary Ann cooked up will work?" White's tone was sceptical.

"There is no way the Governor can ignore what Grant has done. With Pennoyer backing Mary Ann, we can make a case against Grant and take him to trial. With any luck we'll see him swing for his crimes."

White sniffed and spat.

"You place an awful lot of stock in the law," he said. "Rich men don't face justice."

"The rule of law is what keeps us apart from the animals," Stokes said.

"Rule of law," echoed White mockingly. "You ain't been in the West long enough to know the truth about the law out here."

"And what's that?"

White was about to answer when they both heard the scrape of something on a stone. Stokes stopped breathing and listened to the night. Beside him White stubbed out his smoke in a puff of sparks. Stokes followed suit. There were no lights in the house or the bunkhouse, so in the shadows of the porch, they would be invisible to anyone riding into the ranch.

Silently, White picked up the two Winchesters that were propped against the door jamb. He handed the longer of the two, Thornford's rifle, to Stokes. Neither man spoke, each listening intently for any sound. In the darkness, Pincher growled, low and menacing.

Stokes placed his hand on the dog's back.

"Shhhhhh," he whispered, and Pincher fell silent.

For a long time there was no sound. Stokes was beginning to think they had imagined it all, or perhaps it was a coyote or another wild animal out in the night. Then, loud in the dark came the clop of a hoof and the jingle of a bridle.

Letting out a peel of furious barks, Pincher sped off into the darkness. White rose up from his chair, jacking a cartridge into his carbine's chamber.

"Come on," he said, following the dog into the night.

Stokes levered his Winchester and made his way down the timber steps, making no effort to disguise the sound of his footsteps. Out from the dark beneath the eaves, the light of the waxing gibbous moon was bright enough to make out the shapes of two riders. Pincher did not cease his barking, but he kept his distance from the horses, perhaps remembering what had happened to him when he had last snapped at a man's mount.

White moved to the right of the riders. Stokes slid to the left.

"Who are you and what's your business here?" White snapped. "And think how you answer. If I don't like what I hear, I'll put a slug in each of your bellies and still sleep like a babe."

"Don't shoot," shouted one of the riders. "Don't shoot!"

"Give me one good reason why I shouldn't." White whistled. "Pincher, get back here."

Pincher let out a couple more barks as if to remind them how dangerous he was, then trotted back to stand beside White. A lamp had been lit in the bunkhouse, splashing light through the small window.

"You want to know what happened at the Rice spread, don't you?" said the first rider, his voice tinged with panic. "We was there."

"I seen what happened," snarled White. "I don't usually take pleasure in killing men, but if you was there, I'm gonna enjoy killing you."

"Jed, wait," Stokes said, his voice clear and commanding. "Who are you men?"

"Cullen Towns," said the second man. "And this here is Rab Tovey."

Chapter Forty

"You telling me you rode up to the Rice ranch like you was the redskins fighting General Custer and you expect me not to shoot you both?" Jed White took a mouthful of whiskey and shook his head. "Killed some cowards in my day. Even back-shot a few sons of bitches who needed killing. But I can't recall killing anyone more deserving of a bullet than you two shucks."

"We didn't know they was planning on shooting nobody," Rab Tovey whined. His eyes kept flicking from the whiskey bottle on the table to White, then on to Stokes and Lars Giblin, who stood in the shadows at the edge of the lamplight.

They were inside the JT Ranch house. The hurricane lamp glowed brightly in the centre of the table. Tovey and Towns were seated. Both men looked as though they regretted their decision to come to the ranch. Lars, Winchester in hand, was grim-faced, as if he expected to be called upon to perform an unpleasant task, such as slaughtering a couple of pigs. The glint in his eye and the set of his jaw gave the impression he might not be averse to the task as it pertained to the two men sitting at the table.

Van Orman was awake too, but he remained outside in the darkness, watching over the house while the others questioned the two Cabin Creek hands.

"Could be a trap," he'd said. "Others could come while you speak to Towns and Tovey."

It seemed unlikely to Stokes, but they had left Van Orman on guard duty.

"Don't try to sell us horse shit," White snapped at Tovey. "Why d'you ride to the Rices' with so much iron if you didn't mean to use it? I ain't no gump. You might be, but even you ain't that stupid. Grant sends eight gun hands to the Rices', it's pretty clear what they figure on doing. Or did you forget what he hired you for?"

"It's true," Towns spoke for the first time. His voice was deeper and carried none of the whine of his companion. "I knew there might be some lead pushing, but I never thought we'd be shooting at women and children."

"We didn't sign on with Grant for that kind of work," added Tovey. "We ain't murderers."

Without warning, White's ivory-handled Remington was in his right hand and pointed at Rab Tovey.

"Told you not to lie to me," he said, his voice as hard as granite, and as cold. "Done heard about enough of your voice, Tovey. When you get to hell, say hello to Old Scratch."

Both Tovey and Towns were still armed. It would have been safer to have disarmed them, but they were jumpy and it was clear they would never have agreed to come inside the house without their guns. When asked to come inside and speak about what they knew, Tovey had eyed White suspiciously.

"What's to stop you killing us when we get inside?"

White had raised his Winchester to his shoulder and stared at Tovey for several seconds.

"Why make a mess in the house?" he said. "If I wanted to shoot you, I'd do it out here."

"Nobody is shooting anyone," Stokes said. "You have my word. We just want to talk. Come inside and have a drink. Tell us what you know."

"I ain't giving up my gun," Tovey had said. Cullen Towns had said nothing. Stokes couldn't read his expression.

"You can both keep your guns," White had said, and led the way into the house.

Keeping hold of their pistols had made the men feel protected. The speed with which White had drawn his Remington shattered that fantasy. From a seated position, hampered by the table, they had never stood a chance against Jed White. Tovey didn't even try to pull his own gun. He held up his hands and whimpered.

"I swear it on my mother's grave," he said, "we didn't want no part of what happened."

Towns didn't move. He glowered at White, but made no effort to beg.

"You want to shoot us, Jed, you go ahead," he said. "But I ain't sure how that makes us the murderers."

"We didn't kill nobody," whined Tovey.

"Shut up," said Towns, not taking his eyes from White. "You're embarrassing yourself."

Stokes had played this game with witnesses many times before. One officer taking the role of a belligerent, angry and often violent inquisitor, while the other acted in a more friendly manner. Done well, it got results, often more quickly than the simple beating that many of his colleagues in Scotland Yard had been perfectly content to administer. White, with his gruff aspect and mercurial anger, was well suited to play the part of the bad policeman. Stokes slipped into his role easily enough.

"They came to us, Jed," he said. "They could have been halfway to Utah or California. Instead they came here. We should hear what they have to say, don't you think?"

White said nothing. His jaw clenched and unclenched as if he was chewing his own teeth. After a few seconds, he eased the hammer down on his gun and holstered it.

"OK," he said, "start talking."

"What do you want to know?" Tovey said, his tone pathetically eager. Beside him, Towns scowled.

"Who was with you?" Stokes asked.

Tovey opened his mouth to answer, but Towns cut him off.

"Shut your damn mouth, Rab," he said. "I knew we shouldn't have come here."

"If you ain't gonna tell us nothing," White said, "what did you come here for?"

Towns met White's glare without blinking.

"Didn't want you on our trail," he said. "Wanted you to know we were no part of it. Figured we could tell you how it was, and you'd let us ride."

White frowned.

"Only way we let you ride is if you give us names."

"I ain't no songbird," Towns said. "I didn't kill no women or children, but I ain't about to snitch."

"Give us something to take to the law," Stokes said. "Anything we can use against Grant."

Towns shook his head in disbelief.

"You really think you can stop Grant? He owns everything and everybody in these parts. If he don't own it now, he will soon. He won't let the likes of you stop him."

"Then I figure we need all the help we can get," said White. "You gonna help, Cullen?"

Towns sighed.

"I done told you already, I ain't no fink."

White was suddenly very still. Something in his total lack of movement was unnerving.

"Then you better be fast with that Smith & Wesson on your hip," he said.

"What d'you mean by that?" asked Towns, a note of anxiety entering his voice. "You said we could just talk."

White didn't move.

"The Englishman said that. I didn't say nothing about not shooting you."

"Jed," Stokes said, hoping this was an act for Tovey and Towns' benefit, but fearing White was in deadly earnest, "I gave my word."

"I didn't," White replied.

Tovey half stood, then sat back down when Lars pointed his rifle at him.

"You said you wouldn't shoot us inside the house," Tovey said, his voice trembling.

White didn't take his eyes off Towns.

"I said it would make a mess," White said. "I didn't lie. I'd rather shoot you outside. Might break some of Mrs Thornford's china if we start shooting in here. And I reckon your brains, not that you got many, would stain the curtains. But a little cleaning never hurt nobody."

Towns sat up straight.

"You yellow son of a bitch," he said. "Giblin will drill us before we can even move."

White thought about that for a second.

"He might," he admitted. "Tell you what, I'll give you a fair chance. Tell us what you know and you can ride away. Both of you." He flicked a glance at Tovey. "Or just one of you."

Stokes sensed the shift in the atmosphere, as if a cloud had passed before the moon. With a sudden violent motion, Cullen Towns heaved the table over and pulled his gun.

Four shots rang out, so close together it was like a roll of thunder. To Stokes it sounded like a volley from a squad of infantrymen. The small room was instantly filled with smoke. Towns jerked as lead tore into him.

He had been fast. His Smith & Wesson revolver had cleared leather and he had got off one shot, but he fired too hastily and his bullet went wide, smashing one of Mary Ann's pretty plates that stood on a shelf. Jed White had drawn and shot Towns twice in the head. The final gunshot came from Lars Giblin's Winchester. The shell punched Towns in the chest, sending him slumping back in the chair.

The lamp crashed to the floor with the toppled table and shattered, spilling oil that instantly ignited. Hungry flames danced along the floor, licking at the table cloth.

As soon as the action started, without thinking, Stokes threw himself at Rab Tovey, pulling his Colt Lightning as he moved. Tovey was slower than Towns, but he was still fast. He had his pistol out and was about to fire at White, but he sensed Stokes' charge and made the mistake of shifting his aim. His gun barked. It was loud enough that Stokes forgot how to think. Luckily for him, he was acting on instinct, as he often did when things became desperate and the time for talking was over. The smoke from Tovey's gun engulfed Stokes' face. The black powder blast singed his eye lashes and stung his cheeks like a dozen wasps.

Blinded by the smoke and deafened by the gunshot, barely knowing whether the bullet had hit him or not, Stokes crashed into Tovey. The chair splintered beneath them and the two men sprawled on the floor. Stokes was dimly aware of voices shouting and the heat of flames from the burning oil. But he ignored everything except for the man beneath him. Tovey was trying to bring his gun to bear on Stokes. It would be a matter of a second before he was able to press the barrel of his revolver into Stokes and pull the trigger.

Stokes grappled for the gun, but it was too late. He felt the hard muzzle press into his ribs. He hadn't been fast enough. Now he would die. Time slowed and he was aware of every detail of Tovey's pock-marked face. The snarling lips, the brown teeth. He wondered if he would have enough strength to hit back at his enemy after he felt the searing agony of the bullet ripping through his lungs and heart.

Nothing happened.

Tovey's expression of victory changed to one of abject terror as his gun failed to fire. Why it had misfired, Stokes had no idea, but he did not stop to think about the second chance that had been afforded him.

Lifting himself up above Rab Tovey, he brought the Colt Lightning down hard into the man's ugly face. It was not the biggest of handguns, but it was steel and it was heavy enough to split Tovey's lip and break his nose.

With his left hand, he grasped Tovey's gun hand, twisting it painfully backwards until he relinquished his grasp on the revolver. At the same time, he struck Tovey again across the top of the head and then the temple. Tovey went limp beneath him and Stokes surged to his feet, his Lightning, smeared with blood, in his right hand, and Tovey's Colt Army in his left.

His ears were ringing and his eyes stung from the smoke and black powder burns.

Blinking, he took in the state of the room. White still had his gun in his hand. Giblin had taken the table cloth and was using it to beat out the flames. He had it under control, but Stokes waved the bloody revolver at White.

"Help Lars to put that out, then you can clean up your mess," he said, his words clipped. "And don't even think about shooting Tovey. He's much more use to us alive than dead."

White stared at Stokes for a few seconds, taking in the Englishman's dishevelled appearance, the powder burn marks on his cheeks and forehead, the spots of blood on his hands, shirt collar and face, and the mad glint of battle fever in his eye.

At last, he gave a smirk and a desultory salute.

"Yes, sir, Lieutenant," he said, and did what Stokes had ordered.

Chapter Forty-One

After the fire had been put out, Stokes bound Rab Tovey hand and foot and, with Van Orman's help, they half-carried and half-dragged him out to the barn. Van Orman agreed to watch him.

"Just remember," said Stokes, "we need him alive. If we can get him to testify against Grant, that could well seal the man's fate."

Van Orman raised an eyebrow and looked unsure of that outcome, but he nodded.

"I am no fool," he said. "I'm not like Jed."

"No," replied Stokes, "thank God that you're not. One Jed White is quite enough."

When he got back to the house, Giblin and White had dragged Cullen Towns' body out of the back door. There was a bloody streak smeared across the wooden floor and Giblin was in the process of filling a bucket at the pump.

"Best to mop it now," he said, his face sombre. "Before it dries."

Stokes nodded, but did not answer. He glared at White, who was drinking the last of his whiskey. The bottle had fallen when Towns upturned the table, but it had not broken and very little had spilt.

"It's a miracle this bottle didn't break," White said, offering the bottle to Stokes.

After a moment's hesitation, Stokes accepted it, snatching it from the old man's hand.

"A miracle?" he said. "You think God saved your whiskey?"

"Take a drink," White said. "You look like you need one."

"You'd like that, wouldn't you?" Stokes said.

"Don't care what you do, Stokes," replied White, holding out his hand for the bottle. "But piss or get off the pot. If you don't want a drink, give it here."

"Well, I won't drink," Stokes said, barely hearing White. "No matter how much I am tempted. I won't. And you want to know why?"

"Why?"

"Because," shouted Stokes, his fury pouring out of him in a bellowed roar, "I gave my bloody word!" With that, he flung the bottle onto the ground, where it shattered and the remainder of the whiskey seeped into the blood-stained boards.

Stokes turned on his heel and stalked over to the bunkhouse, hoping he would be able to sleep.

They rode into Griffith the next morning. Stokes' anger was still simmering. He had slept poorly. The burns on his face hurt, waking him frequently. He could hear a hissing chiming in his ears even though the night was silent. And when he did manage to sleep, his thoughts roiled and tangled in his mind, filling his slumber with nightmares. His sour mood was not improved by White's complete lack of remorse for his actions.

"Don't know why you're so bent out of shape," White said, as they rode under the cool shade of tall firs and red cedars. "Towns pulled on me. You saw it."

Stokes took a calming breath. He didn't want to argue with White, there were more important things to occupy their attention. But he could not just ignore what had happened the night before.

"What I saw was you goading the man until he went for his gun. Then you shot him."

"Maybe it was like that," White said.

"That is how it was."

White scratched at the stubble growing on his neck.

"Worked out all right though," he said. "Towns was never gonna talk. You heard him. And I wasn't ready to let a man like that ride away."

"A man like that?"

"You seen what they did at the Rices'," White said. "Men like that are worse than animals."

"So you shot him?" Stokes said. "Like an animal."

"Ain't sorry to see him dead. I'd do it again."

"You killed the man in cold blood. What makes you any better than them? Are you not a murderer, Jed?"

Now it was White's turn to be angry.

"Don't you ever compare me to the likes of Tovey and Towns," he snarled. "I ain't like those hard cases. I killed me plenty of men, but none that didn't have it coming. Those boys did nothing to stop the others from burning the house with Mrs Rice and the children inside." He shook his head, his voice choking with emotion. "Nothing to stop 'em killing that girl."

"You think Tovey and Towns could have stopped them if they'd tried?"

"Ain't the point," White said, his anger subsiding. "I ain't a good man, Gabe, but I ain't never stood by and watched little ones or women abused. To watch and do nothing..." He sucked his teeth. "Tovey's a cowardly skunk. But Towns. He was a man. He had himself a gun. Knew how to shoot it, too. Got what was coming to him."

They rode on in silence for a time. Stokes thought about White's words.

"You're so sure of yourself," he said after a few minutes. "Don't you ever question your actions?"

"What's the point in that?" White asked. "I do what I think's best. No use in worrying later if I was wrong. Won't change nothing."

"You're lucky," Stokes said. "I question myself all the time. I wonder if I'm really any different from Tovey and Towns. Would I have acted any differently if I had found myself in the same situation?"

White looked at him. To Stokes' surprise, the older man started laughing.

"What's so funny?"

"That you'd think for a second you'd ever find yourself in that position." White chuckled. "Towns and Tovey had plenty of chances to walk away before they rode down to that ranch. They took their own decisions."

Stokes mulled this over for a while. He supposed White was right. He had made plenty of mistakes in his life, but he would never have allowed himself to be a party to the actions of a man like Grant.

"I just want to see Grant and his men brought to justice," he said. "To pay for their crimes."

"Never did trust in the law much," White said. "A bullet is quicker."

"Civilization needs laws."

White hawked and spat.

"Figure Oregon ain't that civilized."

They rode out from under the trees. The morning sun glimmered on the Grande Ronde River below. The loud rasping and thumping from the sawmills reached them on the light wind. Stokes could feel his anger at White dissolving in the warm sunlight. There was some truth in what the frontiersman said. Towns had stood by and watched horrors take place. He had offered no resistance. Neither had he offered to help bring those responsible to justice. White's summation of the man was accurate. Towns' motive for coming to them had been purely selfish – to try and convince them of his innocence, so they would not go after him.

"Don't make me into a liar again, Jed," Stokes said. "Of all I own, all I truly value is my word as a gentleman."

White kicked his horse into a trot.

"OK, Gabe the gentleman. Deal. So long as you don't herd me into the same corral as men like Towns."

Riding past the station, they saw it was ready for the grand opening in a couple of days. It gleamed bright in the sun and the smell of fresh paint was strong in the air. Hampton waved at them from the door of the livery stable. Stokes returned the wave, but they did not stop.

White made straight for the large house on the edge of town, the one with the brass plaque on the door that Stokes had seen on his previous visits. They swung out of their saddles and looped their reins around a hitching pole beside the gate to the tidy garden in front of the house. As they walked up the path to the front door, Stokes saw that the plaque read: DR D. YARDLEY, M.D. PHYSICIAN AND SURGEON.

He rapped the brass knocker on the door a couple of times and stood back. For a second, he recalled countless such approaches to doors in the streets of London. He was seldom the bearer of good news on such occasions, and now he had the familiar tightness in his stomach as he waited for the door to open.

When it did, it revealed a woman in a dark dress. She had a high-cheeked, open face. Her hair was pulled up in a severe, neat bun.

"Can I help you?" she asked, her tone pleasant.

"Might we speak to the doctor, ma'am?" Stokes said.

"The doctor is with a patient, but you are welcome to wait inside." She stepped aside and led them into a small parlour. There were seats there and she waited, expecting them to sit. When they both remained standing, she frowned.

"We are not unwell," Stokes said. "We just wanted to speak for a moment with the doctor."

Her eyes widened as if she suddenly recognised him, though Stokes was certain they had never met.

"You must be Mr Stokes," she said.

"The same," he replied. "I don't suppose you get many Englishmen around here."

She smiled.

"Not many. No."

"Gabriel Stokes at your service," he said, removing his hat. "This is Jedediah White."

The woman appraised both of them, her eyes lingering on Stokes.

"Beryl Yardley." She flicked a glance at the door that must have led to the doctor's surgery. From behind it they could hear the muffled sounds of talking. Lowering her voice so that whoever was in there with the doctor would not overhear, she said, "Have you come to check on the girl?"

"How is she?" Stokes asked.

"Her burns are bad," she said, her expression grave. "But she'll live. She will never be a beauty though, the poor thing."

"And her sister? Is she well?"

"As well as can be expected. She's not spoken a word since they arrived in Griffith. Though who can blame her for silence? They've had such a wretched time of it. They've been through hell, those girls."

"Can we see them?" Stokes said. "Are they upstairs?"

"They're not here." Seeing his surprise, she went on quickly. "Oh, don't worry. They are perfectly safe. We all just decided they would be more comfortable staying with Mrs Mullen, the school mistress, and her daughter."

They thanked Mrs Yardley and went outside to the horses.

"Would have been better to leave both girls at the doc's," White said, stepping into a stirrup.

Stokes nodded, swinging up into the saddle.

"She said they haven't spoken about the girls to anyone."

"Still would have been safer not to have moved 'em. Hard to keep two girls secret in a town this size."

The schoolhouse was on the far side of town and Mrs Mullen lived in a small house next door, so Stokes and White trotted down Griffith's main street. The town was busier than the other times Stokes had visited. It had a festival air about it. Bunting had been tied across the road between some of the buildings, and ribbons fluttered in the breeze. Several of the stores had freshly painted doors and signs, giving the sensation that the town had just been erected.

The Grand Hotel, though small, was trying to live up to its name. The doors and window frames had been painted in gold and red, and the glass in the windows gleamed.

"All this for Governor Pennoyer?" said Stokes.

"For Pennoyer and the opening of the railroad," White said. "People see it as the moment Griffith is put on the map."

Stokes noticed Mrs McCall peering at them from the recently cleaned windows of the General Store. He cursed quietly.

"I wonder how long till Grant hears of us coming to town," he said.

"Unless he's here already, he won't know about it until someone rides out to the Cabin Creek."

"You think he is in town?"

White scanned the horses tied to the hitching rails along Main Street. There were several in front of the Grand Hotel, many more clustered in front of the Lady Elgin and just one scrawny mule outside the other saloon, The Palace.

"I don't see any horses with the Cabin Creek brand, but that don't mean none of his hands are around. One thing's for sure. He won't want to miss the grand opening, day after tomorrow."

"Do you think anyone saw the girls when they brought them in?"

"No way of telling," White said. "All we can do is watch 'em. Keep 'em safe."

"They won't be safe till Grant's behind bars."

White said nothing.

"Hey there, handsome."

Stokes recognised the Lancashire lilt in the voice and turned to see Bella Sawrey step out of the Lady Elgin. He reined Banner in and waited for her.

"Ain't you popular with the ladies?" White said. "Only been in town a couple of times and you're friends with all the whores."

"Not with all of them," Stokes said, bristling. "Just this one. And don't be so vulgar. She's a nice girl."

White scoffed.

"I bet she is."

Ignoring him, Stokes watched Bella step down from the wooden sidewalk and come across the street to them. She was dressed much as she had been when he had first met her, but then he had not had the benefit of watching her move far. He paid more attention now, enjoying the sway of her hips and the swell of her breasts beneath her tight bodice. He felt his face redden as he thought of Rebecca for the first time in days. He wondered what his wife would think if she could see him now.

"Glad I seen you through the window," Bella said, reaching them and looking up at Stokes, squinting against the bright sky.

"Miss Sawrey," Stokes said, smiling and pulling the brim of his hat. "The pleasure is all mine."

"I don't have no time for flirting, Mr Stokes," she said. "You need to watch yourself."

Stokes' smile vanished.

"Really?"

"People are talking about what happened at the Rice ranch."

"What are they saying?"

"That the place was burnt by Grant's men. That the Rices and their hands were all killed."

"I'm afraid it's true," Stokes said. "A terrible thing."

"That's not all," Bella went on. "Jayson Stockman's been saying that a couple of the Rice girls got away."

"Shit," White said. "That ain't good."

"Reckon it won't be long till Grant hears about them," Bella said, "if he hasn't already."

"Damn and blast," Stokes said. "I apologise for the language. But what is that fool Stockman thinking?"

White shrugged.

"Thing like this," he said, "men take sides. Seems Stockman has picked his. Must have figured the chips will fall Grant's way."

"Thank you for telling us, Miss Sawrey," Stokes said. "I owe you a drink."

"Bella," she corrected. "Just keep those girls safe. When this has blown over, you can buy me that drink."

She smiled and her face lit up, radiant in the sunlight.

"I might just do that, Bella," he said. "Take care of yourself."

"That's one of the things I'm best at," she said.

She watched them ride on for a few seconds before turning her back on the sunshine and making her way once more into the smoke-filled shadows of the saloon.

When Stokes and White reached the small house where the Mullens lived, the first thing they noticed was there was no sign of the ladies' buggy, and no horses outside.

Stokes dismounted, opened the small gate in the garden fence and knocked on the door. There was no answer. He peered into the window, but could see nothing more than a neatly decorated room.

"Let's try the schoolhouse," White said.

They left their horses tethered to the fence and walked over to the plain timber building. As they grew closer they could make out snatches of Abigail Mullen's curt voice. She was telling the children the difference between adverbs and adjectives.

Stokes opened the door quietly, hoping not to draw attention to his presence. But the door opened at the side of the single room and some twenty pairs of eyes looked in his direction as the children all turned to stare. He made out Albert and

Adelaide amongst the students. He smiled a greeting. Albert waved, but neither child smiled in return. Both looked pale and sombre.

Ruby Mullen, however, offered him a broad grin. She was almost as pretty as Bella, he thought. Behind him, Stokes was aware of White shaking his head.

"By God," he muttered under his breath, but loud enough for Stokes to hear, "the young ladies of Griffith are powerless. We might need to lock them up for their own safety."

"They're in no danger from me, I can assure you," Stokes hissed.

Abigail Mullen shot them an angry glance and the men fell silent.

"Children," Mrs Mullen said, "write five sentences using an adverb and another five using adjectives. And no talking. Ruby, watch them please while I step out to speak to these gentlemen."

She closed the door behind her and ushered Stokes and White away from the schoolhouse.

"Mary Ann and the girls are safe in my house," she said, not waiting for them to speak.

"We went there first," Stokes said, "but there was nobody home."

"Looks like they've taken the horses too," White added.

Mrs Mullen offered them a thin smile.

"Then I am pleased our little ruse is working. Come, follow me."

She walked over to her house.

"Please don't tie your horses there," she said. "They will eat my roses. You can turn them out in that corral, if you don't plan on staying long." She pointed to a small, empty fenced-off patch of grass. "But if you are staying, best to take them to the livery stable."

She paused by the gate.

"You want us to move 'em now?" asked White.

"Why yes, if I want to keep any of my roses."

Just as she had predicted, Banner had already started cropping the leaves from the nearest bush.

Stokes apologised and, under the stern gaze of the schoolmistress, he unhitched the gelding and led him to the corral. White came along beside him leading his mare.

"Pity your English charm don't work on her," he said. "She's sourer than a tart cherry."

"It seems what charm I possess is most effective on younger and prettier ladies."

"And whores," White said, closing the gate behind the animals.

"Perhaps you should try your own brand of rustic charm on Mrs Mullen," Stokes said. "I am quite sure she is eyeing you up as a prospective husband."

To Stokes' amusement, White looked back anxiously at the austerely handsome woman waiting impatiently by the garden gate.

"Me?" he asked, sounding rattled.

"Oh yes," said Stokes quietly as they walked back to the widow. "I am certain of it. She has a way of watching your movements. Like a cat watching a mouse."

White swallowed and removed his hat. With his left hand he smoothed his greasy hair.

"Sorry about your flowers, ma'am," he said.

"No real harm done," she said, opening the gate.

Reaching the front door, she knocked four times, paused, knocked twice, then knocked three times. A couple of seconds later, they heard a bolt being drawn back and the door opened. Mrs Mullen entered quickly. Stokes and White followed.

Chapter Forty-Two

The door was opened by Tanner Strickland. As soon as they were inside, he closed it again and slid the bolt into place. There was a chair near the door which was where he had been sitting. An old Henry rifle was propped against the wall beside it.

"Good to see you, Mr Stokes," Strickland said, nodding a greeting. "Jed."

"And you, Tanner," Stokes said. He meant it too. He liked Strickland. Tanner enjoyed a joke as well as the next man, but he was earnest and solid when it mattered.

Mrs Mullen seemed less favourably disposed towards the young man. She frowned.

"Please take care not to scuff the wall, Mr Strickland," she said, her tone sharp.

"Sorry, ma'am," he mumbled.

"No harm done, I suppose," she replied.

Stokes caught White's eye and raised an eyebrow. White scowled and chewed his moustache. Stokes had never seen him so nervous.

They were in a short corridor, at the end of which Amos Willard sat in a chair beside the back door. He held a shotgun across his knees.

"Nice of you to join us, boys," he said. "Wondered when you'd get here."

"We thought it best," Mrs Mullen said, ignoring Amos,

"not to have the horses outside to signpost that the men are in the house."

"What happens if they need to light out of here in a hurry?" White asked.

"We did what we thought was right at the time, Mr White." Her tone was acerbic. She was much more accustomed to giving criticism than receiving it. White looked down, abashed. "It seemed more important that the girls' presence here was not known. I sincerely hope your fears are unfounded, but if it should come to needing to retreat with haste, we will be hard pressed. Cora is in no state to travel far or fast. What she needs is rest."

Before they could reply, Mary Ann came down the stairs. Once again Stokes was struck by how much she reminded him of Rebecca. She looked tired, her cheeks sallow, but all the tribulations of the past weeks could not extinguish her natural beauty.

"Jed," she said. "Gabriel. I'm so glad to see you. Any news?" Before either of them could respond, she held up her hands. "Where are my manners? Would you like coffee? Tea, Gabriel? Abigail has a very nice blend that I think you'll like. You can tell me everything over a drink and a piece of the emery cake Ruby baked with Florence yesterday. There isn't much left, but I thought you'd be coming, so saved some."

A few minutes later, Jed, Gabriel, Mary Ann and Amos were seated around a table in the parlour. White and Stokes had a thick slice of the cake along with their drinks. Amos and Mary Ann had half a slice each. She'd sent Tanner upstairs with some cake for Lenny and the girls. Strickland's piece of cake awaited him on the chair by the front door.

Abigail Mullen had returned to the schoolhouse.

"Goodness only knows what mischief they will get up to with only Ruby watching them," she said as she slipped out the front door. "I swear that girl is worse than the children she is supposed to be teaching sometimes."

They'd locked the door behind her.

Stokes took a sip of his tea. It really was good, more refined and subtle in flavour than the Brooke Bond that had been John Thornford's preference. The cake smelt rich and looked appetising and it was all he could do not to eat it in two quick bites. White and Willard felt no such need for restraint. They each wolfed down their cake in seconds. Stokes took a small mouthful, chewing it slowly, savouring the sweetness. It tasted as good as it looked.

"Delicious," he said. "I'll have to give my compliments to the bakers."

"They'll like that, I'm sure," Mary Ann said.

"How's Cora?" he asked.

"In a lot of pain. And distress. She has some fever. But Dr Yardley is confident she'll pull through. She's in good hands here. Florence and Ruby are both wonderful nurses. And Lenny has not left her side since he got here."

"How is he?"

"I don't know really." She drank some tea. "Quiet. Withdrawn. But he is wholly dedicated to the girl. She's lucky in that at least."

Stokes lowered his voice.

"No trouble between Lenny and Tanner?"

"Trouble?"

"There was some competition between the two of them for the girl's affections."

"Well, it seems Tanner has stepped aside. It is very apparent who Cora would rather have at her side. Tanner is no fool."

"I'm glad to hear that. Squabbling now would be the last thing we need."

"Now that you've had your cake and tea, what news?"

Stokes told her about Tovey and Towns. He chose not to mention how White had goaded Cullen Towns into pulling his gun, or of their disagreement after the event. When he finished speaking, Mary Ann was pale.

"Did you really have to kill him?" she asked White.

"If I hadn't shot him, I wouldn't be talking to you now." He glanced at Stokes as if he expected the Englishman to contradict him.

"What's important," Stokes said, "is that we have a prisoner who witnessed what happened at the Rices'. He might well have witnessed John's murder too. If we can get him to testify under oath, it will be hard for Grant to wriggle out of the charges against him."

"You think Tovey would do that?"

"He might. With the right incentive. One thing is certain though, if Grant finds out we have Tovey, he'll try and kill him."

"Wouldn't be a great loss," Willard said. "Rab Tovey is mean enough to steal the coins off a dead man's eyes."

"He's no use to us dead," Stokes said. "Jed and I are going to stick around until the Governor arrives. We promised Reuban and Lars we'd send you boys back to the JT to watch Tovey and help guard the place, not to mention to watch the livestock. But things have changed. We'll send only two of you back and keep one with us."

"What's changed?"

"People know that Cora and Florence survived the attack."

"What?" Mary Ann's shock was clear on her face and in her voice. "How? We have been so careful."

"Stockman is telling anybody who'll listen. It's only a matter of time before Grant finds out. I still think they are safer here in town, but we'll keep one of the hands with us. I was hoping we could ask Bannon to lend us a few of his men too, but now I'm not so sure. Stockman might not be the only one we can't trust." A sudden thought came to him. "Does Bannon know about the special four-two-three knock?"

"Yes," Mary Ann said, "he came over last night with a couple of his deputies. They helped stand guard. He said he'd send a couple over this evening."

"We need to change the signal. And I'll go and speak to Bannon. Tell him not to send any men tonight."

"Think we can still trust Bannon?" White asked.

"I don't know who we can trust, but we have to keep those girls safe. With any luck, once the Governor hears everything we have to say and has a chance to read the evidence we've put together, Grant will have no place to hide."

"Who you gonna send back with me?" Willard asked.

"Who's better in a fight?"

White and Willard spoke at the same time and without hesitation.

"Tanner," they said.

"My thoughts exactly. So Lenny goes back with you."

"I ain't going nowhere."

Stokes turned to see Lenny McCloskey in the doorway. The boy's face was wan and he appeared to have aged several years in the last couple of days.

"We think it would be best if you went back to the JT with Amos," Stokes said. "Tanner will stay here with us. We'll make sure nothing happens to Cora."

"I ain't leaving her side." McCloskey stepped forward and placed his empty plate on the table. "Thanks for the cake, Mrs Thornford."

"You still work for Mrs Thornford, don't you, Lenny?" Stokes said, the clipped, whip-crack edge of the hussar officer entering his tone unbidden. "If she tells you to go somewhere, you do it."

McCloskey bit his lip.

"Due respect, Mr Stokes, I don't work for you. Mrs Thornford tells me to go back to the ranch, I'll give it some thought. But I can tell you now, I'd rather stay with Cora, so I reckon I'd just ask for my wages. Mrs Thornford, you telling me I have to go to the JT now?"

"No, Lenny," she said. "I'm not."

"Good, then I'll head back upstairs."

He brushed past Strickland, who was coming down the stairs. Tanner raised his eyebrows, but said nothing. Sensing the strained atmosphere, he went to his chair by the front door and the slice of cake that awaited him there.

The four of them around the table were silent for a time after Lenny left. Amos whistled low.

"Looks like the boy found some sand."

"He should know how to follow orders," Stokes said. "To do what's best for everyone, not just what he wants."

"Is that what you did, Gabriel?" Mary Ann asked, not unkindly. "Because John told me a few tales of your time in the military."

Stokes stiffened.

"This is not about what I did years ago," he said, wondering what John had said about his frequent clashes with their commanding officers. "Besides, when it came time for battle, I always did what I was called upon to do."

"I'm sure," she said, patting his arm, "but you are not in the army any longer. And this isn't war."

"You are wrong about that. This is a war. It might not be between armies, but it's a war all right. John knew that. I think that's why he invited me here. And if we can't stop Grant through legal means, more people will die in this war."

"The Englishman's right," White said. "But Mary Ann ain't wrong about one thing. You ain't in the army now, Lieutenant. You can't give Lenny an order and expect him to follow it blindly."

Stokes sighed. He drank some tea. It wasn't hot enough for his liking now, but it still tasted good.

"No," he said, "you're right. I had wanted to keep Tanner here with us, but if Lenny won't go, then Strickland will have to go back with Amos."

White nodded.

"So we guard the girls here, just the three of us. You, Lenny and me?"

"When you put it like that," Stokes said, "it doesn't sound like great odds."

"Ain't so sure," White said. "Lenny has his dander up. Reckon he could take on all of Grant's bad hombres hisself."

Stokes smiled thinly.

"When I speak to Bannon, I'll try to get a sense of where his allegiance lies. Perhaps he'll still be willing to help us."

White looked dubious.

"Perhaps."

"The house isn't very large," Mary Ann said, turning to other practical matters. "We can't stay here forever. Once I've spoken to Pennoyer we'll need to move the girls back to the ranch where there is more space."

"Are you planning on looking after them then?" Stokes asked.

"Of course. They have no other kin. Cora says there is an aunt in Tennessee, but the children have never even met the woman. Until we manage to get word to the aunt and find out her wishes, Cora and Florence will live with us."

"Let's not get ahead of ourselves," said White. "Until you speak to the Governor, we'll be staying here. There's barely room to spread a bedroll in this parlour."

"We can take turns," Stokes said. "One of us sleeping while the other two are on watch."

"I ain't worried about that," White said. "Never did need much sleep. But..." He looked uncomfortable and his voice trailed off. He glanced at each of them, then lowered his gaze. Stokes had never seen the man so unsure of himself.

"What is it, Jed?" Mary Ann asked.

White chewed his lip for a while, before looking up, clearly having decided to say whatever was on his mind.

"I ain't had a drink since yesterday."

"Abigail won't abide drinking in her house," Mary Ann said. "Believe me, I would have liked a drop of something myself."

"Figured the schoolmistress would feel that way. Then I'll need to take a trip to one of the saloons."

"We need you here," Stokes said.

"You don't understand, Lieutenant. Without some whiskey to wet my whistle, I ain't gonna be any use to you or the Rice girls."

White stared imploringly at Stokes. The frontiersman's eyes were bloodshot. A muscle near his left eye twitched.

"I won't have me more than a couple of drinks," White said. "I promise. But look at me." He held out his hand. It was trembling. "I ain't gonna be worth a hill of beans without a drink."

"Surely you can wait for a couple of days, Jed," Mary Ann said.

Stokes sighed. He knew the grip drink had on White. It had taken all his own will power to wrest himself from its clutches, and even now he dreamt of the taste of whiskey, brandy, wine and absinthe. Alcohol was as much a part of Jedediah White's life as the air he breathed. He was right. Without it, he would be worse than useless to them. He would become a sweating, raving, agonised wreck of a man, shaking and weeping, when they all needed to be focused on the task of guarding the girls. Perhaps it would be best to send White back with Amos. Stokes dismissed the thought the instant it entered his mind. He had seen White in action. There was no doubt that Jed White was the man to have at his side if bullets started to fly. But a Jed White who had a couple of steadying drinks.

"Sorry, Mary Ann," White said. He sounded pathetic, and Stokes felt pity for him.

"You'll get your drink," Stokes said. "Just enough to keep you steady."

"Is that wise?" Mary Ann asked.

"We have no choice."

"I'll be back soon then," White said, pushing himself up from the table.

"Sit down," snapped Stokes. "I can't let you go to the saloon."

"You think you can stop me?" White's voice was suddenly chill. Gone was the pitiful drunk of seconds before.

Stokes' mouth went dry. He stared at White unblinking.

"I don't know, Jed," he said. "You planning on getting me to draw on you?"

White held his gaze for several seconds, anger blazing in his bloodshot eyes, before looking away.

"No," he said. "I ain't gonna fight you, Gabe."

"Good. Then here is what we'll do. I'll buy you a bottle when I go to the livery stable."

"Why you heading to the livery?"

"Now that Stockman's spread the word about the girls, there's no point hiding that we're here. I think it would be best to have the horses close, in case we need to move in a hurry."

"And you'll buy me a bottle?" Stokes saw White flinch at the pleading tone of his voice.

"Yes, but I'm not running the risk of you drinking it all at once. I'll ration it for you. Can you live with that?"

"Reckon I can," White said. "But when this is over, I'm gonna kick up my heels and drink my weight in booze."

"If we put Grant out of commission, I'll buy the first round." Stokes snapped open his pocket watch. "No time like the present. If we leave now, Amos and Tanner can be back at the JT before sundown." He stood. Amos rose too, groaning as his back straightened and his knees popped. "Will you be able to hold it together for another hour?" Stokes asked White.

"Ain't about to crack up any minute," White replied, anger crackling in his words. "Could just use a drink is all."

Stokes glanced at Mary Ann. She raised her eyebrows.

"We'll be fine," she said. "Just don't take too long."

"Right you are," Stokes said. "Anything happens, you know how to use that fowling piece. You ready, Amos?"

"Ready as I'll ever be."

"Good." Stokes turned to the front door where Tanner Strickland sat. "If you've finished your cake, get ready to leave."

Tanner stood.

"Where we going?"

"Nowhere," said a voice from the stairs.

Lenny McCloskey stood there. His cheeks were tear-streaked and his eyes red.

"You stay here, Tanner," he said, his voice strained. "And watch my girl."

Stokes smiled, pleased that the more capable Strickland would remain in town.

"You've changed your mind?" he said.

"I ain't changed nothing," McCloskey said. "You want me to head to the JT, don't you?"

"Yes."

"Then there ain't nothing more to talk about. I'm going, that's all there is to say."

Chapter Forty-Three

"Thank you for agreeing to return to the JT," Stokes said to Lenny. "I know you would have stayed with Cora, but Lars and Reuban will be pleased to have your help. There's nobody better with the animals."

Their boots were noisy on the timber sidewalk. Lenny had said nothing since they had left the Mullens' house. Amos, bow-legged and slow behind them, had been quiet too. He seemed to need all his concentration just to put one foot before the other, and Stokes noticed how the old man winced when he stepped up and down from the sidewalk.

They were approaching the Lady Elgin when Amos finally broke his silence.

"If you is gonna buy Jed a bottle of rotgut, I think it only right we get another bottle for me and the boys up at the JT."

Stokes eyed the old man.

"You'll need your wits about you, Amos," he said. "You can't get drunk. Not with Tovey to guard."

"I ain't about to get drunk," Amos said. "But an old man needs a nip now and again to oil the joints. Pretty sure Lars and Reuban would like a taste of whiskey too. It's been a tough few days."

"It certainly has," Stokes said. "Very well. I'll buy you a bottle too, but I'm trusting you not to let anyone drink too much."

"You ain't got nothing to worry about there," Amos said.

They went into the saloon, blinking at the sudden change from the bright sunshine outside. Stokes scanned the faces of the men at the bar and around the tables. He recognised a few of them from previous visits to Griffith, but none of them by name. Part of him had hoped to see Bella again, and his gaze lingered for a second on a lady who was talking to a man in a suit playing Faro. For a second Stokes thought it might be Bella, but then he saw with disappointment that this woman was plumper, older and altogether less appealing than Miss Sawrey. There were no other women in the saloon. He pushed away thoughts of what that meant with regards to Bella's current activity.

The smell of the saloon filled his nostrils. He felt the pang of longing for a drink that gave him an understanding of White's plight. Not wishing to stay for long in the place, he strode straight to the bar.

"Two bottles of whiskey, if you please," he said to the barman.

"You're thirsty," the barkeep said with a grin.

Beside Stokes, a grey-haired man in threadbare dungarees cackled as if this was the funniest thing he had ever heard. Stokes stared at him unsmiling until the man stopped laughing.

"And a shot for the road for me," Amos said, reaching the bar and shouldering the chuckling man aside.

"Two bottles for the English gent," said the man, "and a shot for his servant." He laughed again, clearly thinking his witticisms the height of humour.

"I ain't his servant," Amos said.

"Well you sure look like you are. Carrying his saddlebags and walking on behind him."

"Ignore him," Stokes said. "We don't have time for this."

Amos gave the man a hard stare, then turned his back on him. The man's face grew crimson and he pulled at Amos' shoulder.

"Don't you turn your back on me, you old coot."

Stokes looked around the saloon. The man's raised voice had drawn attention to them. Heads turned and conversations stopped as men peered to see what was happening. His heart sank. So much for buying the whiskey and leaving quickly.

"We don't want any trouble," he said to the stranger at the bar.

"Too late for that," the drunken man snarled. He stepped back, his hand dropping to the gun on his belt.

Without warning, Lenny stepped in close. He moved much more quickly than the old drunk and his pistol was in his hand before the man's gun had cleared his holster.

"Too late for what, old man?" Lenny said, shoving the muzzle of his Colt under the man's chin. "It ain't too late for me to blow the top of your head off. Figure we can take a look and see if you got any brains in there."

The colour drained from the man's face. Lenny's eyes held an edge of madness. He didn't blink and his lips curled back from his teeth in a savage snarl.

Stokes placed a hand on McCloskey's shoulder. The boy was quivering, as taut as a bowstring.

"No need for that, Lenny."

For several seconds nobody moved. The saloon was silent. It felt as though everyone held their breath.

"This son of a bitch was gonna pull on Amos," Lenny said. "Figure I should finish what he started."

"No, Lenny. Put your gun away."

McCloskey trembled. The drunk's eyes widened as he became sure the young man was going to pull the trigger. Stokes was concerned about that very real possibility.

"Lenny," he said. "Come on. You have somewhere you need to be." He searched for something that would penetrate the young man's fury. "Would your girl want you to do this?"

McCloskey shuddered. With a sudden movement, he reholstered his revolver and pushed the old man away from him.

"Don't let me see you again," he said. "I do, I'll bed you down for good."

The grey-haired man stumbled back, face white. He made

no attempt to draw his gun. When he was a safe distance away from the furious young man, he turned on his heel and staggered out of the saloon.

Slowly, the conversations started up once more. Stokes let out a long breath.

"Your whiskey," the barman said, thumping the two bottles on the bar as if nothing had happened. "And a shot."

He poured a measure for Amos.

"I'll take one of those too," Lenny said.

Stokes sighed. The sooner the boy was out of town, the better. There was only so long his pent-up anger could be held in check. Whiskey was a bad idea, but he anticipated the boy would ignore him if he refused him the liquor. He nodded to the barman.

"Just the one," he said.

Amos looked at Stokes, then at McCloskey.

"My lord," he said, "I thought you was gonna drill that old sodbuster." He sipped his whiskey with relish.

"I would have," Lenny said, tossing back his own drink and suppressing a shudder. He placed his hands flat on the bar and took a deep breath, as if he was dizzy. "That fool owes his life to Mr Stokes."

"What did Cora say to get you so riled up?" Amos asked.

Lenny bit his lip and his eyes brimmed with tears.

"Said me watching her all the time made her more sad. Said when she looks in my eyes she can see how ugly she is—" His voice cracked.

Stokes placed a hand on his shoulder.

"She needs time to heal."

"She ain't ugly at all," Lenny said. "But looking at what they done to her, how sad she is, the pain she feels... I... I..." His voice trailed off.

"You're a good man, Lenny," Stokes said, picking up the bottles. "Cora is lucky to have you. I'm sure she knows that. Come on, let's go."

Hampton saw them coming and stepped out into the sun. He shielded his eyes with one dirty hand while the other held a cigarette to his lips.

"Thought it was you," he said, blowing out a long trail of smoke. "How's the girl?"

Stokes sighed.

"Everyone knows about her?"

"About Cora Rice? I was here when Amos brought her in with Mrs Thornford. I helped 'em with the wagon." He held up his hand, anticipating Stokes' next comment. "Don't worry. I ain't told nobody else. Mrs Thornford asked me to keep quiet and when a lady asks Alpheus Hampton for a favour, by ginger he does it."

"Thank you. It seems others do not share your tact."

"Stockman?"

"He's been telling everyone in town who'll listen."

"I heard that. Never did like that no count son of a bitch." Hampton threw away his cigarette butt. "Say, you wouldn't happen to have any of those nice cheroots, would you?"

"I tell you what," Stokes said, "you get these boys' horses saddled and the JT wagon hitched up. I'll have one of those cigarillos waiting for you when you're done."

Hampton grinned. "Right you are."

"Oh, another thing," Stokes said, holding out one of the bottles of whiskey. "Could you hold onto that for me and saddle up Tanner Strickland's horse too? I'll be back in a bit to fetch both the horse and the bottle."

"And you'll have that cigarillo?" Hampton smiled, then his expression changed to one of embarrassment. "And what the JT owes me?"

Stokes hadn't considered having to pay the hostler, but he nodded.

"Of course," he said. "How much does the ranch owe?"

Hampton told him. Even though Stokes had little left of the

money he had brought with him to Oregon, he had enough to pay the livery stable bill.

"Sorry for asking," Hampton said.

"No need to apologise. You run a business. I understand. The JT Ranch's future is uncertain."

Hampton looked glum. He mumbled something that Stokes didn't catch before nodding curtly and disappearing into the shadowed stable building.

"Here." Stokes handed the other whiskey bottle to Amos Willard. "Don't drink it all at once. Stay safe, both of you. Make sure you keep a watch on the ranch and don't travel anywhere alone. We don't know what Grant might try. And watch that bastard Tovey. He strikes me as a weakling, but I have no doubt he'll do whatever he can to escape."

"No doubt," said Amos. "The man's a snake, but don't you worry about us. I'm old, which should tell you all you need to know about me."

"Which is?"

"I'm tougher, smarter or luckier than a lot of men I seen buried. I ain't about to let Grant do anything to the JT and I sure as hell ain't gonna let that skunk Rab Tovey escape."

"Well, take care. Both of you." Stokes clasped McCloskey's shoulder. "Hold onto that anger of yours, Lenny. There might come a time to use it, but for now, keep a tight rein on it and do what Amos tells you."

Lenny nodded, but would not meet his gaze. The ire and angst washed off him like a stink. The sooner he was away from the town, the better.

With a feeling of foreboding, Stokes turned away from the two men and walked back into Griffith.

Chapter Forty-Four

The town was quiet. Clouds had formed over the mountains but the afternoon sun was still warm. A few people walked along the timber sidewalk on the far side of the street. A teamster drove a creaking wagon of lumber hauled behind six straining mules. The colourful bunting and ribbons that had been hung for the railroad opening fluttered gently. The distant thump of the sawmills drifted over the town, a reminder of one of the industries that had given birth to this settlement. A half dozen horses bearing the brands of local ranches stood at the hitching rail outside the Lady Elgin, bearing testament to the other predominant business that kept Griffith alive. As usual, The Palace appeared to be empty. Not for the first time Stokes wondered how long the establishment could remain open with so little commerce.

Griffith gave the impression of a calm, tranquil place. A haven for peaceful, hard-working men and women, nestled in the foothills of the Blue Mountains. Stokes clenched his jaw as he walked. His left leg ached slightly, but he didn't notice the familiar throb, instead thinking about the evil that lurked within half a day's ride of the town. Evil stemming from that most common of motives: greed. There was more than enough wealth in this land's resources for everyone to share. Grant had no right to possess it all.

Stokes smiled grimly to himself, wondering what his father would have thought of such a sentiment. The Stokes family owned a large estate where tenant farmers worked the land. Gabriel's forebears had almost certainly driven men and women from the lush fields of Wessex in just as vicious a manner as Grant. So what entitled Stokes to feel righteous anger? Surely this was simply the way of the world. How things had always been done.

Perhaps, thought Stokes, his hand absently touching the grip of the revolver on his hip, but that didn't make it right. He could not change what atrocities his ancestors might have committed, but he could challenge what was happening right under his nose. He was content in the knowledge that William and Eliza ran the family estate fairly, treating the families that lived on the land with respect and dignity. Here, thousands of miles from that green and pleasant home, he would do his utmost to see that the Thornfords, the Rices, and everyone else in this valley could live without fear, without the threat posed by Grant and his army of gunmen.

Reaching the Sheriff's office, he knocked on the door. When there was no answer, he tried the handle. The door swung open and Stokes stepped inside.

As he entered, Deputy Stockman was coming into the office from a door in the rear wall. Presumably it led to cells, such as he had seen in the Marshal's office in Huntington.

"Oh, it's you," Stockman said, sitting down at the largest of the two desks. His face was flushed and beaded with sweat as if he had been running. Stokes wondered what he had been doing in the back room. Fleetingly, he pondered whether one of the girls from the saloon might be back there. He felt a flash of annoyance as he imagined Bella behind that door.

"Warm day, isn't it?" Stokes said.

"Yeah." Stockman pulled a kerchief from a pocket and mopped his forehead and cheeks. Leaning back in his chair, he put his boots up on the table. They were dusty and Stokes noticed a dark spot on one of them. Seeing it at the same time,

Stockman lowered his feet and used the kerchief to rub at the stain. Folding the cotton carefully, he pushed it back into his pocket. "What do you want?" he asked, his tone gruff.

Anger flared inside Stokes and he considered confronting the deputy with his lack of discretion. But to do so would gain him nothing. He was no foolish boy like Lenny, acting on instinct alone. He had more important things to deal with.

"I'm looking for Bannon," he said.

Stockman's mouth twitched into an expression that might have been a smirk.

"The Sheriff ain't here."

"I can see that," replied Stokes, keeping his voice calm. "Do you know where he is?"

"Can't say I do. I ain't Bannon's keeper. He goes where he wants, when he wants."

Stokes took a calming breath.

"When you see him, please tell him I'm looking for him."

"Where shall I say you're staying?"

Stokes stared at him for several seconds without blinking. He did not want a fight with this man, but he could feel his rage building.

"You know where," he said at last.

"Reckon I do," Stockman replied, a wide grin on his face.

Stokes turned on his heel and made for the door. Just as he reached for the pommel, the door flew open and a man ran into the office. He was about thirty years old, with a full beard and a small cap on his head. He wore dusty overalls and heavy boots caked in dried mud. A farmer perhaps, or a labourer of some sort.

"Deputy!" the man shouted, first looking at Stokes, then, realising his error, swinging to face the desk. "Deputy! Come quick!"

"What is it?" Stockman asked, standing and reaching for a repeating rifle that rested in a rack on the wall behind him.

"It's Sheriff Bannon," said the man. "Come quick." Without

waiting for a response, the man rushed out of the office and ran across the road. Stokes followed him with Deputy Stockman close behind.

There were a number of people milling about outside the Lady Elgin and at first Stokes thought the man was leading them into the saloon. Instead, he shouldered his way through the crowd and headed for the alley that ran down the side of the building. There were more people in the narrow space and the man shouted at them to get out of the way. The alley smelt strongly of stale urine. Flies buzzed in the stench-heavy shade. Stokes brushed them away as he followed the shouting man. Stockman was right behind him and, sensing that a crime had taken place, he started adding his own voice to that of the man who had come to the Sheriff's office.

"Make way!" he bellowed. "Make way for the County Sheriff."

The gathered people parted before them. They jostled and shuffled awkwardly, trying to avoid stepping on what they were all looking at. The space behind the saloon was cluttered with all manner of supplies and refuse. Between the building's back entrance and the outhouse that stood some ten paces away, the ground was littered with bottles and cigarette butts. Piled to one side were several barrels. Next to them teetered a stack of wooden crates. A couple of broken chairs and a table missing a leaf were leaning against the back wall of the establishment.

The area was in deep shadow. Beyond the outhouse the sun shone on some fenced fields and corrals. Stokes could see some of the stockyards in the distance. Pulling his gaze back to the shaded yard, he blinked after the bright hazy sunshine in the street, but he had no trouble making out what was sprawled on the ground.

He let out a long breath.

"Well, Stockman," he said, his tone acidic in its politeness, "I'd say congratulations are in order."

Stockman stood without moving. He stared down at the

body that lay at his feet. Gazing up at them with unseeing eyes, lay Theodore Bannon. His dark suit was smothered in dust from the ground, his white shirt stained crimson. The badge on his chest gleamed despite the shadows, mocking them with its promise of justice and order. The man couldn't have been dead for more than a few minutes. Blood still oozed from multiple stab wounds to the chest and abdomen. Stockman suddenly realised the blood was touching his boot and he stepped back abruptly, bumping into a large bearded man who swore.

"What?" Stockman said, his voice hollow and lost. His face was drenched in sweat and he seemed incapable of looking away from the corpse.

"Congratulations on your promotion, Stockman," Stokes said. "Or should I say, Sheriff Stockman?"

Chapter Forty-Five

They heard the long whistle of the train followed by the hiss and rattle as it huffed past the south of town towards the new station. Stokes checked his watch. Just before eleven a.m. Dimly, through the open window, he could hear people cheering the arrival of the train and the Governor. The grand opening of the station was due the following day, but the people of Griffith were ready to start celebrating. Stokes thought the new sheriff would have his work cut out for him as the saloons filled up with merrymakers and fights inevitably broke out.

"The train's on time," he said.

Mary Ann glanced at him. She was standing by the window and the light of the morning limned her fine features. In her hands she clasped the package of notes they had compiled together; Van Orman's statement and the witnesses' accounts of what they had found at the Rice ranch. There were also records of the activities of the Blue Mountain Sheep Shooters, and the group's association with Tom Grant. The papers also contained written details of the circumstances of John Thornford's murder. That was one part of the dossier Stokes was not content with. What was written was eloquent enough and damning. But Stokes knew there was another, conflicting account. White spoke of several shooters, naming them as belonging to Grant's crew, while Van Orman had told him the tracks showed only one man on the ridge. A lone shooter. Stokes did not like the contradiction, but had chosen not to mention it to Mary Ann. She had enough to worry about and the stakes were too high for uncertainty in the evidence they were presenting. But the discrepancy rankled and he felt uneasy at the omission of Van Orman's description of the tracks at the site of John's murder.

One thing Stokes was sure of was that Grant gained from Thornford's death and he had ordered the burning of the Rice ranch. He had spoken to the man and taken the measure of him. He was ruthless and calculating. More than that, he seemed to enjoy wielding power over those weaker than him. There was no doubt in Stokes' mind that Grant was guilty of many crimes, including ordering murders, and all for financial gain. He just hoped the evidence they had compiled would be enough for the Governor to act upon.

"Should we leave now?" Mary Ann asked.

"The train hasn't even pulled into the station yet," Stokes said, understanding her nervousness, and trying to allay it with a smile. "We'll walk down there so that we arrive just before midday. That is the time Pennoyer put in his telegram, so he'll be expecting you then."

She looked out the window as if she thought Pennoyer, or perhaps Grant, would be standing right outside. She looked exhausted, her eyes underlined with dark bruises. None of them had slept much the night before. They had expected a knock on the door, or worse, a sudden shot in the darkness, or a lantern thrown through a shattered window.

Thankfully, by the time the golden fingers of the last dawn of April stretched across the valley, no attack had come. The Mullens had risen just after sunrise and set about making breakfast for them all. Abigail with her usual terse efficiency, Ruby with friendly eagerness and frequent glances and smiles in Stokes' direction. He was flattered by her attention, but did not respond, not wishing to give any indication that he might be interested in her. She was pretty and would make some man a good wife, but he was already married. Ruby was not a young woman to be ruined with a dalliance. She was respectable.

The thought of Rebecca galled him. He did not blame her for what had happened. She had not told him to leave and it had been his decision to see that she was catered for as she was accustomed. But now here he was in a backwater town on the other side of the globe, surrounded by corruption and violence, just as he had been in London. But here he didn't have the weight of the Metropolitan Police behind him, or access to his family's fortune. He had escaped nothing by fleeing. If they managed to put an end to this, he could not carry on like this. He would have to return to England to sort out his affairs.

"You really think Stockman killed Bannon?" Mary Ann asked, breaking into his melancholic reverie.

"I would place a wager on it," he said. "He stood to gain and I am quite certain it was Bannon's blood I saw on his boot in the Sheriff's office. But there were no witnesses to Bannon's murder. No murder weapon. Without hard evidence, Stockman will say it was some drunk whom Bannon was trying to arrest."

Mary Ann looked out the window again.

"Isn't that where we are with this?" She lifted the dossier. "Supposition and circumstantial evidence? Nothing concrete."

That worried Stokes too. He was sure Grant and his men were guilty of many crimes, but what evidence they had was thin.

"This is a roll of the dice," he said. "With luck, Pennoyer will agree to take it to a judge that is not in Grant's pocket."

"And if he doesn't?"

White, who was evidently listening from where he sat by the front door, spoke up, loud enough for them both to hear.

"Then Grant will have to face a whole different type of justice," he said. "I ain't about to let that bastard get away with what he's done."

"Before it comes to that," Stokes said, "remember the

Governor's telegram. He said he had good news. I'm hopeful. Perhaps he already has other evidence against Grant. Grant's rich and powerful enough to have ruffled plenty of feathers across the state. He must have some influential enemies. Let's hope Pennoyer is one of them."

White didn't say anything further, but Stokes could sense his scepticism. The older man had been surly and ill-tempered all through the night, but a shot of whiskey every hour or two had kept his hands steady, even if it had done little to improve his mood. Stokes knew Jed was desperate to dive into a bottle and it was only sheer force of will and his affection for Mary Ann that was keeping him from losing his head. Stokes could only imagine the scale of debauchery White would submerse himself in when this was all over.

Time passed slowly. Stokes checked his watch frequently and they spoke little. There was nothing more to say. They had done all their talking the previous evening, discussing possible outcomes of the meeting with Pennoyer, the repercussions of Bannon's death, and how Reuban, Lars, Lenny and Amos would be faring back at the JT. Everything hinged on Governor Pennoyer's reaction to their evidence.

Eventually it was time. Stokes clicked his watch closed and slipped it into his pocket.

"Ready?"

"Ready as I'll ever be," said Mary Ann.

"Coming with you," White said, standing up and buckling on his gun belt with the two Remingtons.

"We've talked about this, Jed," Stokes said. "You need to watch the girls with Tanner."

"Been thinking about that. Seems if they didn't come for them in the night, they won't come in the day with the Governor and newspapermen in town."

"Still, I'd feel better knowing you were here."

"And I'd feel better knowing I had my eye on Mary Ann. There are gonna be a lot of people down by the hotel. You ain't got eyes in the back of your head. Comes to a scrap, you'll need me."

Stokes hesitated. He didn't want to leave Tanner alone protecting Cora and Florence, but there could be no denying White's value in a fight.

"Jed's right," Tanner said, from where he sat by the back door, as if he could read Stokes' mind. "I'll be all right. I'll lock the doors. And you won't be long. Anyone come looking for the girls, they won't get past me."

"There's no time to argue about it," Mary Ann added. "I don't want to miss my appointment."

Stokes looked from one to the other, angry, though not surprised, that White had chosen the last minute to voice his plan to accompany them.

"As you wish," he said at last. "Let's go."

Stokes and White walked either side of Mary Ann, who grasped the packet of documents tightly to her chest, as if she thought they might blow away. Wind gusted down from the mountains, and the dark clouds there promised rain. The pennons and ribbons for the celebration snapped and flapped above their heads as they entered the main street. There were a lot more people in the town than the day before. The sidewalks were bustling. Several horses were hitched outside the Lady Elgin and even The Palace had a few horses tied to its often empty rail.

As they arrived at the Grand Hotel, a carriage was pulling up. A thickset man with a handlebar moustache stepped down from it and offered his hand to a well-dressed lady wearing a large bonnet decorated with lace and tulle. The man opened the hotel door and held it for the lady, then followed her inside.

"Look," White said, nodding at some horses tethered to a rail nearby. "Cabin Creek brand."

"Keep your eyes peeled," Stokes said. "We don't need any trouble right now."

White sniffed.

"I never go looking for it, but trouble always seems to find me."

"Let's get in off the street," Mary Ann said.

Looking around for any sign of danger, Stokes stepped up to the freshly painted doors and pulled one open. Mary Ann was about to step through, but White held her back.

"Me first."

He entered, then beckoned her inside.

"Looks like trouble's found us again," he said.

Stokes' eyes took a few seconds to adjust to the dim light filtering through the windows so he was unsure what White meant. Then he understood.

"What in God's name are they doing in here?" he hissed.

Cadmar Byrne rose from where he was sitting on a couch at the rear of the lobby. He was as dapper as ever, his usual smirk on his lips.

"Mrs Thornford," he said, lifting his hat, "you look radiant."

"The pleasure's all yours," snarled White.

Byrne smiled. Bull Meacher and Joaquin Lopez were sprawled on the couch. Jackson Pailing was leaning against the banister at the bottom of the staircase. All three of them eyed Stokes and White like wolves watching antelope grazing.

A hard-faced man Stokes did not recognise stood partway up the stairs, where they turned at a right angle. He was broad-shouldered and tall and wore a plain, smart suit. He surveyed Stokes and White, taking in the guns they wore. Stokes thought he had the bearing of a soldier or a policeman.

"Would you care to sit?" Byrne asked Mary Ann.

"Thank you, but no," she replied. Turning her back on Cadmar Byrne and the other men lounging beside the stairs, she walked to the reception desk. The clerk, a middle-aged man with pomade-slick hair and a suit that looked two sizes too big for his slender frame, was just finishing with the couple who had arrived by carriage.

"I trust you will have a very pleasant stay at the Grand Hotel," the clerk said, and clicked his fingers. A skinny youth came out of a back room. "Show Mr and Mrs Hindle to room three."

The boy led the man and woman to the stairs. The Cabin Creek men watched the wealthy couple pass. Lopez made loud kissing noises at the woman and the portly man wheeled on him angrily.

"You watch your mouth, boy," he said, colour high in his cheeks.

Lopez stuck out his tongue and waggled it lasciviously at Mrs Hindle.

"*You* watch it," he said with a grin. "Like what you see, señora?"

The man appeared about to step down to face Lopez when his wife pulled him back.

"Come on, Charles," she said. "Don't let that horrible man spoil our day."

With apparent reluctance, he allowed his wife to coax him away.

"That's right, gringo," Lopez said, his fingers tapping lightly the gun at his side. "You come at me, I spoil your day like you wouldn't believe."

"I'm sorry about that," the clerk said in a quiet voice that would not carry to the men from the Cabin Creek. "They should be gone soon. How can I help you?"

"I have an appointment with Governor Pennoyer," Mary Ann said. "At midday."

The clerk glanced at a large clock above the fireplace. It was two minutes to twelve. Stokes checked his watch. It was one minute faster than the hotel clock.

"Of course," the clerk said. "The Governor is with another guest. If you would care to wait here, I'll let you know when he is free."

"Thank you."

They stood awkwardly near the fireplace, as far as possible from Cadmar Byrne and the others. The ticking of the clock was loud. From outside came the muffled sounds of hooves and the rumble of wagon wheels, the clump of feet on the wooden sidewalk. Stokes stared at Cadmar Byrne. The handsome gunhand stared back, his infuriating half-smile on his face.

"Bet you a dollar we know who's inside with the Governor," White said.

"I wouldn't take that wager," Stokes replied. "God damn it," he said under his breath. "My apologies for my language, Mary Ann."

"No need to apologise," she said. "I feel like cussing too. How can Grant be in there speaking to Pennoyer before us?"

"More to the point," Stokes said, "what is he telling Pennoyer?"

She bit her lip, nervous and uncertain.

"Should we leave?" she asked. "There is little point in meeting with the Governor if Grant has poisoned him against us."

"Him being here might have nothing to do with you and the JT. The Governor is an important man. Grant is no fool. He wants to be friends with the men at the top."

"That's what I'm afraid of," she said bitterly. "Grant has deep pockets. If he has donated money to Pennoyer's campaign..."

Stokes placed a hand gently on her arm.

"Let's not create things to worry about that haven't happened yet. They may not occur at all."

She sighed.

"You're right. I know you're right. We have plenty to worry about already without me creating more problems, however likely they might be."

Stokes offered her what he hoped was a calming smile, but inside, his stomach churned and his mind roiled. Mary Ann was right to be concerned. Grant's meeting with the Governor could surely not bode well for them.

The clock ticked and time moved as slowly as spilt molasses in winter. At twenty past twelve they heard footsteps on the stairs. The suited guard glanced up and straightened, as if standing to attention. Stokes nodded to himself. The man had definitely been a soldier once. The guard nodded to whoever was coming down. White and Stokes both tensed. Without speaking, they took a step in front of Mary Ann protectively.

Just as they had expected, it was Grant. The big cattleman surveyed the foyer with a glance. Spying Mary Ann and the two men with her, he grinned.

"Mrs Thornford," he said, striding towards her, hands outstretched as if welcoming an old friend. "What a pleasure it is to see you, my dear."

"I can't say the same," Mary Ann said, her voice tight, her words curt.

Grant ignored her tone. His smile didn't falter. He halted a couple of paces away from Stokes and White, but didn't acknowledge either of them. His eyes never left Mary Ann.

"Have you thought any more about my offer? It really is very generous."

"I've told you what I think of your offer," she said.

"Are you sure you wouldn't like to reconsider. It would make everybody's lives much easier. I wouldn't want you to regret your decision, like poor Thomas Rice. I'm sure he regretted not accepting my money. Not for long though." He turned back to Byrne and the others who had risen from the couch and followed him. "What do you think, Cadmar?" he asked. "How long do you think Mr Rice regretted his decision?"

"I couldn't say for sure, Mr Grant," Byrne said. "I would judge it would only be a few minutes before he stopped being able to feel anything at all."

Byrne looked at Mary Ann intently, perhaps to gauge her reaction to his words. Whatever reaction he had expected, his eyes widened in surprise at the one he got. Stokes sensed a sudden movement behind him, then Mary Ann had shoved herself in between him and White. She appeared to be pointing at Grant, arm outstretched. Grant's face paled.

Stokes saw his mistake at once. She was not pointing. In her hand was a tiny pistol. A two-shot Derringer like the one he had taken from Tovey back in Huntington. The gun was small in Mary Ann's hand, but large enough to kill. At this range, she could not miss.

The men behind Grant erupted into movement. Byrne's pistol seemed to fly into his hand. Meacher and Lopez were only a little slower. Pailing stood off to one side. He had not drawn a weapon, but watched on impassively. When Stokes flicked a glance at White he saw that the old man had both his Remingtons trained on the Cabin Creek men. Stokes had not even noticed him moving. His own hand rested on his Colt Lightning's grip, but he did not attempt to pull it free of the holster. The situation was on a knife-edge. Any movement now might see them all killed in a blaze of shooting.

"I should kill you now, Grant," Mary Ann said. There was no trace of fear in her voice, just a simmering rage. "Like the rat you are."

Grant forced a smile.

"If you do that, my dear, my men will kill you, and your two men here."

"But you'd be dead," she replied, each word delivered with the finality of a nail driven into a coffin. "Griffith and this valley would be rid of you. It would be worth it."

He had regained some of his composure now and his smile seemed less affected.

"Sacrifice your own life, Mary Ann, but would you really sentence Jed and your husband's friend to death?"

"Don't worry about me, Mary Ann," White said. "Go ahead and shoot the son of a bitch. I'll kill the rest."

Bull Meacher's gun twitched towards Jed.

"You would risk your friends' lives for what?" Grant

said, ignoring White. "Revenge for something you *believe* happened?"

"We all know what you are!" she shouted. Stokes watched her closely. Her finger was white on the pistol's trigger.

"Not like this, Mary Ann," he said.

"He deserves it," she said. Tears rolled down her cheeks and her hand shook, but Stokes had no doubt that if she fired, her shot would find its mark.

"The law will give him what he deserves," he said. "I know how you feel, but killing a man is not something you can ever be free of. You're not a murderer, Mary Ann. If you do this, you'll be as bad as him. Is that how you want Albert and Adelaide to remember their mother?"

For several seconds she did not move. Her cheeks streamed with tears. Slowly, cautiously, Stokes held out his left hand.

"Give me the gun, Mary Ann. Let the law handle him." She didn't move, but he thought he saw her hand relax slightly. Without hesitation, he lashed out and grasped the Derringer, forcing his thumb underneath the hammers. He winced as she pulled on the trigger and the hammer pinched into his skin. He tugged the gun out of her hand and used his other hand to pull the hammer back enough for him to free himself. The webbing of his thumb was an angry red and throbbed in agony but the skin was not broken. Stokes couldn't be certain if she would have fired if he had not intervened, but if she had, there was no doubt in his mind there would have been a blood bath in the hotel lobby. He hoped he would not regret stopping her from killing their enemy.

"Fun's over, boys," Grant said. "Put your guns away. We're here to celebrate, not get in a fight. Mary Ann, that's the second time you've pulled a gun on me. I won't forgive such behaviour again."

"Next time, I won't hesitate," she said.

"If there's a next time, neither will I." He held her gaze for several seconds. There was no sign of his smile now. "But I

347

doubt there'll be a next time." He touched the brim of his hat. "Have a good day."

He left the hotel without a backward glance. His men followed him. Byrne lifted his hat as he passed.

"Ma'am," he said. "Gentlemen."

Bull Meacher paused in front of them.

"Mr Grant's too soft," he said. "Up to me, I'd have painted the wall with you."

White sneered. Stokes offered Meacher a condescending smile that told the man just what he thought of him.

"Well it's a good thing for Mr Grant you don't run the outfit," he said. "If you'd shot at us, he'd be dead, and most likely so would you. Not that either death would have been a bad thing."

Bull Meacher's mouth worked as his small eyes darted from Stokes to White and then to Mary Ann. It was clear he wanted to say more, but couldn't find the words.

"Run along now," Stokes said, "there's a good chap. You wouldn't want to get left behind."

Seeing that indeed all of his comrades had already left the hotel lobby, Meacher backed away from the trio.

"You'll get yours, Englishman," he spat. "You too, Jed. Then we'll have some fun with her." He stabbed a finger at Mary Ann and she flinched as if slapped.

When he had gone, Stokes examined his hand. It was red and raw and stung like hell. He weighed the tiny pistol in his palm. It looked familiar.

"Mary Ann, where in God's name did you get this from?"

She looked abashed. "Sorry," she mumbled, cuffing at the tears on her face. Stokes pulled out his handkerchief and handed it to her. "Thank you," she said, and dabbed her eyes.

"I ain't usually one to say sorry," White said sheepishly, "but I reckon this is my fault, not Mary Ann's. Though in my defence, I didn't know we'd run into Grant."

"You gave her the gun?"

348

"Took it off Tovey. Thought Mary Ann could use the protection."

Stokes shook his left hand and tested his grip. It was painful, but no lasting damage had been done. He looked at each of them in turn.

"No more surprises?" he asked.

"With the trail we been riding," White replied, "I wouldn't like to bet on that."

Chapter Forty-Six

"Please, take a seat."

Sylvester Pennoyer, Governor of Oregon, gestured to a small couch. He was of medium height, three or four inches shorter than Stokes, but such was his presence and self-assurance that his stature seemed to equal that of the Englishman. He wore a black suit and a crimson cravat. His hair was greying at the temples and his trimmed beard was mostly silver. Stokes judged him to be close to sixty, but still full of vitality and vigour.

Mary Ann, still rattled from the confrontation with Grant in the lobby, mumbled her thanks to Pennoyer and sat.

Stokes looked around the room. It was small and quite sparsely decorated. However, there was a patterned rug on the floor, thick velvet curtains at the window, and the seats were upholstered with padded brocade. It was provincial and austere when compared to his own house in London, or his family's home in Wiltshire, and Stokes was certain the smooth-talking man who stood before them was used to much finer accommodation than this. But it was clean and no doubt it was the best room available in the hotel, quite probably the most luxurious in all of Griffith.

"I'd rather stand," Stokes said.

Pennoyer nodded.

"As you wish," he said. "Would you care for a drink? I know it is early, but you look like you could use one, my dear. I know I need one after speaking to that snake, Grant." He moved to a table where a decanter and a few bottles stood along with several glasses on a tray. Stokes watched him, sizing him up, looking for signs that would show his character. He had become used to dealing with the rough ranch hands and frontiersmen of this Oregon valley, but Pennoyer was no ruffian and would not be so easy to read. This was a slick politician, accustomed to hiding his intentions from men who would look him in the eye and lie without blinking. A man did not get elected to the position of governor without understanding how to play the game. It might be a good sign that he professed a dislike for Grant, but that could just as easily be a ruse to trick them into showing their own cards.

"There's whiskey," Pennoyer said, "what looks like a half decent French brandy, and," he picked up one of the bottles and studied the label, "sherry. I'm sure the locals think the whiskey is good enough, but it smells like paint thinner to me. I'm going to try the brandy."

"Just a small sherry for me, please," Mary Ann said in a timid voice.

Pennoyer looked to Stokes.

"Nothing for me, thank you."

"Signed the pledge, have you?" the Governor said, with a smile. "Not sure I can trust a man who doesn't drink."

The man's oiliness irked Stokes.

"I'm not sure I can trust a man who thinks it's his business what another man drinks."

Pennoyer stared at him for a few seconds, then his smile broadened.

"Fair enough," he said, pouring the drinks. "I guess that's me put in my place."

Pennoyer carried the glass over to Mary Ann, who took it gratefully and sipped at the contents. She gave no indication of her thoughts on the quality of the sherry. Pennoyer moved to stand by the window. He took a gulp of his brandy and nodded appreciatively. The three of them were alone in the room, but Pennoyer had such charisma that he seemed to fill the space.

White was waiting in the lobby. The Governor's man on the stairs would not let them carry any weapons up to their meeting, and White had refused to give his guns up, so he took hold of Stokes' Colt and gun belt, pocketed Mary Ann's Derringer and sat to wait on the couch recently vacated by Meacher, Byrne and Lopez.

"You must be Lieutenant Stokes," Pennoyer said, turning his back on the window and giving them his full attention. "A military man, and a lawman too. And a good friend to Captain Thornford, no doubt."

"I owe him my life," Stokes said. "It is the least I can do to help his widow and children."

"Admirable indeed," Pennoyer said. There was something in his tone that made Stokes think the Governor believed there to be something unsavoury in his presence there. Pennoyer had another mouthful of brandy, then took a deep breath, as if coming to a conclusion about how to proceed. "I was saddened to hear of your husband's death," he said, frowning gravely at Mary Ann. "John was a good man."

"Thank you. And thank you for agreeing to see me."

"I had planned on sending you a telegram the very day your letter arrived. I was most surprised to receive it, I have to say."

"You planned on contacting me?" Mary Ann was incredulous. "Why? I know John had met you a couple of times and he spoke highly of you, but I didn't know you were close."

"We weren't. But I am pleased to say he placed his trust in me with a very sensitive matter. This concerns the good news I mentioned in my telegram." He glanced at Stokes. "It is a sensitive matter that perhaps you should hear alone."

"Whatever you have to say to me, Gabriel can hear too."

Pennoyer raised an eyebrow, perhaps inferring from her use of Stokes' Christian name some impropriety in their friendship.

"I would feel more comfortable speaking to you alone," he said.

"Your comfort is really none of my concern," she replied coolly. Stokes felt a smile tugging at his lips. He forced a sombre expression. "I trust Gabriel," Mary Ann went on. "He has been of great help in obtaining the evidence we have compiled against Mr Grant."

Pennoyer finished his brandy and set the glass back on the table. Pulling a chain from his waistcoat, he produced a silver watch that gleamed in the dull sunlight from the window. He checked the time.

"As you wish, but the news I have for you really has no bearing on the allegations you have made against Mr Grant."

Stokes felt a sinking sensation in his stomach. Something in Pennoyer's demeanour made him uneasy.

"What do you mean?" Mary Ann said. "Why else would you have reason to see me?"

"I am needed at a luncheon at one," the Governor said, ignoring the question. "So I don't have much time. Are you absolutely sure you are happy for Lieutenant Stokes to remain present while I give you confidential information of a personal nature?"

"I can step outside," Stokes said, not wishing to place Mary Ann in a difficult position.

"No," Mary Ann replied, "you stay." She was pale, but the sherry seemed to have calmed her. Stokes looked at the brandy on the table. He longed to reach out and take a long pull from the bottle. Instead, he clenched his hands at his side and didn't move, apart from giving a curt nod.

"Very well," Pennoyer said. "Although what I have to tell you is not directly connected to your problems with Mr Grant—"

"Problems?" interjected Stokes. "You think murder is merely a problem?"

"Please, let me continue." Pennoyer looked fixedly at Mary

Ann, who nodded for him to carry on. "Nothing can change the past, Mrs Thornford. I was saddened to hear of John's death and I realise nothing can bring your husband back. However, your husband made provision for you and your family to be cared for in the event of his death."

"I don't understand."

"When Captain Thornford was last in Salem, he requested a meeting. I knew of some of the..." He hesitated, searching for the right word. "Some of the issues of the land rights here and the clashes between the cattlemen and the sheepherders. I thought Captain Thornford wanted to discuss something to do with that difficult situation. Instead he asked that I would be witness to some legal documents."

"What documents?" Mary Ann asked, her confusion evident.

"A life insurance policy. You are the beneficiary."

"John took out a life insurance? Why did he not tell me any of this?"

Pennoyer shrugged.

"That I cannot answer. All he said was that he wanted to make sure you and the children would be provided for if he died. He asked for me to hold onto the policy and to make sure you received the papers in the event of his death. When I heard he had been killed I decided I would give them to you in person. I thought it would be better for me to deliver such news face-to-face than in a letter."

Mary Ann was pale.

"I understand this is a shock," Pennoyer said, "but it is good news. Of that I am certain."

Mary Ann seemed unable to speak. She was staring at the Governor as if his words made no sense to her.

Stokes broke the silence.

"How much is the premium?" he asked.

Pennoyer ignored Stokes, but by way of an answer he took an envelope from the table and handed it to Mary Ann.

Silently, with trembling hands, she opened it and pulled out some papers. She scanned them and her eyes widened.

"Good news, as I said." Pennoyer seemed pleased with himself. "I know your circumstances must have been looking grim and I apologise for not letting you know about this sooner, but as I was already scheduled to come to Griffith, this seemed the perfect opportunity."

Mary Ann did not speak. She was still reading from the papers, trying to digest what she had just learnt.

"This is good news," Stokes said. "I can see that. But how does it help with Grant?"

Pennoyer briskly smoothed his moustache and beard with his forefinger and thumb. It was a small gesture, that could have meant nothing, but his jaw tightened and his eyes narrowed for an instant. It seemed to Stokes the Governor was trying to hide his annoyance at the Englishman's involvement in this conversation.

"It doesn't directly," Pennoyer said, "but Mrs Thornford now has more than enough money not to worry about the ranch any longer. As I understand it, Mr Grant has made a generous offer on the land that he is still willing to honour. I suggest you accept it, my dear, and move somewhere far from here. Somewhere safe. Your children can go to the best schools and you can live in leisure. You will be the mistress of a modest fortune."

Mary Ann carefully folded the papers and slid them back into the envelope.

"It is quite something to be surprised by one's husband from beyond the grave, but I cannot be angry with him for this. He must have had his reasons for his secrecy. But this is not why we wanted to see you." She smoothed her skirt over her knees. "You received my letter. In it we laid out many of the crimes linked to Mr Grant and the Cabin Creek Ranch. Since then there have been more, even worse crimes in which he has been involved. We have documented them all. We would like you to help us take this before a judge. Someone neutral who will weigh up the evidence fairly. It is a badly kept secret that Judge Selby is in Grant's pay. With your backing, I'm sure people will listen and Grant can be made to face trial." She held out the thick packet of papers Stokes and she had compiled. Pennoyer made no effort to accept them. Instead he walked to the window and stared out at the street below.

The sinking feeling in Stokes grew stronger.

"Don't you understand?" Pennoyer said. "With the insurance and the money Grant will pay for your ranch, you need not worry any more about disputes over grazing rights, water rights, land boundaries. It is my sound belief that you should accept his offer and move away. Be done with all this. It is no life for a member of the fairer sex."

"It is no life for my husband either," she said, her bitterness making her words cut like knives. "Or have you forgotten that John was murdered? And what about the Rices? Grant ordered their ranch destroyed. Mr and Mrs Rice died in the fire, their ranch hands were gunned down. One of their daughters was killed, another badly burnt. I cannot turn my back on all of that. I simply cannot."

Stokes felt a great pride swelling in his chest at her words. It might be folly to remain here, but like Mary Ann, he could not walk away without seeing justice done.

"Whatever evidence you believe you have, it will not be enough," Pennoyer said. He did not meet her gaze.

"You haven't even looked at it," she said. "Your mind was made up before we came into this room. Just look at the evidence. And there is more. We have a witness?"

"A witness?"

"One of his men," Stokes said. "He has ridden for the Cabin Creek during all of this and has been involved in several crimes."

"And this man is now willing to talk out against his employer?"

Stokes thought of Rab Tovey, bruised, bloody and trussed up in the JT Ranch barn.

"He'll testify," he said.

Pennoyer pondered this information.

"If you can get this man to testify, there might be a chance. Where is this man?"

"He's safe," Stokes said.

Pennoyer nodded thoughtfully.

"No, it is no good. It will be one man's word against Grant's. And he will produce dozens of witnesses who will declare his innocence."

"He should stand trial for what he has done," Stokes said.

"I don't disagree with you," the Governor said. "But you don't understand. Grant has many friends. I have no love for the man, but my hands are tied. This is an election year. I cannot stand against him."

"Cannot, or will not?"

"I cannot!" He sounded desperate, his controlled facade slipping. "I too have children."

"Grant threatened you?" Stokes asked.

Pennoyer took a deep breath, regaining control of his emotions. He poured himself a finger of brandy and swallowed it down in one gulp.

"I cannot help you, Mrs Thornford," he said with finality. "But you have the means to move on with your life. Many who deal with such men as Grant are not so lucky to get a second chance. Take it and never look back."

A crashing sound outside in the corridor interrupted them. Shouting, furious and shrill, permeated the thin wood of the hotel door. A man and a woman were fighting, loudly. Frowning, Stokes went to the door and opened it. He recognised one of those voices.

"Bella?"

Bella Sawrey was being restrained by the Governor's bodyguard. She lay sprawled on the ground at the top of the stairs.

The strong man had a hold of one of her feet. Her skirt and petticoats had ridden up as they struggled, exposing her long, lithe legs.

"Let go of me!" she screamed, kicking out and connecting with the guard's chin.

He relinquished his grip. She sprang up and ran towards Stokes who stood in the doorway.

"What is it?" he asked.

"You got to come quick, Mr Stokes," she said, her breath coming in great frightened gasps. The guard was right behind her. His face was red and he thundered down the corridor, looking as if he would kill her if he got his hands on the girl.

Stokes stepped past Bella and held out a hand.

"Halt!" he snapped in his best officer voice.

Without hesitation, the guard stopped running. To Stokes' amusement, he even came to attention and began to bring his hand up to salute, only at the last second realising what he was doing and instead touching his fingers to his bloodied lip where Bella had kicked him.

"Goff, what's the meaning of this?" asked Governor Pennoyer from inside the room.

The guard looked at his fingers. They had come away from his mouth dotted with blood. He glowered at Bella and said, "This strumpet was demanding to speak to the Englishman."

"And she got past Ichabod Goff, the great hero of the Battle of Cedar Creek? Perhaps I should employ *her* as my bodyguard."

"Sorry, sir," Goff said. "It won't happen again."

"I should hope not. Though I understand the sentiment of not wishing to strike a lady."

"This one ain't no lady," the burly guard said. "Come on, you." He reached for Bella, but Stokes interposed himself.

"Wait," he said, still using the voice he had perfected on the parade ground. "I would hear what she has to say."

"It's Jed White," Bella said breathlessly. "I didn't know what else to do, but I seen you with him."

Stokes felt suddenly cold.

"Jed's in the lobby," he said, "what seems to be the trouble?"

Bella shook her head emphatically.

"He ain't downstairs," she said. "He's in the Lady Elgin. Must have drunk a bottle of whiskey in the time it takes most men to drink two shots. He's yelling at the Cabin Creek boys, calling them all manner of things. It's like he wants them to pull on him. I know he's supposed to be fast, but Cadmar Byrne, Bull Meacher and the rest of the Cabin Creek crew are in there. There's no way on earth he can hope to take them all."

Stokes cursed. He had been a fool not to see that White would head straight for a saloon as soon as he was out of their sight. And he knew just how the old frontiersman liked to goad others into action.

"Mary Ann, stay here," he said. "Pennoyer, can you see that no harm comes to Mrs Thornford?" There was no time for niceties and contemplation.

"Of course," Pennoyer said. "You have my word."

Stokes held the man's gaze for a second, then nodded. He hoped he was judging Pennoyer correctly. The Governor might not be about to help them bring Grant down, but he seemed to truly dislike the cattleman and would not wish to see Mary Ann hurt. Besides, John Thornford had trusted the man and Stokes knew no better judge of character.

"Out of my way," he snapped at Goff, shoving the guard aside and rushing down the stairs as quickly as he was able.

Chapter Forty-Seven

Stokes leapt from the last step into the dimly lit lobby of the Grand Hotel. The couch was empty and he cursed again his own stupidity at allowing White to come with them. The clerk watched him, open-mouthed.

"The man that was here with us," Stokes said, "did he leave anything for me?"

"Why no, sir."

He hadn't really expected otherwise. It had been a vain hope that White might have left his Colt with the clerk. But he had grown so used to the gun on his hip that now, running towards possible danger, he felt the lack of the weight of it keenly. Stokes said nothing more to the clerk. His mind was racing as he bounded across the lobby and pushed through the door.

The warmth of the afternoon, the bustle of the town and the bright colours of the store signs, ribbons and bunting assailed his senses. The sweet pungent smell of freshly dropped horse manure hung in the warm air. He hurried along the sidewalk, weaving past a man and woman perusing the wares in the window of Hansen's Drug Store. Stokes' boots thudded noisily on the timber boards. The old wound in his left leg throbbed in protest but he did not slow.

As he ran he listened for the report of firearms that would signify he was too late. He had no idea what he would do when he arrived at the Lady Elgin, but he knew he could not stand by and allow Jed to be shot down. The man was cantankerous, rude and frequently drunk. And yet he had saved Stokes' life and had stood by the Thornfords when it would have been easier to run. And, like Governor Pennoyer, John had trusted the man.

Stokes was almost at the saloon now. There had been no gunshots, just the usual sounds of the town. People, horses, the distant thump of the mills. He caught snatches of piano music wafting through the open door of the Lady Elgin. He frowned as he ran. The music struck him as strange. If things were as Bella had described, surely the pianist would have stopped playing and most of the patrons would have fled onto the street, terrified of being hit by stray bullets.

But there were only a couple of men outside the saloon. They were leaning against the hitching rail, smoking idly and chatting. They didn't give the appearance of men who had just witnessed Jedediah White insulting the Cabin Creek hands with his colourful language. If the saloon was about to be filled with clouds of black powder smoke and the thunder of gunfire, those two cowhands would not be standing so calmly a few paces outside the door.

Stokes began to slow his pace. Perhaps the situation had already been diffused. But he could not imagine how. He wondered if White might have backed down, but he could not believe that. Nor could he envisage Meacher, Byrne and the rest of the hard men who worked for Grant stepping away without answering the old man's taunts. No, something else must have happened. Maybe the new sheriff had been called. That was a possibility, but somehow Stokes found it hard to think that Stockman could control White and the Cabin Creek crew if they had already locked horns and were set on a fight.

Well, he would soon find out. He passed the bakery, the last building before the Lady Elgin, stepping down from the wooden sidewalk where there was a gap into the alley between the buildings. He was still looking intently at the two men outside the saloon, pondering what might have occurred, when

361

he sensed a sudden movement from the alley. He had been distracted, but he still had sharp instincts from years in the military and the police. He flinched away from the dark shape, swaying his head back without thinking to avoid the blow that he sensed more than saw.

Light burst behind his eyes and his head blazed with agony as the long barrel of a Colt revolver clattered against his temple. It had not struck him as directly or as hard as his attacker had intended. If it had, Stokes would surely have been knocked unconscious instantly. As it was, even though the blow had been glancing, his vision blurred and his legs buckled.

Lashing out a fist blindly, he felt it connect. Someone grunted. Stokes staggered out into the street, shaking his head in an attempt to see straight. But it was no good. All he could make out were the smudged shapes of men closing in on him. A punch flew at his face and Stokes caught it on his left forearm, countering with a right cross. His fist slammed into someone's face and one of the adversaries crowding him fell back, leaving a bright space ahead of him. If he could push his way through the gap and make his way inside the saloon, perhaps he would be able to clear his head enough to defend himself properly.

He was dimly aware of screams and shouts around him, but the voices were muffled by the roar of his blood in his ears. He lunged forward, but strong hands grabbed him. Kicking out, he caught someone on the knee, then clattered an elbow into another opponent. But there were too many of them. Dragging him away from the possible sanctuary of the saloon, two men pinned his arms, while another pummelled his body with solid, thumping blows, driving the air from his lungs. Through the pain, his vision cleared slightly and he saw that the man punching his ribs and stomach was Bull Meacher.

"Told you you'd get yours," Meacher said, grunting with the effort of punching Stokes.

Stokes struggled weakly against the hands that held him, but his head swam and Meacher's blows were taking their toll, sapping the strength from him. He could feel warm blood trickling down his face from where the gun barrel had split his scalp.

He presumed that the men holding him were Joaquin Lopez and Jackson Pailing because he could see Cadmar Byrne standing in the alleyway, watching the proceedings with his habitual smirk. Evidently, he was above getting involved in such vulgar things as brawls.

"What's wrong, Meacher?" Stokes said, spitting out blood. "Scared to fight me on your own like a man?"

"I'm man enough to whip you," snarled Meacher, landing another powerful punch to Stokes' stomach.

He could feel his gorge rising. He wanted to answer Meacher, but his words wouldn't come. His vision was ringed with shadows, as if staring into a tunnel. He would faint soon and if these men didn't stop hitting him then, they might well kill him. Ineffectually, Stokes tried again to free himself, but the men that held him were too strong and with each passing second he grew weaker.

The sound he had been listening for as he ran along the street now rang out, tearing the afternoon apart and shocking everyone into a momentary silence. The gunshot was loud and the air was suddenly thick with the rotten egg smell of burnt powder. Stokes felt the men behind him tense, holding him more tightly, perhaps thinking to use him as a human shield. Meacher stopped beating Stokes and spun around, dropping into a crouch and pulling his revolver from its holster. He was fast, but a hard voice made him hesitate.

"Put your gun away, Bull," said the voice. "You done enough damage with those fat fists of yours. No need to start shooting with your swollen fingers. You might miss me and plug Byrne instead."

Stokes peered groggily past Meacher. In the shadows of the alley between the buildings, Jed White had come up behind Cadmar Byrne and must have done to him the same as had been done to Stokes. Cadmar's hat was in the dust at his feet and blood tricked down the side of his face. His eyes were glazed and he seemed about to swoon. He might well have fallen if not for Jed White's firm grip on his collar. In his other hand he held one of his big Remington pistols.

"Now," White said, "let the Englishman go and you boys can be on your way."

"You old bastard," said Meacher, "I ought to shoot you right now."

"Go ahead, Bull. Take your shot." White's voice was cold. "Are you ready to die today?"

They stared at each other for a time. Meacher didn't answer and Stokes sensed the man had made a decision not to risk it all with Jed White's gun already trained on him.

"Reckon Cadmar here could use a lie down," White said, some humour creeping into his tone. "How about we finish this another day, Meacher?"

After a few seconds, Meacher nodded curtly.

"Let the Englishman go," he said.

"Wise decision," White said. "Have the bean-eater and the darky get your ponies. Cadmar's not gonna be walking any-where. Might have popped him a bit harder than I needed to."

"Go ahead," Meacher said to Lopez and Pailing. "Get the horses."

The two men released Stokes and he almost fell. He saw that Lopez's nose was bleeding and Pailing walked with a slight limp as they made their way to the Cabin Creek mounts.

Staggering forward, Stokes pushed past Meacher to lean against the wall beside White and Byrne. He was dizzy with the effort of walking those few paces.

"You gonna pass out?" asked Jed in a hushed voice.

"Maybe," Stokes said. "But not yet."

"Good," White said. "Your Colt's in my belt. Take it."

Stokes did. The cool grip and the weight of the pistol felt good in his hand. He aimed it at Meacher, though his eyes did not seem to be working properly. Everything was blurred and growing dark. He leant against the wall, forcing himself not to drop the gun.

White shoved Cadmar Byrne towards Meacher as Pailing and Lopez rode up leading their horses. As Byrne stumbled forward, tripping over his hat and sprawling in the dust, White drew his second pistol, pointing them both at the four men. Stepping forward, he kicked Byrne's hat at Meacher, who retrieved it and jammed it on the slim gunhand's head.

Meacher had to help Byrne into the saddle, but when the young man was on his horse, he seemed to regain some of his strength. He wiped at the blood on his face, smearing it across his cheek with the back of his hand.

"You're a dead man, Jed White," he said through gritted teeth.

"Funny," White said, sounding as if he was holding back laughter with difficulty. "Feel mighty alive right now."

Meacher mounted and pointed his gun at White.

"This ain't over," he said.

"You can count on that," White said, grinning.

The four men wheeled their horses around and galloped north along the street. White watched them go, ignoring the horrified stares of the onlookers.

"How you holding up?" he asked Stokes.

Gabriel Stokes heard the question and tried to reply, but darkness finally engulfed him and he slumped to the ground against the wall of the Lady Elgin. White stooped to pick him up, and smiled to himself, an unfamiliar tingle of pride warming him.

The Englishman still clung to his gun.

Chapter Forty-Eight

Gabriel Stokes woke slowly. He lay in a comfortable bed in a small, clean room. Patterned curtains covered the window and it must have been night for no light shone from behind them. What little illumination there was came from the door that stood ajar. Voices murmured out there. He recognised Mary Ann's tone speaking to another woman, Abigail Mullen perhaps, but he didn't think so.

He looked around the room, unsure where he was. In the shadows he could make out a dresser and a small table upon which rested a vase of pink peonies and a china jug. He had seen every room in the Mullen house and he was sure this was not the school mistress's home.

His head throbbed. The effort of looking around the room made his vision blur. Lying back down, he took stock of the pains that afflicted his body. His stomach and ribs were tender. He took a deep breath and winced at the ache in his side, but he didn't think any bones were broken.

"Was beginning to think you'd never wake up."

The voice, very close and loud in the quiet room, startled Stokes. Craning his neck painfully and propping himself up on an elbow, he saw that Jed White was seated in the deepest shadow in the corner between a dark mahogany wardrobe and the wall.

Holding his weight up, Stokes found his arm hurt just like the rest of him. The pounding in his head grew more intense. Letting out a groan, he lowered himself back onto the bed.

"How long have I been out?" he asked.

White reached over and lifted Stokes' watch from the bedside table. Opening it, he held it to the dim light filtering in from the part-open door.

"Nine hours, give or take," he said, returning the watch. "Was quite some crack on the noggin you took." He reached down and picked up a whiskey bottle from the floor by his feet. He didn't bother with a glass, just tugged the cork out, lifted the bottle to his lips and took a large swallow.

From outside came the distant crack of gunfire. Stokes tensed.

"Just some cowboy letting rip in town," White said. "Some high spirits tonight. With any luck that bastard Stockman will get himself shot up." He shifted to show the back of the chair he was on. Stokes' gun belt hung there. "Don't think you'll need it tonight, but your gun's here."

Flashes of that afternoon's fight came back to Stokes.

"Thanks for your help," he said.

White wiped his mouth with the back of his hand. "Would have been happy to watch, but never could abide seeing a man beat when he was down."

"But I wasn't down."

White raised an eyebrow.

"Hit from behind and then held by Lopez and Pailing while Meacher whaled on you. Didn't seem right to me. If they hadn't bushwhacked you, let you defend yourself and fought like men, I'd have left you to it."

Stokes reached up to touch his head. It was swollen and sore. Part of his scalp had been shaved and he could feel the prickle of stitches.

"I could have taken them," he said, "if they hadn't hit me from behind. That's just not cricket."

"Ain't got no idea what cricket is, but it sure was mighty yellow-bellied of 'em. As if four against one wasn't enough of an edge."

Stokes offered him a thin smile. Even that hurt his face and he wondered how many times he'd been punched before Jed had stepped in.

"I suppose they needed to even the odds somehow. And you have my sincerest thanks for returning the favour to that Byrne fellow. I hope his head hurts as much as mine. You've made an enemy there."

Stokes scoffed and took another swig from the bottle.

"He didn't seem all that friendly before I tapped him on the sconce."

Stokes lay back and closed his eyes. Slowly, as if rising up out of a swamp, the memories of the day's events floated back to him.

"How is Mary Ann?" he asked.

"Shook up from what Pennoyer told her, but she's fine. She's in the kitchen talking to Mrs Yardley."

Stokes thought of the revelation of John's life insurance policy. It must have come as a shock, but it was good to know Mary Ann and the children would be provided for.

"This is the doctor's house?"

White nodded.

"Ain't too far from the Lady Elgin and figured it the best place for you. After he patched you up the doc wouldn't let me move you."

"And Tanner? And the children?"

"Doc agreed to put us all up for the night. Figured it best to keep everyone together. Easier to watch that way. Alpheus helped me with a wagon. The girls and Albert are sleeping in the parlour. Tanner's watching the door."

"Any more trouble?"

"You mean since Pennoyer declined to help with Grant and then you got your brains scrambled?"

Stokes smiled weakly.

"Yes."

"All quiet," White said, "but I ain't sure how long it will

stay that way. I told you the law wouldn't help with Grant. There's only one way to put an end to this. You might not like it, but it's the only sure way to be done with Grant."

Stokes lay in silence for a few minutes, mulling over what had happened, trying to make sense of things and plan for their next step. He wouldn't admit that White was right. He couldn't.

"There has to be a better way," he said at last. But no matter how he looked at things, he couldn't think of how to rid themselves of Grant and the threat posed by his men.

White sighed and pushed the cork into the almost empty bottle. His eyes gleamed and Stokes wondered if he had drunk all of that whiskey alone.

"Grant had the right idea," White said.

"What do you mean?"

"He sees you as a threat now, so he told his men to take you off the board."

Stokes felt a stab of sadness as he recalled how he had been duped.

"Bella said you were in trouble at the Lady Elgin. You think Grant arranged for her to do that?"

White shrugged.

"Grant? Byrne? Meacher? Who cares who told her to go to you? Worked, didn't it? Almost got you killed."

The thought that the girl had betrayed him saddened Stokes. It must have shown on his face for White sighed and said, "You ain't the first man to be fooled by a pretty girl, Gabe."

"I thought she might be different."

"Thought you could save her, did you?"

"I don't know what I thought. I just didn't like the idea of her working at the Lady Elgin."

"Don't feel too bad about it," White said. "She was probably put up to it. What else could she do? Grant owns the Lady Elgin. Owns her too."

Stokes was thankful for White's words. It hurt less to think

Bella had been coerced into tricking him rather than doing it willingly.

"You must think me a soft fool," he said.

The gruff frontiersman chuckled.

"That ain't got nothing to do with you falling for that slommack. You can't help being a soft Englishman. Give me a few years, might be able to toughen you up."

A thought came to Stokes and he sat up, immediately regretting the sudden movement.

"Take it easy," said White. "Doc says you need to stay in bed."

"Has Grant made his offer for the JT to Mary Ann again?"

"Don't think Grant's gonna be making Mary Ann any more offers. Not after she stuck a pistol in his face."

"Is he still in town?"

"Reckon he is. Staying at the Grand ready for the station opening tomorrow."

"What about his men?"

"Ain't seen 'em since they lit out of town after trying to split your skull. But I been busy and I ain't been looking."

"We should get back to the JT," Stokes said. "I've got a bad feeling about this."

He was about to say more when the door swung fully open. A man entered carrying a lamp. The warm light bathed the man's angular, clean-shaven face. His hair was black, thick and wavy, his eyes dark and intelligent. He was in his late thirties, slim and of middling height.

"I thought I heard voices," he said, placing the lamp on the table. "Mr Stokes, I'm Dr Dillon Yardley. How are you feeling?"

"As if my head has been used as a football. I wish we were meeting under better circumstances."

Dr Yardley smiled.

"One of the downsides of my profession," he said, "is that

I frequently meet people when they are unlikely to offer much in the way of sparkling repartee. Let me take a look at you."

Jed White rose. Shaking the almost empty bottle, he said, "I'm going for another drink." When he had left, Dr Yardley whistled. "It's a miracle he can function at all after everything he's drunk this afternoon."

"He's got to slow down," Stokes said. "We might need him to shoot straight."

"You can tell him that," Yardley said. "I very much doubt Mr White would listen to me."

"I can't say I hold out much hope that he'll pay any mind to me either. But if it comes to a fight, I'd rather not get shot by my own side."

"I'd rather nobody got shot," Yardley said. "I make enough from gout, stomach complaints and rheumatoid arthritis without having to cut bullets out of people."

After taking a close look at the stitches in Stokes' head, the doctor examined the rest of him, prodding here and there and asking if it hurt. The truth was it hurt almost everywhere, but Stokes did his best to make his answers useful for the doctor. Yardley held up the lamp and stared into his eyes, moving the light to the left and right.

"Any dizziness? Blurred vision?"

"Some," Stokes said.

"How much?"

"A little."

The doctor's eyes narrowed as he detected the lie.

"The good news is you won't need to worry about Mr White's shooting ability tonight."

"Why's that?" Stokes was still groggy, his mind slow as if each thought were struggling to pull itself from a mire. He wondered if the doctor had overheard their previous conversation and knew something about Grant's plans.

"Because you won't be going anywhere tonight," Yardley

said. "I would recommend at least a day in bed. You are concussed and your head needs time to recover."

"Nonsense," Stokes said, "I have already been in bed for hours. I'm no use to Mrs Thornford lying here." He swung his legs round and placed his bare feet on the floor. Standing, he felt a sudden rush of nausea and lost his balance. Dr Yardley caught his arm and lowered him down to the bed once more.

"You'll be no use to anyone in this state," he said. "Rest until morning and we'll see how you feel then. A good night's sleep will work wonders. But you should refrain from any arduous activity for the next few days."

Stokes sagged back onto the bed, feeling useless and disheartened.

"I can see why you and John were close," Yardley said, looking down at Stokes.

"You knew the Captain?"

"I did, though not as well as I would have liked. He had the same strength of will, the same fierce determination to do the right thing, no matter the cost to himself." Taking the pitcher from the table, he poured a glass of water and handed it to Stokes. "Here, have a few sips."

Stokes drank a little and set the glass on the bedside table. He lay his head back on the pillow. The water revived him somewhat, but he knew the doctor was right. He was in no state to go anywhere, let alone to ride through the night to the JT Ranch.

"I wish I'd had a chance to know him better," Yardley said. "He seemed like a fine man."

"He was. Perhaps the best man I've ever met. He saved my life in Afghanistan."

"I was very sorry to hear he had been killed," Yardley said. He stared wistfully into the lamp's glow. "Though I suppose it was for the best."

The doctor's words were so incongruous that for a few seconds Stokes thought he must have misheard.

"What do you mean by that?" he asked, his voice cold.

The colour drained from Yardley's face.

"Sorry. I misspoke."

Stokes glowered at the man.

"I would say you did, yes."

"No, no, you misunderstand me," Yardley said. "I am tired. I should not have said that."

"But you did, Doctor, and it sounded for all the world as if you were pleased for my friend's death."

Yardley was aghast.

"That is not what I meant at all."

A dark idea flashed into Stokes' mind. If the doctor was in Grant's employ it would explain why he was glad that John had been killed. John's murder would allow Yardley's patron to swoop in and snatch the land from Mary Ann.

"Then be so kind as to explain what you did mean," he said.

Yardley bit his lip and shook his head, as if searching for a way out of this. In the end, he sighed.

"I gave my word to John not to mention it to his wife, but I suppose I did not promise him I would not speak to you about it. Though I am not so sure I can absolve myself of wrongdoing based on such a technicality."

"You have said too much to turn away now, Doctor," Stokes said. "What secret did John share with you?"

Yardley hesitated once more. Then, seeming to decide there was nothing for it but to come clean, he took in a deep breath.

"When I said John's death was for the best, I did not mean I was happy he had been killed, just that the manner of his death was preferable to the alternative."

"Alternative?"

"When he was murdered, John had only weeks, or perhaps months, to live. They would have been long, painful weeks, filled with misery. A bullet was surely a more merciful end."

"I don't understand," Stokes said, though he thought he was beginning to. Even in his addled state with the throbbing pain in his head, he could feel pieces of the puzzle falling into place just out of reach. "What was wrong with John?"

Yardley, resigned to giving up a confidence shared with a dead man, said in a heavy voice, "John was dying of cancer."

Chapter Forty-Nine

Mary Ann brought Stokes some thin broth shortly after the doctor left. She was nervous and awkward with him. He wondered if she was planning on changing her mind and accepting Grant's offer, or perhaps simply taking the insurance money and leaving.

"Things have changed," he said. "Nobody will think badly of you should you decide to leave. In fact, I think it might be what John would have wanted. He would want you to be safe."

Mary Ann hesitated. She would not meet his gaze.

"You need your rest," she said. "Let's talk in the morning."

He watched her leave the room, her slender form silhouetted momentarily in the doorway. His head ached and he wondered what she would say after sunrise. For his part, he didn't think it was his place to tell her about John's diagnosis. He could not see how the knowledge of her husband's illness could benefit Mary Ann, and Yardley had made it very clear that John had wished it kept a secret.

Outside in the night, several horses galloped in the street. Men whooped and hollered, and pistol shots rang out. Stokes listened for signs of imminent danger, but nobody stirred in the house and he put the sounds down to raucous merrymaking.

He lay in the bed and stared up at the ceiling. Mary Ann had left the door slightly open and a crack of light shone in from a lamp outside the room, slicing across the dark ceiling like a bright sabre blade. His head throbbed and the thin soup churned in his stomach. Thoughts rolled over each other in his mind, never quite settling, but every now and then offering him a tantalising glimpse of order, some way the events of recent weeks might slot together and make sense.

The letter inviting Gabriel to Oregon... John's illness... the life insurance... Mary Ann... Albert and Adelaide... The image of the ravine where John had been shot surfaced in his mind... Van Orman showing him the shooter's boot prints...

There was more to John's death, Stokes was certain of it, but no matter how he tried to position the pieces of the jigsaw puzzle, his addled mind would not fit them together.

He closed his eyes but could still see the afterglow of the stripe of light against the darkness of his eyelids. If only he'd arrived in Oregon sooner. He had been so looking forward to seeing his old friend. The thought that John had known his days were numbered and had written to him so that they might spend some of his final days together filled Stokes with sorrow. He wondered at the state of John's mind, knowing his death was imminent. It did not surprise him that Thornford had approached the situation with his customary courage, energy and zeal. It appeared he had gone about preparing the way for those who would remain after him, not falling into wallowing despair as many might in such circumstances, but instead becoming filled with a driving purpose.

Stokes sighed, seeing visions of his father's dour visage and recalling the portrait of his brother, Michael, frozen forever in the prime of his youth, handsome and dashing in his dress uniform. That painting had shaped his life. Michael had gazed down on him as he grew up, a constant reminder of how a son should look; what it meant to be a man.

Looking inside himself, Gabriel doubted he would have acted in such a noble fashion as John. No matter how hard he tried, he was too much like his father. Even now he could feel the familiar melancholy reaching out its cadaverous fingers and caressing his mind. He could hear the intimate whispers that it would be better to flee, to ride away, to smother his fears with intoxicating spirits and opium. He had always thought his father too weak to deal with the death of his beloved first son. In the end his grief had consumed him, driving him to take his own life. But now Gabriel asked himself if he had been faced with months of painful torment, whether he would have acted any differently. The answer was plain to him. Whenever things had grown too difficult he had run away. He had lost Rebecca when he had fled into the stews and opium dens of London. Then, after the horrors of Jane Adams' murder and his rage-filled attack of Fred Bullen, he had fled west, hoping that the distance might be enough to escape his demons. But of course, those demons rode within him, as much a part of him as the memories of his father and the painting of Michael.

The scraping of a chair in the room brought his thoughts back to the present. He opened his eyes and realised he must have been dozing. The flame in the lamp on the landing had been lowered and the light on the ceiling was now a honey-coloured smudge.

Jedediah White was once more sitting in the chair beside the wardrobe. He had a fresh bottle of whiskey and when he saw Stokes was awake, he held it out to him.

"Look like you could use a drink," he said.

Stokes' hand moved of its own volition, taking hold of the cool glass. The weight of the bottle was reassuring and the smell of the liquor within was almost unbearably enticing. It took all Stokes' willpower not to raise the bottle to his lips, but rather to shove it back towards White. With a shrug, Jed took it and drank.

Stokes eyed White's grizzled face in the gloom. He couldn't read the man's expression. Just as when he was playing poker, White gave away little of his thoughts.

"Feeling sorry for yourself?" White said. "Sometimes a man needs a drink to take his mind off things."

Stokes was startled by White's words, spoken so matter of factly.

"The problem is that if I start, I know I won't stop. And I think I might need my wits about me. Grant hasn't gone anywhere."

"Lucky for you, drunk or sober, I can shoot straight."

Stokes watched as White took another swig from the bottle.

"Do you drink to forget, Jed?" he asked.

"Ain't gonna forget nothing by drinking. Been doing it too long to know that." He sipped from the bottle. "But if memories are knives, whiskey makes 'em blunt, so they don't cut so deep."

"I've found opium does a better job than liquor."

White chuckled.

"Tried that a couple times down in San Francisco. Didn't agree with me. I can shoot drunk, but after a pipe of that Chinese Molasses, I didn't know which way was up. A grizzly could have started eating my feet and I would have smiled and offered him some salt for his meal."

"Exactly," Stokes said. "Opium deadens the senses to such an extent I could forget who I was. What I'd done. What I'd seen."

"Know who I am," said White, growing sombre. "And I'm OK with that. But some of the things I seen... Those I'd rather forget."

"Such as?"

White grimaced. "Just said I want to forget 'em. Think I want to talk about the past?"

Stokes thought of Jane Adams' dismembered body. The defiled corpses of the Ripper's victims.

"You make a good point," he said.

They sat in silence for a time, each lost in his own thoughts. The night was quiet now. Perhaps the revellers had finally grown tired and gone to their beds, or collapsed somewhere in the town.

"We're not so different, you and I," said White without warning, his husky voice rasping in the darkness.

"How so?" Stokes could not imagine what similarities the man saw between them.

"I know we ain't alike in many ways, you being an English gentleman and all, but I seen enough of you to know we ain't so different. We were born into different worlds, but I see some of myself in you."

"Oh you do, do you?"

"Yes, I do." White's words were stumbling and slurred. He took another drink from the bottle. "You don't back down from a fight, no matter the cost."

Stokes smiled without humour.

"I suppose that's true."

He thought of the skirmishes in Afghanistan, where he had galloped through the dust and smoke towards the screaming enemy soldiers. He recalled confrontations with the Dove-row gang and the Bow-commoners in the East End. He'd taken a few knocks and been reprimanded by his superiors for reckless behaviour at times, but his fellow police officers knew they could always count on him if things got sticky.

"I see something needs doing," White said, "I do it. Just like you. If that means a man needs killing, so be it. You got that same toughness in you."

Stokes said nothing. He watched the liquid sloshing in the bottle. White's eyes glinted in the dim light from the door. The older man waved the bottle at Stokes.

"Want to know the difference between you and me, Gabe?"

"Just the one?"

White went on as if he hadn't heard him.

"You do what needs to be done, but you think about it afterwards. Ain't no point looking back. Can't change nothing, so why think about what might have been?"

"You don't ever look back?"

"No. Make a decision and move on. That's where we're different. You let your thoughts get to you."

"Why do you drink then?" Stokes asked.

White laughed, a sudden barking cough.

"So my thoughts don't get to me!" he said. "You got me there."

They fell silent and Stokes pondered what White had said. Were they alike? There seemed little similarity between them, but he could not deny they were both men of action. Perhaps it was what drove them that set them apart from each other.

"The worst thing I found with drink," Stokes said, "and even opium, was that when I stopped, in the cold light of day, my memories had not gone. Nothing was better. In fact, my life was worse than ever."

"There's a solution to that problem," White said, raising the bottle aloft as if in salute and then taking a mouthful of whiskey. "Don't stop drinking!"

Stokes didn't smile. He sighed.

"I tried that for a time, but one day I woke up and knew that if I truly wished to be rid of my nightmares and never to have to face my darkest memories, there was really only one way out. And I am not prepared to take the coward's way. I will not take my own life."

White stood, groaning as his knees and ankles clicked. He went over to the window, pulled the curtains apart and opened it. Thin, silver light from the moon washed into the room. He must have been rolling cigarettes while they talked, for now he handed one to Stokes and stuck another one in his mouth. He struck a match on the window frame, the flare bright in the darkness. He lit his cigarette and held the flame out to Stokes.

"I've known men put a gun up to their eyeball and blow their brains out rather than be tortured by Comanches," White said, sitting down again. "Didn't seem so cowardly to me."

Stokes took a deep pull on his cigarette. The coal glowed a brilliant, ruby red.

"Suicide is the craven's escape," he said.

"You ain't seen what the Comanche can do to a man. If

you had and you faced capture, you might well have pulled the trigger on yourself."

Stokes blew out a cloud of smoke. His head ached less and he was glad of the cigarette.

"Perhaps," he said. "I suppose it could be said that such an action was depriving the Indians of sport."

"Didn't figure you for a religious man, Gabe."

Stokes frowned.

"I fear God, but I don't believe anyone would describe me as religious. The last time I was in church was on my wedding day."

"Who committed suicide?"

Stokes stared at White in surprise. Despite his obvious intoxication, White clearly still had his faculties.

"My father," Stokes said. "After my brother died he was never himself. I only knew him as a shell of the man he had been. Melancholy had a tight grip on him. I feel that same melancholy threatening to drag me down into despair. I've come to understand the drinking and drugs only serve to make that part of my character stronger, the dark moods darker, the hopelessness more acute. That's why I stopped and vowed never to start again.

"It's not God or concern for my mortal soul that would stop me taking my life, Jed. It certainly isn't fear of death. Having lived through my father's suicide, I would never wish that upon my family. My sisters have had to deal with enough heartache without me adding to it."

"What about your wife?"

"Rebecca might shed a tear or two. But she would inherit everything, so I imagine she would get over her grief soon enough."

The coal of White's cigarette burnt brightly for a second, lighting his craggy face in a ruddy warmth.

"So you came here. If you couldn't end things, you could at least travel as far away as possible."

That White understood him so clearly annoyed Stokes. Was he so transparent?

"I came to see John," he said, taking another puff of his cigarette, "but I would be lying if I hadn't thought about disappearing. Leaving my old life behind and riding towards the sunset. The land here is vast. I had vague ideas of riding out into the wilderness and being lost forever."

"You could do that, though I dare say your sisters would miss you. Many a man has disappeared in the mountains, plains and deserts of the West. But you ain't no fool and I reckon you know the truth of it, Gabe."

"What truth is that?"

"Some things you just can't run from, my friend."

They finished their cigarettes in silence, stubbing them out on the window ledge and tossing the butts into the garden.

White was right. There could be no escaping his own thoughts and actions. Riding off into the wilds of America would be no less cowardly than putting a bullet in his brain. No. When all this was done, he would have to return to England and put his affairs in order. Perhaps then he would return to this land that had so taken a hold on his heart, but he could flee from himself no longer.

White had closed his eyes and seemed to be dozing.

Stokes' head ached and his battered body cried out for rest, but still sleep eluded him. His thoughts returned doggedly to the problems at hand, away from the self-pity that had enveloped him.

Jed wanted to finish this affair once and for all in the most final of ways; taking the law into his own hands and killing Grant. Stokes despised Grant, and the thought of the cattleman living in luxury, free to torment and abuse whosoever he pleased, filled him with fury. There must be a way of bringing him down. But he could not see how. Grant was able to brush aside with impunity any who stood against him, shielded from the law by friends in high places and the power he held over them. If the law could not be relied on, what could? Surely there was nothing more potent than the courts. Stokes could not countenance the idea that law and order might not prevail in this land, no matter how civilized it professed to be, with its railroads, banks and the soaring buildings of the cities on the east coast. Oregon was as far removed from New York as London was to Kabul. Although part of the same United States of America, Oregon could just as well have been a different country.

An idea came to him then. A spark that began to light up the recesses of his mind with its possibilities. There was perhaps one thing that even men as powerful as Thomas Grant feared; a power strong enough to topple governments.

Stokes lay in the darkness, listening to Jed's snores as his ideas grew and flowered. Reporters from all the local and some national newspapers were in Griffith to write up the story of the opening of the station and the arrival of the railroad. There would be nothing they would like more than a juicy tale of a rich man, bullying and murdering his opponents to further his own ends, perverting the course of justice by threatening politicians and even resorting to killing innocent children to pursue his nefarious goals. Reporters would want proof before printing, but they would be less scrupulous than a judge and the dossier he had compiled with Mary Ann would give them more than enough evidence to join the dots and create a sensational story. If they could speak to the right reporter, they might be able to bring about such a swell of emotion against Grant that Pennoyer would be compelled to act. Judges outside of Griffith County would take an interest. Perhaps they would be able to bring Grant down without another shot being fired.

He should have thought of this sooner, but his disdain for the type of reporting that might now help them ran deep. He wanted nothing to do with men like Bullen and their ruthless, sometimes even fraudulent pursuit of stories to sell more copies of their newspapers.

And yet perhaps the press might be just what they needed

now. He had witnessed first-hand how newspaper stories had whipped the public into a frenzy over the Whitechapel murders. They had printed letters and the wildest theories. The reporters and the public had been obsessed with salacious details of the murders. It disgusted Stokes that men would profit from such crimes, just as Fred Bullen had done, feeding people's insatiable appetite for gossip, the more prurient the better. But maybe the press could bring about some positive change, to do what corrupt officials and fear were preventing.

In the morning he would find the reporters in town and offer them a story that could make careers, and hopefully ruin Grant. He began to lay out plans in his mind, sure that he would be well enough by the morning to make his way about town, no matter what the doctor said. It was an opportunity he could not afford to miss.

With these thoughts swirling in his head, his injuries and weariness finally got the better of him and he slid into the darkness of a deep sleep.

It seemed to Stokes he had only been asleep for a matter of minutes when a clatter of hooves, loud through the open window, woke him with a start. For a second he lay in the darkness, his thoughts muddled, unsure where he was. Then a banging on the door below brought him fully awake. He sat up quickly, the ache in his head returning sharply with the sudden movement.

Outside in the dark of the night, someone was shouting.

"Open up!" The voice was harsh, brash in the stillness. The hammering of a fist on the wooden door was repeated. "Open up!"

Jed White jumped up from the chair. He staggered woozily, leaning on the wall with his left hand, but Stokes noticed with surprise that one of his big Remington pistols was already in his right hand.

"Wait here," White growled, and, without another word, he left the room.

There were other voices in the house now, women and men. Stokes heard Tanner Strickland shouting from downstairs, asking who was outside. The response was muffled. Stokes' head swam. He was dizzy, but he would not lie in bed if their enemies had come for them. Swinging his feet to the floor, he stood, letting out a grunt at the pain he felt. He tottered over to the chair and pulled the Colt Lightning from its holster. The world tilted and he feared he would fall. He steadied himself on the chair-back for a second until the floor righted itself, then, taking a deep breath, he followed White out of the door.

Lamplight shone brightly from below, illuminating the landing. A door opened and Dr Yardley came out, dressed in a nightgown. He glanced at Stokes, taking in the gun he held. He said nothing about his patient being out of bed. Stokes followed him to the stairs. By the time they reached the top, the banging and shouting had ceased. Yardley trotted quickly down the stairs.

"What is the meaning of this?" he asked.

Stokes followed him down more cautiously, holding the banister in his left hand. With each step his head pounded, and he felt a stabbing from his bruised ribs.

The hall before the front door was crowded with people. White and Yardley were closest to Stokes. Beyond them, Strickland had opened the front door and a strong man stepped inside from the night. His blond hair was bright in the lamplight and, as he moved from the shadows, Stokes recognised him at once.

Lars Giblin ignored Stokes and his fellow ranch hands. His eyes settled on Dr Yardley.

"You got to come quick, Doctor," he said, his voice anxious. His eyes were wide and red-rimmed, his face pale.

"What is it?" Yardley asked, his voice calm and commanding,

now that he realised they were not under attack. This was a man accustomed to being awakened in the night for medical emergencies.

"It's Lenny," Lars said. "He's in a bad way."

Chapter Fifty

They rode hard through the darkness. Behind them the sky was lightening above the mountains in the east, but it was still dark under the trees. Stokes gritted his teeth against Banner's jolting gait. The gelding was sure-footed and normally a comfortable mount, but now Stokes' head throbbed and his bruised body complained with each new stride of the animal.

"You OK?" Tanner asked, riding close, his face just a smudge in the gloom.

"I'm fine," Stokes lied. His voice was almost drowned out by the thunder of the horses' hooves that reverberated within the benighted forest, but Strickland appeared to have heard him and accepted his words, for he nodded and spurred his own mount to greater speed.

Stokes grimaced, clutching the reins tightly. He was glad of the darkness that hid his pained expression and thankful for the deep-seated saddle that held him on Banner's back. Without it, he feared he might have fallen more than once.

Dr Yardley had told him he was in no fit state to ride, but Stokes had been stoically stubborn, pulling on his clothes and boots and following the rest of them out of the house and striding towards Alpheus Hampton's Livery and Feed Stables.

He looked at the shadows of the men riding beneath the trees. Just ahead of Strickland, Jed White on his sorrel mare led the group with Lars who was mounted on a fresh horse provided by Alpheus Hampton. Dr Yardley brought up the rear of the group, riding awkwardly on a barrel-chested horse that had seen better days but didn't look as if it had ever been much in the way of horseflesh. The doctor was clearly not a natural horseman, but he did not complain and managed to keep up the pace set by Lars and Jed.

Stokes wondered what they would find when they reached the ranch. Not for the first time he questioned his stubbornness in riding along with the others. Perhaps he should have remained with Mary Ann. The pounding in his head was not getting any better, but at least the nausea he had felt at first had passed, which was an improvement. Banner knew the way along the road and was content to follow the other horses, leaving Stokes able to grasp the saddle horn and think about what Lars had told them.

Lars had breathlessly recounted the events of that evening for them as they had hurried to get ready and he sipped a cup of coffee Mrs Yardley had made. He told them how several men had ridden into the ranch just after dark. They had made no effort to hide their identity. It was Meacher, Lopez, Byrne, Pailing and a couple of others. Perhaps they had underestimated the resistance they would face, or they had deadened their caution with drink. Whatever the reason, they rode boldly up to the ranch house and demanded that Rab Tovey be turned over to them.

"Tovey?" Strickland said. "How did they know about him?"

Stokes cursed. "It must have been Pennoyer," he said. "We trusted him far too much it seems. After we spoke to him he must have relayed what we had told him to Grant."

"Never mind how they knew," spat White. He had already pulled on his boots, belted on his guns and held his carbine, ready to leave. Stokes could scarcely believe it, but the man showed no signs of having overindulged. "Tell us what happened."

Mary Ann poured more coffee into his cup and Lars took a mouthful before continuing with his tale.

"Amos came out carrying his coach gun. He told them to be on their way. Tough old coot didn't show a sign he was scared at all. Meacher said they weren't leaving without Tovey. That's when Lenny came out of the barn. For a moment I thought he was going to hand Tovey over and I couldn't blame him. That bastard wasn't worth risking our lives over. But Lenny didn't give them Tovey."

"What did he do?" Stokes asked.

"He was raging and screaming. Telling them they were all sons of bitches." He hesitated, embarrassed. "Sorry," he said, glancing at the ladies present. Mrs Yardley waved away his apology.

Mary Ann placed a hand on his arm reassuringly.

"Go on," she said.

"I don't reckon the Cabin Creek boys expected any resistance," Lars went on. "And Lenny surprised us all. He dragged Tovey out of the barn, all the while insulting and abusing Meacher, Byrne and the others for murderers and scum. Things were looking dicey, and I figured there'd be shooting, no matter what."

"Where were you?" Strickland asked, tugging on his boots.

"Inside the house, watching from the window with my Winchester. Reuban was in the bunkhouse with his old Springfield rifle. Things were going to go south and I was just wondering whether it wouldn't be better if one of us started things off. I was considering shooting that smug bastard, Meacher, when Lenny beat me to it."

"Lenny shot Meacher?" White asked. He sounded amazed.

"No, he shot Tovey. He dragged him out of the barn and busted a cap right up in his head." He indicated his own temple. "Damnedest thing."

Stokes thought of the strange tension in Lenny before he left. He had thought the boy had been upset to be sent away from Cora's side. Evidently his fury had simmered since he had seen the girl's disfigurements and it had boiled over in a savage blast of anger.

"Things got confused then," Lars said. "Everybody started

shooting at once. When the smoke cleared, Amos was in the dust, dead as a post." He shook his head and bit his lip. "Lenny was lying on top of Tovey. Gut shot."

"What about the Cabin Creek boys?" White asked.

Lars looked sheepish.

"I would have sworn I had Meacher in my sights, and when the shooting started, I didn't hold back. Thought I'd drilled him, but he rode away with the others. Pretty sure at least one of them was injured though. There was some blood on the ground. But only one they left behind was Adney Fretwell. Reuban plugged him right through the spine."

"Pity you didn't get more," said White.

Lars frowned, perhaps sensing a rebuke in the words.

"You did your best," said Mary Ann.

The blond man stared into his coffee cup. Stokes felt sorry for him.

"Sorry we weren't there to help," he said. "How was Lenny when you left?"

Lars loured.

"Looked bad to me, but I ain't no doctor. We carried him inside and I rode straight here. But Reuban's no slouch when it comes to patching up critters and people. He ain't no doc though. Reuban said the bullet was still in Lenny. Needed to come out."

Lars had started his account in a hushed whisper, but as he recalled events, he relived the anger and fear he had felt, causing his voice to rise in volume. His last words must have travelled to where Cora was resting, for her wailing cry reached the men and women huddled in the kitchen.

Mrs Yardley hurried off to see to the girl.

When Stokes had made his way upstairs to retrieve his clothes, moving with awkward stiffness, Mary Ann had followed him.

"You should stay," she said, looking into his eyes with obvious worry on her face.

"No," Stokes replied. "I'm a part of this now and I'm not turning away. Even when you leave, I think I will stay and try to finish what we have started. I owe it to John. I need to see Grant finished." Jed had been right about him. He could not turn away from a fight.

Mary Ann held his gaze.

"Who said I am leaving?"

"You're not?" He was surprised. "I thought with the insurance money you would."

"I thought about it, but no. John and I worked hard for what we have. I will not be chased from my land."

Stokes felt fiercely proud of her in that moment. He wished to embrace her, but instead fastened his gun belt and donned his hat. His head hurt where the hat band pressed against the stitches.

"I'm glad to hear that," he said. There was no time to spare, so he told her quickly about his plan to take their evidence to a newspaper reporter.

"You think it will work?" she asked.

"It might," he said.

Along the landing, they could hear Cora's weeping and Mrs Yardley's soothing tone as she sought to console the poor girl.

"It would have been easier with Tovey to back up the story," Mary Ann said.

Stokes scowled. He had the sensation that things were unravelling too quickly. He was uncertain of the best course of action, but he had made his decision and would stick with it, move forward and try not to look back.

"Do your best," he said. "And be careful. Yardley thinks you'll be safe here. Find the reporters and stay close to them. With so many people in town, I can't see Grant trying anything today."

"What do you think happened at the JT then?" she asked. "Grant doesn't seem to fear anything or anybody."

He thought of her words as they rode out from beneath the

pines. The sky in the east was bright now. The sun had not yet risen above the mountains and the valley was still in shade, but after the deep shadows under the trees the early morning light made the riders blink.

At first, as the JT Ranch came into view, Stokes could see nothing amiss. The barn and ranch house faced each other over the flat stretch of earth. Lambs and ewes dotted the field behind the pens and corrals. It looked as peaceful as ever until Stokes noticed the shapes lying on the earth outside the house. Two men were stretched out there. They had been covered by a canvas sheet, but the wind had picked up in the night and pulled the edge of the paulin away, exposing the grey, gaunt features of Amos Willard. His eyes were half-open, glazed and unseeing.

As always when he saw a dead body, Stokes was shocked by how different the removal of life had made the man. Old Amos had been testy and irascible, but he had been full of vitality, despite his age. With the removal of that energy, his body seemed to have withered, as if the soul itself had given him weight and substance.

The riders dismounted. Tanner looked down at Amos, his face almost as pale as the corpse's. Jed's face was set and grim. Lars moved to where the dead men lay and pulled the sheet back over Amos' face.

Without warning, the door of the house opened. Stokes' hand dropped to the gun on his belt and he saw the other men stiffen too. All except White. He walked towards the house without hesitation.

Reuban Van Orman stood in the doorway, his expression grave. Pincher and Tooyakeh shot out of the house, Pincher bounding towards the newcomers on his three legs, tail wagging furiously. At a command from his master, Tooyakeh dropped down on the porch, eyeing them all with keen interest. Stokes was surprised to see Tooyakeh, but there was no time to ask how the big dog came to be there.

"You must have ridden fast," Van Orman said to Lars, nodding his approval. His gaze shifted to White, who was approaching the porch steps. Seeing something in his expression, White halted.

"There's nothing for you in there," Van Orman said. "You want to kill someone, those who did this rode out of here like coyotes with burning tails. Headed for the Cabin Creek Ranch, I reckon."

White hesitated. He frowned, but said nothing. Stokes wondered if the amounts of whiskey he had consumed were finally taking their toll, for he was uncommonly quiet.

"You have a patient for me?" snapped Dr Yardley, pushing past White.

Van Orman stepped aside, opening the door wide.

"This way, Doctor," he said.

Yardley did not acknowledge him. Grasping his medical bag tightly, he stepped briskly into the dark interior of the house.

Chapter Fifty-One

Lenny McCloskey's pale form was stretched out on the table in the middle of the room. A red-stained bandage swaddled his stomach.

Dr Dillon Yardley removed his coat and jacket. He began to examine Lenny as he rolled up his sleeves.

"Soap and water," he snapped.

Without a word, Van Orman went to the kitchen and brought back a ewer filled with water and a cake of lye soap. Yardley scrubbed his hands and rinsed them.

"You cleaned the wound?" Yardley asked, indicating the blood-soaked bandage wrapped around Lenny's middle.

"Yes, sir," Van Orman said. "Used a clean cloth and boiled water."

Yardley took scissors from his bag and cut away the bandage. Van Orman had wadded the wound with a folded cloth that came away sodden and dripping red. The doctor dropped the crimson rags into a bucket.

"If he lives," he said, "he'll owe his life as much to you as to me."

Tanner's eyes were wide as he took in the amount of blood on the bandage.

"Why'd he do it?" he asked. "Why shoot Tovey in cold blood?"

Van Orman's features were hard.

"Revenge," he said.

"Revenge?"

Van Orman nodded sombrely. "He's a brave boy, and we all know he's in love with Cora."

Tanner bit his lip.

"You think he did this for Cora?" he asked.

"I know he did. Before he passed out, Lenny asked me to tell Miss Cora he'd kept his word to her."

Stokes sighed. "She didn't send him away, did she?"

"Perhaps not in the way you thought," said Van Orman. "When she heard we had one of the men who'd attacked her family, she asked Lenny to deliver justice. He'd do anything for that girl."

"Including murder," said Stokes, his voice not much more than a whisper.

"This weren't no murder," Tanner said. "Tovey got what he deserved." He stared down at Lenny's pale body. "What chance does he have, doc?"

"I'll be honest," Yardley said. "It doesn't look good. But there is no time to waste. I need to remove whatever is in there and do what I can to repair the damage and stop the bleeding. After that, the boy will be in the hands of God. But he is young and strong."

Stokes glanced at Pincher, who now lay by the oven in the kitchen. He had been quite sure the animal would die, but he had been proven wrong. He hoped Lenny would be another miracle.

"Boil more water," Yardley ordered. "And bring that light close."

Van Orman went back to the kitchen for the water. Strickland picked up the lamp and held it close to the table. Stokes' head ached. He had decided he was no use standing where he would only get in the way, so he'd seated himself in a chair in one corner of the room near the back door. But now, as he watched Tanner looking down at his stricken friend, he saw the young man's face drain of colour. Pushing himself up with a stifled groan at his body's pains, Stokes moved to the table.

"Why don't you see to the horses?" he said. "We rode them hard and you know Lenny wouldn't want them left untended."

Tanner nodded his thanks.

"I'll do that," he said, almost tripping through the front door in his haste. Stokes caught a glimpse of Jed White leaning on the porch railing smoking a cigarette. After a brief look at Lenny, the old man appeared to have decided he could be of little use inside, or perhaps, thought Stokes, Van Orman's cold attitude towards White had deterred him, though that seemed unlikely.

Lars Giblin for his part seemed utterly spent. His face was wan and pale and he slumped in a chair, his eyelids already drooping.

Stokes held the light steadily and gritted his teeth. He had witnessed his share of injuries and death, but seeing someone so young and full of the passions of youth, laid low in an instant and struggling to hold onto life itself, unnerved him. Stokes felt feeble and trembly after the beating he'd received, followed by the ride through the night, but he refused to show any sign of weakness. The injuries he had suffered at the hands of the Cabin Creek crew were nothing compared to the gunshot wound Lenny had sustained.

The wound was clearly visible. It was a small hole, the flesh around it dark and bruised. As soon as Yardley removed the pressure of the bandage, blood began to ooze from the wound.

"Help me turn him," he said.

Setting down the lamp, Stokes did as he was asked. Lenny's skin was hot and feverish. They rolled him on his side and Yardley snatched up the lamp to look more closely. After a few seconds, he indicated that Stokes should allow him to roll back.

"Gently now." Blood, dark and viscous, welled from the wound. Van Orman returned with a bowl of steaming water. Into this Yardley poured a small amount of carbolic acid from a brown glass bottle.

"Clean around the wound," Yardley said. "I'm going to

open it a bit more so that I can get a clear view." He pulled a lancet and some other instruments from his bag and lay them on the table. "I need to find the bullet and any cloth that might have been pushed into the body, if he is to stand any chance. He is going to bleed more once I start. I'll need you to swab. Are there any clean towels?"

Van Orman had dipped a cloth into the hot water and acid solution and was already busy wiping Lenny's midriff.

"I think there are some in the chest at the foot of the bed in there," he said, signalling with his chin at the door to the main bedroom.

"I'll get them," Stokes said.

The first thing he noticed in the bedroom was the smell. After the copper tang of blood and the stale sweat of the men in the other room, the bedroom smelt fragrant and fresh. It was clean and tidy with many feminine touches. He took in at a glance the crocheted counterpane on the bed, the lace curtains and the wilting wildflowers that stood in a china vase on the small table under the window. Beside the vase was a porcelain potpourri jar with a delicate pierced lid. No doubt the soft aroma of herbs and flowers emanated from this.

On the bedside table there was a framed photograph of John standing tall and proud in his full dress uniform beside a serious-looking seated Mary Ann in a fine dress. They made a handsome couple and Stokes felt uncomfortable entering their private quarters. He had the sensation he was intruding. But he had a good reason to be here.

Quickly looking to the foot of the bed, he saw the chest. He was surprised to also see that John's uniform hung on the door of the wardrobe. His fabulous sabre, in its engraved metal scabbard, was propped there too. But there was no time now to admire the sword. Pulling open the chest, he found it replete with folded sheets and towels. The scent of lavender, rose and cedar wafted out of the chest. As he pulled out the towels, a small cloth bag of potpourri fell to the ground. It was sealed with a violet ribbon. He smiled ruefully to think of how a woman will change a man. He could not imagine the John Thornford he had known in Afghanistan and India bothering with the scent of flowers on his sheets.

Setting the towels on the bed, he stooped to retrieve the small muslin bag. He was already embarrassed at coming into Mary Ann's room, without her finding her things carelessly dropped on the floor.

"Where are those towels?" called Yardley from the other room.

"Coming," Stokes said, depositing the potpourri pouch back in the chest and closing it. As he bent down, his head throbbed worse than ever, as if pressure were building behind his eyes. But thoughts of the pain vanished as something caught his attention. Beside the wardrobe, in the shadows, were a pair of boots. At first, Stokes thought they must have been John's, as they were beneath his uniform. But he quickly saw he was mistaken. Even in the dust and heat of Afghanistan, John's boots had been cleaner than these muck-caked things. And there was something else. Stokes took a step closer and knelt beside the boots. He didn't wish to soil his hands or the towels, so he did not reach for the dirty footwear, but he could see well enough in the morning light streaming through the small window. These were not the kind of riding boots worn with a hussar's uniform, but the high-heeled boots favoured by cowboys and frontiersmen.

And the heel of the left boot was badly split.

The pieces of the puzzle rattled in his aching head, but Yardley's angry voice cut through his thoughts.

"God damn you, man, where are those towels?"

Without a word, Stokes hurried back to the other room where Dr Yardley was poised to make an incision. The doctor did not waste time asking what had delayed him, he merely gave Stokes and Van Orman their orders as he went about the bloody business of cutting out the bullet.

Soon his hands and forearms were smeared in blood. Lenny

McCloskey had not awoken, but every now and then, as the doctor probed deep inside him with long forceps, the young man moaned.

Stokes' mind reeled. He longed to speak to Van Orman; to confront White with what he had discovered. But for a time it was all he could do to follow the doctor's orders. His headache was worse than ever and he feared he might lose his balance, upsetting the table and putting Lenny's life further at risk.

It was some time later, as Yardley was sewing up the cut he had made in Lenny's side, that Van Orman and Stokes were finally able to step away. Van Orman carried the bloody water to the back door and tossed it outside. Stokes followed him, dumping the bucket filled with blood-soaked towels on the back step.

"I'll boil more water to soak them," Van Orman said.

As he turned away, Stokes caught his arm.

"Whose are they?" he asked. "The boots in the Captain's room?"

Van Orman did not appear surprised by the question.

"They are Jed's old boots," he said.

"Why are they in the Thornfords' bedroom?"

Van Orman sighed and for the first time, out here in the sunshine, Stokes saw the lines of worry and exhaustion on the shepherd's face.

"When Jed brought the Captain's body home," Reuban said, "Mrs Thornford saw he was limping. His heel had split, so she gave him the Captain's boots. Jed's feet were the same size and John had no use for boots anymore."

Stokes took a deep breath, hoping his conclusions were wrong.

"Are those the boots worn by the Captain's killer?"

Reuban didn't hesitate.

"They are."

Stokes still hoped he was mistaken, that somehow he had misunderstood matters in his weary state.

"Are you telling me Jed shot John Thornford?" he asked.

"That's what the sign told me."

"Could the sign be wrong?"

"Perhaps," replied Van Orman. "But I don't think so. The tracks were as clear as a buffalo walking in mud."

Stokes' voice rose as the reality sank in.

"Why didn't you say anything?"

Van Orman's expression was impassive.

"It was not my place."

"Not your place?" yelled Stokes, his head feeling as if someone had split it with an axe. "You knew I was looking for John's murderer. Why didn't you tell me it was Jed?"

"Because I don't think Jed murdered John Thornford."

This made no sense. Reuban's calm demeanour exasperated Stokes. Much more of this and he might punch the man.

"But you just said yourself that Jed shot him."

"Yes, but don't mistake me," Van Orman said. "I don't like Jed White. The man's rude and hates my people. But I don't think it was murder. It confused me, still does, but I read the sign and know how it went down."

Stokes let out a long sigh.

"Speak plainly, man. What do you mean?"

"I'm sure Jed shot Captain Thornford. But I also think John waited for White to take his position. He stood still while White aimed."

"What are you saying?" Stokes asked, already knowing the answer.

"John wanted Jed to shoot him."

Chapter Fifty-Two

Gabriel Stokes sprinted through the house, past Lars who was dozing in a chair and the doctor whose face was drawn with fatigue, and ran out onto the porch. There was no sign of Jed White outside. The bright morning light sent lances of pain into Stokes' head as he scoured the ranch for the old frontiersman.

Tanner was over by the barn. He had unsaddled the horses and was brushing them down. On hearing Stokes' heavy footsteps on the porch, he looked up, his features twisted with a mixture of hope and trepidation.

"How is he?" he asked.

"He's still alive," Stokes growled. He noticed White's sorrel mare tied to the hitching rail and tensed. He was unsure what he would say to the man. He had an inkling of what had transpired between John and him, but he had to hear the explanation of what had occurred from White's own mouth. "Where's Jed?" he snapped.

"Gone," Tanner replied.

Stokes scowled.

"What do you mean, gone? His horse is there."

"He took Amos' old nag. Slung his saddle on her and lit on out."

Stokes cursed. He was too late. White must have realised he was onto him and perhaps doubted Gabriel would be inclined to sit and talk things over.

"Why didn't you stop him?" he asked.

"Because I like living," Tanner said. "I seen what Jed can do and he looked fit to shoot anyone who got in his way."

Stokes took a deep breath, forcing himself to slow his thoughts.

"Did he say where he was going?"

"No, but he gave me a message for you."

"What did he say?"

"Told me to tell you he was sorry for how things worked out. And I ain't never heard Jed apologise before."

Stokes scoffed.

"I can imagine," he said. "What else?"

"Said he had only done what John wanted, but now he would make things right. Finish things once and for all."

"Is that all he said?"

"Yeah. He was all fired up over what had happened to Amos and Lenny. You know what he was talking about?"

Stokes bit his lip. The pieces of the jigsaw were finally clicking into place.

"I think I do," he said. "Now, saddle my horse. I'm going after him."

He hurried back into the house. He picked up John Thornford's Winchester rifle from where he had propped it by the door then, on a sudden whim, he went into the master bedroom. Striding to the wardrobe, he took the sabre that rested there, tugging the gold and red belt free from where it hung with the uniform.

Buckling it round his waist, he connected the sabre's scabbard rings to two of the slings. The gaudy sabretache of the Tenth Royal Hussars was already attached. The bag was clumsy, but he didn't pause to remove it.

"Look after the boy," Stokes said to the amazed-looking doctor, then went back outside.

He was pleased to see that Strickland had obeyed his command and was tightening the cinch on Banner's saddle. Beside the gelding, Reuban Van Orman was saddling his own

402

squat pony. A bleary-eyed Lars was also there. As Stokes approached, Giblin heaved his heavy saddle up and onto his horse's back.

"What are you doing?" Stokes asked.

"What does it look like?" Reuban said.

"I'm not riding to stop Jed," Stokes said.

"I know why you are riding. Figure you could use me to make sure you don't get lost."

"I thought you hated Jed."

"I don't like him. That don't mean I want to see him killed." He shrugged. "He's one of the JT crew and, as far as I see it, that makes him family."

"What about you?" Stokes asked Lars. "You look done in."

"You should take a look at yourself," Lars said. "You ain't no picture. I can still ride and shoot straight enough." He spat. "And Mary Ann might be in danger."

Tanner Strickland finished saddling Banner and handed the reins to Gabriel. Sliding the Winchester into its scabbard, he swung up into the saddle. He noticed that Tanner had lifted his own saddle and thrown it onto his mount's back.

"Tanner," he said, "this isn't a good idea."

"If it's good enough for you, Lars and Reuban, figure it's good enough for me."

"We're riding after Jed," Stokes said. "He's gone to kill the Cabin Creek crew. There are a lot more of them than there are of us."

"Reckon you need all the help you can get then." Tanner didn't smile, but there was humour in his tone.

Tanner tightened his saddle straps, secured his rifle and climbed into the saddle. Tooyakeh came out of the house and ran over to the men. Banner snorted and pawed the earth.

Reuban knelt and whispered to the dog.

"Stay here and guard the ranch."

The dog looked up with sad eyes as his master put his moccasined foot in the stirrup and stepped into the saddle.

Stokes met the gaze of each of his companions.

"Are you sure about this?"

"It's about time Grant got what was coming to him," Reuban said. "He's been making war on the people of this valley for too long."

"You can count on me," said Lars.

"And me," added Tanner.

"I know," Stokes said. "But I don't know if we'll come back from this."

"Reuban's right," Lars said. "This has gone on too long. It's high time someone put a stop to it."

"And reckon we can help some," Tanner said, slapping the stock of his Winchester. "Even the odds."

Banner, sensing the nervous excitement of his rider, pranced and stepped, turning in a tight circle. The sun gleamed from the sabre's polished scabbard and the gold thread of the sabretache.

"Figure on a sword fight?" Tanner asked.

Stokes glanced down at the weapon. The weight of it was familiar where it rested against his thigh. The sabretache hung against Banner's flank.

"This was John's sabre. The weapon of an officer of the Tenth Royal Hussars. It is apt I should carry it now."

"But where we're going, figure there'll be bullets, not blades."

Stokes thought on that. Ever since arriving in Oregon he had been avoiding the truth. But now it was clear to him. When the law did not serve, it was still possible to mete out justice. At such times, men were called upon to bear arms to defend themselves, their loved ones and their lands.

"It is a soldier's weapon," he said at last, pulling Banner's head around and kicking him into a canter. "And we are heading for war."

Chapter Fifty-Three

They had not ridden far when Reuban called out for them to halt. They reined in their mounts and Van Orman leaned out of his saddle. He scanned the road for a few seconds, then handed his reins to Tanner and slid down from his horse.

"We're wasting time," Stokes grumbled.

Reuban ignored him. He walked slowly along the edge of the trail, stooping to examine a leaf here, a broken twig there. After what seemed a long time, but was in reality only a matter of a minute or two, he climbed back onto his horse.

"I was wrong," he said. "They didn't ride for the Cabin Creek Ranch. They headed for Griffith."

"Wouldn't we have seen 'em on the road?" Tanner said.

"No," Lars replied, shaking his head. "Think about it. I rode off some time after them and it was dark. They could have ridden anywhere." He took off his hat and scratched at his blond hair. "Guess I'm lucky they didn't lie in wait for anyone who might follow them."

Stokes' stomach tightened.

"Mary Ann and the children are in town," he said, his clipped tone betraying his anxiety.

"Jed will be there too soon enough," Reuban said. "He stopped here and read the sign. Then he set off at a run towards Griffith."

They kicked their mounts into a gallop. There was no time

to spare. Stokes was furious with himself at having left Mary Ann and the children unguarded. What a fool he had been.

The sun was warm in the sky, the light flickering through the tree canopy as they rode. Now and then they passed into a clearing where the sunlight made them squint, and they could feel the heat of it on their faces in spite of the breeze created by the speed of their passage.

The horse Hampton had loaned Lars Giblin was already showing signs of tiring. It was blowing hard, its eyes rolling. The JT mounts were better stock and kept up the pace without complaint. Banner seemed unaffected by the night-time ride and this frantic dash back down towards town. Again, Stokes marvelled at the animal's seemingly limitless energy. Banner appeared eager to reach whatever awaited them. Stokes felt his own blood thrill at the prospect of battle. He could see no way to avoid conflict now, and part of him, the dark part he tried to smother with drink and drugs, revelled in that knowledge.

But perhaps all was not lost. If they could reach White before he found Grant, they might yet curtail further bloodshed. Maybe there could still be a peaceful resolution to this, with Grant brought to justice. Anything was possible, Stokes told himself as they galloped on, but he did not truly believe it.

And what of Jed White? He too must be held accountable for his crimes; made to face a jury of his peers. White was a killer, no doubt, and he appeared to have fired the shot that had taken John's life. And yet, here in the mountains, far from city courts, perhaps a man like White was needed. Maybe Jed had been right all along and the only justice Grant could face would be a bullet.

The cattleman and his gunmen had governed the valley with violence for too long. Stokes recalled Amos' unseeing eyes, the charred remains of the Rices' ranch, Elsa's burnt and shattered body, Cora's scarred, raw face. Leaning low over Banner's sleek neck, Stokes urged the gelding on to greater speed. His head throbbed with each pounding hoof beat, and as the miles passed by in a blur, he wondered whether they rode towards justice or a reckoning.

The four riders thundered out from the tree cover and careened towards the town. Stokes could see great plumes of smoke rising from the station where a train engine stood. The sawmills were silent. Everyone had been given time off to attend the opening. There were dots of colour on the station and the buildings of Griffith, where the red, white and blue bunting fluttered in the midday breeze.

Even from this distance, Stokes could make out the throngs of people gathered before the station. He was riding too fast to risk pulling out his watch, but the sun was high in the clear sky and he estimated it must be close to midday, the time of the grand opening. Not a cloud besmirched the perfect azure of the sky. The newly painted buildings of Griffith glimmered like jewels against the slope of the mountains in the distance. The sun shimmered from the waters of the Grande Ronde River beyond the town. It was a perfect day for a celebration.

Nothing appeared out of place and he wondered fleetingly whether perhaps they had somehow missed Jed. Maybe he had veered off in a different direction or perhaps Reuban had misread the sign.

Then he heard the sound of gunfire, followed by the thin, reedy noise of distant screams; the collective sound of fear and outrage uttered by a large crowd. Small puffs of grey smoke emanated from the people outside the station, the reports of the guns reaching the riders a second or two later. The citizens of Griffith and the visitors who had flocked to the town for the festivities shifted and rippled as if pushed by a great wind. From this distance they reminded Stokes of a large flock of many-coloured sheep being chased and herded by a sheepdog. But rather than the nipping bite of a dog's jaws, the people were fleeing from the flash and crack of guns, and the very real fear they might be caught in the crossfire.

Stokes spurred Banner on once more. The beast responded

valiantly. Whatever thoughts Stokes had harboured of resolving this without further bloodshed had dissolved when he heard the first gunshot. Jed White had reached Griffith before them and had removed any peaceful option that might have been available.

There was nobody on the road, everyone having gathered at the station. Stokes galloped on, Banner breathing hard beneath him. Reuban was some way behind him, his smaller mount not as fast. Next came Lars. His horse was all but played out and Stokes thought the animal might well not survive this run. Still, Lars whipped it on and the beast bravely laboured to obey its rider. Tanner Strickland's horse was a fine animal and kept pace with Banner.

Stokes scanned the station, the train on the tracks before it, and the mass of people gathered for the opening ceremony. He was riding along beside the tracks, coming at the train from behind and the station building from the side. The area of open space in front of the station had been packed with people, but now it was clearing rapidly. Men, women and children rushed towards the station building, some pushing through the doors, others running around the station and stumbling onto the tracks. Yet more were climbing into the train's carriages, seeking refuge within the vehicle. Stokes noticed one woman fall sprawling to the ground. A man returned to her, pulling the woman to her feet and urging her on. The hubbub of voices raised in fear reached him like the far-off roar of waves on a shingle beach.

And still gun shots rang out, the sounds ever closer to the clouds of smoke that were discharged, as Stokes and the other riders drew nearer.

A small platform had been constructed on the station steps, no doubt for the Governor and other notables to stand and pontificate over the crowd in the way of politicians, extolling the virtues of the Oregon Railroad and Navigation Company and declaring the station open for business. The platform was adorned with bright ribbons and banners, but was now devoid of spectators. People were cowering behind the timber construction now. There were too many of them in front of the station for it to have completely cleared and, as Stokes got closer, he heard more shots and saw several puffs of gun smoke rise above the few who remained as men there opened fire. Stokes was close now, and there was no perceptible gap between seeing the smoke and hearing the guns' reports.

The object of the shooters by the station was some thirty or forty yards from the station steps. Stokes recognised Amos' old horse. It lay still in the dust. Behind it crouched Jed White. As he watched, Jed rose and let off a quick shot with his carbine, then dropped down behind the protection of the animal and the thick saddle. He levered a fresh cartridge into the Winchester's chamber. The men in front of the station returned his fire, their bullets thumping into the horse. Seeing Stokes' galloping towards him, White grinned savagely.

"Couldn't miss the fun, eh?" he shouted.

Between White and his enemies a body lay sprawled in the dirt, a rifle by his dark outstretched hand.

Jackson Pailing.

Stokes saw everything clearly. As ever, when faced with combat, his mind seemed to speed up. His headache, and the aches and pains from the beating he had received, were forgotten. Now was the time for action.

He was close enough to recognise faces in the crowd now. He saw Jayson Stockman raise his pistol and shoot at Jed White. Deputy marshals were scattered about the steps, some stretched out flat, others kneeling, but all laying down fire at White.

Joaquin Lopez and a couple of other Cabin Creek hands were pinned down near the platform. No doubt Grant was there too, but Stokes did not see him. There was no sign of Mary Ann either, and he prayed she had already got clear of the fight.

Fleetingly, he had entertained the idea of giving White up to the authorities, but he discarded the thought immediately. Stockman was corrupt, in Grant's pocket and likely a murderer himself. There was no law here and White had saved his life more than once. It was as Reuban had said. Whatever he felt about the man, White was like family.

Seeing Stokes and the other JT riders speeding towards the station, Lopez and the Cabin Creek boys turned their fire on them. Stokes felt rather than heard the fizz of bullets flying past. Something tugged at his sleeve.

There was no time to plan, but they could surely do better than riding in guns blazing, which was evidently what White had done. If they remained in the open they would be cut down as surely as White's horse had been.

Stokes turned in his saddle and bellowed at Tanner.

"Spread out and find cover at the livery stables and those buildings across the street. Cover Jed and make a killing ground. Like I showed you at the JT."

"What about you?"

"I'm going to outflank them," he shouted. "Just don't shoot me."

"I'll try," Strickland called back, pulling his horse off to the right and away from Stokes.

Stokes didn't wait to see how Lars and Reuban would respond to his commands and whether they would listen to Strickland. He kicked his heels into Banner's sides, dragged on the reins and sent the gelding leaping over the tracks.

Chapter Fifty-Four

Banner's hooves clattered along the hard earth beside the tracks, the staccato sound echoing the rapid gunfire.

For an instant Stokes was transported back to a time a decade earlier. The screams and cries of the people streaming into and around the train carriages, the thunder of his horse's hooves, the crack of pistols and rifles and the whiff of black powder smoke on the air all conjured in his mind visions of that fateful day at Maiwand when he had galloped towards danger on a different horse in a very different land.

But there was no time now for memories.

Moments after crossing the tracks, the train carriages were flicking by in a blur. He glimpsed vague shapes in the windows, pale faces staring out at him. But he was travelling too fast to take in any details.

The thrum of Banner's hooves was loud, reverberating from the carriages' polished walls. The gunfire was muffled by the bulk of the train. Motes of soot from the train's chimney fluttered down into Stokes' face. The huge engine let out a sudden loud hiss. Banner tried to shy away, threatening to baulk at rushing headlong into the huge plume of vented steam before them.

"You can do it, old boy," Stokes whispered, leaning low so that the animal might hear his words. He could not be certain Banner paid his voice any heed, but he noticed that the horse's ears turned at the sound and the brave beast ceased fighting his rider. Lowering its great head, Banner sprang forward into the billowing cloud and was instantly past the train and into the bright sunshine once more.

There were people here, running round the engine in order to place its massive bulk between them and the shooters. A woman let out a shriek of terror as Stokes, astride the bay gelding, burst forth from the steam. Snatching the hand of a small boy dressed in an expensive-looking frock coat, she yanked him out of their path.

"Make way!" Stokes cried. "Make way!"

The crowd parted before him, more than one of them falling painfully onto the tracks. Thankfully Banner avoided them all and nobody was trampled beneath his hooves.

As soon as they were clear of the people, Stokes hauled on Banner's reins, sending him wheeling to the right. Effortlessly, the horse jumped across the tracks and carried him back towards the station from the far side. Stokes could still hear gunfire, though it seemed more sporadic now. He thought of what he had said to Tanner. When he cleared the station building he would come out to the far side of White's attackers, which would put him in the line of fire of the JT hands. He would have to put his faith in their good aim and providence. He could not halt now and lose this chance at surprising his quarry and perhaps putting an end to this. If this shooting continued, it was only a matter of time before some innocent observer would be shot, if such a tragedy had not already occurred.

There was little movement on this side of the station building. The Cabin Creek men, and Stockman and his deputies, were at the front, spread around the raised platform. Whatever reporters, dignitaries and other guests of the opening ceremony were left at the front of the station were now prostrate, hoping the bullets would fly harmlessly over their heads. Whoever was going to run had already done so and was now in the lee of the building or swarming around the train for added protection.

412

"Not much further now," Stokes said, patting Banner's neck and slowing his careening run slightly.

They were approaching the side of the station now, and in moments Stokes would have sight of the men shooting at his friends. Taking the reins in his left hand he reached down to draw the Lightning from its holster.

A figure emerged from the far end of the building. It was a man, moving with a stealthy gait, as if he wished to be hidden from view, though he was in plain sight. Stokes put this down to not wishing to be seen by any gunman and mistakenly shot as a result. Stokes could not blame him for wishing to seek cover, but there was something familiar about the stocky figure. The man looked towards the sound of the approaching horse and his eyes locked on Stokes'. They recognised each other in the same instant.

Beauregard "Bull" Meacher already had his six shooter in his hand and Stokes was in the process of pulling his own gun from its holster. The flash of recognition flickered like electricity between them, then, without hesitation, both men fired.

Chapter Fifty-Five

Bull Meacher was fast. His gun boomed and he was immediately partially obscured in a cloud of smoke. Stokes felt the punch of the bullet to his left shoulder. He had not had time to cock his own pistol and was pleased the Colt possessed the newfangled technical development of double action. He jerked hard on the trigger. Too hard. The gun discharged, but his shot flew wide of its target, splintering the wood beside Meacher's head.

Meacher flinched. This involuntary movement, coupled with Banner's speed, made his second bullet miss. Stokes felt the heat of the projectile whistle past his face. But he did not shy away. He would not miss a second time. Allowing Banner to carry him forward, he took careful aim and then fired twice in quick succession. The double-action mechanism worked perfectly and Stokes' aim was true. Both his bullets slammed into Meacher's thick chest.

Meacher fired again, but it was a wild shot. Already his fingers were growing numb and the pistol fell from his hand.

"Damn you," Meacher snarled, sinking to his knees. "Damn you to hell."

Stokes glanced at him as he cantered past, making sure the burly man was no longer a threat.

"Looks like you got yours in the end," he said. "Thought you said you could whip me."

Meacher glared up at him, but didn't reply. Slumped against

the station wall, blood smearing the fresh paint, he was already dead.

Dropping down out of the saddle, Stokes edged his way forward, clutching the gelding's reins in his left hand, the revolver in his right. He was aware of a growing pain in his left shoulder, but he pushed the throbbing ache out of his thoughts. The arm still worked and there would be time to worry about the damage Meacher's bullet had done when this was over.

If he survived.

Stokes inched slowly up to the corner, wary his approach and the gunshots might have alerted the men on the station steps to his arrival.

Passing slowly from the shade at the side of the building, Stokes surveyed the scene before him quickly so that he could make the best decision on how to proceed.

There were still some two or three dozen people scattered about the steps and the platform. Men in suits and women in their best dresses lay flattened against the timber steps and walkway. Some of them whimpered and cried out with each new booming gunshot, but amazingly, nobody seemed to have noticed him. He shifted his gaze to the men looking away from his position, guns raised. The stink of powder smoke was strong and a thin fog of the stuff hazed the air. Evidently they had been shooting continuously all the while as he'd ridden around the track side of the station building and his and Meacher's shots had been masked by the general tumult of the skirmish.

In the distance, he saw Jed White rise quickly from behind his felled horse and snap off a shot. A couple of the deputies returned his fire, their bullets kicking up dust or thumping into the horse's flesh. Near the platform, Joaquin Lopez must have been waiting for just this moment. Before White could drop behind the protection of his saddle and horse, Lopez squeezed off a shot from his rifle. White reacted, jerking as if slapped by an invisible hand, then fell back out of sight.

Stokes only had two shots left in his pistol, but he would make them count. He swung the muzzle up to point at the Mexican, but before he pulled the trigger, Lopez tensed, dropped his rifle and staggered back, clutching at his neck where great gouts of blood gushed. Stokes flicked his gaze to where the shot had come from. He saw the puff of smoke at the far side of the street and, beneath it, he briefly registered Tanner Strickland's red shirt before the JT hand disappeared behind the cover of a building.

Sweeping his gaze across to the livery stable on the other side of the street, Stokes could just make out Reuban Van Orman peeking out from around the corner of the tall structure. He could not see Lars, but he was content that they had listened to him, spreading themselves so that their enemies could not focus their fire and also so that they would be able to cover as many angles as possible.

Lopez was making choking, gurgling sounds, grasping at his neck in a vain attempt to halt the flow of his blood. The Cabin Creek men and the town deputy marshals redoubled their efforts, letting out a rolling barrage of gunfire reminiscent to Stokes of a platoon of infantrymen. The air before the steps became thick with gun smoke, partly obscuring the view of White and the others.

After a few seconds, the shots slowed as men ran out of ammunition. They fumbled for new cartridges, pulling them from belts and pockets, then shoving them into their Winchesters and pistols. They were vulnerable in that moment, but there was little that White, Tanner, Lars or Reuban could do to capitalise on the situation. Stokes didn't know how badly hurt White might be. Perhaps he was close to death, or maybe he too was reloading. Or perhaps the constant hail of lead had done the job of subduing him and the rest of the JT crew.

Whatever the reason for the lull in shooting, as the smoke

cleared, Jayson Stockman raised his voice so that everyone might hear.

"Throw down your guns, White," he shouted. "Rest of you JT boys too. Come out with your hands raised. We can talk all this over. You have my word you'll be treated fairly."

None of the JT crew showed themselves, but a second later White's gruff voice, strong and loud, came from behind the dead horse.

"Like Bannon?" White shouted. "You gonna drag me behind the Lady Elgin and stick me like a pig? That's how you did for the sheriff, ain't it?"

Shocked silence followed White's words, then one of the deputies, Seb Mooney, stern-faced as ever, thick moustache bristling, spoke, his voice carrying to everyone gathered there.

"What's he talking about, Stockman?"

The other deputies turned to look at the new acting sheriff. Nobody uttered a word, waiting to hear Stockman's reply. Lopez's bubbling wheezing was frantic. None of the Cabin Creek crew offered him any aid or comfort. After a few seconds, the Mexican shuddered and lay still. A shiver ran through the crowd. Somewhere, a woman let out a sobbing cry.

"Don't listen to him," Stockman said at last. "He's lying. Desperate. He's trying to make us fight each other 'cause he knows we have him."

"Why don't you tell 'em about Bannon's blood on your shoes?" shouted White. "How come you had it on your shoes before anyone reported finding his body?"

A murmur ran through the crowd.

"Is that true?" Mooney asked, his words rasping with dark emotion.

"Course it ain't true," Stockman said, his tone increasingly nervous. "That's Jedediah White! The man's a God-damned killer and a known criminal!" His voice had risen in pitch until he was screaming, spittle flecking his lips with each word.

Without warning, someone from the mass of people cowering on the steps rose to their feet. It was a woman in a dark dress. With a jolt like a punch to his stomach, Stokes realised it was Mary Ann Thornford.

"A known criminal, you say, Sheriff Stockman?" she said.

"Yes," he replied. "A thief and a back-shooting killer."

"You could be describing another known criminal," she said. Mary Ann's face was pale, but she held herself tall and straight, as if daring to be shot. Her jaw jutted in defiance. "None other than Thomas Grant!"

"Shut your mouth," snarled a voice.

It was Grant. Stokes saw then that the cattleman was only a few paces from Mary Ann. He had been hidden from Stokes' view until now by the Cabin Creek men and the timber construction of the platform.

Mary Ann ignored Grant, but she noticed Stokes standing in the shadow of the station and their eyes met. He was horrified at the risk she was taking, but his heart swelled with pride at her bravery. She had clearly decided this was the best possible moment to expose Grant and his crimes. When could they hope for more witnesses? When would there be dozens of reporters surrounding her, ready to listen to her every word. She offered Stokes a determined nod and continued to speak in a firm, loud voice, ignoring Grant's protestations.

"Thomas Grant pays these men," she waved a hand to encompass the gunmen surrounding Grant, "and this man who murdered Sheriff Bannon, and the county Board of Commissioners who appoint men to the post of sheriff. Everyone knows Grant wants to own all the land in this valley and that he'll do whatever it takes to do so. How many sheep have the Cabin Creek hands shot in the last year? How many so-called accidents must there be before someone stops them?"

"Shut her up," Grant growled at his men, but none of them moved.

"What do you think they're going to do, Thomas?" Mary

Ann said. "Shoot me in front of all these witnesses? But that's not how you operate, is it?"

"I'll pay you double what I offered," Grant said. "Just stop talking."

Mary Ann actually laughed then and Stokes marvelled at the woman's courage.

"Oh, I don't think so," she said. "You murdered my husband, but you can't silence me. Not now. Listen, everyone." She raised her voice to a shout. "It was Grant's crew who burnt down the Rices' ranch. They killed their hands, murdered Tom and Winnie Rice and poor little Elsa too. Cora, their eldest, is badly burnt. Scarred for life. And all of this done on Grant's orders. And for what? I'll tell you for what. More money. More power. Enough land to be able to deliver on a government beef contract."

"I'll kill you," Grant hissed, his voice quiet and dangerous. Stokes heard the deadly madness colouring Grant's words, but Mary Ann seemed oblivious, or uncaring of the danger she faced. Now that she had started talking she would not be quieted.

"No, you won't," she replied with the utmost disdain, like a mother berating a spoilt child. Turning to address the crowd, she held aloft the parcel of papers Stokes recognised. "It's all in here," she said, triumph in her tone. "All the evidence." She swept the onlookers with her gaze. "Which one of you reporters will write this story? Which newspaper will take it? The *Oregon Statesman*? Perhaps you, from the *Examiner*? Or you, from the *Seattle P-I*?"

With a sudden roar like that of an angry animal on discovering it is cornered and the only hope for its survival is to kill those who stand before it, Thomas Grant surged up from where he had been crouched. His huge Colt Dragoon was in his hand.

Stokes swung his gun, ready to shoot the man, but despite his bulk, Grant was quick, and he had already closed with

Mary Ann. Stokes dared not pull the trigger for fear of hitting her.

Grant wrapped one of his bear-like arms around Mary Ann's neck and thrust his gun into her ribs.

Chapter Fifty-Six

"I told you to shut your mouth," Grant growled, pulling Mary Ann onto the tips of her toes and dragging her down the steps. The packet of papers fell from her grasp.

"Let the lady go," said a tall, broad-shouldered man, who rose, aiming a pistol at Grant. The gun, a small calibre revolver, was dwarfed in his meaty hand. Both of the man's eyes were surrounded by mottled bruises where Bella Sawrey had kicked him in the face, but if he felt any discomfort from this injury he showed none. His aim did not waver. It was Ichabod Goff, Governor Pennoyer's bodyguard. The Governor looked on from the ground where no doubt Goff had shoved him as soon as the shooting started.

"It's all lies," Grant yelled. "This woman is trying to ruin me. Her accomplices are murderers. Look about you. See what they've done."

Jackson Pailing's corpse lay for all to see. Amos Willard's old, gore-streaked horse, behind which Jed sheltered, projected from the flat earth. Beside the timber platform, Joaquin Lopez stared up with vacant, sightless eyes, his head resting in an ever-expanding pool of crimson. There could be no denying that the arrival of Jed White to the festivities had precipitated chaos and death. A grumble of dissent rippled through the crowd.

Sensing that perhaps the tide was turning in his favour, Stockman spoke up.

"Listen to the man," he said. "You know him. This is

Thomas Grant. Without him there would be no Griffith. We wouldn't be here celebrating the opening of the station and the arrival of the railroad. Mr Grant's no killer. He's an innocent businessman."

"If he's so innocent," called a man Stokes did not recognise, "how come he's the one holding a gun on a woman. I for one would like to see that evidence. If he's as innocent as you say, he's got nothing to fear."

The man made a move to retrieve the parcel of papers from the steps. He wore a black suit and a small hat. There was no gun on his belt. He had the look of a city dweller, thought Stokes. A reporter perhaps. Stockman aimed his gun at the man.

"Don't touch that," he said, pulling back the gun's hammer.

The man's eyes widened.

"Are you gonna shoot me?" he asked, squaring his shoulders in an effort to put a brave face on it, but his voice cracked, spoiling the effect.

"Move and find out."

Another gun cocked, the click of the hammer loud behind Stockman's head. Seb Mooney pressed his pistol's muzzle against the nape of the sheriff's neck.

"Give me your gun, Stockman," the moustachioed deputy said. "You ain't killing nobody else."

"I didn't kill Bannon," Stockman said. "I swear it."

Mooney leaned around Stockman and took the pistol from his hand.

"That's to be seen, but I'd hear what White has to say on the matter first."

"You can't do this," Stockman said. "I'm the acting Sheriff of Griffith County."

Mooney tugged the badge from Stockman's lapel.

"You ain't nothing till I hear what happened to Bannon," he said. "He was a friend of mine."

Taking advantage of the distraction, Grant had continued to

move down the steps and then away from the station, pulling Mary Ann along with him as they moved slowly towards Hampton's livery stable.

Ichabod Goff's gun was trained on Grant, following him step by step.

"If you've nothing to hide, Grant," Goff said, "why are you trying to run?"

Grant's features were contorted with rage.

"Reporters twist anything," he said. "They can make lies of the truth, and truth of lies. Who's to say what stories they will spin about me? Look! Men are dead. These people want to see me killed too. I'm not safe here."

"No, you're not," yelled Mary Ann, bursting into life. Twisting her body and pushing Grant's gun away from her, she produced her tiny Derringer pistol from the folds of her dress. Both her small gun and Grant's massive Dragoon fired simultaneously, the noise shockingly loud.

The blast from the Dragoon was so close to Mary Ann's skirts that the cotton was set alight. The Derringer's bullet slammed into Grant's thigh. He staggered, but he did not relinquish his grip on her.

The two of them struggled, smoke wafting about them, from the shots and the smouldering cotton of Mary Ann's dress.

Goff tensed, hoping for a clear shot at Grant, but, seeing none, holding his fire. Likewise, none of the distant JT men chanced a shot with their rifles. The risk of hitting Mary Ann was too great.

Goff and the mass of people on the steps were between Stokes and Mary Ann, so, without hesitation, Stokes leapt into the saddle once more and kicked Banner around the station steps and towards the pair.

He had barely begun to move forward when there was another report from a gun. Stokes' breath caught in his throat, imagining the devastation the Dragoon would wreak on Mary Ann's fragile form at such close range. But as he rode closer, his mind cleared. It had not been the thundering crash of Grant's long pistol he had heard, but the smaller, less powerful discharge of the Derringer's second shot.

The small Derringer round did not carry a potent load of powder, but it was strong enough at close quarters and, whether by luck or design, Mary Ann's shot hit true, smashing into Grant's gun hand. With a scream he dropped the big Dragoon into the dust at his feet. His right hand was a bloody mess.

"You bitch," Grant said, his teeth bared like a wild animal. Pulling back his left hand, he punched Mary Ann savagely in the face. She sprawled in the dust, unmoving.

On seeing Mary Ann struck, Stokes urged Banner into a gallop, the gelding springing forward with his hugely muscled hind legs. Stokes would reach Grant in a matter of seconds, but it was unlikely he would be needed, for already, even as Banner carried him forward, Stokes heard the crack of Goff's small pistol and saw Grant's body jerk with the impact of the bullet.

Grant bellowed, more in angry disbelief than pain, it seemed to Stokes. The small calibre round appeared to do nothing to slow the big man, and in a rage, Grant reached for the fallen Dragoon pistol.

From behind the dead horse now surged up Jed White, face pale and shirt wet and dark with blood. He had his carbine pointed directly at Grant's face. There was a savage joy on White's features as he pulled the trigger, then an expression of shocked disbelief as the hammer fell with an impotent click. His Winchester was empty.

All this happened in a blur, but Stokes saw every detail. He watched as Grant stooped for his pistol, shrugging off another shot from Goff's revolver. Banner had borne Stokes across the distance in a few bounds and it seemed the Englishman's intervention would be needed after all. He aimed his Colt carefully, tightening his finger, ready to fire the remaining two bullets into Grant. At such close range, and already injured as he was, this would surely finish the tall cattleman. But as Stokes pulled on the trigger, he felt something within the gun give way, and nothing else happened. By God, the mechanism had broken, just as White had predicted. He had told Stokes never to trust a double-action revolver and now his misplaced faith in the gun was going to cost Mary Ann her life.

Grant's fingers closed on the Dragoon and stiffly he pulled himself to his full height, his face dark with murderous fury.

Feeling a familiar weight hanging against his thigh, Stokes tossed the useless pistol away. With a motion practised countless times on the drill yard, he drew forth John Thornford's sabre. Fleetingly, he noticed that Jed now had one of his Remington pistols in his hand. Banner charged forward. Stokes was almost on Grant now. If Jed fired he might well hit Stokes, but he cared nothing for that. If White had the chance to save Mary Ann he should take it. Besides, it was too late now to slow the gelding. The horse sped him towards his quarry like one born and bred for the cavalry charge.

Grant, having shed all pretence of the law-abiding citizen as a viper sheds its skin, aimed the Dragoon at Mary Ann's still form. He pulled back the pistol's hammer and sneered, his features twisted with an expression of gleeful victory.

Captain Thornford's sabre had been kept razor sharp. Stokes barely felt any resistance as the blade took Grant's head from his shoulders. Blood spurted into the warm air and the Dragoon fell from the man's senseless fingers, discharging with a booming flash of smoke and dust.

Stokes reined Banner in and leapt from the saddle, staggering slightly as the old wound sent a jolt of pain up his leg. Rushing to Mary Ann's side, he found her already coming to. Her lip was split and already swelling. Her eyes were not quite focused.

"Are you shot, my dear?" he asked. When she did not reply immediately, he repeated the question more anxiously. "Are you shot?"

"I'm well," she replied, and his heart soared at the sound.

"Thank God," he said.

"I will," she replied, with a lopsided smile. "And I would thank you too." She glanced at Grant's severed head. It lay in the dust, blood oozing from the neck. Grant seemed to be snarling at them, his last moment of hatred frozen on his coarse features. She shuddered. "And it would seem I owe my life to good English steel too."

Lars Giblin reached them then. Shouldering Stokes aside, he knelt beside Mary Ann.

"Thank the Lord," he said, tears streaming down his face. "I had feared the worst."

Movement behind him made Stokes turn. Jed White was stepping past the dead horse.

"If old Amos needs a horse in heaven," he said, "he's welcome to that nag."

White's shirt was sodden with blood, and his face was pale, but he seemed hale enough. A wave of emotion washed through Stokes. He wished to confront White about his part in John's death; to rage at him for putting Mary Ann and all of them in danger. He glanced at where Lars was tenderly helping Mary Ann to her feet. He took a calming breath. His questions and his anger could wait. Perhaps it would be best if Mary Ann did not hear that conversation. Looking back at Jedediah White, he realised with a shock that the overwhelming emotion he felt was relief that the old frontiersman yet lived.

"Told you we were not so different, you and I," White said.

Stokes grimaced.

"Is this the way of the West you keep talking about?"

White took in Grant's corpse and the head that lay several paces away from it.

"I know you English police do things differently. I wouldn't have used a sword," he said. "But you got the job done. I'll give you that."

Stokes shook his head. It hurt terribly. He still gripped the sabre in his hand. There was a thin smear of fresh blood on the blade.

"I would have used my gun if the infernal thing had worked."

"Should have listened to me."

"Perhaps if you weren't drunk so much, I would listen more."

White laughed, then winced.

"You need to see the doctor," Stokes said.

White nodded at Gabriel's shoulder.

"What about you?"

Stokes looked down and saw his sleeve was wet with blood. In the same instant the pain hit him.

"By George," he gasped. "That smarts. That bastard Meacher shot me."

"It happens," White said. "That bean-eater Lopez got me."

"If it's any consolation, their shooting days are over."

Jed White nodded slowly.

"You know what? That does make me feel a mite better." He coughed, grimacing. "Reckon a whiskey would fix me right up. Come on, Gabe. I'll buy you a drink."

Chapter Fifty-Seven

Stokes leaned back against the wall of the small parlour and closed his eyes. Perhaps if he'd permitted himself to drink some of the whiskey Jed had offered him he might have been able to sleep too, just as the frontiersman was doing. But despite the pain of his wounds, Gabriel had remained firm in his resolve. All he had drunk since the shooting at the station was coffee. Jed White on the other hand had been true to his word and had quickly procured a bottle of whiskey.

"I ain't letting the doc cut me sober," he'd said, before taking a long draw on the bottle.

Barely a mouthful of whiskey was left now in the bottle on the floor beside Jed's chair. White was slumped, head back, mouth open, snoring as he dozed. His face was almost as grey as his hair and Gabriel questioned the older man's stoicism in refusing Dr Yardley's treatment until everyone else had been tended to.

Not that Stokes had been any less stubborn. His shoulder throbbed with each beat of his heart and it was only getting worse. It seemed to him that both of them bore the pain of their wounds as a badge of honour. Or perhaps as penance.

When the dust and smoke had settled on the gunfight outside Griffith Station, Seb Mooney and the other deputies had managed to round up and disarm the few remaining remnants of the Cabin Creek crew. There had been many innocent onlookers injured in the fighting, some seriously, others with minor abrasions and bruises. Mooney had sent men out to the

JT to bring back Dr Yardley. In the meantime, Mrs Yardley had done her best to care for the people that crowded her house.

Dr Yardley had not slept and was clearly exhausted, but he did not shirk from his duty and had diligently attended to everyone who had been brought to him. On seeing that Jed and Gabriel had both sustained gunshot wounds, he had said they should be treated at once, but both men had been adamant that they would wait until everyone else had been seen. The doctor had not been happy about it, but he was too tired to argue. He checked that Mrs Yardley had cleaned and bandaged their wounds, then ordered them to wait in the parlour.

That had been hours ago. Since then Dr Yardley had seen dozens of patients. Now only Mr McCall remained before Gabriel and Jed. The shopkeeper's leg had been grazed by a stray bullet.

"You look like death, Mr Stokes," McCall said. "So does your friend here. The doctor should see you both before me."

"Mrs McCall wouldn't agree with that," Stokes said.

"No, she wouldn't." In the aftermath of the shooting, Mrs McCall had screamed a tirade of abuse at Stokes, as she had led her crying sister away. Grant's sister-in-law seemed to hold Stokes personally responsible for everything that had happened. Now, Mr McCall offered Stokes a mischievous smile. "But Mrs McCall isn't here. And I never did like that bastard husband of her sister's. In fact, if I had one with me, I'd give you one of those Cuban cigars you have a taste for."

"I would appreciate that," Stokes said, surprised, but gratified by McCall's comments. He was not the first person to voice such an opinion since Grant's death, but he was certainly the closest relation. "But don't worry about us. We've waited this long. We can wait a few minutes longer."

Beside McCall, Jed broke wind and grunted in his sleep. McCall grimaced and shifted his position.

"What I worry about are your friend's innards," he said.

Stokes said nothing. He stared at Jed White and wondered

whether he could ever consider the man a friend after what he'd done.

They had spoken little since the gunfight. The parlour had been crammed with people all that long afternoon, leaving little room for the kind of conversation they needed to have. Apart from the general hubbub of the shocked and injured townsfolk, the time had passed slowly, with little to punctuate the passing hours apart from watching Jed White becoming increasingly more inebriated.

A couple of reporters had stopped by, eager to interview Stokes and White, but Gabriel had sent them away. He would give his account of events later, if doing so would help Mary Ann, but he could not bring himself to speak to the newspapermen yet.

Two other incidents had caused a commotion and consternation. First, the barman from the Lady Elgin had been carried in drenched in blood. Mrs Yardley had knelt beside the man and peeled back his sodden shirt. Stokes had thought he must have been hit by one of the many bullets from the gunfight, but the barman hadn't been shot. He'd been stabbed. He was in a bad way, pale and woozy from loss of blood.

"Who did this to you?" Stokes asked.

The barman grasped Stokes' sleeve with blood-smeared fingers.

"That whore, Bella," he hissed.

"Bella Sawrey?"

The barman coughed, wincing in pain.

"Emptied the cash box," he said. "Did this when I tried to stop her." He looked down in disbelief at his blood-soaked clothes. "Don't know why I bothered. Not my money..." His voice trailed off and he coughed again.

"Where did she go?" Stokes asked.

"How in hell should I know? She lit out with that son of a bitch, Byrne."

Stokes' mind was reeling. Questions thronged his mind, but

before he could marshal his thoughts, the barman had passed out. Mrs Yardley had the deputies who'd brought him in carry him quickly through to the examination room.

Shortly afterwards, those same men had carried the barman back outside, his body and face covered by a blood-stained sheet.

One of those same deputies delivered the news that Alpheus Hampton's corpse had been discovered in the livery stable. The hostler had been shot in the head and two horses had been stolen. Cadmar Byrne had not been seen since the first shots were fired at the station and it was presumed he was Hampton's killer.

Gabriel brooded over both incidents as he waited for Dr Yardley. He had liked Hampton. He was a decent man. As for Bella Sawrey, he was furious with himself for believing she might be anything more than a strumpet, happy to take whatever she could and to side with whoever would offer her the best prospects.

Hearing of Alpheus Hampton's murder, Bella Sawrey's treachery and her escape from Griffith with Cadmar Byrne, had done nothing to improve Gabriel's already dark mood. Now, with the sun low in the sky and the ruddy light of the sunset tingeing the room in a golden hue, Stokes could feel his anger simmering just below the surface.

The door opened without warning, jolting Stokes from his reverie. Mrs Yardley stood there, her features drawn and wan.

"My husband will see you now, Mr McCall," she said, moving to assist him to limp into the next room.

At sound of the door closing behind them, Jed White stirred. Looking groggily about him, he saw he was alone with Stokes. Reaching for the bottle at his feet, he let out a groan, placing his left hand over his bandaged wound.

"Looks like we're up next," he said. He emptied the bottle with a swig, dropping it so as to avoid bending again.

Stokes had been surprisingly glad to see White survive the

battle, but his fury with him had soon returned, and it had grown more intense all that afternoon. He had been waiting for this moment for hours. He leant forward now, ignoring the stab of pain from his shoulder.

"Why did you do it?" he snapped.

White let out a long sigh. The warm camaraderie between them in the initial moments after the action at the station had dissipated quickly. Now it had evaporated entirely. White might be drunk, but he recognised Stokes' anger well enough, and made no attempt to joke.

"John knew I needed the specie," he said simply.

Stokes stared at him. He had suspected as much.

"John paid you to kill him?"

"He did. Truth is though, would have done it anyway, if he'd asked me. He was a good man. Always treated me well." He gave Stokes a sharp look. "What would you have done, Gabe? Figure you know by now why he asked me. Reckon I was doing right by him."

"The insurance?"

"Told me he was sick, but the insurance wouldn't pay out if he killed hisself."

Stokes took a steadying breath.

"Why not wait for the cancer to kill him?" he asked. His shoulder burnt with a searing agony, and he thought of John's pain. "I would never have wished him to suffer, but surely that would have been the right thing to do."

"You and your cricket," White said, looking forlornly down at the empty bottle. "Might have been the right thing to do, but John didn't believe he could wait, not with the way Grant was. Knew he would get weaker and weaker. Grant would swoop in and take the ranch. Who knew how many people he might kill along the way?"

"So you killed John instead."

White sniffed.

"Your fault really."

Stokes could scarcely believe his ears.

"How in God's name can I be held responsible for you shooting John?"

White shrugged, flinching at the pain the movement caused him.

"You can't," he said. "Not really. But when you wrote to him about your troubles, the Captain saw a way to get the insurance for Mary Ann, and to finish Grant once and for all."

Stokes stared at him for a long time. Slowly, the truth dawned on him.

"He wanted me to investigate his murder and bring Grant to justice."

"Said you would never rest knowing he'd been killed. Knew you well." He offered Stokes a twisted smile. "Seems he didn't know just how persistent you'd be. When I figured you'd found my old boots, knew you'd put it all together. Decided to take matters into my own hands. But you have to know, I only shot John because he asked me to. Would never have killed him otherwise. And this way he didn't suffer."

As the final pieces of the puzzles clicked into place, Stokes let out a ragged sigh.

"So in the end I killed an innocent man."

White was incredulous.

"Innocent man? Grant? Come on, Gabe. Grant didn't shoot the Captain, but he was as crooked as a barrel of snakes. He did all those other things you and Mary Ann wrote up in your little dossier."

It weighed heavily on Stokes that Grant would not face trial, but White was right. The man had been evil, bloated with greed and power. He would have stopped at nothing.

Gabriel was about to say as much when Dr Yardley stepped into the room. His eyes were dark with weariness, and there were blood spatters on his shirt sleeves. McCall hobbled out with the aid of a cane. He glanced at White and nodded once at Stokes.

"You're next, Jed," Yardley said.

"See to the Englishman first," White growled.

The doctor sighed.

"If you want to die, White, why don't you just put a bullet in your skull? I'm too tired to argue with you."

Stokes fixed White with a cold stare that brooked no dissent.

"Go with the doctor now, Jed. We can carry on our conversation another time."

Jed White held his gaze for a long while, then pushed himself to his feet with a grunt. Stokes watched him shuffle out of the room. Dr Yardley closed the door behind them without another word. Stokes stared unblinking at the painted wood. He knew he would not speak to White again about his involvement in John's death. There was nothing more to say.

With a sigh, he looked down at the empty bottle beside White's chair. The evening sunlight illuminated a drop of amber liquid that had pooled within the glass. Stokes imagined the burning taste of it on his tongue to distract from the pulsing heat in his shoulder. Holding himself still, he counted the minutes until it would be his turn to be seen by the doctor.

Chapter Fifty-Eight

Gabriel Stokes stood in the yard behind the building and shivered. Looking down at the watch in his hand, he saw it was only just after four in the afternoon. Darkness was still hours away, but while it was still autumn down in the valley below, up here in the Sierra Nevada mountains there was already snow in the air and the wind that blew down the pass carried the sharp bite of ice.

He watched the second hand ticking round. He had promised Jed he would wait for a full three minutes before entering the establishment, but he was regretting that decision already. He calculated how long there was left of the allotted time and slipped the watch back into his pocket.

He shoved both his hands into his coat pockets in an effort to warm them. If he were to be called on to use his guns, he would like to be able to feel his fingers.

The yard was piled with chopped timber, ready for the harsh winter ahead. Jed had told him about the long winters in the Californian mountains. Of how the snow piled up more than the height of two men. He had not really believed him, but now, feeling the icy chill in the air when midwinter was still months away, Jed's tales seemed less fanciful.

Wishing he had bought a warmer coat when they had stopped in Alturas, he clapped his arms about his chest, trying to stave off the shivering. His shoulder ached at the movement. Meacher's bullet had nicked the bone, but Dillon Yardley had done a marvellous job of removing the lead ball and the small sliver of bone. Stokes considered himself fortunate to only have one more scar and another limb that ached in cold weather. Jed had been lucky too. The bullet that had hit him had missed his vitals and he had nothing but a puckered scar to remind him of the action in Griffith.

It could have been much worse for both of them, Stokes thought, recalling Alpheus Hampton and the barman of the Lady Elgin.

The story of Grant's crimes had been picked up by all the newspaper reporters at the scene. The man from the *Oregon Statesman* had even offered to pay for exclusive access to the dossier they had compiled. Mary Ann would not take his money, but had the reporter agree that the *Statesman* would pay Dr Yardley's fees for treating the JT crew and Cora Rice.

Stokes had been impressed with Mary Ann before that day on the station steps, but from that moment on, she was a revelation. Having made the decision to stand up in the face of such danger and speak out for justice, she had become more self-assured and secure in her role of ranch owner.

Another revelation had been Cora. She had moved out to the JT Ranch along with her sister, Florence. Mary Ann treated the girls like her own family. It was agreed Mary Ann would administer the Rices' land until the girls were old enough to inherit, and Cora set about learning the ways of governing a large spread right away. She would follow Mary Ann around, earnestly scribbling notes in a small notebook that Gabriel had given her. She was sombre and grave, her raw, scarred face rarely smiling. The only time she seemed truly happy was when she looked at Lenny. The young man had pulled through and was as besotted with Cora as ever. In fact, he had asked Mary Ann if they could be wed, and a date had been agreed for the following summer.

Nobody brought it to the new sheriff's attention that it had been Lenny who shot Rab Tovey, or if they did, Seb Mooney, who had been appointed to the post without contest, never brought charges against the young man, seemingly content to sweep Tovey's death away with all the others killed that spring in what the newspapers liked to refer to as the Griffith County War.

Stokes shivered. It was hard to believe he had been too hot to wear a jacket only days earlier when they had traversed the edge of the Black Rock Desert in Nevada. He thought about checking his watch again, but decided against it. Enough time had passed and there had been no sounds of gunfire or fighting. Surely all was well inside and he was tired of waiting. Perhaps next time he would go in first and Jed could wait outside in the cold, with nothing but the stink of the outhouse for company.

He pulled the Colt Lightning from the new holster on his right hip and moved close to the door. He'd had the gun repaired by a gunsmith in Boise, much to Jed's amusement. Truth was, when the gun worked, it was a joy to use, and so Gabriel stuck with it. On his left hip though, he carried Meacher's single action Colt Frontier. He had learnt his lesson and would not make the mistake of relying solely on the Lightning again. If both pistols should prove unreliable, he also carried the large cavalry sabre. Mary Ann had given the sword to him, and he was honoured to carry it, a constant reminder of his old friend. He had left behind the elaborately decorated belt and sabre-tache, preferring to wear the sabre on a plain leather belt slung over his shoulder.

He'd bought the sabre belt from the same saddle-maker in La Grande who had sold him his gun belts. He'd returned the one he'd worn at the JT to Albert before he left.

Picking up the Winchester from where he had leaned it against the log pile, Stokes reached for the door handle. Before he could touch it, however, the door swung open and a man stepped out quickly into the cold afternoon. Stokes took a step back, warily raising the gun in his hand.

The man who had come out of the building was tall and barrel-chested, his size emphasised by the great buffalo skin coat he wore and the high-crowned hat on his head. Seeing Stokes armed with the Colt, the giant held out his hands.

"Easy there," he said. "I don't mean no trouble. I'm just heading to the necessary."

"I'll not stand between a man and his business," Stokes said, relaxing somewhat and letting the man pass.

Once the big man was inside the outhouse, Stokes stepped into the saloon. It was gloomy inside, little more than a shack, but Stokes was pleased with the heat at least. A pot-bellied iron stove provided enough warmth for the small room. In the depths of winter it would no doubt struggle to keep out the cold, but this afternoon it did a good job and, after the cool breeze outside, Stokes felt sweat break out on his forehead.

On the far wall was a window and a door that was closed to the street. To Stokes' right were a few chairs and tables, each of different size and shape. Men sat at a couple of the tables, nursing drinks. At the largest table, three men sat with cards and chips before them. The fourth chair was empty, no doubt recently occupied by the man in the buffalo coat.

To Stokes' left was a bar made out of a couple of barrels between which an old door had been laid. A slim, pasty-looking man stood behind the bar. In front of it, with his back to the barman, stood Jed White. Stokes noticed he already had a glass and a bottle in front of him. Sighing, he moved to the bar.

"That was a long three minutes," White said. "What if I'd needed help?"

"I'm sure you would have made me aware of your predicament," Stokes said. "I see you didn't wait for me before ordering a drink."

"Don't like to waste time." White turned to the barman. "Sarsaparilla for my friend."

The barman stared at White as if he had spoken in Chinese.

"I got whiskey or beer," he said.

White grinned at Stokes.

"Lucky for you really," he said. "That stuff will kill you."

"Do you have coffee?" Stokes asked.

"I ain't got none made."

"Could you make some, please?" Stokes took a quarter eagle from his pocket and placed it upon the door that served as a bar.

"Coffee it is," said the barman, palming the coin and rummaging about for the pot and coffee grinder.

White sipped his whiskey and the two of them surveyed the room. They watched the buffalo-coated man come in out of the cold and sit back down at the poker game.

"No sign of either of them?" Stokes asked.

"Not sure they were ever really here."

"That mule skinner said Byrne was playing cards here. The girl he saw with him sounded like Bella Sawrey."

"Any whore would sound like Bella," White said. "Might have been Byrne, might not have been. Only thing I can tell you for sure is they ain't here now. And seeing the place, even if they came all the way up here, can see why they didn't stay. This place is played out. Not enough money here for someone like Byrne. Not enough people. No, reckon he's headed for the coast. San Francisco'd be my bet. We'll head west tomorrow. Be glad to get out of the mountains before the first snows too."

Stokes watched the men playing cards. The big man had removed his buffalo coat and left it on the floor by his feet. It looked like a huge dog sleeping beside the table.

"You think we'll find them?" he said after a while.

"We'll find 'em," White said, "if we keep looking long enough. Either that or we'll hear they got themselves killed. Man like Cadmar Byrne don't usually live to a ripe old age."

It had been months already, following the trail from one small town or mining camp to another. A couple of times they'd been close, but it seemed they'd headed the wrong way when they'd come up into the Sierra. Stokes wondered if Byrne knew they were on his tail and had paid the skinner to put them off his scent. He had to know there would be someone following him after what he'd done.

Sheriff Mooney had been happy enough to let Byrne and Sawrey go. He had a lot on his plate, what with Stockman's trial for Bannon's murder and sorting out the mess left behind in Grant's wake. Stokes and White were less forgiving. As soon as they had recovered from their wounds, they had saddled up and ridden out in pursuit of the pair. It meant they would miss Mary Ann's wedding, but neither of them was particularly bothered by that thought, though Jed did bemoan missing out on all that free booze.

In a surprising turn of events, two days after the shootings, Lars Giblin had proposed to Mrs Thornford and she had accepted. Lars was a solid, serious man and Stokes was sure he loved Mary Ann. Whether she loved him, he was not so certain, but he wished them both well and meant it.

It had been the same day that Lars proposed to Mary Ann when they had learnt that the charges against Jedediah for the shooting of Wycliff Furlong had been dropped. Governor Pennoyer no doubt had something to do with that. It was one of the ways in which he showed his gratitude for the removal of Grant. They never did find out what Grant had on the man, but it was clear the second that Grant was killed a weight had been lifted from the Governor's shoulders. Stokes had heard that Pennoyer's campaign for re-election was also going well. He was predicted to win by a large majority.

The barman carried a blackened coffee pot over to the stove and placed it on top.

"Won't be too long now, fellas," he said, returning to his position behind the bar.

Stokes nodded his thanks.

"Don't include me in this," White said. "Coffee's all for him. I'm gonna have a good evening with this here bottle. Hey, what are you staring at?"

A pale-faced man had been watching Stokes and White from

where he sat at a table. White's shout startled him. Nervously, he pushed his chair out and made his way across the room to them.

"That's close enough," Jed growled when he was still a few paces away. "What do you want?"

"Begging your pardon, gents," said the man, eyeing Stokes' sabre in its burnished scabbard. "Might you be Lieutenant Gabriel Stokes the man they call the Hussar of Griffith County?"

Stokes sighed. The newspapers had coined the name for him, blowing his exploits out of all proportion and making him sound like some hero in a fanciful adventure story such as those Albert liked so much.

"Mr Stokes here don't like people using that name for him," White said with a grin, "but it's him right enough."

"And you must be Jedediah White."

"'White by name, black by nature'," Stokes said, quoting the newspaper articles. "How did the *San Francisco Examiner* put it? My 'faithful hound'? 'Squire of the gallant English Knight'?"

"I'm Jed White," snarled Jed, and it was Stokes' turn to smile. "Ain't nobody's hound."

"Quite so, quite so," said the man. He was very nervous, stepping from one foot to the other, clearly unsure how to proceed.

"Shit or get off the pot," White said.

"Of course," the small man said. "Might you gentlemen be in search of employment?"

"What kind of employment?" White asked.

"The kind for which the two of you are admirably and eminently qualified."

"We're not hired guns," Stokes said. This was not the first time they had been approached and offered money to settle someone's grievances.

"Of course not. Quite so," said the man, his cheeks flushing.

"My name is Anthony Lombard and I have been robbed, you see."

"Robbed?" Stokes asked, his interest piqued. "Tell us more."

The man started to speak, but White cut him off.

"Wait a minute, Gabe. I thought you said we needed to find Byrne and Bella as quickly as possible and then you were heading back to England."

It was true. He had said exactly that not two months earlier. Stokes recalled the last letter he had received from Eliza enquiring after his health and clearly wishing for him to return home. And then there was the letter from Rebecca that had reached him just before they left the JT Ranch. In her message, his wife had begged for his forgiveness. On reading the letter he had at first been filled with a burning desire to rush back to London with all haste, but as the days passed, so his ardour dimmed and the thought of returning to Rebecca and all he had left behind seemed an ever-distant dream; something to be thought of, but perhaps best left unfulfilled.

Gabriel Stokes let out a long breath. The barman brought him his coffee and he accepted it with a thin smile. It smelt good and the cup warmed his hands.

"I will need to go back eventually, I suppose," he said. "But there is plenty of time for that. Besides, there is much of this country I have yet to see. Let's hear Mr Lombard out. England can wait."

Author's Note

Ihave always wanted to write a western. But it has taken me several years and thirteen novels to build up the courage to set one in the American West during the second half of the nineteenth century. Nevertheless, it has long been apparent to me that all of my previous books, even though set in the early medieval period (or Dark Ages), are essentially westerns at heart. Instead of guns they have swords, spears and axes, but other than that, and other obvious differences in technology and culture, many of the themes and even plots are reminiscent of classic westerns.

The seventh century of my Bernicia Chronicles series was a violent time, where races clashed and kingdoms were created and destroyed through bloody conflict. Men with ambition ruled kingdoms with small numbers of warriors. Although they professed kingship tracing their claims all the way back to the gods themselves, there is really little to separate them from the cattle barons of the American West. Each vied for dominance over the land, clashing with other rulers in battles which were in essence nothing more than turf wars. In the case of the cattle ranchers, they literally fought over turf and grazing rights.

Throw into this maelstrom of war, racial and religious tensions and the expansion of the Angles, Saxons and Jutes, subjugating the older, native inhabitants of Great Britain, and you have a situation not dissimilar to the American West. Invaders from the east, with superior fighting power destroying a proud culture that inhabited the land long before they arrived. As in the "Wild West" of cowboys and Native Americans, men and women who wished to live outside of the laws laid down by their societies gravitated into the power vacuums that formed along the frontier, where any semblance of control from the different factions was weak at best and, at worst, totally absent.

The Superintendent of the United States Census of 1890 declared "there can hardly be said to be a frontier line, in the discussion of its extent, its westward movement, etc., it can not, therefore, any longer have a place in the census reports". The frontier line was defined as a point beyond which the population density was fewer than two persons per square mile. Because of this declaration by the Census Bureau, 1890 has often been cited as the year the American West was effectively tamed. However, the reality was that in many areas things were far from safe. This was a country recently ripped apart by civil war, and many of the men had fought and had first-hand experience with firearms. Following the American Civil War, the Indian Wars raged on for decades until effectively ending on 15th January 1891, with Kicking Bear's formal capitulation to General Miles, shortly after the tragic massacre at Wounded Knee.

Gun ownership in the American West was high, and in a land full of dangers, ranging from other people to wild animals, such as wolves, bears and mountain lions, it is not surprising that people would wish to be armed to feel secure.

As you would expect, firearms feature heavily in the book, and as part of my research I shot several guns from the period, including replica Remington and Colt revolvers, '66 and '73 Winchester rifles, shotguns and even an original 1875 .577-450 calibre Henry-Martini British Army rifle. What struck me most was how much smoke is generated with each shot. Modern smokeless nitro powder, originally cordite, was only used from the end of the nineteenth century, and all the guns in Oregon in 1890 would have used traditional black powder, with the copious clouds of smoke it produces and its very particular sulphurous smell.

Into the often violent and savage frontier world of the American West steps Gabriel Stokes, with his dark memories and chequered past in the British military and police. The Tenth Royal Hussars were deployed in Afghanistan during the Second Anglo-Afghan War, and participated in the victory at Ali Musjid (Ali Masjid) in the Khyber Pass, for which those who took part received a campaign medal. After the campaign, Queen Victoria graciously permitted the 10th (Prince of Wales' Own) Royal Hussars to bear the words "Ali Musjid", "Afghanistan, 1878–1879", upon its appointments.

After Ali Musjid, the regiment was unable to participate in the continuing war due to reduced numbers and ongoing sickness, and it remained at Rawul Pindi (Rawalpindi). However, four officers and five non-commissioned officers and men of the Tenth were employed by other regiments in the second campaign in 1880. I have chosen to have Captain Thornford and Lieutenant Stokes added to that small group. The Battle of Maiwand on 27th July 1880 was a catastrophic defeat for the British. Some 2,500 British soldiers were confronted by 25,000 Afghan warriors. The battle led to a disastrous rout with about a thousand British dead. The Afghan force lost twice that number, but still carried the day, with the British fleeing the battlefield in disarray.

Two Victoria Crosses were awarded for acts of valour during the battle and the subsequent retreat to Kandahar. One was awarded to Sergeant Patrick Mullane, for attempting to save the life of a wounded colleague; the other went to Gunner James Collis, who drew the attention of enemy fire upon himself and away from wounded colleagues. I have added a third Victoria Cross for Captain John Thornford for rescuing the wounded Lieutenant Gabriel Stokes during the retreat.

Following his discharge from the army, Stokes became a policeman in the Metropolitan Police Force in London, where his intelligence, tenacity and sense of justice saw him rise quickly to the rank of Detective Inspector. London in the 1880s was a crowded, violent place, and Stokes found himself investigating some of the most infamous murders of all time: those attributed to the serial killer, Jack the Ripper.

The case of the brutal murder and dismemberment of Jane Adams that haunts Stokes is loosely based on two similar cases from the nineteenth century: the murders of seven-year-old Jane Sax in 1866 and eight-year-old Fanny Adams in 1867. Those crimes, like those committed by Jack the Ripper, were horrific, made even worse by the fact they were perpetrated on young children. Gruesomely, the terms "Sweet Fanny Adams" and "Sweet FA" are derived from the Fanny Adams murder and relate to the way the child's corpse had been hacked into so many pieces that sailors in the Royal Navy would darkly joke that the tins of beef they received in their rations were actually parts of the poor dismembered and disembowelled girl.

Reading about these crimes, it is easy to imagine the toll they would have had on the mental health of the police officers and others involved in the investigations and subsequent trials.

It is from these horrors that Stokes escapes to Oregon, where he yearns to find a bucolic wilderness. The country itself is everything he had hoped for, vast, beautiful and wild. Unfortunately, it is populated with men and women who are not so different from those he has left behind in England. Despite the pristine landscape, the same crimes and evils are present in this far-off land.

Just like London, the American West was a melting pot of different nationalities and ethnicities, and political and racial tensions were rife. The victory of the Union in the War between the States might have freed the slaves, but racial discrimination was still the norm, rather than the exception.

One of the largest, non-native, ethnic groups affected by such racism in Oregon in the 1880s was the Chinese. Following the gold rushes of the mid-1800s, there had been a huge influx of Chinese workers, welcomed into the States to work in all manner of business, from laundries to laying the tracks for the railroads that would connect the east and west coasts, effectively shrinking the country in a way never before possible, reducing travel from coast to coast from months to a few days. Many thousands of these Chinese immigrants settled all along the west coast of America, and soon became the focus of populist leaders; a handy scapegoat to rile up the masses and win votes. Sylvester Pennoyer himself won his first election to the governor's office in 1886 as a leader of the anti-Chinese crusade in Oregon.

Following the Chinese Exclusion Act of 1882, anti-Chinese sentiment grew stronger, and between 1885 and 1887 mobs forced Chinese immigrants out of several cities and murdered Chinese labourers in Oregon and other states. The 1882 Chinese Exclusion Act meant Chinese immigrants could not leave the United States and then return without first applying for a re-entry certificate. In 1888, this was made even worse with the passing of the Scott Act that prohibited re-entry altogether. This was not repealed until 1943.

As with all my historical fiction novels to date, many of the principal characters are fictional, but the world they inhabit is based on reality. As well as Governor Pennoyer, Reuban Van Orman also existed.

Much of Van Orman's known background is described in the novel itself. His family were killed in a massacre on the Snake River in 1860. Young Reuban was only about ten years old when he was forcibly retrieved from the Shoshones and Bannocks in Cache Valley, Utah in 1862. Many people had been involved in his rescue, including his uncle, Zachias Van Orman, Major Edward McGarry and a detachment of cavalry troops. During those two years, Reuban had been a part of Chief Bear Hunter's tribe and the boy actively fought against his "rescuers" when separated from the Native Americans he had bonded with.

Henry C. Haskin described the incident in the 20th December 1862 edition of the *Napa County Reporter*: "He was dressed and bedaubed with paint like an Indian and acted like a regular little savage when given into our possession, fighting, kicking and scratching when the paint was washed from him to determine his white descent."

J. H. Martineau, a local militia officer and pioneer surveyor, also wrote of the child's "light hair and blue eyes" that "betrayed its race".

After being taken from Bear Hunter's people, Reuban's story goes dim and disappears entirely after his colourful childhood.

There are many accounts throughout the history of the American Frontier of children being taken by Native American tribes, and when I discovered Reuban Van Orman during my research, I knew I had to include the adult he might have become in my story.

Most of the places and towns in the story are real. The names of the ranches are my invention, as is the town around which most of the action takes place. Griffith is loosely based on the town of Elgin, but apart from its location, timber providing its main industry, and the arrival of the railroad in 1890, any other similarity is purely coincidental. As a nod to the real town, I've called the main saloon that features in the story the Lady Elgin.

Incidentally, the Oregon town of Elgin received its name from a ship, PS *Lady Elgin*, that sank on Lake Michigan in 1860. SS *G. P. Griffith* was the name of another ship that sank on Lake Erie in 1850, which is how I came up with the town name.

Huntington, Oregon is a very real town and was an important stagecoach station before the arrival of the railroad in 1884. It had its share of saloons, opium dens and gunfights, and by the end of the nineteenth century Huntington had developed a reputation as a "Sin City".

Cattle and sheep wars in America in the late nineteenth and

early twentieth centuries claimed the lives of fifty-four men and over 100,000 sheep. More than a hundred such engagements were recorded across eight different states. The problems would often begin with the arrival of sheep onto public land, as the sheep had a tendency to overgraze, making the open range unusable for cattle for months afterwards. There was also a fear of disease, such as sheep scab, that could infect the water sources that cattle drank from.

Perhaps the most notable, and certainly the bloodiest, conflict and feud between a cattle rancher and a sheepherder occurred in Arizona and became known as the Pleasant Valley War. It was fought between the families of John Tewksbury and Tom Graham and started when a Basque sheepherder working for Tewksbury was murdered in 1885. By the time the Pleasant Valley War was over in 1892, some twenty-five men had been killed, including all of the men in the Graham family and most of those in the Tewksbury family.

Oregon saw its share of sheep and cattle wars too. When the Cascade Forest Reserve was created in 1898, sheep owners who had used the Cascade Mountains for their summer range were forced to look elsewhere to graze their flocks. This resulted in a sudden increase in sheep numbers in the Blue Mountains, disrupting the balance that existed there between cattlemen and local sheepherders.

Eventually, the cattlemen organised themselves into groups known as "Sheep Shooters" with the goal of driving sheep owners back from the range they claimed for their cows. They created what they called a "deadline", across which sheep men were not permitted to graze their sheep. Trees were marked with notices tacked on the sheep side of the line.

Several mass killings of sheep occurred in Central Oregon as a result of the increasing tension between sheep and cattle operators, the largest slaughter taking place in 1903, when nearly 2,400 sheep were killed.

The Blue Mountain Forest Reserve was established in 1906.

This soon became the Deschutes and Ochoco National Forests, and the government granted grazing allotments there by 1907, which controlled the number of livestock that could be grazed and the location of animal grazing. This ended the major conflicts between cattle owners and sheep owners in the area.

The power of the press burgeoned in the nineteenth century. Numerous periodicals vied to capture the attention of a voracious readership. In this period of nascent mass media, with competition growing ever more intense, some newspapers used increasingly lurid stories to gain attention. The term tabloid journalism was not coined till the twentieth century, but it quickly became evident that a scoop, particularly one that drew on the public's darker imagination, could change a newspaper's fortunes. *The Star* was launched shortly before the Whitechapel murders, and after it published letters purportedly from the murderer himself, the paper saw its daily sales rise to more than 230,000.

Those sensational letters, supposedly penned by Jack the Ripper, were thought by many, including high-ranking police officers, to have been created by the very journalists who profited from their publication. The prime suspects were Frederick Best of *The Star* and Tom Bullen of the *Central News Agency*.

Taking inspiration from these journalists for the fictional reporter Fred Bullen, I had him print fake letters from Jane Adams' killer in the extremely popular weekly *Illustrated London News*. The founder of that newspaper, Herbert Ingram, coincidentally died in 1860 in the *Lady Elgin* accident on Lake Michigan!

Life insurance policies had not been mainstream finance products until the mid-1800s when insurance companies started appealing to the moral duty of husbands to provide for their families in the event of premature death. This led to a boom in the life insurance industry with many of the companies formed in that period still in existence today.

By the end of *Dark Frontier* Gabriel Stokes has found out

what happened to his old friend and he has ended Tom Grant's reign of terror in Griffith County. But will Jed and Gabriel catch up with Cadmar Byrne and Bella Sawrey? What will happen if they do? These questions and many more will have to wait for another day and another book. I for one can't wait to continue exploring the American West alongside the Hussar of Griffith County and his faithful hound. I hope when the time comes, you'll saddle up and ride with us.

Acknowledgements

Firstly, thank you, dear reader, for taking a chance on this book. I truly appreciate that you have spent the time, and hopefully your money, to read this story. (Unless you've borrowed it from a library – that's fine too!) I hope you've enjoyed it. If you have, please take a moment to leave a review on whichever online store you bought it from, or shout about it on social media, or tell your friends and family how much you liked it.

Reviews and word of mouth really help.

Moving into what was for me a completely new location and period of history was daunting and I needed to do quite a bit of research. Several people helped me with that, but of course, as ever, any mistakes in the final book are mine alone.

Thank you to Phil Morgan and Charlie Morgan of The Single Shot Black Powder Cartridge Rifle Club of Great Britain, who were kind enough to invite me along to the National Shooting Centre at Bisley, Surrey and show me the awesome power of the 1874 Sharps rifle at 300 and 600 yards. The size of the .45-70 cartridges was impressive, as was the rifle's and shooters' pinpoint accuracy at such huge distances.

I am also indebted to Richard Smith and all the members of the British Western Shooting Society, who warmly welcomed me to one of their competitions and allowed me to fire some of the iconic guns of the American West that went on to feature in the novel.

Thanks is due to fellow historical fiction author Prue Batten, who, along with her husband and son, runs a sheep ranch in Tasmania. She very kindly sent me a comprehensive description of a sheep farmer's life and what sheepherders might expect to be doing in each season in Oregon.

To get a feel for the land and a small taste of what it would have been like to ride the hills around Griffith, I spent some time at Wilson Ranches Retreat near Fossil, Oregon. Thanks to Kara Wilson, Morgan Smith and Chantelle Sorensen for their hospitality and for answering all of my questions about horses, cattle and ranch life in Oregon. And thanks to Cochise, the lovely gelding that carried my not inconsiderable bulk over the rocky slopes of the high desert.

Thanks to Steve Litteral for sending me links to useful websites and for sharing his vacation photos of some truly stunning American Western scenery.

Extra special thanks must go to Jon McAfee and Mary Faulkner, and all my other patrons for their ongoing generous patronage. To find out more about becoming a patron, and what rewards you can receive for doing so, please go to matthewharffy.com.

Thanks to my friends and test readers, Gareth Jones, Simon Blunsdon, Shane Smart, Jacqui Surgey and Alex Forbes. Their input on the first draft was, as ever, extremely useful.

Thank you to Steven A. McKay, author and co-host of *Rock, Paper, Swords! The Historical Action and Adventure Podcast*, for listening to my rants, for making me laugh and for sharing the podcast journey with me. Steven is a great guy, and a wonderful writer too. Read his books and listen to our podcast!

Beyond the writing of the manuscript, tons of work goes into getting a book published. Thank you to my editors, Nic Cheetham and Greg Rees, for adding polish and focus to the story, and thank you to all of the wonderful team at Aries and Head of Zeus.

Thanks to the online community of authors and readers who

connect with me regularly on the ever-expanding list of social media platforms, such as Facebook, X (or the social media platform formerly known as Twitter), Mastodon, Instagram, Threads and TikTok. The list seems to go on forever, but it is always great to hear from like-minded individuals. So don't be shy.

Finally, but never least, my undying love and thanks go to my family. To Elora and Iona, for frequent doses of reality, and to my wife, Maite (aka Maria), for always guiding and supporting me, for getting up on a horse in Oregon with me, and above all, for listening even when I am sure she is fed up with hearing about my latest book.

Matthew Harffy
Wiltshire, September 2023

About the Author

MATTHEW HARFFY grew up in Northumberland where the rugged terrain, ruined castles and rocky coastline had a huge impact on him. He now lives in Wiltshire, England, with his wife and their two daughters. Matthew is the author of the critically acclaimed Bernicia Chronicles and A Time for Swords series, and he also presents the popular podcast *Rock, Paper, Swords!* with fellow author Steven A. McKay.

Follow Matthew at @MatthewHarffy and
www.matthewharffy.com.